Praise for Dian

On Winding Hill Road

"A wonderful mix of gothic melodrama and contemporary romance . . . Ms. Tyrrel writes an incredible story . . . this is an excellent read and if you like deep, dark, and gothic, do not pass this one by."
—*The Romance Reader's Connection*

"[An] entertaining gothic romance . . . Fans of modern-day gothic romantic suspense will enjoy the drive in, around, and on Winding Hill Road."
—*Midwest Book Review*

"A gothic romance in the classic mold . . . The story is well-written, and the author has an engaging style . . . an entertaining read."
—*All About Romance*

"*On Winding Hill Road* is rather reminiscent of all those Barbara Michaels novels I read . . . Tyrrel has an eloquent style and evokes a wonderful sense of place. The northern California coast with its rock cliffs and ocean views seems right at home with that traditional gothic setting—Victorian England . . . Those who remember the gothics of a bygone era should get ready to welcome a new writer with open arms."
—*The Romance Reader*

"Readers are sure to enjoy *On Winding Hill Road* . . . it encompasses romance, mystery, and an excellent story. Fans will enjoy reading this new gothic."
—*Romance Reviews*

"Ms. Tyrrel has created a true modern-day gothic romance. It has all the nuances of the gothic tales of old with a fresh, introspective present-day twist . . . All of her characters are intriguing and complex, and it's fascinating to uncover not only the mysteries, but the people themselves. It's entertaining, innovative, and lingers in the mind like literary ghosts waiting to be discovered. A definite winner, it's hard to put down."
—*Fresh Fiction*

continued . . .

"The story moves along at a steady pace. The primary mystery is quite intriguing . . . Tyrrel, as always, nails the perfect gothic tone."

—*The Romantic Times*

"Ms. Tyrrel has written another keeper in this gothic romance. Dark and gloomy at times, with engaging, mysterious characters and backdrops . . . fans of the genre won't be disappointed."

—*Romance Junkies*

On the Edge of the Woods

"*On the Edge of the Woods* marks the memorable fiction debut of an author in striking command of all the gripping essentials. Tyrrel offers up likeable, compelling characters; vivid settings; a host of stormy and steamy relationships; and a chilling mysterious thread that keeps the reader turning pages until the shocking twist ending."—Judith Kelman

"Classy, sexy, and deliciously suspenseful. Don't miss it!"

—Linda Castillo

"Readers will enjoy this absolutely enthralling . . . gothic romantic suspense that reads . . . like a modern-day *Suspicion*."

—*Midwest Book Review*

"Takes plenty of time to build the tension and suspense . . . The mystery elements are all used to good effect and will please fans of gothics . . . the twists at the end are worth the effort. This is an author to watch."

—*The Romance Reader's Connection*

"Grabs readers from the start . . . this tale of suspense will keep readers on the edge of their seats . . . Readers looking for an engaging tale that will have them biting their nails one minute and rooting for the main characters the next should pick up a copy of *On the Edge of the Woods*. This reviewer is looking forward to more stories from Ms. Tyrrel."

—*Romance Reviews Today*

"Tyrrel has a descriptive writing style . . . She has a fine attention for detail . . . [and] also populates the story with an array of characters, making the red herring possibilities endless." —*The Romance Reader*

"A world-class gothic novel."

—*Romance Junkies*

The Inn at Half Moon Bay

Diane Tyrrel

BERKLEY SENSATION, NEW YORK

THE BERKLEY PUBLISHING GROUP
Published by the Penguin Group
Penguin Group (USA) Inc.
375 Hudson Street, New York, New York 10014, USA
Penguin Group (Canada), 90 Eglinton Avenue East, Suite 700, Toronto, Ontario M4P 2Y3, Canada
(a division of Pearson Penguin Canada Inc.)
Penguin Books Ltd., 80 Strand, London WC2R 0RL, England
Penguin Group Ireland, 25 St. Stephen's Green, Dublin 2, Ireland (a division of Penguin Books Ltd.)
Penguin Group (Australia), 250 Camberwell Road, Camberwell, Victoria 3124, Australia
(a division of Pearson Australia Group Pty. Ltd.)
Penguin Books India Pvt. Ltd., 11 Community Centre, Panchsheel Park, New Delhi – 110 017, India
Penguin Group (NZ), Cnr. Airborne and Rosedale Roads, Albany, Auckland 1310, New Zealand
(a division of Pearson New Zealand Ltd.)
Penguin Books (South Africa) (Pty.) Ltd., 24 Sturdee Avenue, Rosebank, Johannesburg 2196, South Africa

Penguin Books Ltd., Registered Offices: 80 Strand, London WC2R 0RL, England

This book is an original publication of The Berkley Publishing Group.

This is a work of fiction. Names, characters, places, and incidents either are the product of the author's imagination or are used fictitiously, and any resemblance to actual persons, living or dead, business establishments, events, or locales is entirely coincidental. The publisher does not have any control over and does not assume any responsibility for author or third-party websites or their content.

First edition: September 2006

Library of Congress Cataloging-in-Publication Data

Tyrrel, Diane.
   The inn at Half Moon Bay / Diane Tyrrel.
      p. cm.
   ISBN 0-425-21165-7
   1. Motels—Fiction. 2. Single women—Fiction. I. Title.

PS3620.Y63155 2006
813'.6—dc22

                                    2006019257

PRINTED IN THE UNITED STATES OF AMERICA

10 9 8 7 6 5 4 3 2 1

For J

ACKNOWLEDGMENTS

I am grateful for the support and enthusiasm of my extended family, especially those we've lost along the way; you will always stay beside me.

And Paige Wheeler, my beautiful agent; Cindy Hwang, my editor at Berkley; and for all of you working behind the scenes at Berkley.

For Nancy Berland and Matthew Tamayo, for helping me get the word out; Cheryn English, my first friend, for your love of reading; Jocelyn Forrester, for years of friendship and selling my books in your shop; Patti and Larry Magid, for that first computer, childcare, and your love story; Freyja, for fire ceremonies and my first book-signing party; Aleta Bloch, for your friendship and soul-satisfying photography; and Annie Nuestadter, for your help.

And for my three girls . . . Ashley, for asking me if I was still writing, way back when; Burgundy, for what you said about *On the Edge of the Woods*; and Sierra, for being my most brutally honest reader (and making me read Harry Potter).

And my hubby, David, for supporting the writing even though you liked the painting better.

And J-mom, (step)mother and friend . . . always so encouraging, loving, and accepting.

With all of you, and all my good friends and readers, I am blessed.

Thank you.

Chapter 1

THE first time I came to the inn, I saw the motel first, and I immediately discounted it. Not what I had in mind. It was a stucco rectangle painted a shade of pink something between salmon and flamingo, with faded turquoise accents, doors, and shutters. The neon Motel sign was vintage; the Vacancy light was on. There was a parking slip at each door and a small swimming pool on the north side of the building. I thought of the motor hotel in *Dr. Seuss's Sleep Book*.

Addie and Bill O'Mally treated me like a long-lost daughter come home—or maybe I should say *grand*daughter. I was not yet thirty and they were in their late seventies, having finally reached the top of the waiting list for the retirement community where they planned to spend their "golden years." But before they moved on, it was very important to them that they find the right owner to take over their beloved inn.

"Bill, it's her," the woman whispered to her husband the first time we met, staring at me with big soft eyes. "It's our mermaid."

"Now, Addie, don't," he scolded her, but there was some strange excitement in his expression, too, as he looked at me.

Mermaid. It wasn't the first time I had heard the comparison. The long, wavy red hair often attracted the question "Is your hair really that color?" One poetic admirer had told me my hair was melted brown sugar, my eyes as deep and blue as the sea from which I had emerged, and my skin as flawless and white as the sand on a virgin beach. Then again, a drunk guy at a party once said I looked like I'd been dead a few hours.

Addie and Bill thought I was one of their own, an Irish lass. There *was* a little Irish in me, as well as some German and French. A touch of Persian, too, according to my mother.

A little Irish was enough for Addie and Bill. They took to me instantly, and I to them, but the inn was something else entirely.

THE motel stood on a bluff above the ocean with a gully running between the motel and the farmhouse. The old highway curved past the inn, the farmhouse, and cottages, and the cluster of farm buildings on the hill that had once belonged to the inn property. On one side of the road lay the dunes, on the other, ranch land, pastures divided by lines of eucalyptus and groves of giant pines, with the blue-tan bulk of the hills behind them.

I'd driven up to the motel with the real estate flyer I printed from the Internet on the seat beside me, wondering if I should just turn around and head home. I wouldn't have wasted much time— it was less than an hour's drive over the mountains from Palo Alto, which was amazing considering the remote feel of the place. Still, an hour out was an hour back, and since I'd come all the way here I thought I might as well take a look at it.

I parked my car and got out, breathing deeply of the ocean-scented wind. The drone of a vacuum cleaner sounded from within one of the motel rooms; a cart stacked with linens stood by an open doorway. I looked into the room and was startled by the immensity of the blue ocean through the open windows on the western side. The view was spectacular.

"Can I help you?" A woman slightly younger than me, with eyes like Cleopatra and a thick black braid of hair hanging down her back, came out of the room next door.

"I'm Kelly Redvers," I said. "I have an appointment with Addie and Bill O'Mally, to look at the property."

"The office is in the farmhouse, down that way," she said, nodding toward the gully. "You can drive your car down there or you can walk over the bridge."

"Okay, thanks," I said. "So, you work here . . ."

"Yes," she said. "I run the housekeeping staff. I am Anita Hernandez."

"Pleased to meet you," I said, offering my hand.

She raised her hand slowly, even reluctantly, it seemed, to take mine.

"Do you plan to stay on after the place sells?" I asked her.

She looked at me, dignified, with what might have been a deliberately blank expression. "That all depends," she said.

"Can I take a look in one of the rooms?" I asked.

She hesitated a moment before answering. "Yes, go ahead."

The room was modestly appointed, and the furnishings worn, but it was clean and the mattress on the bed was firm. Two young girls of seventeen or eighteen were in the room, one making up the bed with fresh linens, the other vigorously scrubbing away in the bath. They seemed relaxed, content, and professional, though when I tried to talk to them, they just giggled. I guessed they knew little English, and I knew very little Spanish, though learning the language was on my list of things to do.

I walked to the window and stood looking out at the view. It kept surprising me.

"Do you like it here?" I asked Anita on impulse when I walked out the door after looking at the room.

She continued what she was doing, tending to something on her cart without breaking her rhythm, sparing me a quick look of mingled amusement and wariness. "You see I am here," she replied.

She pushed the cart along to the next room.

I left the motel and walked down the slope on a stone pathway to the gully. When I glanced back, Anita and one of the younger girls were standing close, whispering together, watching me.

I cautioned myself not to make too much of it. Must be strange for them, I thought, with the place up for sale. No job security there.

I crossed the arched stone bridge, and through the trees the old house came into view: a lovely Queen Anne farmhouse, graceful and welcoming, with Adirondack chairs on the front lawn and wicker furniture scattered over the wide front porch. The hand-lettered sign on the top gable read:

THE MAGIC MERMAID INN
MOTEL & COTTAGES

I almost laughed out loud. The Magic Mermaid Inn. *How cheesy is that?*

But despite my cynicism, I was enchanted. I could hear the waves on the beach below, and as I climbed the stone staircase built into the hillside up to the house, the view became even more expansive. I could see honey-colored cliffs curving away to the north and the massive bulk of the coastal mountains rising up behind the bluffs. In the other direction, miles to the south, the coastline faded into the mists.

If the motel was kitschy and retro, the farmhouse was warm and charming. A small driftwood sign over the entry door said: Sea House.

I went up the steps to the front porch slowly, taking it all in. The Adirondack chairs and wicker couches were deserted, but I could imagine guests spending lazy afternoons lounging around, enjoying the clean ocean breezes. The front door stood open, braced by an antique iron Scotty dog doorstop, and I wandered in.

Off to one side of a generous entry hall, a sitting room had been converted to a front office, with a huge oak desk and antique filing cabinets. The door opposite opened into a large, comfortably furnished parlor that was now the common area for the inn, with an old upright piano in the corner, a fireplace, and casement windows looking out over the front lawn to the ocean. The entry hall, which was cluttered with small tables, side chairs, an umbrella stand, and racks of tourist literature, had an odd, if not unpleasant, smell.

The first thing I'd do, I thought, is clear out some of this stuff here. *Open up the entry a bit.*

But of course I had already decided against this particular establishment.

MY impression of a Dr. Seuss world had increased upon inspecting the property. It wasn't just the motel—the house had some of that whimsy, too. Nothing about it seemed quite square. And the O'Mallys were Dr. Seuss characters. Addie was scrawny and sweet and wore her metal-yellow hair in a messy topknot; Bill was cheerful and curved, like a fat Kokopeli with huge feet.

Addie and Bill were so warm and enthusiastic about me right from the start, I began to regret that I must eventually disappoint them. We walked around the property, Bill hobbling along ahead,

Addie by my side, chattering away. "You should see the birds we get here," she said. "I keep the feeders full for the greedy things. Our guests love them. We have lots of squirrels, of course. Raccoons, too. They can be a nuisance. That's where the girls do the laundry."

We were walking by a small building with gingerbread detailing. It looked like a witch's cottage.

Check into cost comparisons, doing laundry in-house versus contracting it out.

Bill played tour guide. "This here's Starfish Cottage, which you can look inside if you want, and that one is Pelican Cottage, and up the hill there is Sea Horse, which is our honeymoon cottage. Can't show you that one, because I believe we have some honeymooners in there right now. And way up there on the edge of the cliff, that's number nine—that's where Grendel lives."

"Number nine? But all the other cottages have names. Doesn't number nine have a name?"

"We've always just called it number nine," Addie replied. "All the other cottages have numbers, too, but we call them by their names. All but number nine . . ." She looked at her husband for help, but he just shrugged.

"You said someone—*lives* there?"

"Yes." She nodded. "We have one full-time lodger. He's very nice, but I'm afraid he's rather lonely. That's his cottage, number nine. He pays by the month."

Though number 9 perched high and solitary on the cliff above the others, most of the cottages were clustered together in a friendly way, built at various levels to take advantage of the views. Some of the cottages were attached, like building blocks stacked down the hillside, but each was situated so that they all had a private deck overlooking the ocean. The huge old trees that shaded the property also enhanced the feeling of privacy.

"The motel is going to need reroofing one of these days." Bill spoke up on practical concerns. "Some of the cottages are okay, some of them aren't. We have our man Nick McClure help us out from time to time. Local fella. If we could afford to have him full-time, we could keep him plenty busy. He takes care of the plumbing and electrical work, carpentry, whatever's called for. We pay him time and materials, so you could just pick up with the maintenance like that, when we transfer the property title."

"Oh, and our staff is wonderful!" Addie said. "Especially Arturo, our breakfast chef, and Anita, she runs the housekeepers."

"Yes, I've met Anita."

"I do worry about Anita," Addie said. "I think she's got her problems. But she's a very good worker."

What sort of problems?

"And, Kelly, you'll love our regulars." Addie was on to other things. "So many really lovely people. You'll see."

What I was really loving, at that moment, was simply being there. It smelled so good, the wet salty tang of the ocean on the fresh wind, the scent of sun-baked pine needles rising from the earth. The air was full of quiet sound—the muted crashing of the ocean waves, the wind in the high branches of the cypress trees near the house, birds rustling in the shrubbery.

As they showed me around, Addie waxed poetic on the virtues of the Magic Mermaid—really selling the place—but she obviously loved the inn, and she was so guileless, it was impossible to think her insincere. And Bill seemed to want me to understand exactly what a new owner would be getting into.

"Utilities are in pretty good shape," he was saying. "New hot water heaters, and the electrical has all been upgraded. But there's always something going to pot around here. These old structures, you know. If it's not one thing, it's another."

I understood. But that wasn't the reason I had decided against this place. I simply wanted something else. Something more elegant, less rustic.

And yet the house was wonderful, with the sea glinting off the beautiful glass panes in the windows, and the lawn that fell away from the wide front porch and sloped down through the woods to the cliffs and the beach below . . .

"See the widow's walk up there?" Bill pointed to the balustrade that ran along the roof above the front porch. "They say Mrs. Worthington used to stand up there, staring out to the west, waiting for her husband to return from the sea."

"Mrs. Worthington?"

"She lived in this house over a hundred years ago. She was a fine lady from the East Coast and her husband was a lusty sea captain. He built the place and gave it to her for a wedding present. Folks say she loved the house, all the more so because it was a gift from him, though the number of nights they spent together beneath its roof you could count on the fingers of one hand."

"So he was lost at sea?"

"He sailed away and never returned." He added with a sly grin, "But whether he was lost at sea or simply decided he wasn't cut out for holy matrimony—that we'll never know."

His delivery was flawless. Obviously he had told the story many times.

"All right then," he said, ushering me along. "Almost finished with the tour."

The entry hall with its odd smell and its clutter and jumble of tourist brochures led on to a steep, curved staircase. Between the parlor and the big farm kitchen was a huge formal dining room with banks of windows looking out on the ocean side.

It was remarkable how little had been done to the house in converting it to an inn. The architecture retained all the original charm of a bygone era, with simple but generous detailing, wide moldings, and high ceilings.

"We do happy hour in the parlor," said Addie, "or out on the porch if the weather is nice. Dessert and coffee in the dining room . . . but of course you'll set it up however you like, won't you?" Her voice trembled a little, and her husband laid his hand on her arm.

They showed me the apartment they lived in, a comfortable if uninspired space in an annex off the back of the house, added on in the '70s, from the look of it. The air smelled like spiced apples, and a pair of blue parakeets cooed and screeched softly from a cage on a stand in the living room. I could feel the love permeating from the walls of this home, but aesthetically it was a nightmare, with cheap aluminum windows, peach carpet, and splashy floral wallpaper in tones of peach and baby blue. As the manager's apartment, this was where I would live, if I bought the property.

I tried to imagine it without the clutter of cute knickknacks and the throngs of sun-faded family photos covering every available surface in the room. It helped that the apartment had a sheltered deck with incredible ocean views off the living area and a similar deck off the bedroom. With the wallpaper gone, a coat of white paint, bare wood floors, new windows and French doors—it just might work.

I had already decided against the place, yes, but . . .

We went out through the garden and back into the main house and continued our tour up the steep curved stairs to the second floor, where a large landing connected three charming guest rooms.

"Most of the antiques will stay with the property," Addie said. "These things have been in the rooms so long, they seem to belong here. And we won't have space for them where we're going . . ."

She looked at me with big eyes. "But of course you will furnish the rooms as you see fit."

No, it won't be me, I said silently. But her look of pathos touched me. "I wouldn't change a thing in here," I said honestly, looking into a comfortable, sweet, and surprisingly spacious room, which had a view of the ocean, and its own bathroom with a claw-foot tub and vintage pedestal sink.

Guests go nuts for this sort of stuff.

I didn't realize it until later, but I was beginning to soften.

Addie and Bill weren't exactly pushy about their assumption—that I was the one for the place—but they were fixed on it for some reason, and had been from the moment I came into their office. It was flattering; the place was charming and well priced—I knew they would probably receive multiple offers.

The tour of the property ended in the big farm kitchen, where Bill made us coffee. At that point I was still set against the place, or thought I was.

"I just really had something else in mind," I heard myself saying.

I hadn't intended to lay it out there like that. I had planned to simply smile and say thank you and move on. Why get into it?

"Something a little more modern," I explained. But somehow the word modern sounded lame when I said it.

"Are you thinking you would tear the place down, then?" Bill asked with a rather worried expression. "We already got an offer from a fella who would like to tear it down and put up something new. That's not what we'd like to see happen here."

"Tear down the place? No, that would be a shame. Its age is its charm. No, anybody who'd want to tear this place down would be missing the point."

Addie and Bill looked at each other with relief.

"Kelly," said Addie, "you'll take good care of this inn. I know you will."

"Now, you're not listening, Adelaide," said her husband in a reasonable tone. "The girl says this place isn't what she had in mind, even if she can appreciate its appeal. And you know as well as I do that it would be a lot to take on, especially for one person alone. Your heart's got to be in it, one hundred percent."

"It's a perfect job for a couple," Addie said, looking at me hopefully. "Ideally, a family."

"No," I said. "I have no husband. No kids."

"Ah," she said, looking down at the ground and nodding gravely, as if I had told her I had a terminal illness.

"You are rather young to be taking on a project like this, aren't you?" Bill suggested in a fatherly way.

"Maybe." I had already considered this. Already decided it was probably true. The sort of project I had in mind was too much for one person to handle, but I had to do it anyway. My father said I had always been an early achiever, if not an overachiever. I finished college in three years, went to engineering school, and started working for a top engineering and design firm in Palo Alto when I was twenty-three. When I was twenty-eight I was promoted to head of my department. I survived the dot-com bust, one of the lucky ones who got out of it with my job intact.

I loved the design, the actual work of creating something new. And I had become very good at it. I had been promoted, and I was soon overseeing others doing the job instead of doing it myself. I got good at that, too. And then I realized I didn't want to do it anymore.

I tried to explain all this to Addie and Bill. They sat at the kitchen table with their coffee mugs, listening politely. I had no idea what they were thinking. I wondered why making them understand even mattered to me. I would never see them again.

"Anyway, that's all a roundabout way of saying I'm ready for another challenge."

"And you've never married, never had children?" asked Addie.

"No," I said. "I don't plan on ever getting married, or having children. I like my independence."

"I should think that would be so lonely," Addie said.

"Now, my dear, not everyone thinks the way we do," said her husband.

"Lately," I said, "I have been feeling a little . . ."

Lonely. I pushed the word aside, didn't utter it aloud.

"I'm ready for a change," I told them. "I want to take up watercolor painting and arrange flowers and furniture and nurture people with good food and comfortable surroundings. That's why an inn would be just the thing for me—people around all the time, but always gone again, too. Relationships without the permanence."

Addie and Bill exchanged a private, meaningful glance. For the first time, they both looked doubtful.

Suddenly I was afraid they wouldn't let me have the inn. That was the moment I realized I wanted it.

"I'm not trying to say that I don't have *any* permanent relationships," I added hastily. "I'm really close to my parents and my sister, and I have lots of good friends. It's just that I'm not looking for the live-in-the-suburbs kind of life, with a husband and a nine-to-five-job and two-point-five kids and a dog—"

"Don't you like dogs?" asked Addie.

"I *do* like dogs," I said with a laugh. "I had dogs, when I was a kid. I like men, too. I hope to have one in my life again someday soon—"

"A dog, or a man?"

"Um . . . both, I guess! Why not?"

"Well, life here at the Magic Mermaid certainly isn't your traditional life in the suburbs," said Addie.

"And it isn't an easy life. There's always work to be done," Bill added.

"I'm not afraid of hard work."

Somehow, and rather abruptly it seemed, I had gone from arguing against buying the inn to arguing for it.

"It is hard work, but it's worth it," said Bill. "This is a special place."

"Yes, it is something special." I got up from the table and walked to the window. I looked out over the grounds, suddenly doing some serious thinking. I had envisioned plush carpets and gleaming fixtures. Elegant couples dressed for dinner. High society and high rates. Trade that for bare sandy feet, rusty plumbing, and family discounts? I was beginning to think . . . *yes*.

"So, you know what it is you want out of life, eh, little girl?"

I turned away from the window to see Bill's eyes narrowed on me, shrewd. I smiled, feeling shy with his penetrating attention focused on me.

I was silent a moment, feeling the beating of my heart, the excitement. "This place you have created here is magical," I said. "I don't know how else to describe it. I want to stay here."

"It is a magical place, isn't it, Bill?" Addie said. "You'll fall in love, Kelly, if you take it on."

The word *if* annoyed me. *If you take it on.*

I was already beginning to consider it mine.

The Magic Mermaid Inn wasn't what I'd had in mind—it was even better.

Chapter 2

"ARE you included in the price of the room?"

The guy was my grandfather's age, pale hair thinning, yellow teeth showing a harmless grin. His wife was sitting in the car outside the office.

"You're all set, Mr. Keefer," I said with a wry smile, handing him his key. "Enjoy your stay."

Almost two months had passed since the day I first came to the inn, and now it belonged to me.

A Lexus sedan was pulling into the parking area near the main house—from the office windows I had a good view out to the old highway. *A return customer.* Most new guests drove up to the motel when they arrived and were directed down to the office in the old farmhouse. We had signs out at the road, but visitors often missed them.

I added it to my already too-long mental list: *Put up more effective signage for the front office.*

The woman stepping out of the car was tall and sophisticated-looking, with black hair cut short and artfully spiked. Her lithe body was overdressed for the woodsy beachside setting, but striking in a skin-tight gold T-shirt, black leather trousers, and high-heeled boots. Her leather bag was cherry red, and her lipstick matched it perfectly.

"Hello, welcome," I greeted her when she came into the office. She sized me up in a way only another woman can, examining me critically and yet somehow approvingly.

"Welcome yourself—you must be the new owner of the inn," she said. "It's Kelly, right? I'm Paula Watson. Hello. Great to meet you." Passenger doors opened on the Lexus and two young boys slowly emerged. They looked red faced and rumpled, like they'd been asleep.

"Oh, yes—Paula," I said. "And your two boys. Rocky and—"

"Dean, right. Very good."

"Addie says you're her favorite guests." It was a PR line, sure, but it wasn't a lie. Addie had actually said that about a lot of her patrons, and I believe she meant it sincerely every time.

"Addie and Bill do take care of us. My ex-husband has the boys most of the time, and when I have them for the weekend, what are they going to do? They go postal after about an hour in my apartment. So we've been coming here two or three weekends a month. It's worked out pretty well. I mean, eventually I'm going to have to get a bigger place of my own, but right now this is our home away from home."

"How old are your boys?"

"Rocky's eleven, Dean is almost ten. We like Dolphin Cottage, but we didn't get it this weekend, called too late, forgot it was Labor Day. Pelican is nice, too, though, so I don't mind. We stayed in Schooner Cottage one weekend, and I swear I heard this eerie, sad moaning all night long. I'm sure it was the ocean or the wind or something—but it really freaked me out. So now when I call I always specify, don't put me in Schooner, *please.*"

"I'll remember that," I said with a laugh. "But you don't have to worry. I'm staying in Schooner now."

"Really?" she seemed surprised. "You're not using the apartment behind the main house, then?"

"Addie and Bill are staying on for several months, so the transition will be easier for all of us, hopefully."

I got Paula and her boys settled into Pelican Cottage. Other guests were arriving and the staff was bustling. Bill came hobbling in to help me at the front desk. The inn had a three-hour window for check-in, which was convenient in some ways, but it meant we were usually swamped between three and six.

Addie rushed into the office, breathless, cradling a bottle of champagne in her arms. "Kelly, dear, would you be a lifesaver and run this up to Sea Horse on your young legs? One of our regulars is bringing his fiancée to the inn for the very first time, and I'm afraid they'll be here any minute, and I haven't—I meant to do it myself, earlier, but . . ."

"Yes, yes." I took the bottle. "What about a champagne bucket?"

"Well, there's the plastic one in the room . . ."

"Right."

Provide silver buckets for champagne.

I headed up to Sea Horse Cottage, which was toward the rear of the property, higher up the hill behind the house. Pathways of weathered stone edged with clumps of tiny daisies and sweet alyssum meandered between the cottages and through the trees.

As I came around a turn, I was met with a strand of caution tape and my purposeful stride was checked. I stopped so abruptly, my hands slipped on the wet champagne bottle, and I was just barely able to save it from crashing to the ground.

"Hey, are you okay?"

The painter stood on a ladder, paintbrush in hand, working on the window trim of Starfish Cottage. He was a little older than me, with a scruffy beard and white, paint-spattered coveralls. Though his hair was tied back in a bandanna, a dark curl managed to escape at his brow. His mouth was set, expressionless, but his eyes laughed at me, lines radiating out from them like sun beams drawn by a kindergartner.

"I almost stepped into the paint can," I said. "This is a walkway, you know."

"Well, that's why I put up the tape."

"I'm Kelly Redvers," I said as I cradled the champagne in the crook of an arm, and offered my hand in what I hoped was a friendly but businesslike gesture. "I'm the new owner of the inn."

"You're—oh. Hi. Good to meet you." He stumbled over the words, unable to hide his surprise. Holding the paintbrush in his left hand, he reached down with his right hand and we shook, firm and quick. My hand must have been wet and icy to the touch, from the champagne bottle. His was dry, warm, and strong.

"I'm Nick McClure. I do the maintenance for the place."

"Yes, Bill told me about you."

"Well, don't look so dubious. I'm all right, really."

"Is it necessary to set up right here in the walkway?"

"If you want this side of the building painted, it is."

"It's Friday afternoon on one of the busiest weekends of the year, and suddenly you choose this moment to do your work?"

"Well . . ."

"I've been here full-time for over a week now and this is the first I've seen of you, though I was told you were contracted out to paint these buildings over a month ago—"

"There's really no contract," he said calmly. "But yeah . . ." His voice rose into a question. *So?*

"So it would be nice if you could plan your job around normal business hours. Would that be possible?"

"It would be, yes. With certain exceptions." Those laughing eyes again.

"Such as this week, apparently."

"Yes, ma'am." He was making fun of me now.

"You had another job?"

"That's right."

"And that work took precedence over us here."

"Yeah. It did."

He didn't back off from my gaze, and he met my challenge with poise. His mouth seemed to be pressing back mirth, and his eyes held mine and seemed to be asking me to dance. He didn't appear to be overly tall or heavily muscled, but he had the advantage in height over me now, standing on his ladder. I understood the importance of establishing authority with subordinates, and I sensed I was failing with this one.

Scruffy beatnik.

"Make way!" Paula came prancing up the path in a black and white one-piece swimsuit and red mules, a red sarong loosely tied across the slight swell of her hips. Didn't take *her* long to strip down, I thought. She looked good, too, with her long neck, her long legs and—well, her long *everything* except the short black hair, which set off black saucy eyes. She didn't have breasts to speak of, but with legs like that she didn't need them.

"I think the fog's coming in, and I'm freezing, but I am determined to go swimming!" she exclaimed. "The boys are ahead of me, but I think I went the wrong way."

"Just go on back down there," I said. "The path loops around. Watch out for wet paint."

"Right. I'll find it. It's not like I haven't been to that pool a hundred times already. The boys will swim in any weather." She picked her way past us in her red heels, smiling at us both.

High heels with a swimsuit? *Red* high heels. I was impressed. That was taking your feminine side to an extreme. In my jeans and flip-flops, I suddenly felt insignificant.

Nick McClure was watching Paula now, his gaze following the stride of those long legs. He looked like a billy goat, his dark beard jutting off his chin.

"Don't fall off your ladder, Nick," I said.

I went into Sea Horse and set the bottle on the table by the window with the note Addie had provided in an unsealed envelope. I opened it to see what she'd written. Pretty soon I would be the one writing these notes to my guests.

I was surprised to see the unfamiliar handwriting.

Kyra—hope you learn to love this place as much as I do.
Eli

So this was not a gift from the inn. I guiltily slid the note back into the envelope and took a better look at the label on the champagne bottle, feeling doubly glad I hadn't broken the bottle.

Eli and Kyra. How romantic. I surveyed the room, which was perfectly done up; I smoothed the already-smooth coverlet on the bed and checked all the details again. I loved the nubby texture of the old creamy white cotton chenille, and the look of the iron bedstead against the unpainted walls, golden cedar planks polished with beeswax.

So he was bringing his fiancée to the inn for the first time. Yes, it was a perfect romantic escape. The views of the ocean, the big comfortable bed, the private patio with its honeysuckle-draped picket fence and arbor, flowers spilling color out of window boxes. Who wouldn't want to spend an idyllic weekend with one's lover in such a setting?

Not Alex. Alex had had no feeling at all for the romantic gesture. Alexander Jones, my most recent live-in love. Not that recent anymore; it had been over a year now. No, if we had stayed together in a place like this, he would be itching to get home, to get back to his computers. He was an absentminded genius who had a high-paying job doing something for NASA he couldn't talk about. He had come after Andy Shane, a perpetually broke guitarist, who had come (following a lengthy interval of casual dating) after Brad Suzuki, my college boyfriend, a fellow engineering student and a really good guy.

They were all good guys.

I had been faithful to each of them in reverse order for four years, two years, and six months, respectively—and I remembered each relationship with fondness. I truly loved them all, and felt their love for me. And yet with each of them I had known, in the part of my mind and heart and soul that knows these things, that we would eventually part.

Alex was probably my favorite of all—terribly funny, horrendously intelligent, and hopelessly unromantic. No candlelit dinners. No thoughtful little gifts. No wild weekends away, just the two of us. Was that part of the reason we eventually called it quits? Certainly not. I was no romantic, either.

But I did appreciate the occasional romantic gesture.

I got out of the cottage just in time; as I was latching the door I heard giggling and footsteps coming up the path. I wanted the champagne to be a surprise, for the girl at least, so I slipped through the gate and moved behind the arbor just as they appeared, arm in arm. He carried a small travel case; she carried nothing but a tiny handbag.

As I peered at them through the tangle of honeysuckle vines, he had my attention at once—something about him struck me as familiar. He was a big, broad, good-looking guy with a jutting Dudley Do-Right chin, ruggedly casual in hiking boots, indigo jeans, and a forest green puffy jacket. His nose was large and straight, his eyes slightly squinty, like he was used to gazing out upon vast distances. The girl was petite and pretty, golden blond and milky, her exotic catlike eyes roving over the landscape, narrowed and considering. Two attractive people, but they didn't seem to go together quite right, like a mismatched pair of salt and pepper shakers. He was huge and rugged and friendly looking; she was petite and rare, like something kept behind glass in a gift shop.

"Well, here it is," I heard him say to her. He paused at the gate and gazed at the cottage. "Sea Horse." He sounded wistful. "I sure had a lot of great times here when I was a kid."

"You keep saying that, Eli. You had a great time here as a kid. But is this the *honeymoon* cottage. What's that about?"

"Well, I mean I've had some great times here . . . at the inn. I've probably stayed in every room and cottage they have."

He held the gate open for her and she passed through with a regal glide.

Bill came slowly up the pathway toward Sea Horse, bent beneath the weight of two large, heavy-looking suitcases. The lovebirds stood cooing at each other on their charming little porch, too engrossed in each other to notice the old man hauling their stuff. I immediately disliked them for this. I was about to step out into the open and give Bill a hand when Eli suddenly noticed him.

"Hey there, I'll take those."

Okay, so the guy wasn't so bad after all. But proud Bill shook him off and completed the journey to the porch with the heavy bags. The girl stood watching him, and Eli opened the door with his key. She went in first, followed by Bill at Eli's insistence.

Look into hiring a local teenager to porter luggage.

ELI. Where had I seen him before? How did I know him? I didn't know an Eli. I walked down the path to the front office. The painter had disappeared, though his equipment still cluttered the pathway. The sun had dropped low over the ocean, now faded beneath a curtain of mist. I could hear laughter and shouting from across the gully, but the pool would soon be deserted.

I noticed movement behind the windows in cottage number 9, and for a moment I thought I saw a face peering out at me. Number 9, set off by itself against the steepest part of the hillside, on the edge of the cliff. Number 9, a source of irritation for me, because it wasn't rented by the day or week, but by the month. I had seen the records, and I wasn't too happy about that. Even in the off season we could get more for the cottage than we did now, with this arrangement.

I had yet to meet my "tenant," and I was already set against him. Addie had described him as "shy," and, when pressed, "a very nice, rather eccentric young man." I was mildly curious to see who Addie would describe as eccentric—or young, for that matter. J. G. Greenfield—his name as it was registered in the books—never seemed to be around during the day. Until now.

But there was too much to be done at the moment for me to pop in and introduce myself. Bill was busy with the lovebirds, and another car had just pulled in: first-timers, from the look of it. I walked up toward the motel to welcome them.

AFTER checking in the latest arrival, I perused the guest register to see if I could discover Eli's last name. I was sure I knew him from somewhere; maybe his last name would tip it off. But the couple in Sea Horse wasn't listed in the guest register. The reservation for Sea Horse simply noted *E* and the date. Apparently the couple hadn't even checked in yet, which was odd, since Bill had already carried their bags up to the cottage.

The front door banged shut; somebody came into the entry and I looked up. Eli himself stood there in the office.

"Hello," I said. "May I help you?"

"I'd love it if you would," he replied, looking at me with open curiosity and a flirty half smile. "How are you doing?"

"I'm doing fine," I said, automatically pulling back a little in reaction to his decidedly male summation of my assets.

"Is your hair really that color?" he asked.

"Yes, it is."

"A true redhead. Beautiful."

"Thank you. Would you like to check in?"

"Actually, I just wanted to see if I have any messages."

I looked at him blankly.

"Oh, hello Eli," Addie bubbled and chirped, hurrying into the office. "There are some messages here for you . . ."

She snatched a handful of Post-it notes from behind the desk and thrust them at the man. He was tall; Addie looked like a gnome beside him. He glanced at the notes, then at Addie, and said, "Thank you, Mrs. Addie."

"You're welcome, Eli."

"Addie knows I'm always forgetting my phone," he said. "Or losing it somewhere. I hate phones, so I think subconsciously I'm always trying to ditch mine. She makes sure I get my messages."

"So! This is your girl's first time," Addie said to Eli. "How does she like it so far?"

"Her first time, yeah." Eli glanced at me with a faint smile. "So far, so good," he said. "But Kyra's a hard sell. We'll see." He turned to go out, thought of something, and turned back.

Yeah, you forgot to check in, Eli.

"Oh, and Addie," he said, "you might tell McClure to be more careful. Kyra almost fell over his ladder out there."

"Oh dear," Addie gasped. "I'm so sorry."

"No harm done."

When he had gone out the door I turned to Addie. "Addie, who is that guy?"

"Well, he's one of our guests, of course . . ." she answered slowly, as if it might have been a trick question.

"Why didn't he check in? I see he's already settled into Sea Horse, but he didn't—"

"Oh, that's Eli." She waved her little hand by way of explanation. "He's been coming here since he was a boy, first with his mother and father, then on his own. We never require him to check in."

"What do you mean, you never *require* him—"

"Well, it's just the way it's evolved. He leaves *enormous* tips for the housekeepers, and—"

"Well, he still has to pay for the cottage, doesn't he? And what if—"

"Of course, of course. Don't worry. He's always very generous."

I went to the window and watched him walk up the path until he disappeared behind the laundry cottage. What kind of business do we run here, I wondered, that we don't require guests to check in?

But others were arriving and I didn't have time to think about it.

Chapter 3

THE system around here is entirely too lax, I said to myself, not for the first time. Not even for the first time that day.

It was late Saturday afternoon. During happy hour a boy who couldn't have been more than sixteen had parked his bike by the rear entrance to the house and had availed himself of the wine and cheese we put out for the guests on the wide front porch.

I knew the boy wasn't staying at the inn; one pointed look from me and he disappeared, bike and all, only to be replaced by the painter Nick McClure, in his spattered overalls and his bandanna. He had started work early that morning and kept at it steadily, which I appreciated, except when he was getting in the way of the guests. He did take a break to instruct Paula's two young boys in the manly art of sanding and caulking; then he put them to work. The kids seemed to be having a great time, and Paula was loving it, having her children occupied, but I was pretty sure my insurance didn't cover child labor.

Now my painter-handyman was helping himself to a bottle of beer from a tub of ice near the table.

So we provided wine to the neighborhood teenagers and iced beer to tradesmen who worked whenever they felt like it. No wonder the legitimate guests were nowhere to be found. Scared away, no doubt.

Ah, but there was Paula, swirling up the steps in a full-skirted sundress. The bright red and white print set off her smooth tanned skin to perfection, and I found myself sneaking a glance at Nick to gauge his reaction to this striking female specimen. But his head was down. He seemed to be studying the paint on the porch.

Nope—there was a quick glance, he couldn't resist.

One of Paula's sons, a striking copy of her, with black eyes, black hair, and that beautiful sharp-featured face, came running full speed across the lawn and up the stairs to the front porch. In response to one look from his mother he stopped abruptly, and then sedately climbed the steps behind her. Following along at a more leisurely pace came a dreamy-eyed blond boy, a contrast to his larger brother in both looks and mood.

"Boys, have you met Ms. Redvers?" their mother asked as she poured herself a glass of wine and sat down at one of the small round tables on the porch.

"Hi, guys," I said. "You can call me Kelly."

"Hello, Kelly," they said in unison, nodded politely, and looked away quickly.

"And here's Nick." Paula indicated the painter, who stood near the drinks table and had just popped open his beer.

"Hey, Nick," said the dark-haired boy.

"Hey, Rock. Dean." Nick spoke easily to the boys, his voice low and lazy as he crossed the porch to take a seat in the corner.

"Hi, Nick," piped the little one.

"So, you guys gonna help me trim out Starfish tomorrow?" Nick asked the boys, casual.

"Anytime." Rocky shrugged. "You name it."

"Come here, I want to show you something." The boys rose automatically and went to sit with Nick at his table.

Eli and Kyra came strolling down the pathway and up the porch steps together, holding hands. Polite greetings were exchanged all around and more wine was poured. Eli and Kyra seated themselves at a table off by themselves.

Looking at Eli's profile, I was once again struck with a sense of recognition. I had forgotten to ask Addie his last name.

"I'm so jealous," Paula murmured to me behind her hand.

"What?" I slid into the chair beside her.

"When I see couples like them." She rolled her eyes discreetly in the direction of the lovebirds. "I feel like all the good stuff is passing me by. I fear celibacy may become my permanent condition."

"I wouldn't think *you* would have to worry about that."

"Thank you, but . . . honestly? Things were awfully dry for at least a year before the actual divorce, if you don't count the relapse on the day we signed the papers, which I don't. And *that* was months ago."

"Seriously?" I asked. "You haven't been with anyone since your husband?"

"No," she replied flatly. "Not even a date."

"I can't believe that."

"Believe it." She sipped from her wineglass and I admired her long, well-manicured fingers with their cherry-glazed tips. "I don't know. I can't explain it. I just don't feel attractive anymore."

"Well, McGruff there finds you attractive." I nodded toward Nick, who was deep in conversation with Paula's two boys, planning the painting strategy for the cottages. No wonder so little work had been done! I had a beatnik and two kids for a painting crew.

"Oh, you mean Nick," Paula exclaimed, loud enough for half the porch to hear.

Nick lifted his head and looked at us, then looked away again.

"The two of you are well acquainted, obviously."

She lowered her voice again. "Mmm, yes, I have run into him a few times about the place. I think he's a doll."

"A doll?" *A rag doll, sure.*

"Does that surprise you? Why? Check out those eyes. Have you noticed how green they are? Like translucent jade."

"Well, why don't you go for it?"

"What? Oh, no."

"Why not?"

I thought she would say Nick was a bit greasy for her taste, but instead she exclaimed, "Because! I am *so* finished with men."

"Come on."

"No, really. I am. Men are the scourge of my existence."

"Your sons are men," I pointed out.

"I know they are," she conceded with a tragic sigh. "And they're wonderful. I don't deserve them. I'm not a natural mother, though I do try very hard. When we first separated, I thought Rocky and Dean would be better off if Blake had custody. He's so much more normal than me. Homework, regular bedtimes, dentist appointments, he's always on top of all that. But now I don't know if it was such a good idea, letting them go. I miss them so much, and they're growing up so damn fast—I go a week without seeing them and they look taller."

"Is there a ladies' room in the house that I might use?" Kyra rose and asked no one in particular, and several of us pointed the way. When she had gone inside, her beau—the mysteriously familiar Eli—came to sit at the table with Paula and me, pulling up an empty chair.

His presence was commanding, large, healthy, and virile, and there was a faint scent of something masculine and delicious about him.

"You didn't tell me you were the new owner of the joint," Eli said to me. He was looking at me intently with his bold eyes, pale hazel and completely compelling. When he flashed a smile at me, that heroic chin jutted out a little farther.

"You were so busy acting like you owned the place," I teased him, "I never had the chance to tell you *I'm* the one who owns the place."

Paula snorted with laughter.

The painter looked up, watching us.

Uh-oh, I thought. Obviously it was going to take some getting used to, remembering my place as innkeeper. I couldn't just say the first thing that popped into my mouth anymore.

But as Eli looked at me, a long, slow grin spread over his big boyish face. He replied in a tone of gallant bantering, "Then I guess I'm lucky you didn't have me arrested for trespassing when I refused your offer to check in."

I laughed. "I thought about it."

Paula pulled her chair closer to the table. "Don't be too hard on him, Kelly," she said. "There's just something about the Magic Mermaid, I don't know what it is. But it makes you feel like it belongs to you."

"That's true," said Eli. "I've always felt like this was my home away from home. More so than some of the houses I've owned. I love this place."

I was beginning to like this guy.

Nick McClure went back to his powwow with the kids, showing them a trick with a pencil and paper and some scribbled lines and dots. Paula and Eli launched into a friendly argument, comparing and contrasting the charms of the various cottages and motel rooms, each of them vying, it would seem, for the title

of guest-who-has-stayed-in-the-most-rooms at the Magic Mermaid Inn.

Other guests appeared and joined in the discussion, and I was
warmed to feel the affection they all seemed to have for the place.
A middle-aged black man in a gray business suit and a bowler hat
stood near the motel, just beyond the swimming pool, looking off
to the east, his back turned toward the ocean. He was one of our
guests; Bill had checked him in earlier. But he did not come up to
the porch.

I glanced at Eli and saw that he was studying me. And I was
more certain than ever that I knew him from somewhere. I decided
not to ask him; I wanted to figure it out. Besides, it was such a
cliché. Don't I know you from somewhere? I rose, excused myself,
and went into the office.

Through the window I heard a bored-sounding feminine voice.
"Oh, it's unbelievable. Seriously."

Kyra was just outside in the garden, talking on a mobile phone.
"So, I'm like, *this* is the place he comes to several times a year? It
would drive me crazy. You know? Forget room service, we'll be
lucky if they don't have crabs in the bed." She giggled. "No, of
course I'm exaggerating. It's not really that bad; actually it is rather
romantic, with the ocean just outside and everything. But I tell you
what, Adrian, after we're married, when we go to the beach it's
going to be the Ritz!"

She paused to listen for a moment. "Oh, I know. But how often
do we get to the islands? It's been months. And he's having the La-
haina house done over, so it's sort of a mess anyway. But come *on,*
this guy can go anywhere in the world. He can do anything he
wants. You know? And he comes *here?*" Another pause. "I know.
I know. It amazes me. But it's kind of sweet, I guess. It's like me
with Boo Boo. I could've had the most beautiful purebred Persian
kitten, but I wanted Boo Boo. Maybe that's why I'm in love, you

know? He's just so cute like that—anyway, I just wanted to remind you that we really have to nail down the caterer on the individual tortes. Well, of course we'll have a cake, too, but it would be perfect if we could also have the tortes, and Mario's going to do something that's just so cute, these little cupcakes that look like they're wearing tuxedos . . ."

I went back out to the porch. Eli was talking to Paula and another guest, an older woman who came every year for whale watching. He was telling them about how he and his sister used to hunt for shells on the beach below the motel. He was clearly in love with the place, which gave him points in my book, but I found the disparity between his attitude and that of his fiancée rather jarring.

It looked to me like I was about to lose one of the inn's oldest and best clients, and I hadn't even been in management a week.

Paula and Eli began talking about computer systems and software, and in no time they were exchanging business cards. I resisted the impulse to sneak a peak at Eli's card.

Kyra returned from "the ladies' room" and cut her fiancé out of the general conversation, which was too bad. I liked his gregarious, warm manner; Paula had drawn him out the most, but I felt he had been directing some indefinable, subtle attention toward me.

Nick finished his beer and walked down to the parking area below the house to put away some tools in his truck. I left the party on the porch and wandered up toward the trees on the hill above the inn to catch a moment of solitude. A feeling of peace washed over me and I felt a rush of certainty that I was in the right place, doing the right thing with my life. And that was not a feeling I could say had been all that steady recently.

As I came back down the hill after my walk, I circled to the front of the house and saw a strange sight in the flower garden. Addie and Bill, thigh deep in daisies, were struggling with a half-grown Holstein calf who obstinately resisted their best efforts to remove her from the garden. She had a look of comical defiance on her sweet cow-face and a revolving mass of Addie's precious posies in her mouth.

I had realized early on that becoming an innkeeper meant I would be constantly handling any number of small emergencies. But a cow in the cutting garden? This was one crisis I had not foreseen.

A small crowd was forming at the white picket fence sur-rounding the flower garden. Some of our guests had come out to witness the entertainment, including Eli and Kyra, Paula and her boys, and the man in the bowler hat. The teenager I had shooed away from the drinks table sat on his bike, watching from a dis-tance. He was skinny and sullen looking, peeking out from under a wing of glossy black hair. Anita and the maids came out to see what was going on, and the paint-spattered Nick was there, too.

Hasn't he gone home yet? Something about Nick McClure an-noyed me.

Then again, maybe it was good he was there. He crouched down by the picket fence, examining the broken rails.

But where had the calf come from?

"Don't worry, Kelly," Bill said when he saw me. He and Addie exchanged glances, and I knew they were worried about my reac-tion to this latest minor catastrophe at the Magic Mermaid. "Grendel's gone off to get Earl."

Grendel . . . my mysterious tenant. I imagined a brooding, soli-tary writer with muscular arms and a penchant for bourbon. But who was Earl?

I found out a few minutes later, when a big GM pickup pulled into the parking area next to the house. The vehicle was shiny and immaculate, and the bed of the truck was empty but for a welding torch on a cart. The man who climbed down out of the cab was probably in his early fifties. He wore brand-new Wrangler jeans, cowboy boots, a red and white western shirt with pearl buttons and piping over the pockets, and a Stetson hat.

First a cow, I thought, and now—a cowboy. Cow plus cowboy equals all our calf problems solved, right?

"Oh, lookie there," said the man in a deep, easy drawl. "Seems we have got ourselves a situation."

A woman climbed down from the passenger side of the truck, shaking her tight brown curls, folding her arms and looking at the man reproachfully, as if to say, *I told you so.*

Addie and Bill introduced us after the calf had been expertly extricated from the muddy garden with a halter, a lead rope, and a neat bit of pushing and shoving.

Earl and Maxine owned the property that bordered the inn, acres of ranch and farmland, and wild open space. They ran a few head of cattle and grew pumpkins, Christmas trees, and ollalie berries.

They welcomed me as the new innkeeper, and Earl apologized for the mishap, said someone had left the pasture gate open—his wife had warned him he should put a lock on it—and they hoped there wasn't too much harm done. "It's a darned shame," he said, shaking his head. "I remember a time you didn't have to worry about locking everything up. But nowadays . . . you just can't trust people."

"What happened to Grendel?" Addie asked.

"Oh, you know Grendel," Maxine said. "We asked him to ride over in the truck with us, but he wanted to walk."

I glanced at Eli through the small knot of people and found him staring at me with a strange expression. He looked away quickly and wandered off with his fiancée.

A few minutes later Maxine was leading the calf away down the road, small and strong looking in her Pendleton shirt and her jeans cuffed up over her boots, and the show was over.

"I'll be along," her husband called after her. He turned to us and apologized again.

Bill assured him that we would recover just fine, but Addie stalked off with a scowl pressed down over her brow, the least forgiving I had ever seen her. It was apparent she felt the damage to her flowers irreparable, not to mention the picket fence—though Nick had spoken up quietly and assured us he would have the fence fixed in no time.

"*I'll* fix up that fence, don't you worry," Earl Johnson interrupted. His amiability faded and for a moment I almost thought he was annoyed by Nick's offer to repair the fence.

"It's no problem," Nick said. "There's a stash of extra pickets at my house, from when I built the fence. I'll just go get what we need and nail 'em up."

Earl seemed to want to argue this plan, but he closed his mouth, hard.

Nick looked at him with defiance. The two men stood there as if ready for a face-off, the huge, older, neat-as-a-pin rancher with his tightly buttoned and belted western garb, and the smaller, stockier young man with his baggy paint-spattered overalls, greasy bandanna, and shaggy beard. I looked at the welding torch with its tanks for oxygen and acetylene. Watching Nick and Earl together, I thought of that combustion when the two gasses come together, two elements, each controlled and contained, but capable of flaring up hot when combined.

There's something there between those two, I thought.

The party was breaking up. The kid with the wing of black hair had taken off on his bike. Nick went back to his truck. Paula and her kids wandered off toward the house, and Bill and Earl stood talking for a while. I left by the frontage path to check the fence between the rancher's property and inn.

A man came walking toward me down a narrow trail through

the cypress and pine woods. He wore all white: white trousers and shoes and a white silk shirt with a Mandarin collar. The clean white was a contrast to his deeply tanned, golden skin. He was completely bald, and the skin on his skull was shiny.

I hadn't seen him check in to the inn, but the locals sometimes used the trails that wound through the inn property, in and out of the woods and along the cliffs.

When our paths crossed, he nodded at me politely. I thought he would pass on his way, but when we came close, he said softly, "I'm a creature of habit, I'm afraid. Rather worried about change."

I took a good look at him, startled. He was in his late forties, I judged, with an earnest expression, and thick lashes setting off his eyes, which were an extraordinary color—deep blue and slyly tipped at the corners. He was almost handsome, but his chin was narrow and his mouth was small and pretty, as if it belonged on a little girl.

"I'm your tenant in number nine," he said, extending his hand with shy courtesy. "People call me Grendel. You are the new innkeeper, aren't you?"

"Yes, I'm Kelly. Pleased to meet you." My handshake was firm, and I tried to suppress the tangle of feeling number 9 always raised in me. I was itching to get that cottage back on a daily cost basis. I wanted to be an innkeeper, not a landlord. He didn't have a lease, I had been pleased to learn, but meeting him in the flesh disturbed the easy flow of my eviction fantasies. And dashed my tenant-as-sexy-tortured-artist fantasies, too.

"So you're the one who ran for help," I said. He looked confused, and I added, "With the calf—"

"Oh, yes. Well, one does try to be useful."

"So how long have you been living at the inn?" I asked.

"Several years. It's a simple life, but it suits me. I am a great advocate of the benefits of a frugal existence. My cause, if you will, is to help people live longer, healthier lives; I am rather obsessed with matters of diet and exercise." He smiled bashfully. "I'll tell you all about it sometime over a glass of pinot noir. My only vice." He was mocking himself now.

The sun still hovered above the horizon, but the earth had cooled. Grendel spoke a few lines of what might have been Thoreau, looking out to the trees and the meadow beyond.

"I know I am fortunate to live here, in my little cottage." He looked at me sideways, like a child. "Of course I will flow with whatever changes come my way."

I had the eerie impression that he knew all about my feelings for number 9 cottage—though I'd never voiced my misgivings aloud to anyone, not even Addie or Bill—and he seemed to be asking me to reconsider my position.

"I'm not planning to make any changes right away," I said truthfully. "I'm giving myself a few months to observe how things are run around here. After that, I will make changes as I see fit."

"Fair warning," he said with a sad smile.

Before parting ways, we stopped near the edge of the cliff and stood together, watching the waves roll in below, and the vast dark plain of the ocean, the horizon gilded by the setting sun. There was something a bit odd about him, but Grendel struck me as a very gentle, sweet man. I felt a little less dissatisfied now about renting out the cottage on a month-to-month basis.

Chapter 4

ON Saturday night I went into the parlor, and there I found Paula's two boys sitting alone in the dimly lit room, playing chess. I was impressed to see these young boys sitting still and silent, gazing down at the chessboard with intense concentration. From the looks of it, they had hardly touched the platter of fat, fudgy brownies Arturo had baked earlier in the day. Addie set out dessert for the guests every evening at eight o'clock, with coffee, hot water for tea, and cider.

I made myself a cup of tea and sat down near the front window. I could hear a woman's voice—Kyra's, I realized, after listening a moment. She must be out on the front porch, talking to someone, but I didn't hear any other voice. Apparently she was chatting on her little flip phone again.

I watched the boys play chess and listened idly to bits and pieces of Kyra's one-sided conversation.

"So I said, fine, as long as it's film and not video. Well, there is a *huge* difference, you know. Video can look really cheap. You see some of this stuff, it has no depth. I mean, this is my *wedding*. I don't want it to look like a tacky talk show or something. But Ben says the stuff they're doing nowadays with digital is absolutely amazing . . ."

Ah, wedding plans again. I understood that preserving the documentary evidence of one's nuptials was crucial. In my grandmother's day, it was done with photography. My sister's wedding had been videotaped. But none of that, apparently, was good enough for Kyra.

"And so the producer says to me, what about a magenta wedding gown? It would look so striking against the green. And I'm like, what? Are you *kidding* me? But what do you think, Adrian? Am I crazy or is he?"

Producer? Didn't they call them wedding planners anymore?

"That was cool today, when that little cow came into the garden," remarked Rocky, his fingers gently tapping his knight.

"I know," said his brother.

I could never remember the little one's name.

Bullwinkle always popped into my mind when I saw him, instead of his name. Or rather, just Winkle. He was a charming, fragile blond boy and he made a cute little Winkle.

"Addie wasn't too happy about it," I said. The boys looked up at me for the first time.

"She was so mad," said Rocky.

"Well, that calf ate her flowers," I reminded him.

"Hey, she just cuts them anyway." He pointed at one of Addie's arrangements, a tall spray of flowers in a lovely vase on a polished tabletop.

"And dat poor whittle cow was hungwee," said the younger boy, affecting a rather more childish voice than he actually had.

"She grows them just for that reason," I told them. "For her flower arrangements."

"Don't you think that's strange?" Rocky posed the question. "We grow the sex organs of plants to use as decorations in our homes. I mean, when you think about it, it's kind of creepy."

For a moment, in that old-fashioned, dimly lit parlor, sitting there alone with these two odd young men, it did seem rather creepy. The flowers in their urn stood clumped in shadow and resembled some kind of shaggy monster.

Then Kyra's voice cut through the atmosphere. "And I can't believe Eli doesn't think we need a DJ *and* a band. With that many people, and such a mix of ages, it only makes sense to have it like a festival, you know, like with a main stage, and then at least one other venue—at *least* one other."

"Yes, that's downright spooky indeed," I said.

"I think this place is haunted," said Winkle.

"I think so, too," said Rocky, matter-of-fact.

"You do?" I said.

"I know it is. The place is eerie."

"Well, it's just old," I said.

"The first time we came here, these guys we met told us there was a man's hand in the stagnant water around the slough. They said you could see it sticking out of a bunch of branches that got stuck near where the stream goes down into the ocean. So we walked down there, and we saw it, and it really did look like a dead guy's hand, all puffy and white, with fingers."

"But it turned out to be a rubber glove," said Winkle.

"Ha," I said. "That's pretty good."

"Nah, there's way better stuff than that," said Rocky. "Real stuff."

"Like Mrs. Worthington, pacing the widow's walk, gazing out to sea, looking for her lost husband?" I said. "You think she haunts the place?"

Rocky shrugged, clearly unimpressed with Mrs. Worthington. "Yeah, maybe. But there's other stuff, too."

"Like what?"

They both focused on the chessboard, thinking a moment.

Rocky moved a black castle. "Nick's got some good scary stories."

"Really good," added Winkle with a shudder; the admiration in his voice was unmistakable.

"Ah . . ." I said, "ghost stories bore me."

They glanced up at me, surprised.

"You know, the kind they tell around campfires?" I said. "I hate those. They always go on and on, and it's totally unbelievable, and the only reason they get a scare out of you is because at the end they say boo or something really loud and shocking after lulling you into a trance with the long boring ghost story."

"Well, there's one we heard about," said Rocky, "that's supposed to be true. And not even Nick will tell us the whole story, though he knows more than anyone."

"Why, what did he say?" I asked.

The two boys exchanged wary glances.

"Come on, tell me."

"A lady who stayed here went missing," Rocky said in a low voice.

"A lady who stayed here? At the inn?"

"Yeah."

"Was he trying to scare you, telling you this?" I asked.

"Who, Nick? No . . . I think he was more like trying to warn us or something."

"Yeah? So what's the story?"

Rocky scowled down at Winkle's move on the chessboard. "Like I said, I don't know very much about it."

"A woman disappeared. That's it?"

"She was staying here—at the hotel—like us," Winkle piped up. "Right before she vanished into thin air."

"Really?" I said. "When was this?"

"A long, long time ago."

"Was she ever found? Or—her body?"

"No . . ." Rocky faltered at this point. "I don't think so."

Winkle said in his baby voice, "She stayed here and then she disappeared and never came back!"

"Who was she?"

The boys shrugged, thin shoulders up and down in sloppy choreography. "Just some lady," Rocky said.

"But they say she was *beeyooteefool!*" Winkle exclaimed.

"Oh, God, don't remind me. It's so wretched. It's just *got* to grow out before filming begins, or we're going to have to resort to extensions." Kyra's voice, which somehow managed to express both excitement and boredom at the same time, carried into the parlor. "But did I tell you? I just found out they want to shoot all this background, you know, like with the pastry chef, and the designers, and the flower growers and everything, a behind-the-scenes sort of thing . . . Oh, I *know.* I know. Yeah, so, I told them we don't want to do it like a reality show, you know, it's got to be more like a documentary . . ."

The boys had forgotten about me and were reabsorbed in their game. I left the house by the kitchen door so I wouldn't disturb Kyra on the front porch, and I set out walking up the hill to the cypress woods on the north side of the property, thinking about what they had told me.

The foghorn called mutely from a distance. As I rounded a turn in the path, I came across a hunched figure sitting on a bench. It was Eli, in his puffy jacket, his arms resting on his knees, looking out to the ocean. He sat facing the darkness to the west, his head slightly cocked, like he was listening for the foghorn to sound again. He turned his head at the sound of my footsteps and watched me approach.

"What are you doing out here on a Saturday night? Shouldn't you be with your fiancée in the hot tub? You know you have one, on your private patio." The teasing words just slipped out before I could censor myself.

I'd like to think I wouldn't ordinarily talk to a guest in such a familiar way, even though I was new at this business of being an innkeeper. I wasn't sure what came over me with him.

But after hearing his fiancée discussing her wedding plans, I figured the guy deserved a little harassment, if only for hooking himself up with *that*.

"Hot tub, huh?" Eli said slowly. "I'll keep it in mind." There was enough humor in his tone to let me know he had taken my comment in the right spirit. But there was something else there, too, some sadness that melted me a little. "Although at this rate I'll be sitting in the hot water all by myself," he added.

"I guess wedding plans keep people pretty busy," I said.

"You have no idea. Or—maybe you do?"

"No, never been married."

"Me neither," he said grimly.

"Hey, come on," I said. His melancholy mood made me want to cheer him up. "You might as well enjoy it, right? You're only gonna do it once. Supposedly, anyway. Actually, I guess you do have more than one shot at marriage, if you really blow it."

He started laughing. "That's a comforting thought."

"Unless you're devout Catholic, that is."

"I wouldn't know—my father's mother was Jewish, and his father was a Southern Baptist minister. My mother's family were Presbyterians. My parents joined the Hare Krishnas in the seventies, but they dropped out of that and now they're Mormons. I myself am a Buddhist." He was grinning at me now.

"Is that all true?" I asked, amazed.

"No. None of it. Well, actually, *some* of it is true."

"Which part?"

"My mother's family were Presbyterians. Mom says she doesn't have a religion anymore, but she's spiritual. My dad's always been an agnostic, but then again, we've always celebrated Christmas and Easter, and he gets into it the most. How about you?"

"Your average middle-class white Protestant background. My mother claims to be Zoroastrian, but she made me go to Sunday school when I was a kid. My dad, the practical engineer, says you might as well hedge your bets and believe."

We were both smiling, enjoying the back and forth of quick conversation. I liked the feeling of ease and attraction that I felt when around him. I liked the way he looked in his puffy jacket and his jeans. I liked his Dudley Do-Right chin. And I really liked the way he took my teasing in stride. Too bad he was engaged to be married.

"Anyway," Eli said, "As far as marriage goes, I think even the Catholic church has an escape clause, but you have to prove somehow that you weren't actually married, and they call it annulment, not divorce, and it's complicated—"

"Divorce is always complicated."

"I know." He was suddenly serious. "And I'd hate like hell to fail at marriage. I'm really scared I'm gonna screw it up."

"I always figured I probably *would* screw it up, which is one of the reasons why I decided a long time ago that I'm never going to do it."

"Never going to get married? Really?" He looked at me, impressed.

"What?"

"Well, it's just that most women—" He stopped himself.

"What?"

He laughed. "Never mind."

"Oh, okay," I said knowingly. "And what about most men? If you ask me, it's the men who all want to get married."

"Well, I think most people, male or female, want that. They want to get married. They want to start a family, and why not? That's a fine thing to want."

"It is."

"I don't mean to sound defensive about it. Well, maybe I do. I have to admit, I've been having second thoughts . . ." He trailed off, looking guilty.

"Oh, *there* you are, Eli."

The fiancée appeared on the pathway, light from the house shining a halo around her, throwing her delicate figure into silhouette. She seemed unreal, just a cameo in a shining setting of gold, not a flesh and blood human being. Or maybe I just didn't want to think of her as a flesh and blood human being.

"Finished with your calls?" he asked her politely.

"I hope so." She smiled, apologetic.

"We were just talking about how much work it is, putting together a wedding," I said.

"Not to mention the marriage," Eli murmured.

"All right, mister," said Kyra. She walked purposefully to her man and held out her hand to pull him up from the bench. "Enough spending your romantic weekend hanging out with pretty redheads you aren't engaged to. You and me have a date with the hot tub."

"Have a good one," I said cheerily, glad they were going to enjoy their sensual, private hot tub in my inn after all; but for just a moment I wished it were me he was going away with, my hand he was holding.

He shot me a quick, moody glance before he walked off with his fiancée.

Chapter 5

I found out who he was the next morning.

I was sitting at a table on the front porch with a cup of coffee and the Sunday *Chronicle*. Eli's photo was on the front page of the business section.

"Bay Area Business Moguls: Fortune's Five."

So *that's* who he is, I thought.

Eli was *Eli Larson*. THE Eli Larson.

I knew who Eli Larson was. I had never met him, but I certainly knew of him.

Eli Larson's photo was the largest on the page. Well, of course. In the aristocracy of Bay Area entrepreneurs, he was royalty. His software company, Estreya, had helped put Silicon Valley—that mythological kingdom on the peninsula somewhere between San Francisco and San Jose—on the world map. Eli's empire was one of those begun-in-a-garage enterprises that had grown exponentially each year of the dot-com boom, making its founder incomprehensibly rich. And Estreya was one of the few tech businesses in the area that hadn't imploded during the dot-com bust. Eli's company was quite healthy—even robust, employing thousands of people and putting out innovative products. Some of my best friends worked for Eli Larson.

Eli himself had become something of a personality in recent years. Stories about him showed up regularly in the business and style pages of the *San Francisco Chronicle*, not to mention the national press. He was young, good-looking, and sporty. He raced cars. He sailed. He climbed Mount Everest. He traveled to poor countries and donated untold millions to help needy people. And his press agent made sure all his doings were well documented. His recent engagement to socialite Kyra Jennings had rated respectful media coverage.

Wow, I thought. Eli Larson. At my inn. One of his favorite places since he was a boy. That's the kind of clientele you wanted. Well, it was nice while it lasted, but it wouldn't last much longer, not with Kyra as Mrs. Larson.

I flipped to the local gossip page, but there was nothing there about Eli Larson or his fiancée. Well, she would remedy *that* oversight soon enough, I had no doubt, with a few well-placed phone calls.

I flipped back to the photo of Eli Larson.

"Doing research on your guests?"

It was Nick, in his inevitable splotched overalls, though today he wore a baseball cap instead of a bandanna. He had appeared from nowhere and jumped up on the porch, taking the steps two or three at a time. He walked past the table where I sat and poured himself a cup of coffee from the carafe on the table and swiped a muffin from the basket Arturo had set out.

"Hello, Nick," I said, forcing a smile. It had been such a lovely quiet morning. Addie and Bill had the office, which left me sitting in the sun on the porch, drinking Arturo's excellent coffee, reading the paper. In solitude.

Nick certainly was an early riser. And he had ignored my request to work only during regular business hours.

I should just be glad the work is getting done, I thought, damping down my annoyance.

"Notice how they put his picture larger than the others?" Nick leaned over me and pointed to the photo of Eli. For a moment I felt possessed of a strange urge to bite into his lean, muscular arm.

"Yes, actually, I did notice that," I said.

"It's because he's got the big bucks."

"Yes."

I drew back so he wouldn't touch me, and he gave me a look of amusement, sun-ray lines radiating out around his eyes. Green eyes, like clear jade, just as Paula had said. It was that same look he had given me the other day, like he was laughing at me but trying his best not to. I don't know why he bothered to hide it. I didn't care.

"It's the same in medieval art, you know," he was saying, "how they would have a queen and a servant standing side by side, and they make the queen all big, and the servant small, out of proportion to the queen, because the queen is the important figure—"

Nick's art history lesson was interrupted by a soft shriek.

"Oh, look." Addie pushed her little body between us to get a better look at the photo spread on the table. "It's our Eli, isn't it? I don't know if that's a very good picture of him."

"Addie, did you have any idea who he is?" I asked her. "You said you've known him for years."

"Who, Eli?" she asked with her characteristic placid innocence. "Well, yes, we've known him since he was a boy. I had heard that he's done very well for himself, selling computers, isn't that it?"

"Not computers exactly," I said. "The software that runs in them."

"I don't know much about computers, to be honest," she said. "And I don't really want to, either."

I already knew that. The front office was woefully under-computerized—another thing for my ever-growing list of things to do something about. Here at the Magic Mermaid, we took reservations and registered guests the old-fashioned way: with a pencil in a book. We had no Internet advertising, and no website for the inn, which was a shameful lost opportunity, as far as I was concerned. But I planned to change things.

"Don't tell Eli I said that." She smiled, looking down at his picture.

"Don't tell Eli you said what?"

It was Eli himself, standing behind us. The porch suddenly seemed crowded. He tipped his head over Addie's shoulder to see what we were all looking at. The distress in his voice was comical.

"Oh, man," he said.

Later, in my room, I cut the photo of Eli out of the newspaper. On impulse I stuck it up into the frame of my dressing table mirror. I stood there and looked at his face for a long time.

Chapter 6

I was alone in the office late Monday morning when Kyra and Eli came in. I waited to see why they had come. Not to check out, surely—since they had never checked in.

I looked up over the desk at Eli as he discreetly slid me an envelope. "We had a great time," he said. "Thank you for everything."

Kyra said charitably, "It's very peaceful here. And the paintings in the cottage are wonderful."

"They're new," said Eli. "I never saw them before. They must be one of your touches."

"Yes, one of the few things I permitted myself to change right away," I said, "was some of the art around the place."

"Kyra here is an artist," said Eli.

She shook her delicate blond head. "I dabble," she said modestly. "I'm nowhere near as good as that." She nodded at a watercolor on the wall above the front desk. "Who is the artist?"

"Kenneth Bing," I said. "He's a local artist."

"Wonderful. It's almost abstract, yet it manages to completely evoke the feel of the California landscape. The paintings in the cottage are his, too, aren't they? The two over the bed?"

"Yes, they are. You have a good eye."

"What was his name again?"

"Ken Bing. He'll be here at the inn in a couple of weeks, doing a weekend workshop, if you're interested. We have a special promotion for rooms—" I caught myself. Special promotions meant nothing to these people. "Here's the brochure. There are still one or two spots available in the workshop."

"Oh, well, thank you!" Kyra said, a little too brightly, clutching the brochure. They both thanked me again and said their good-byes, and went out to their car, a little silver bullet of a Porsche. This time Eli carried the luggage.

I opened the envelope and counted out a tall stack of crisp one-hundred-dollar bills. Okay, I thought, dazzled. Addie was correct: Eli Larson was a generous guest. I opened the drawer to put away the money, wondering what my accountant would say about this, and was surprised when the door banged open again.

Eli reappeared, breathless.

"Hey, Kelly," he said. "Put us down for a reservation the weekend of that painting workshop, for Sea Horse again, if it's available. I'm going to surprise Kyra. I think she'd like to do that."

I had my doubts, but I wasn't about to discourage him. "Okay," I said. "Sure thing." I jotted his name down on the list.

Ordinarily, I would have asked for a deposit, but in this instance, I would waive it. I would make an exception for Eli Larson. Just like Addie.

"Yeah, she's going to like that, I think," he said again, as if trying to convince himself. "Besides, it will give us an excuse to come back again soon."

"Well, great," I said, sounding more dubious than I intended. But my money was on Kyra. He might be one of the richest and most powerful guys in California—or the world, for that matter—but he was still a mortal man, a flesh and blood human being with a rather sturdy fiancée, even if she did resemble a piece of delicate Dresden china.

"HEY," said Nick from behind me the moment Eli had gone out. Startled, I whipped around to see him standing in the kitchen doorway, leaning against the jam. Spattered overalls, greasy do-rag, bushy dark beard. He'd come into the house and through the kitchen so quietly, I hadn't known he was there.

"You sure do make yourself at home around here, don't you?" I snapped, wanting my annoyance to show.

"Do you object?"

"When it comes to you, the word *object* does come to mind, yes," I said.

"And here I was hoping to be the *ob*ject of your affections," he said with a grin.

"Don't hold out any hope for that. From what I see, you're more of a liability than an asset. You're always in the way, you get very little done around here, and you appear to consume far more than your share of the inn's resources."

"A harsh and undeserved criticism, my lady. But alas, I didn't come in here just now to enjoy the privilege of receiving your insults."

"Why did you come in here?

"I have need of your authority. Your decision-making powers. There are some details on the back of the cottages and around the windows, painting details, what should be white, what should be blue, that sort of thing. It's a judgment call, and I thought you might want to make it."

He said the last bit softly, and I looked at him sharply. There was something frank and down-to-earth about him, which was disarming, but at the same time he was too smart, too wily to be trusted.

"So who made these decisions before I came along?" I asked him as we walked up the path together between the cottages. "Addie or Bill?"

"Well, neither, if I could help asking them. Bill doesn't care about aesthetic details, and Addie, well, Addie would give her heart and soul to each question of detail, so much so that a decision might take days. Weeks. Months. It might never get decided. So I learned not to need to know, as much as possible."

"I see. But you're taking a chance on me."

"I figured better safe than sorry, though I could still be sorry, no doubt. But I don't know you well enough yet to know."

"To know if I can make good decisions?"

"Exactly. Or any decisions. Turns out Addie didn't really want those decisions to make, anyway. But a girl like you would probably get touchy if she wasn't at least asked."

"Yes, a girl like me probably would."

As we turned off the path and walked behind the cottages, I saw a lot more had been done in the last couple of days than I had realized. The backs of the cottages sparkled.

"Well, I must say, the backs of the cottages look very nice," I told him.

"I figured over the weekend you'd prefer me to stay out of the way as much as possible, so I concentrated on the rear of the buildings, discreet side walls and such. Don't worry, I tried to be sensitive to the comings and goings of the guests, and I didn't look in anyone's windows. I'll move on to the fronts at the beginning of the week, when fewer guests are around."

He showed me the windows and trim in question and we

quickly reached a consensus about what should be painted blue and what should be painted white.

"There," he said. "That's what I would have done anyway. I needn't have asked for your opinion."

"But it's good you did."

"I thought so."

"Anything else I can do for you?"

"I'm good for now," he said in his laziest voice.

"Maybe you can do something for me."

"Sure."

"Try to keep in mind that when you make up stories about the place, you're reflecting on the reputation of the inn."

He looked at me blankly.

"I think it's great, the way you've taken Paula's boys under your wing, teaching them about things, letting them help you work and everything. They said they loved your ghost stories. But maybe you should be careful about what you put out there, you know—"

"What did I put out there?"

"They said you told them a lot of good scary stories, and that there was one in particular, about a young woman who stayed at the inn, and then went missing . . ."

He didn't say anything.

"I mean, they implied it was a murder—do you know what they were talking about?"

The sun rays around his green eyes deepened. "I wouldn't put too much importance on the stories kids tell, if I were you," he said.

He seemed suddenly restless, eager to get back to work.

Then I remembered what one of the boys had said—something like, *Nick won't even tell us the whole story, even though he knows more than anyone—*

"So, this story about a missing or murdered woman—is it a fictional story or is it something that really happened?" I prodded him.

"Either way, it could be bad for business," Nick replied in a low voice. "Isn't that right?"

"Nick?"

It was sultry Anita, with her big dark eyes and her white shirt-sleeves rolled up over the lean, compact muscles of her hard brown arms. "Nick, I need you to look at something for me," she said. "The door latch in Dolphin is acting up again."

She glanced at me, but didn't respond to my smile. Her face remained expressionless.

"Sure," said Nick. "I'll come take a look right now. I can take a break here, let some of the paint set up before I get on with the trim."

He walked past me and I was annoyed at how easily, and abruptly, he finished with me and went on to her. And was it my imagination, or had he deliberately evaded answering my questions about this story of a missing woman?

I decided I would ask Addie about it.

LATER I was walking down to the house when I noticed Anita and Nick together by the flower garden, looking at something on the side of Schooner Cottage, the cottage I was living in until I made the transition to full-time manager of the inn. Their intense focus on whatever it was they were looking at got me curious and I took the left fork of the path.

Something—some symbol—had been scrawled on the newly painted siding, some spray-painted graffiti. It was a ragged red circle with a big letter A sprawled over it, about two feet high on the back wall of the little cottage. A long drip of red paint had run down the wall and dried like blood.

"Is that some kind of satanic thing?" Anita was asking Nick.

"No, it's the symbol for anarchy," he replied.

"For what?" Anita looked confused.

"It's a political thing," he told her. "I think the philosophy is like total freedom. Break with government and its restrictions. Something like that."

"Freedom!" I moaned. "Freedom to paint crap like this on my building?"

"Hey, it's okay, boss." Nick reached out and grabbed my shoulder, gave me a gentle shake. "I'll take care of it. Fifteen minutes from now you won't even know it was there."

"But who did this?" I cried.

"Punks. Don't even worry about it."

"Do we have gangs here?"

"Gangs are everywhere," Anita said portentously.

Nick and I looked at each other and started laughing; the way she had said it just sounded so funny. She seemed a little offended.

"Give me a minute, Hernandez," he said playfully, and now his hand was on Anita's slender shoulder, giving her a squeeze. "I'll just paint over this masterpiece, and be right with you."

NICK came into the office on Tuesday morning to pick up a check. He looked so different, I didn't recognize him for a moment. He had shaved his beard and mustache. He wore no hat or bandanna and his hair was trimmed short. Instead of coveralls, he wore faded jeans and a cambric shirt, and for once he wasn't all spattered with paint.

I found him disappointingly normal looking without the scruffy beard and the greasy hair curling out from beneath the bandanna, and decided I'd liked him better before the makeover.

"I wanted to let you know," he said to me, "I've got to go to court. I'm going to be out of town for a couple of days, so I won't be working on your place."

"Court," I said. "Why does that not surprise me? You, going to court? For a couple of days?"

"It's in Nevada County."

"Oh. So, what they get you for? Armed robbery? Murder? Aggravated assault? Or just plain aggravation?"

"I'm not the defendant," he said. "I'm an expert witness."

I couldn't decide if he was joking or not. I was about to prod the answer out of him when we were interrupted by a delivery. A lanky kid came into the office with an enormous bouquet of pale pink miniature roses.

"Kelly Redvers?"

"Yes, that's me," I said wonderingly.

He set them on the desk and was gone.

Baffled, I slit open the envelope. "Thanks for a wonderful weekend," I read aloud. "Signed, E.L."

I frowned, thinking.

A *wonderful weekend*. "This must be from one of our guests," I said. "E.L.?"

"Eli Larson," said Nick, leaning against the desk, chewing on a toothpick, watching my face.

Eli Larson! I felt my face grow hot, and turned away so Nick couldn't see me blush, but he was canny enough to notice the force of my reaction, and just enough of the devil to find it amusing. There was that holding-back-laughter expression about his eyes, and even with the scraggily beard gone, I recognized the smug expression, which was now accented by a deep dimple on the left side of his mouth.

"He's got a fiancée," said Nick.

"What?" I scowled at him.

"You know what I'm talking about."

"It says thanks for a nice weekend. That's all. He's a classy guy."

"Right. A classy guy with a fiancée."

"Which means he isn't married yet," I pointed out.

Nick shoved off from the desk, flicked his toothpick into the wastebasket, and threw me a withering look. "I gotta go," he said. "See you later, Kelly."

"Have a good time at court," I called after him.

I watched him walk out to his truck, and through the open window I heard him tell someone to get out of his seat. I moved closer to the open door, looked out, and discovered the someone was a dog; I could see pointed ears and a long, grinning face.

E.L., I thought. E.L.

Pink roses.

I turned back to smell the roses again. They were gorgeous, tiny, and perfect, and there were dozens of them. I hadn't even known I could be so moved by such a thing as a delivery of flowers.

Chapter 7

NICK stayed away longer than "a couple of days," and the work stopped dead on the maintenance projects. While he was gone we had to call in rooter service when the plumbing stopped up in one of the cottages. And the wayward calf made a return appearance in Addie's flower garden, smashing through the fragile old picket fence that Nick had already repaired.

Addie was a little high-strung, but she proved to be game under duress, and Bill was a stalwart companion during times of crisis, and so was Grendel, who appeared whenever he could be of help. When Addie's garden was again trampled and she needed a shoulder to cry on, his was available. He was a calming, organizing presence. His sweetness might have been cloying but for the fact that he usually made himself scarce; when he wasn't needed, he'd fade away.

To make amends for their calf, Earl and Maxine invited Addie, Bill, and me to dinner Saturday night. The Johnsons had a comfortable ranch house in the fold of the hills on the east side of Highway 1. Old orchards flanked one side of the house, pastures on the other. Down the road lay the pumpkin fields and across the gully, the Christmas tree farm. The couple had no children; their dogs, a springy border collie and an old basset hound, were their babies.

The dinner was excellent; they had produced almost everything we were eating, including a roast of their own private reserve beef.

"Sure is good," said Bill wistfully, savoring every bite. Addie didn't let him have much red meat.

"You know," said Earl, "we should have asked Grendel to come have supper with us tonight, too, but then, he don't eat meat at all. Hell, I don't know what the man does eat anymore. He's a vegetarian, you know."

"He's a vegan now," said Maxine.

"That's what I said."

"No, a vegetarian eats eggs and milk, and he doesn't."

"Well, a vegan is a vegetarian, right?" I said. "Though a vegetarian isn't necessarily a vegan. Or is it the other way around?"

"It's the wrong way around, I'll tell you that much," Bill said jokingly.

"Don't you make fun of our Grendel," said Addie. "He's very healthy on his diet, and he hardly costs us a dime to feed. You know, Anita's son is a vegetarian, too."

I didn't know Anita had a son. Arturo was always talking about his wife and kids, but Anita never mentioned her family. Then again, Anita never spoke to me if she could help it.

"Arturo deliberately adds milk and eggs and meat to his dishes, just so Grendel won't eat, to keep costs down," Bill said.

"Oh stop it, Bill," said Addie. "You know Arturo makes Grendel that special bag lunch every day."

"This is America," said Earl. "Grendel can eat whatever he wants to. They haven't made a law about that yet, have they?"

"Earl," said Maxine warningly, "you are not to talk politics tonight. You promised me."

"What did I say that was politics?" Earl asked innocently.

"It's the local politics that really get him going," Maxine said, ignoring his question. "He's been in a tizzy lately about this local land-use referendum they're all talking about."

"What's that?" I asked.

"It's not a big deal, though Earl would like to make it into one," said Maxine. "It's nothing more than an opinion poll, really. They're not passing any new laws—"

"You will learn, Kelly," Earl said to me, interrupting his wife, "not everyone around here sees eye to eye on certain particular issues."

"Now you've got me curious," I said.

"My wife won't allow me to fill you in on the particulars, 'cause I'm not allowed to talk politics at the dinner table. But if you'll come to the meeting at the old church next Wednesday night, you can participate in the forum. You're eligible to join the community association and vote now that you're a property owner here, and you might want to look into it, as this issue pertains to you. If you ever want to make any changes around your place you'd better speak out now and help us stop these fellas who'd like to control everybody else and keep us from using our own land the way we see fit."

"Now, Earl," said his wife. "Don't you be trying to convert Kelly to your way of thinking. She can make up her own mind about things."

"Leave him alone, Maxine," said Bill. "Let him blow off steam if he needs to. Kelly won't pay him no mind."

"If you encourage him, Bill, you're only going to make it worse."

"So now it's my politics?" Earl asked his wife, feigning hurt. "I thought it was my stories you didn't like, Max."

"I heard a story recently," I said. "About a young woman who stayed at the inn and then disappeared. I wondered if it was something that had really happened, or . . ."

I got no response but the shrugging of shoulders. The room was silent for a moment.

So much for that idea. I had thought these old-timers would be the ones to ask. Either they didn't know what I was talking about, or they were pretending they didn't.

"Well, I guess it's just a ghost story or something," I said. "According to some kids who stayed at the inn last weekend—Paula's boys—Nick tells some good ones."

Earl Johnson gave a snort, leaned back in his chair, and folded his arms. "Nick McClure? Yeah, he tells some good ones, all right."

"Earl!" Maxine's tone was sharp. "Don't you go gettin' started up about Nick. This is neither the time nor the place."

Earl pretended he didn't hear her. "Kelly," he said, "you watch that Nick McClure—he is a slick one. You keep an eye on him and don't let him put one over on you."

"Nick is a nice young man," Addie said with a worried look. "He's very good."

"Addie likes Nick. But then, she likes everybody. Don't you, my dear?" Bill ruffled her hair affectionately. "Though I didn't think she'd ever forgive you, Johnson, when that calf got into her flowers again yesterday."

"It's all right," Addie said softly. "I'm working on forgiveness in my visualization class."

"Your what?" Earl snorted.

Addie drew herself up, dignified. "The countess's visualization class. I'm learning to create my own reality."

"The countess!" Earl shook his head. "Another one of our colorful coastside characters." He passed Addie a plate of Maxine's homemade bread, which he knew she loved. "Here ya go, darlin'," he said. "This here's reality. And I am sorry for the mess that heifer made of your garden. I'll make it up to you somehow. You'll see."

LATE Wednesday afternoon I was in the office catching up on some paperwork when I heard a deep rumble in the yard. I looked out the window to see a man in dark sunglasses and black leathers dismounting a big silver Harley in the parking area in front of the house. He removed his helmet and I realized he was Eli Larson. I stepped back into the room, my heart beating hard.

I heard his boots on the steps. He entered the office and our eyes met with an impact that felt almost physical. I was grateful for the desk between us.

"Hi," he said. "Remember me?"

"Hmm," I said. "You do look familiar. I think I've seen your picture before, somewhere."

"Mug shot, probably."

"Thank you for the flowers. They really brightened up the office."

"Well, good, I'm glad you think so, because coincidentally, I'm here because I want to do something else for your office. I want to upgrade your computer systems. And build you a website for the inn."

"Well, we need it, that's for sure. I am aware that we do need— I was going to say an upgrade, but frankly we have nothing to upgrade. And yes, we need a website."

"Great. So we're thinking alike here."

"But I just bought this place, and right now I have to pace myself, and my resources—"

"I want to make a gift of it," he interrupted. "For the inn. Will you let me do that, Kelly? I've got the best. Web designer, technicians, all state-of-the-art stuff . . ."

I shook my head; this was so unexpected, I wasn't sure how to respond.

"As my gift to the inn," he said.

"I couldn't accept that."

"You could," he argued. "But if you won't accept a gift, what about a trade? I'll set you up with the network, and you can offer me a night's free lodging. Okay, a week's lodging! Two weeks. A month! Forever! Hey, listen." He spoke softly now. "Think about it, okay?"

"Umm . . . okay."

Nick chose to make his reappearance right then, coming in through the kitchen, looking dusty and rumpled in his coveralls. No bandanna this time; his dark head was shorn and his face clean shaven, which surprised me. I'd forgotten he'd done that.

"Hey, guys," he said amiably.

Of course he hadn't been around for days, when we could have used him around the place. *And now he appears, just when he's most in the way.*

"Hello, Nick. You have sawdust in your eyebrows."

"Nick." Eli nodded politely, but it was plain he didn't welcome the intrusion, either.

Nick looked at Eli, dressed in his full leathers, and me, behind the desk. "Bad time?" he asked.

I looked at him, exasperated. "What is it, Nick?"

"I'm taking off now," he said.

"I didn't even know you were here."

"I just wanted to warn you that the steps behind Gull Cottage are wet. I had to replace one of the treads, and it's just been painted. It'll be okay to walk on in an hour or so, but you really should stay off it until tomorrow."

"There's no one in Gull tonight, so we should be all right, thanks."

"Good enough. See you later, then. Larson."

"McClure."

The two men shook hands in a friendly way, and Nick went out through the kitchen.

"Addie's going to set out drinks in a few minutes—would you like to have a glass of wine?" I asked Eli.

"Sure," he said. "But I was really hoping I might be able to take you to dinner tonight. Talk more about this system I want to have set up for you."

"Oh, you want to take me out to dinner on your bike?" I smiled at him.

"Sure, if you're the kind of girl who likes to ride." He gave me a teasing wink. "If you aren't, I could call us a car."

"I have a car myself, actually," I said. "But the thing is, I have plans tonight."

"Oh. Can't rearrange them, then?" He looked at me soulfully.

"No, I really can't . . ." Well, I *could,* I thought. I didn't need to go to the community meeting, though I was eager to acquaint myself with local politics, especially issues affecting my business. I was sorely tempted to forget about the meeting and go out with Eli. He was a tall, good-looking, and good-smelling male presence standing in my small office, cajoling me with his smooth voice, intently watching my expressions. But all the reasons why I shouldn't loomed large, the largest being the fact that this was a man who was locked into another relationship. I knew he was living with Kyra. And he was engaged to her. To be married.

So I opted for the glass of wine on the porch instead of the dinner.

"Eli, there's something I'd like to ask you about."

"Sure, of course. Anything."

"Ordinarily I wouldn't ask something like this of a guest," I said. "But you've been coming here a long time, right? You must have heard something about a woman who stayed at the inn, and then went missing? What I heard was just kids talking, you know, but I'm curious if there's anything to it, or if it's just one of those stories that get started."

"Yeah. No, I think I remember hearing something about that."

"Was she a tourist, or . . . ?"

"I think she was, yeah."

"Maybe it's a morbid interest, but anything connected to the inn interests me. I mean, not that I want there to be any connection with the inn—"

"Oh, I doubt there's really any connection to the inn," he said.

"So what happened?"

"I really don't remember it very well. It was a long time ago."

I got the impression he didn't actually know anything about the so-called missing woman. But why would he say he did? To move the conversation along? Or because he wanted to appear well informed? I suspected the latter.

"Does your fiancée know you're here?"

"I rarely give her a detailed itinerary of my plans for the day," he replied dryly. "Though I often fill her in later. And yes, I will tell her I came here."

"Give her my regards."

He looked at me with a grave expression. "Kelly, you know I've come to the conclusion that I have to end it with her."

"No, I didn't know that," I said coolly.

"Well, you know it now."

"I think you'd better think about it long and hard before you . . . make a decision you may end up regretting."

"Once I make a decision," he said, "I rarely have regrets."

Thankfully it was time to get ready for the meeting, and I still had work to do in the office, so I cut it short with him. We walked down to the parking area together.

"Think about my offer," he said, slinging his long, well-muscled leg over the saddle of his bike, fastening his helmet. "I'll be calling you."

I watched him roar off on the big, shiny, powerful-looking machine, and I asked myself—just what *was* he offering me?

THE little white country church was full when I arrived for the meeting. I stood at the door, looking over the heads of those already seated in the neat rows of aluminum folding chairs. At the front of the room, a woman in a gray suit fumbled with a microphone attached to a podium and a deep amplified thump echoed through the room.

I'd come too late; it was standing room only.

Nick suddenly appeared at my side and touched my arm. "Hey, Kelly."

I blew out a sigh. "Oh, it's you," I said.

"Where are you sitting?"

"Nowhere, it seems."

"Don't worry, I'll take care of you. Come with me." With his hand on my arm, he guided me through the crowd to the far side of the room, where two chairs on the aisle were empty but reserved with his jacket. He indicated one for me and he took the outside. We settled ourselves down and in a few minutes the meeting began.

The woman in the gray suit spoke; she formally opened the meeting, and some items of business that she called "housekeeping" were discussed.

For some reason I felt acutely aware of Nick's leg beside mine. In fact, I found myself more focused on the sensation of heat from Nick's warm body than on what the speaker was saying.

I might have experienced the warmth of Eli's body tonight, I thought, if I had taken him up on his offer. Straddling his bike, wrapping myself around steel and leather and him, like a girl on the cover of some trashy pulp fiction paperback . . .

The imagery struck me as more comical than sensual.

I tried to calm down, but I felt restless. Beside me, Nick remained still. He seemed to be listening intently to the woman in the gray suit.

When the discussion tightened in on the land-use referendum, I began to pay closer attention. Several people spoke, including Earl Johnson, expressing their opinions on the issue. I found Earl an effective, persuasive spokesman for his cause. The land use restrictions along the coast had gone too far, he said, and those with property needed to stand up for their rights. He warned that coastal land owners wouldn't be able to get building permits, or use their land the way they saw fit, if others had their way. By the time he was finished, I was convinced he was right.

"Any more comments before we close the discussion period?" asked the woman in gray.

To my surprise, Nick stood up.

"With all due respect to my neighbor," he said in his low-pitched, deliberate voice, "I believe the issue has been somewhat misrepresented. The current provision under discussion has no bearing on parcels of twenty acres or less. Nothing changes there. What it does do is, it proposes to lift the restrictions on development of large parcels of land, land that is currently zoned for agriculture and open space. This proposal advocates that we abolish the process by which the community considers large building subdivisions and tracts. In other words, if we want to preserve the rural character of the coast, we currently have the tools at our disposal. If we pass this referendum, we're saying we're okay with giving big developers a free rein."

I could see Earl, sitting a few rows up beside his wife, shaking his head. Now I understood some of the friction between Nick and Earl. I listened to Nick, proud of him, suddenly; he was so at ease with himself, standing and speaking before all these people, articulate, sure of himself, even charming.

He finished his piece and sat down beside me. I noticed, again, the heat. The presence of his vital body in the chair beside mine seemed to radiate, and I had the urge to simply lean into him and touch that heat.

It's just because it's freezing in this room, I thought, annoyed with myself for these thoughts. *Why don't they shut the doors?*

After the meeting we pressed out with the rest of the throng, and I felt Nick's hand on the small of my back. Just down from the steps Earl Johnson stood as if waiting for us, and he said loudly, jokingly, "So, you think you should be able to tell me what to do with my land, is that right, McClure?"

"Yeah, Johnson, why don't you just sign over the deed to me now?" Nick replied with an easy smile, resting his free hand on the rancher's shoulder as we passed by.

"You watch it, buster." Earl Johnson smacked Nick's hand away.

Nick turned to face Earl, instinctively positioning himself, it seemed, to shield me. Those milling around near the church doors stopped their conversation and turned to look at the two men.

"You got a problem with me, Earl?" Nick asked quietly.

"Yeah, I have a problem with guys like you trying to tell me what to do with my own property. We'll just see what the people have to say about this."

"Yeah, let's see what the people say," agreed Nick.

"Listen, you cocky son of a—" Earl suddenly lost control and took a swing at Nick, who jerked backward just in time to avoid the impact of Earl's big fist slamming into his jaw.

In the space of a split second, Nick's body had taken on a classic fighter's stance. His feet danced under him, his hands fisted, and I watched in fascinated horror as he drew back his arm to throw a punch.

But he caught himself just before he let go with the blow—I swear I saw it in his eyes, the decision *not* to swing—and before another moment could pass, Maxine and several large men had grabbed Earl and were hauling him away.

Nick was shaking; he looked down at his still-clenched fists as if expecting to see steam rising off them.

I ran my hand down his arm to get his attention. He snapped into focus, staring at me intently. "You okay, Kelly?" he asked me.

The question struck me as hilarious. "Yes," I replied. "Are you?"

"Nick." Maxine reappeared, grabbed Nick's hand, and shook it hard. "Thank you," she said softly.

"For what?" He frowned, looking annoyed.

"For not hurting him."

He patted her shoulder, embarrassed.

"I know how easily you could have decked him—and he would have deserved it."

"Don't worry about it," Nick said.

Seeing the gentle way he handled the older woman—the caring, warm way he touched her, his hand lingering on her shoulder, made me think perhaps I had misread something in the way he had touched me on one or two occasions. I thought maybe he had been flirting, but apparently it was just his way. He had even tried to touch Earl, in kindness, before the guy had lost his temper and swung at him.

"So, you're a lefty," I said to Nick. We were alone in the church parking lot in the orange glow of the streetlight, standing beside my car.

"Are you talking about my politics?"

"I was talking about this." I touched his arm. "You're left-handed."

He grabbed up my hand playfully and held it. "How did you know that?"

I tried to let go of his hand, but he seemed to be in no hurry to let go of mine.

"That punch you didn't throw," I said. "It was a left."

I thought he was about to say something, but we were interrupted by the crunching of boots over gravel, and I turned to see a police officer approaching us. I felt a bit alarmed at the sight of him, with his direct, grave expression trained on us, but Nick remained relaxed, leaning against my car.

"Hi, folks."

"Hello," I said.

"Hello, Bernie," said Nick. He obviously knew the cop, but he didn't sound thrilled to see him. "What's going on?"

"Wanted to talk to you about your little run-in with Earl Johnson a few minutes ago. You know we like to maintain a security presence at these public gatherings."

"What about it?"

"Johnson assaulted you back there by the church doors, a few minutes ago, is that correct?"

"Is that what you saw?"

"Well, I didn't witness the actual incident myself," Bernie admitted. "Though I did hear Earl's voice raised in anger. But from what bystanders tell me, Earl threw the first punch."

"There was no punch," Nick said.

"Will you consider pressing charges?"

"No."

"Well, let me tell you something, Nick. Maybe you had better press charges before he does."

"Did Earl say he's going to press charges?" I spoke out, incredulous.

Nick laid his hand on my arm. "Bernie," he said with a sigh, "everything's okay. Nothing happened, all right? Don't worry about it. No one is pressing charges."

"Fine!" The officer raised his hands and backed away. "If that's the way you want to play it." He nodded at me and walked off, shaking his head.

"Do you think Earl would really press charges?" I whispered. "I just can't believe—"

"No. That's just my old pal Bernie Hollinger," Nick reassured me. "If there isn't any trouble, he tries to stir some up. Really, Kelly, don't even worry about it."

"All right, but if you need me, Nick, I'm your witness. I saw the whole thing and I will defend your innocence."

He laughed. "That's nice. You're nice."

"Why do you say it like that? Why are you surprised? Don't you think I can be nice? I'm nice. I know you think I'm bossy, but I am a boss, you know, I'm running that inn, and in a couple of months I'll be completely in charge."

He laughed heartily and rested his hand on my head for a moment. "Shh," he said, and I stopped talking.

In the silence, crickets chirped.

"Nick!" A new voice.

"Aaron?"

"Hey."

There was no big display of affection, no hug or handshake, merely a subtle, low bump of fists. Aaron was smaller than Nick, with thin straight hair tied back in a ponytail, a goatee, one gold hoop earring, and several cameras strapped over his thin chest.

Nick introduced us. "Aaron, this is Kelly, the new owner of the

Magic Mermaid Inn. Kelly, my buddy Aaron here is the annoying photographer for the *Weekly Coast Sunflash*—"

"I'm also the annoying editor, publisher, advertising director, distributor—"

"So beware and don't let him take your photograph unless he pays you."

Aaron executed a low bow and doffed an imaginary hat. I imagined an ostrich plume brushing over the ground as he continued to list his credentials: "—resident astrologer, advice columnist, and, my current favorite moniker, critic at large. And at the moment," he added, "I must say I find absolutely nothing to criticize. Charmed."

"Pleased to meet you . . . all."

"Don't be afraid, Kelly," Nick said. "All his personalities are really very well integrated."

"Hey, so what happened?" Aaron asked Nick. "I was in the can and I missed the excitement. Is it true Earl Johnson kicked your ass, McClure?"

"Why, is that what you heard?"

"Yeah. That he trashed you within an inch of your life."

"Well, that's pretty much how it happened," I said.

Nick's nonchalance was replaced by hurt astonishment. "Kelly! You said you would be my witness!"

Aaron belted out, in song: "Can I get a witness? *Oh can I get a witness*—"

Nick glared at me. "Now he's *singing*."

"Like that's *my* fault?"

Aaron stopped singing. "Why do you need a witness?"

"Earl's going to slap him with a lawsuit," I said. "The policeman said so."

"Bernie?" Aaron shook his head sadly. "Bad news. You're going down, bro."

"Thanks for your support," said Nick. "But if I'm going down, I'm taking you with me."

"Seriously," said Aaron. "What happened with Earl?"

"Hate to disappoint you, bro, but nothing happened. There's no story."

"Nick," said Aaron, "there's *always* a story."

Chapter 8

THERE was an old water tower on the inn property, a tall building with a stairway going up through the middle, and sloped walls that had been enclosed and converted to living space. It was unused nowadays, except to store furniture. I had looked inside it when I toured the property, but the unit was cluttered and impossible to get around in without climbing over furniture. It was dusty and dark and full of cobwebs, the stairs were steep and unlit, and the bed that filled the little second-floor room was a sprung mess. I wondered why Addie and Bill had let the place go. It wasn't like them, letting an opportunity pass to rent out a room.

Eager to take on the project and get the water tower ready for guests once again, I decided I would take inventory and see what I needed to do to get the place in shape. So when I had a free half hour, I walked up the slope.

It was early in the day. The grounds seemed deserted but for the bees dancing over the blossoms in the gardens. The water tower stood surrounded by a picket fence, sagging and faded, its white paint peeling. The wood siding and trim on the water tower had been painted the same soft blue and white of the inn and cottages, but it had been neglected in recent years, and now the building was overgrown with brambles.

I loved the tower, the whimsical shape of it, the decorative brackets beneath the cornice, the shingled roof, and the long rectangular windows. I particularly loved it this way, faded and peeling, draped with sprays of unkempt rose, thick clusters of small, pale pink flowers, and I almost hated doing anything to fix it up. But I knew the fix-it-up impulse would win out.

I pushed open the door and heard voices. They spoke so softly, I couldn't catch their words, but apparently they heard me, too, and abruptly stopped talking.

As my eyes adjusted to the darkness, I could see Anita sitting on the back of a sofa that had been shoved at an angle against one sloped wall of the room. Nick was standing beside her, leaning against an armoire.

If I had startled them, or embarrassed them, they quickly covered it. It was funny, and awkward. Finding them here together in the close, dark, musty space made me want to turn and hurry out.

I tried for my best dry tone and said, "You know, I did think it was a shame this building wasn't being used . . . but I guess I needn't have worried."

Anita slid off the sofa and walked to the door. She lowered her eyes as she passed by me and went out.

That left me with Nick.

"Shall I explain?" he asked, with only his eyes smiling.

"It's none of my business. But maybe I ought to deduct the price of a room from your pay."

"You can take all the deductions you want, boss. But don't try to deduce anything about Anita and me from what you just saw here."

"Like I said. It's none of my business. Except that now that it is my business, I should tell you I plan to renovate this water tower building." I thought it best to change the subject.

He nodded. "Okay."

"From a professional point of view, what are your thoughts on the matter?"

He seemed unable to think of anything.

On the floor, leaning against the wall, was a piece of flat driftwood with letters burned into it and hooks drilled into the top. I picked it up and examined it. It was the name sign for the water tower unit. I rubbed the dust off the sign. "Number fourteen, Lighthouse," I read the name out loud. "Funny. Addie and Bill don't call this one Lighthouse or number fourteen. It's just the water tower."

"Number fourteen," Nick repeated. "Which is actually number thirteen, right? Because Dolphin is number twelve and Starfish is fifteen . . ."

"People think it's bad luck to have a motel room numbered thirteen."

"Thirteen, the number of the goddess," Nick said. "Maybe it's bad luck to exclude her. You know, like not inviting the bad fairy to the party?"

"Looking around this place, it would seem the bad fairy was not pleased. She put everyone to sleep for a hundred years. So . . . how much work does it need?" I asked.

"It's a mess," he replied. "The stairs are unsafe and the roof leaks and the whole thing is infested with mice and black widow spiders and rats."

"That sounds encouraging. Should be able to get it fixed up and rentable again in no time."

"Well, of course you can do anything you want."

"Anything?" I said archly.

"Sure. It's all a matter of time and money, right?"

"Well, okay, but . . ."

"So let me know. I'll do my best to help you get what you want. All right?"

"Okay . . ."

And with that, he flashed me a smile and was gone, leaving me standing in the water tower room alone, feeling frustrated. I wanted *help* here.

I picked my way through the cluttered, crowded space, moving aside some chairs and framed pictures that had been put in the room for storage. I would get rid of most of it. The pictures were clunky reproductions of the masters and most of the furniture was dark, cheap, and tacky. I knew I wouldn't put any of this stuff back into the guest rooms. I began making a pile of all the things I intended to throw out.

When I opened the closet between the kitchenette and the little sitting room, I was surprised to see a big suitcase, an overnight bag, and a little pink backpack, all sitting neatly together, all covered with a thick layer of dust.

I pulled the backpack out of the closet and found it heavier than I'd expected. Dumping the contents out on a chair, I found an assortment of personal items—toothpaste, tissues, lip gloss, sunglasses with one of the lenses popped out, some old receipts and papers, a couple of take-out menus, some plastic bangles, and a tiny beaded purse on a silver chain.

I opened the overnight bag and found a hair dryer and curling iron, some silky women's underclothing, and an old glamour magazine. The suitcase was packed with tiny flirty skirts and skimpy tops, jeans, workout clothes, and several pairs of cheap but fashionable shoes. Nothing that Addie would wear. So who, then?

People sometimes did leave stuff behind when they checked out of the inn, but ordinarily they didn't just up and leave *everything*. Perhaps this was simply a collection of items left over the years. But didn't we have a lost-and-found box in the office for that sort of thing? I thought about the story of the missing woman. These things had belonged to a woman, that much was obvious; probably young, definitely slender and flashy. Not too rich—most of the stuff was pretty cheap. What money was spent on clothes was spent on lingerie.

The small beaded bag had been used as a coin purse, apparently—there was some change inside it. It looked like something you might find in an antique store. I held it in my hand, enjoying the weight of the little thing.

I put it back in the backpack, and I packed the bags up and left them in the closet just as I had found them.

WHEN I asked Addie about the things in the closet, she said, "Oh, people leave things here all the time. We try to reunite our guests with their lost belongings, but sometimes they never come back for them. I know that old water tower is filled with junk," she added apologetically.

"I'm surprised you haven't been renting it out, Addie. It's actually quite spacious, considering—"

"Yes, yes, well, but it needs work. I'm sure it could be very nice again with a little tender loving care. Be careful, in the meantime. It's really not safe. We'll just get rid of anything you don't want to keep, Kelly. Ask Anita to help you sort through it, and Nick will haul everything away."

Walking past the water tower later in the afternoon, I was struck again by how beautiful the building was, with its bracket details, one sloping side in shadow and the other lit up by the sun, gold glinting from the narrow rectangular windows.

But Addie was right; it needed a lot of work. Nick had confirmed that. If the roof leaked, I'd have to see to it immediately, before there was more damage. And the stairway would have to be made safe; otherwise it was a liability. But my feelings for the place had endured a subtle change. I no longer felt inspired to do anything with it. Maybe I'd be smarter to put off the project for the time being. For now it was a useful storage area.

Later, I thought. *I'll get to it later.* For now I had other priorities.

IT was Thursday evening, and the inn was quiet. Addie and Bill were in their apartment off the main house. I could see the flickering of the television through the drapes drawn over their living room windows as I came down the hill from a hike, having timed it so that I arrived home just at dusk.

It was good to get outside, to work the muscles and breathe the wild air. I had been too tense, anticipating the weekend. Eli Larson was coming. Bringing his fiancée for the painting workshop.

In the lonely woods above the inn, I sat for a long time in the low crook of an ancient tree, just gazing out to the horizon. But my meditative lull was shaken by a strange crashing sound in the bushes, very near and too large to be anything but human, I thought, or possibly a deer.

"Hello!" I called softly.

With a quick retreating crunch-crunch-crunch through the shrubs, before I could spring down from my perch and peer through the branches, whoever or whatever it was had disappeared.

It was a deer, I told myself. But my heart was pounding. That had not sounded like a deer.

I'm just jumpy, I thought. And not just about Eli.

Lately I was more paranoid than usual. I didn't go around

worrying about my own safety, but I was starting to wonder if I should. Maybe I was too trusting, too naive. This place was idyllic, or seemingly so; but what if Paula's boys were right? That a young woman staying at the inn had disappeared, and had never been found—and no kidnapper or murderer had ever been apprehended. That meant there could still be somebody out there—

I headed back to the inn, and I heard the door to the apartment shut as I passed Addie and Bill's. Addie came out and leaned off her deck and waved down to me as I walked by on the path below her deck.

"That Grendel," she said. "Do you know, he is just the darnedest. He stopped by here not five minutes ago and dropped off a basket of fruits and things. He knows we're supposed to eat more fresh . . ."

I stood for a while and listened to her chatter.

". . . try to improve our habits, but I'm lucky if I can get Bill to eat a single bite of anything but canned peaches . . ."

At one point I realized that I had stopped hearing her; I was drifting into my own thoughts, wondering about the woman who had gone missing. Was she real, or merely the creation of someone's vivid imagination? Who was she? Had she ever been found? Why didn't anyone want to talk about it? Because she never existed? Or was there some other reason?

We said good night, and as I turned down the path to my own cottage, I saw a teenager on a BMX bike shoot from the parking area out to the main road. He wore no helmet, and when he jumped the bike up the curb instead of swerving around it, black hair went flying like sleek raven's wings. We made eye contact, and I recognized him as the kid who hung out around the inn from time to time, the same one I'd shooed away from the drinks table at happy hour. He was lithe and slender, and he wore all black, loose trousers and T-shirt. He stared back at me with blazing eyes, and then he was gone.

I thought of the graffiti spray-painted on my cottage, and what Anita had said about gangs. I thought about the presence in the woods. I thought about the missing woman and a man's hand in the slough that turned out to be a rubber glove. And I decided I was being overly fanciful, looking for dark connections where none existed.

Chapter 9

KYRA and I were in danger of becoming friends during the painful bloodletting that was the painter's workshop. We both recognized a certain magical quality in the work of certain other artists, like that of Kenneth Bing, who was leading the workshop, and we were both very much aware that we fell far short of achieving that quality in our own work.

I took breaks from painting when I was needed in the office, and Kyra took breaks from painting to talk on the phone. "I actually try to take care of all my calls when Eli's not around," she confided to me as we sat together on the front porch with our easels, trying to paint the ocean. "It drives him crazy after a while, listening to me, but I tell him he's a hypocrite, 'cause he's worse than me when it comes to being on the phone! If he didn't constantly lose his phone, he'd never be off it." Her phone began to ring as she spoke.

"Hello? . . . Hey . . . Oh! Okay . . . No, I told you . . . No. We are not using that caterer again." Her voice grew deathly patient. "Because, as I already explained, I'm using Brittany's people . . . No . . . *No*. Salmon and tri-tip? Listen, I am not hosting a chuck wagon at a dude ranch, Adrian."

To me, Kyra sounded semi-crazy when she was going on about her wedding preparations, but when she let fall the occasional comment about her job in the city planning department, it was obvious she was smart and effective. She laughed at her own painting, and disregarded anything our instructor advised us to do, which I admired about her; I tried desperately to do everything exactly the way he suggested it should be done.

Just when I was beginning to think I might rather have Kyra as a pal than Eli as a paramour, I overheard her disparaging the inn again.

"Well, I'm *trying* to make the best of it."

I was in the office and her voice carried in from the parking area, clear and strong.

"But oh my *God*. It's so provincial. There's like, no room service, and the sheets are like sandpaper. And you know how it is when management tries to get chummy? The innkeeper is suddenly my new best friend."

You would think she'd have the sense to keep her voice down.

"Well, you know, Mother, he was just trying to be nice. He knows I want to paint more, and this artist Ken Bing *is* rather good, though I can't speak to his instructional capabilities—my painting seems to be getting worse, rather than better!" She paused to listen, laughed. "Me? Oh my God, no, I suck."

Yes, you do, I agreed with her, bitter. Sheets like sandpaper?

Eli cornered me near the laundry at dusk and made me look at him, his fingers brushing over my arm to stop me when I would have moved past him.

"Kelly," he said. His hands moved over me with startling familiarity, though he broke no taboo, just lightly brushing his hand down my arm. "I've been thinking about you nonstop."

I stared at him, wondering if I should slap his face.

"And I have definitely decided to call off the wedding," he added.

That was all. He dropped his hands and turned away, but he let his gaze linger behind him.

"Wow," I said out loud when he was gone. Was he simply a cad? Or was this a significant moment, one of those crossroads where life unexpectedly turns in a completely new direction?

For the first time, I seriously envisioned myself connecting with this man.

Eli Larson. And me.

Alone in my cottage that night I studied my reflection in the mirror. A few hours in an expensive salon and I could give Kyra a run for her money. I was the right height; tall but not too tall. The right age; young but not unformed. Could be the right look; he seemed to approve. Definitely something to work with. We had sparked off each other instantly. And how else might we click? The possibilities were intriguing.

My gaze shifted from my own image to that of Eli himself, in black and white, staring out of the photo I had clipped out of the paper and stuck in the mirror frame.

Eli Larson and Kelly Redvers. A red-hot affair. He travels over the mountains to the inn by the ocean, just to see her again. He whisks her off to Tahoe in the winter. Tahiti in the spring . . .

But what would it be like, really? Being with him . . . hanging out with him? Living with him? I couldn't quite picture it.

And I shouldn't spend my time trying. At the moment, Eli was engaged. He was another woman's fiancé. Strictly forbidden. And I wasn't one to engage in idle fantasies, as I reminded myself yet again.

I lifted my hand to the photo, thinking I should pull it out of the mirror frame and tuck it away in a drawer.

But his earnest, handsome face arrested me, and my hand fell away. I left the picture stuck on the mirror.

NICK McClure, after having spent the afternoon working on the antiquated plumbing in Gull Cottage, hung around for happy hour (just to annoy me, I was certain) and came back later to play chess with Kenneth Bing, who had already played and beaten another guest. Rocky was playing Eli now. Rocky had beaten Winkle and, according to the convoluted protocol of this impromptu tournament, winner of the current game played Nick for the title.

I felt vaguely annoyed with Nick, though I wasn't sure why. Then again, I was usually annoyed with him, wasn't I? I sat propped up against the padded arm of the comfy couch, looking across the room at his profile. His nose was mostly straight, but slightly dented in where it joined the plane of his forehead. He sat near the little table watching the game, waiting for his turn to play again.

The chess tournament had gone on for hours; it was late and most of the participants and spectators had gone to bed.

I yawned and stretched. "Not sure I'm going to be able to stay up to see Rocky kick your butt, McClure," I called to him across the room.

"And here I was hoping to be your champion, Kelly," he replied in his laziest voice.

"Well, I for one have had enough!" Kyra popped up from the chair she had positioned to look over Eli's shoulder. "I'm off to bed."

No hot tub tonight?

"Night, babe," Eli mumbled. "I'll be in soon."

"No problem, sweetie," she chirped. "Enjoy yourself."

He lifted his face to let her kiss him on the forehead.

"Wow," Paula murmured, for my ears only. She was sitting beside me on the couch. "Did you see that? What do you want to bet that sweetness was one hundred percent acting on her part?"

I shook my head and didn't answer, but I had to stifle a laugh with my hand over my mouth. I had given up trying to pretend I was the prim innkeeper when I was hanging out with Paula. But sometimes she did make things awkward.

"Hey, marriage has to involve acting sometimes, right? See," she added with some bitterness, "I was never good at acting. I mean, I *can*, when I have to . . . but I don't *like* to and I can't keep it up forever. Rock," she said loud enough for her son to hear, "I'm going to bed. Don't you stay up too late."

" 'Kay, Mom," Rocky said without looking up.

Paula got up and poked at her younger son, who was curled up in a chair. "Come on, Deanie Beanie, time for bed."

Winkle let out a whimper of protest, but he allowed his mother to herd him off to their cottage.

Nick got up from his chair and came to sit beside me in Paula's place.

"You girls whispering secrets again?"

"Who? Me and Paula?" I gave him a knowing look, wondering if he was fishing for information about Paula. "Oh, yeah," I said. "Secrets. Dark secrets. No, actually we were just debating the theory that successful marriage requires a certain kind of dishonesty."

"Does it? What kind of dishonesty would that be?"

"Oh, you know. White lies and pretense. Not that I would know, but Paula said—"

"Maybe that's why she's not married anymore," he interrupted me. "Too much of the white lies and pretense."

"She said it didn't work because she *couldn't* lie and pretend."

"Hmm."

"You know, I'm surprised *you* aren't married, Nick."

"Why, because I'm such a great catch?"

"Sure," I said. "Aren't you?"

"Well, I'll tell you how it is, Kelly. I *was* married, once. To a beautiful, accomplished woman. She was a doctor of veterinary medicine; I met her when I brought my dogs to her."

"What happened?"

"My wife left me for one of my own clients. And it all went downhill from there."

His obvious effort to sound nonchalant raised an unexpected compassion in me. "White lies and pretense?" I asked gently.

"Sure. On both sides. And some major deception on hers."

"I'm sorry."

"I guess we didn't have that much in common, besides the animals, but we had fun. We had a good life. Or so I thought. One day I land the biggest contract of my life. A custom home in Atherton for some corporate big shot. I'm ecstatic, right? A year later when I finished building his house, she moved into it with him."

Ouch, I thought. That would have to hurt.

"That was five years ago. And basically, I haven't trusted a woman since." He gave me a look of humorous contempt, as if to press home the fact that I was among the set he despised.

"Five years!" I cried. "Understandable, your taking it so hard, but don't you think it's time to get over it?"

"I *am* over it," he replied coolly. "Believe me. What about you? You're not, uh, with anyone that I can see."

"No, I'm not. Up until recently—well, actually it's been over a year now—I was living with someone. But we ended it."

"Why?"

I was surprised by his blunt curiosity. "Well . . . because I didn't want to get married."

"You mean he wanted to marry you?"

"Yes. He wanted to get married and start a family."

"And you didn't?"

"No."

"Why not?"

"It wasn't anything against him, personally. I just don't want to marry anyone. I never have."

"Don't you want kids?"

I shook my head.

"Never? Ever?"

I shook my head. "Never ever," I said firmly, though even as I said it I felt a twinge of doubt at my own assertion. After all, never ever was a long time. "Why?" I asked. "Do you?"

"Yeah," he said. "I do."

"Even though you haven't trusted a woman in five years?"

"I said I didn't trust women. I didn't say anything about kids. So is that why you broke up with your boyfriend? He was pressuring you to get married?"

I thought about that. "He gave me an ultimatum," I answered, remembering. Alex had taken me out for coffee, midmorning, very unlike him. The coffee hadn't even cooled; I had burned my mouth on it, taking a sip too soon. He came right to the point. *I want to start a family, Kelly, and if that's not something you want, then we will have to reexamine the relationship.*

I smiled, thinking of Alex's serious, bookish expression when he uttered the phrase *reexamine the relationship*. At the time the words had hurt, but now they seemed funny to me.

"Interesting. So it was a real ultimatum?"

I nodded.

"So you didn't like him?"

"I *did* like him," I insisted. Nick was asking a lot of questions. "I loved him. I loved other men, before him. And I hope to love again."

"So—you just love 'em and leave 'em, is that it?"

I matched his ironic tone. "Pretty much."

He said in a low voice, "What about Mr. Silicon Valley there?" He nodded in the direction of Eli, who sat coiled over the chessboard, focused on the configuration of the chess pieces. He was intensely competitive, and this was a competition after all.

"Would you marry him?" Nick asked me.

"I said I don't want to marry anyone. Weren't you listening?"

"Are you telling me you wouldn't consider it? Guy like that?"

"Look, setting aside the fact that he already happens to be engaged, I have told you my thoughts on marriage. Now, are you suggesting I should reconsider my position?" I looked hard at him.

"Only if he proposes to you."

"Oh, so what?" I said, pretending to be indignant. "You think he wouldn't? You don't, do you? *A guy like that.*"

He shook his head. "No, you got me all wrong, Kelly. Seriously. He would be lucky to get you." Nick was looking at me earnestly now, and for some reason, something in his green gaze shook me a little, flustered me. I didn't trust him.

"The truth is," he whispered, "you're too good for him."

"Oh, is that right? I'm too *good* for him. And I suppose I'm too good for you, too, huh?" I asked teasingly.

"It's not that he's not good enough for you," Nick answered quickly, sitting up straight. "It's just that he's wrong for you."

And yes, I'm wrong for you, too. I could read his thoughts. As he could read mine. Though why I would even speculate whether Nick was right or wrong for me was puzzling. Obviously right or wrong didn't enter into it. It would just never happen.

"It's no concern of yours," I said. "I'm not looking for Mr. Right, so what difference does it make if he's wrong for me?"

He shrugged. "I like you, Kelly. I want something good for you. That's all."

"You like me, huh?" I looked at him skeptically.

"I do. Though I am not unaware that whenever you see me coming, you suppress a shudder, and you are thinking to yourself, Oh God, please, not *him* again!"

I couldn't help laughing out loud, so accurately had he read me. For a moment, the chess players on the other side of the room looked up at us curiously.

"But I said to myself," Nick continued on in his low, slow voice, "there's something there, in that one. I'm not going to give up so easily."

"Even though you think I'm a bitch?" We were almost whispering now.

I waited for him to comment, but he only grinned.

"Ah, and you're pretty smart not to go there!" I teased him, punching him lightly on his arm. "Well, Nick, I think you should get over this thing you have about not trusting women, and dare to risk your heart again."

"Oh, yeah?"

"Yes. Especially since you yourself have said you would like to have kids. You want to raise a family with someone, someday, right?"

"Uh, sure," he agreed warily.

"Okay. So it's time to get started."

"Okay," he said. "What do I do?"

I hesitated; but Eli and Rocky were engrossed in their game, and they couldn't hear what we were saying anyway. "Ask Paula out," I whispered.

"Paula!" He looked alarmed.

"Hey, I know you think she's sexy. Don't deny it."

"I wouldn't deny Paula is sexy. But . . ." He shook his head.

"Is it because of her boys?"

"Her boys are cool. I don't have a problem with the fact that she has kids. Though when I said I'd like to have kids, I meant, like, in the *future*."

"She's a lot of fun."

"Yeah. I know." He sounded dubious.

"Well, what's the problem?"

"I just don't think I'm her type."

"She thinks you're hot."

"No, she doesn't." He was blushing now. And awfully cute.

"I think you should go for it. I think she'd appreciate it, if nothing else. She claims she hasn't been feeling that attractive lately."

"She claims. I think she likes to flaunt it, actually."

"Nothing wrong with that. If you've got it. Right?"

"Right . . ." He leaned away from me as if to end the conversation, pretending he was trying to look across the room at the chess match.

He glanced at me. "So why don't you go for *him?*" He nodded in Eli's direction and said quietly, "You think I should go for her. Okay. Why don't you go for him? You like him."

"I do like him." I shrugged, ignoring the fact that my heart was beating harder at these words of his. *Does it show?*

"Well, hell," said Nick. "It's obvious."

It is?

"I mean, what woman wouldn't go for Eli Larson? He's rich, he's a nice guy, he's good-looking, right? He's engaged—but he isn't married yet, as you so aptly pointed out. He's still technically available to anyone who can get him. Why not you? I've seen the way he looks at you."

Why not me? Indeed, I had begun to ask myself the same question. But I couldn't admit that to Nick.

"So," he said. "How about this. You go for him, and I'll go for her. Whoever achieves the goal first has to buy the other dinner at Charlene's."

"Charlene's?"

"A little hole in the wall up above Half Moon Bay, with spectacular sunsets and the best seafood you've ever had. It's astonishingly expensive, and worth it."

"Uh . . . okay," I said. "But what, exactly, is the object of the game here, specifically?"

"What do you think?" His expression was owlish.

"Sexual conquest? Like in *Dangerous Liaisons?*"

"Yeah," he said, "only now that you put it in those terms, it is obvious that you have the advantage."

"What terms?"

"Sexual conquest. Women always have the advantage in that."

"Always?"

"Well, usually."

"Ah!" I said drolly. "So imagine the depth of my humiliation if I attempt the seduction, and fail."

"Huh. I can't imagine that at all. I have a feeling you tend to get just about everything you want, Kelly."

"Seriously, it's completely weighted on your side. Paula is just dying for a little encouragement. She's starved for it. Eli Larson, on the other hand, is extremely unavailable. There are ethical issues."

"Right. I have to wonder just how unavailable he actually is."

I wondered the same thing, watching Eli playing chess with Rocky.

"But the point is," I said with sudden conviction, "as long as he's with her, there's going to be nothing going on between Eli and me."

"You'd be doing her a favor, you know," said Nick.

"Who?"

"His girlfriend."

"Nick, shut up."

"So are we on?" he prodded me.

"You really want to do this, then?" I looked him straight in the eye.

He shrugged. "What have I got to lose?"

"Only your lonely freedom."

He thought a moment. "Unless you want to raise the stakes and make it really interesting."

"How do you mean?"

He let a moment pass. "Make it marriage." He looked at me with that wily expression of his, the sun rays around his eyes deepening. "You marry him, I marry her. First to get to the altar wins. Oh, yeah, I forgot, you don't want to get married, do you?"

"Uh, yeah, no . . . let's say we stick with the lesser goal, so to speak. We see how that goes. We can always go double or nothing."

"Good enough," he agreed, and he reached out for my hand, to shake on it. I felt awkward, remembering perhaps too late that the characters in *Les Liaisons Dangereuses*, Valmont and that horrible Marquise de Merteuil, were amoral, appalling creatures, and their sordid competition was appalling, too. And it had ended up destroying them all . . .

I shivered. My hand in Nick's felt cold and small, and he seemed to hold on to it for a moment longer than necessary, a strange comfort.

The lengthy battle on the chessboard had found its conclusion, and young Rocky emerged victorious. Eli was gracious, but it clearly bothered him to lose the game—I could see it in the tense hunch of his shoulders as he said his good nights—and I sensed that need to win carried over into everything he did.

Before Nick rose to take his place across the table, I whispered to him, "Rocky may be your future stepson, you might want to let him win."

"*Let* him win," he muttered back. "Right. Haven't you noticed? The kid is a prodigy."

Chapter 10

"He wants to go out with you," I told her.

"Get out," she said.

It was early Sunday morning and I sat with Paula on the front porch; we were having our coffee together. A tantalizing smell, like a beckoning cartoon cloud-hand, wafted from the kitchen; Arturo was preparing breakfast with his assistant, Juan. Addie and Bill were busy in the front office.

I knew there would be a lot less leisure time for me when Addie and Bill retired in January, so I relished the moment of relaxation with Paula and a fragrant cup of Arturo's coffee.

With subtle finesse I had brought the conversation around to the subject of Nick.

"Seriously," I said. "I talked to him last night."

"He wants to go out with me? Well, why doesn't he ask me, then?"

"He's shy. Maybe you should encourage him."

"I don't know." She stared off into the distance. "He's not what I usually go for. I like 'em clean-cut. Suits, you know."

Nick had picked up on that himself. Perhaps my matchmaking instincts were flawed.

"But you know," she said, "I haven't had much luck with professional men; maybe I *should* give the blue-collar guys a try!"

"He's pretty clean-cut now," I said.

"And he did clean up nicely, didn't he?" Paula sipped her coffee, thoughtful.

I thought of a few other words of encouragement, things I could say to Paula, to urge the process along. Nick was smart; that much I could tell her. I suspected he was largely self-educated, but he was educated. He was self-assured, and that was sexy in a man. He stood up face-to-face with larger men, in stature and status, and he looked them straight in the eye without flinching. He had a sense of humor, which was attractive in anyone. All these things I could point out to Paula, and more, by way of encouragement.

I could have Nick owing me that dinner by midnight tonight, if I worked it.

She sat across from me, one long slender finger looped through the handle of her coffee cup, black eyes pensive, and I could see she was toying with this new idea. She was just open and eager enough to hear more of why she should give Nick a chance. I thought of other positive attributes I might mention to her; Nick's clear green eyes came to mind. But she already knew about his green eyes. She was the one who had pointed them out to me. *Translucent* was the word she had used, to describe Nick's eyes.

"Maybe I'll ask Bill for the boys next weekend," she mused, thinking out loud. "That'll give me an excuse to come back next week . . . and you'll make sure Nick's working here, say, Saturday afternoon?"

"Oh, yeah," I said. "I have complete control over Nick's schedule."

"By the way, Kelly, Eli was up here earlier, looking for you."

"Earlier this morning? Was there some problem?"

"No, he was on his way to take a run on the beach, and he stopped in, and I heard him talking to Addie, he had some silly question or other, but I had the feeling it was you he was after."

A pleasant warmth spread through me. "Why would you say that?" I asked innocently.

"I don't know. I've got a sixth sense about these things. And I believe Eli Larson is falling in love with you."

"Right. We're talking about the billionaire with the beautiful fi-ancée?"

"Trust me. *That* relationship is like a lingering head cold. It'll be all over with soon enough. I know these things. But isn't he al-most too much?" She laughed. "He's got it all—the money, the power, the car, the cleft in his chin!" She gave me a coy look. "Any woman would be a fool not to jump at that, right?"

"Well, why don't you?" I put it to her.

"No. No more diva boys. Eli Larson is the kind of guy who would always have to be the headliner. Blake was the same way. I can't hang with that type, not romantically. When it comes to busi-ness, on the other hand, I am very open . . . As a matter of fact, I'm supposed to meet Eli for coffee next week, or the week after, to talk about work. Who knows? I'd love to network with Eli Lar-son, you know?"

"*Network*, right."

"Believe me. I may have been lying when I told you I was fin-ished with men—okay, so I was lying—but I am definitely not lying when I say I am finished with rock-star types."

"Kelly!" I heard Addie's voice from the office.

"Coming!" I called. "I'd better get to work," I said.

"Hey, thanks for the tip on Nick," Paula whispered.

I nodded, uncomfortable, not sure it was a good thing I had done or not, encouraging her with Nick.

I hadn't seen much of Eli over the weekend. Actually, I'd seen more of his fiancée, than I'd seen of him. The more I knew her, the less I understood how she and Eli had become an item in the first place. She was beautiful and vivacious, but she was also intense and nervous and obsessively preoccupied with things that would make me want to scream, personally, if I had to live with her, like the length of her fingernails or the exact number of carbohydrates in a small banana. She had wit, though, and I had to admit she was fun to hang out with.

I rejoined the painting class Sunday morning after finishing some office work. I set up my easel near Kyra's on the wide front porch and propped up my board with the taped-down watercolor I had been working on. I arranged my water bucket, my paint box, and my paper towels, and set to work.

"That's beautiful."

I looked up at Grendel, who was staring down at my painting with his vivid blue eyes.

"You have a gift," he added.

I looked down at my painting, cocked my head. "Thank you," I said. My mother had taught me to accept compliments graciously. But I knew the painting wasn't very good, and if I had a gift, I wasn't displaying it here.

When he had wandered away, I turned to Kyra and said, in a deep, calm voice: "I have a gift."

Nick came bounding up the steps, grabbing an apple from the basket on the table by the door, not dressed as a painter today. Today he seemed more slender, less stocky than I tended to think of him. He wore jeans and a white oxford shirt unbuttoned over his faded blue thermal undershirt.

"Great," I said to Kyra. "Here comes another art critic." I said to Nick, "Grendel says my painting is beautiful. He says I have a gift."

Nick stood behind me, looked down at my painting and said nothing, crunching his apple.

I looked up at him. "Well? What do you think?"

"It looks like a paint-by-number."

"You are too kind."

"Just calling it as I see it," he replied. "Hey, do you know where Paula is?"

"I think she went up to the pool."

"All right, thanks. See you later." He was off again, as quick as he'd come.

"Have fun!" I called after him.

"That guy just doesn't recognize genius when he sees it," Kyra said.

"Obviously."

But he did recognize opportunity, apparently. And wasn't shy about taking advantage of it.

RACCOONS had scattered some trash around the cottages at the rear of the property, and I had just finishing bagging it all up when Eli came up from the beach, looking windblown and harried.

"Hey," I said.

"Hey," he answered, sounding breathless. "I've been looking for you. Take a walk with me? I need to talk to you."

I tied up the trash bag and left it beneath a tree, hoping the raccoons wouldn't find it before I came back, and we took off up the hill, away from the inn, and soon we were walking along the cliff path on the edge of the cypress wood. We entered a shaded grotto where the sand was white and soft beneath a ring of ancient low-hanging trees, and he stopped and turned to me, looking at me intently.

"It's beautiful here, isn't it?" he said, his voice soft.

"Yes, it is. And aren't you the sensitive one, for noticing?" I teased him, nervous.

He's a guest, I told myself madly. I can't be doing anything unprofessional . . .

"What?" He pouted, feigning hurt. "Don't you think I'm a sensitive guy?"

"I have my doubts."

"Why do you doubt it?"

"You brought your fiancée here, to the Magic Mermaid Inn, for the second time in a month. You, who could *go anywhere in the world*—I'm quoting her now. Don't you get it? She doesn't *like* it here. If you were truly a sensitive guy, you would know that."

"I do know that. In fact, I think the moment I really knew it was over between Kyra and me was when I saw her turn up her nose at this place I love so much . . ." He was silent a moment, then said, "I only booked this painting seminar for her so that I could come back and see you again. Don't laugh. Kelly, I'm crazy about you. Have been from the moment I laid eyes on you. I'm completely serious." He moved closer and I stepped away from him, overwhelmed by his intensity. He clasped my arm to check my flight, and gently laid his fingers over my lips. "It's okay," he said. "Don't be afraid. Please, don't say anything . . ."

His fingers slid over my lips and chin, and trailed down my throat. "I know you're worried," he said. "You hardly know me."

"And you hardly know me."

"Ah, but you're wrong about that . . ." He brought his mouth close to mine and I felt his breath warm on my lips, his hand still holding my arm.

Poised to flee, I nevertheless allowed the momentary absence of space between us. I told myself I would stop him if he tried to kiss me.

"I don't know what I'm going to do about this," he said.

He let go of my arm and drew away from me and I breathed again.

"But I do know I have to do something," he said vehemently. "And I can't even talk to you about it, until I do something."

"Then you'd better do something. And then"—I had to take a breath—"we'll talk about it."

I was doubtful; I had seen the size of the rock in the ring, the determination in the woman. This wasn't an engagement to be broken easily.

And he was probably only toying with me, anyway.

"Kelly, I am dying to kiss you. God, I need to know if you feel the same way I do."

I took in a deep, sharp breath, and turned away from him, partly because I sensed he was asking me to help him control this.

"What a mess," I said. "You're in the middle of all your wedding plans . . ."

"The wedding is a long way off," he said darkly. "Months. Right now, the big thing is my grandparents' fiftieth anniversary party. It's coming up in a couple of weeks. We've been planning it for a long time. Relations are coming in from all over the country. If I say anything to Kyra now, I'm afraid she'll make a scene and ruin everything. If I could just put off breaking up with her until after this party . . ."

A wave of irritation rolled over me. I turned back to face him. "So why are you saying all this to me?"

"I just want you to wait for me, Kelly. I know I can't ask it of you, but I want it. That's all. I have this fear that while I'm tying up loose ends, some other guy will come to the inn and sweep you off your feet."

"I can promise you I will remain as single as you are now, Eli, for the next few weeks, at least."

"This is ridiculous. I'm just going to tell her. Now."

"Look," I said. "You've been with her how long?"

"Three—almost four years now."

"So give it a little more time," I said. "Make sure you really want to do this. Make it easy on your family, do it after the big anniversary party. Because if you're expecting to get out of that with her, and then right into something with me, I can't promise you— because you're right. I hardly know you."

"I'm not asking anything of you, Kelly," he said swiftly. "Not until I can. You understand, this thing with Kyra and me, it hasn't been right with us for a long time. It's not really about you."

"I know. You can't be breaking up with her because of me, right?"

"Exactly. And yet . . ."

"Everyone always says it's not because of another person, when they break up, have you noticed that? And yet there's often another person already involved."

"Yeah."

"Let's not have that be the case, in *this* case."

"Agreed."

"Okay." I tried to walk on, thinking it was time we got out of the grotto, but he checked me with his hand on my wrist.

"Maybe the other person simply acts as a catalyst for something that has to be done anyway," Eli said. "But I have to admit, I don't remember being so sure I couldn't be with her until I met you . . ." He seemed to surrender some inner discipline, because suddenly he was moving closer again, his arms snaking around me.

Why did it have to feel so good? *God help me.*

"What was that?" I twisted out of his arms and tried to push him away, but his hand clung to mine.

"What?"

"Someone's there."

He let go of my hand and turned in the direction I was looking and scrutinized the woods.

I suddenly felt cold. The distinctly human movement I had seen through the trees had me spooked.

"We'd better go back," I said.

"I almost don't care who sees us together, Kelly," he said in a low, ardent voice. But he was careful not to touch me again, and we walked together up to the inn, and parted with one last lingering look.

I returned to my cottage, flushed with the grand drama of it all, but strangely lacking in emotion. It was the strangest declaration I had ever received. The timing had shocked me. And the thing about his grandparents' fiftieth anniversary was a little weird.

I supposed I respected Eli for how he planned to break up with his fiancée. Taking everyone's feelings into consideration. If he really did plan to break up with her. It was, after all, a long-term relationship. Those usually went on far longer than they should anyway. What was another few weeks?

It was gratifying, knowing that my suspicions had been correct: Eli wanted me.

And I think I want him, too . . .

If I felt guilty about Kyra's feelings, at least I had the satisfaction of knowing that I was essentially helping her avoid a terrible mistake, that of marrying a man who didn't really love her.

A few weeks, he had said. A few weeks.

*   *   *

FROM the looks of things, Nick had a bit of a head start on me.

Eli and Kyra left around noon, and not long after that I saw Nick and Paula together down below in the parking area. He was helping her pack up her car, and they were talking casually, smiling and laughing together, and he ruffled little Winkle's hair before shutting the car door and waving them off.

I've heard it said that for a single woman, having kids is considered a negative on the asset sheet when competing in the dating market. But Nick accepted Paula's children without reservation. Though they were good kids, they were kids nevertheless, who could be annoying and whiny attention-seeking monsters, but Nick seemed to take them in stride, whatever the mood.

A guy like that shouldn't be wasted, I said to myself. It was good I set them up.

"They're well suited, don't you think?"

I gave a start, and looked up at Grendel, who was standing behind me at the window in the parlor and was seeing what I was seeing. The edge of his smooth egg-shaped head was gilded with sunlight.

"Nick and Paula?" I shrugged. "We'll see."

"Come now, I know you've been trying to do some matchmaking."

Matchmaking and match-splitting, I thought guiltily, thinking of Eli and Kyra.

"Well, why not?" Grendel smiled at me kindly. "It would be nice to see her with someone who can help her with those boys. And for him, too. Maybe she can straighten him out."

"Straighten him out? How do you mean?"

"Well, you know, he is a bit of a shady character. He's a good guy, but he's reckless. Got himself into a bit of trouble, a while back . . ."

"You mean with the law?"

"I think he's always managed to stay one step ahead of the law. But there are many ways you can get yourself into trouble, Kelly. Still, we all deserve a chance to start anew. That's my philosophy. So, what do you think of Eli Larson?"

This abrupt change of topic in the conversation left me stammering for a reply.

"He's very charming," I blurted finally. "But I don't think he's happy in his relationship . . ." I instantly regretted saying that, and tried to recover. "He seems to be searching."

"Well, but that's just Eli Larson, isn't it?"

"How so?"

"He's been plying the trade of seduction, with you as his latest object. Am I right?"

I didn't answer, but Grendel wagged his head knowingly, as if I had. "Well, you'd have to be insulted if he didn't, wouldn't you? Larson always goes for the interesting and unusual. For that I'll give him credit. His fiancée is actually surprisingly pedestrian, in comparison to some of the others. You wouldn't believe the women he's brought here over the years—yes, even after he was living with his girlfriend—a different young woman every time. All of them stunning and accomplished. Why do you think it took him so long to introduce *her* to this place? She's the fiancée, the others are the others. Up until now he's been able to keep them separate. I suppose he thinks he's entitled. Maybe he is."

"But he seems so . . . sincere."

"It's a game to him. He considers his prey, discovers her weakness, and he plays it however she—whoever the latest *she* happens to be—however she needs it. He's a shrewd businessman, Kelly, and his priority is always to get exactly what he wants. In any arena. Why do you think he appreciates this modest family get-away on the coast? It's not just for the sea air and the great views. It also happens to be just far enough from the city life that he can use it with impunity for his assignations. Nobody would think to look for him here."

"And you are personally acquainted with his habits, apparently," I said coolly. I didn't like this unsolicited assessment of Eli's character, or Grendel's reasons for why Eli happened to appreciate my inn.

"Actually, I am well acquainted with him," Grendel replied in his modest way, which, at the moment, I found irritating. "I've seen him come and go, many times. We've occasionally shared a glass of pinot noir of an evening. We even went surfing together once. He wasn't very skilled, but I have to admit he's fearless. He's a bit of a braggart with the lads, I'm afraid. But then I suppose he can't help it, with the tales he has to tell."

"What does Addie have to say about all this?" I asked, indignant. I couldn't imagine her being so fond of Eli and approving of this sort of womanizing.

"Well, Eli Larson is discreet when he needs to be. Of course he doesn't parade the women past Addie, and Addie, bless her heart, isn't the most observant in these matters, anyway. But Bill . . ." Grendel smiled. "Bill knows all about Eli."

I wasn't feeling very friendly toward Grendel after this conversation. I didn't want Eli to be a player. Especially in light of what he had been doing with me, which only supported Grendel's claims. But what did I know of Grendel, anyway? How did I know if his word could be trusted?

Later, alone in the office, I pulled Grendel's file. I'd gone over his information weeks earlier, when I was first getting to know the inn operation, and a second perusal didn't change my perceptions. The rental application listed his age to be nearly fifty. He worked at the Cielo Shores Clinic, which was just up the highway a mile or two. His income was modest. No job title was listed; I assumed he was some sort of medical technician. His credit was good. He was single. In his file was a letter from a former landlord, a glowing report.

I found nothing in Grendel's information that gave me any reason to doubt his word on Eli.

It didn't matter, I said to myself. Eli's character will be revealed by his actions. If he kept his word, and broke up with Kyra, I would know in time. If he didn't, I would know that as well.

But Grendel's words wounded me. And haunted me. And echoed my own inner voice of warning. *Best forget Eli Larson altogether.*

Write him off completely.

But I didn't, of course. I couldn't. Not yet. I had to admit, I was having some pretty wild thoughts. Even if what Grendel had said about Eli was true, I reasoned, how many rogues throughout history had been tamed by the right woman?

If I were the right woman . . .

Why not Eli?

Chapter 11

ONE afternoon a few days later I found a dog wandering around near the garden where the Johnsons' calf had broken in, a red and black German shepherd whose name, according to the bone-shaped metal tag attached to her collar, was Maggie. I had no leash, but the dog seemed content to follow me when I invited her along, and we walked together a half mile up the old highway to the address on the tag.

The house was set well off the road on a rise overlooking the ocean. Surrounded by pines and cedars, it was a modest cottage in the same style and vintage as the inn, charming and well kept. The long narrow driveway curved through the woods, and as I walked up to the house I caught sight of a sheltered front porch and a massive stone chimney.

The dog trotted up the steps to the porch and stood expectantly at the door, looking back at me, waiting for me to join her. The house had an open view of the ocean and the headlands to the north. It was situated like the inn on a slope above the water, but even more secluded and private.

I knocked on the door and heard the sound of approaching footsteps. Maggie waved her tail.

The door opened and Nick was standing there.

"Hello," he said with surprise.

"Nick! Is this your house?"

He looked at me oddly. "Yes," he said with a laugh. "This is my house. Maggie! What are you doing out there?"

"I met Maggie here wandering around by the inn," I said. "I got your address from her tag."

"And here you are. Hmm. I never dreamed putting that tag on Maggie would result in having a pretty girl show up at my door, but . . . okay, cool." I thought he was about to invite me in, but instead he brushed past me, crossed the porch, and jumped down the steps, striding purposefully toward the side of the house.

"How did she get out, I wonder?" I heard him asking himself.

I followed him down the steps and around the corner of the house, into the side yard where his familiar truck was parked. The wood and wire gate enclosing the rear of the property was standing open.

"Damn," he said. "When did I leave that gate open? Where's Freesia? Why didn't you dogs stick together, Maggie?" He whistled and called out, but only Maggie responded, wagging her tail.

"You're missing another dog?"

"Looks that way." He pulled keys from his pocket and unlocked the cab of his pickup. "Come on," he said to me. "I'll give you a lift home, and on the way you can help me look for Freesia."

At the snap of Nick's fingers, Maggie jumped into the back of the pickup, which was covered with a camper shell. I climbed up into the cab of the truck with Nick and we rolled off down the driveway. The truck was old, but the cab was roomy, comfortable, and high, and Stevie Ray Vaughan was playing the blues on a good sound system.

But at the road Nick swung the vehicle to the left, the opposite direction of the inn. *So much for giving me a lift home.*

"I should have known better than to get into a truck with you," I remarked.

"Relax. I think I know where she went," he said. "It's not far."

"Sure," I said.

He turned up the radio.

"Okay," Nick said, slowing down, scanning the fields alongside the road with his sharp, hawklike gaze. "Shouldn't be long now . . ."

We came around a curve and sure enough, there she was, an aging, stout German shepherd, wandering along beside the old highway. Nick slowed the truck.

"She likes this spot for some reason. I think she found a salami here once."

The dog noticed the truck and gave a friendly but unconcerned wag of her tail. She continued nosing around in the dirt, but then she readily obeyed Nick's command to jump into the back of the truck with Maggie. He helped her with the final scramble, as she was not as agile as the younger dog.

He got in, turned the truck around, and we headed back in the direction of his house, and beyond that, the inn.

"So you never told me the story of the missing girl," I said, looking out the window at the windswept fields sloping down to the sea.

"What?" he cried. "Didn't you forbid me to talk about that?"

"Please. Tell me."

"I told the kids some ghost stories, that's all. And I understand you aren't interested in ghost stories."

So Nick's been talking about me with the boys.

"But I *do* like stories about the inn," I replied. "And I understand there is one in particular, about a young woman who went
missing after she stayed there . . . Is it a true story?"

"You probably have a lot to learn about that inn, Kelly. Lots of
stories. Joe DiMaggio and Marilyn Monroe once slept in Sea
Horse Cottage. Did you know that?"

"Come on," I said. "I have a right to know. There were no
murders mentioned in the disclosures when I bought the property."

"All right. Since you really want to know, I'll tell you. She
stayed in the motel a few times, and then she disappeared. That's
all I can tell you."

I looked at him, startled. He wasn't joking now.

"That's all?" I asked, my voice sharp.

"That's all."

This sudden burst of information left me silent for a moment.
So it was true, then. I hadn't really thought it would turn out to
be, for some reason.

"When was this?"

He shrugged. "A while ago, I don't know. It's in the past."

"Well, who was she? What happened to her?"

"Why are you so interested?"

"Wouldn't you be, if you were me?"

"Maybe."

"The boys say she was beautiful."

"Yeah? What else did they say, Kelly? Did they say she was
young, about your age? That she was a redhead, like you? Did they
tell you that? That she was trying to start a new life. Also like you,
maybe? Maybe running from something . . ."

I crossed my arms, suddenly cold.

"She came, she stayed a short time . . . and then she vanished."

"So you knew her quite well," I said dryly.

He shook his head. But for a guy who didn't know much, he seemed to know a lot. I didn't know if he was deliberately trying to spook me, but I found myself smoothing down goose bumps on my arms.

"That's all I can tell you," he said abruptly when I opened my mouth to ask him more questions.

He pulled up into the driveway beside his house, apparently having forgotten his promise to take me home. We climbed down from his truck, and he said, "Come on in, I'll make you a cup of tea," which I found quaint. I might have been tempted to say yes, because I wanted to check out his place, which was so like my own, on its wooded hill above the Pacific Ocean, but something held me back, and I thought of how little I actually knew of him. There was something about him I just didn't trust. The way he had compared me to the missing woman was disturbing.

"I need to be getting home," I said. "But thank you anyway."

"Come on, Kelly, I won't hurt you." He grabbed my hand in a playful manner and was leading me up the steps to his front porch before I could think of a more effective way to refuse him.

THE sun had gone down below the rim of the ocean. Nick lit a few lamps and the cozy old house glowed. He made me peppermint tea while I walked around his living room, looking at his things, increasingly astonished with him.

"So you collect Native American art," I said when he joined me with two steaming mugs in hand. I knew enough about art and antiques to realize the objects he had in that room, sitting on shelves, hanging on the walls—pottery, rugs, and beadwork—were the real thing, old and authentic and worth real money, not the sort of souvenir the average tourist picks up while on vacation in Santa Fe.

"I don't collect anything." He said. "It's stuff from my family. I got Indian blood on my mother's side."

"Yeah, Sitting Bull McClure, that's you." I laughed, because somehow I didn't buy it, taking in his Anglo-Saxon fairness, his jade green eyes, the day's growth of beard shadowing his jaw, and the chestnut brown hair with just a hint of curl on his neck.

"Sitting Bull was Hunkpapa Sioux," he replied. "My people are Blackfoot, mostly."

Certain he was putting me on, I nodded solemnly. "Sure. Everyone tries to claim some Indian blood these days."

He looked surprised. "Really?"

"Yes, it's very *in* right now."

"This was my great-great-grandmother's," he said. He showed me a beaded white leather bag he kept in an oak and glass case in the corner of the room. "See, this is the double four-winds design . . ." As he stood there, pointing out the intricacies of the beadwork and fringe, his voice lost a little of its habitual drollness, and excitement came into his expression.

He had stories for all his possessions, and he seemed eager to share each one with me.

"Now, this belonged to my father," he said, showing me an old brass compass. He held the disk up to the light, which flashed from its golden sides.

"When he died, it was the only thing of his I really wanted. I have a state-of-the-art, lightweight compass that I usually bring with me into the wilderness, but this one is still my favorite. When I have it I know I won't get lost."

"Just how often do you actually venture into the wilderness?"

"Oh, fairly often."

"How did your father die?"

"He rolled a bulldozer, clearing brush off a hillside. Six years ago."

It was a startling image. I said, "And this compass was the only thing of his that you wanted, to remember him by?"

"Well, he didn't have much. The compass and the bulldozer, that's about it. And I sure didn't want the bulldozer."

"What about your mom?"

"She lives up in Canada." He pointed to a photo of a beautiful woman with dark hair and solemn eyes. "My parents got divorced when I was in my twenties."

"What went wrong?"

"Well, with my mom and dad, I think they just had to go their separate ways. They grew apart. Literally. She was spending more and more time in Canada, where she works trying to set up these programs for her people. My dad didn't want to be in Canada. She says her work is there. So they eventually split and my dad married Irene a few years later."

He showed me another photo, this one of a younger blond woman. "Irene was a nice lady. I liked her. But that marriage didn't last long. She wanted kids. She was younger and ready for prime time, but he'd already done the dad thing with my older brother and me, you know, the diapers and the terrible twos, teenage rebellion, all of that. He didn't want to go through it again."

"Not even for love?"

"The funny thing is, they each knew exactly how the other felt about it when they got married, and they both thought the other would eventually change their mind. Didn't happen."

"That's sad."

"Yeah, it was awful there for a while, during the split. 'Cause I think they really loved each other a lot. And they ended up hurting each other." He returned the compass to its place on the shelf. "She came to his funeral, and it turns out she got what she wanted, she had a little boy. But she didn't seem too happy with her new husband."

The dogs came dashing into the room, excited and playful. Nick lovingly scolded them and told them to go outside. He went to open the back door to let them out. I waited for him near the cold stone fireplace.

"It's a chilly evening," he said when he returned to me. "I think I'll light a fire."

"I have to go."

He stopped and looked at me a moment, jammed his hands into the front pockets of his jeans.

He was stocky, I thought, although not as stocky as I was used to thinking of him. His dark shorn head was square. I'd be taller than him in high heels. There was nothing remarkable about his face, except for those green eyes, and the way he leveled them on me at times, steady on, amused, like right now.

"Yes," he said softly, using his laziest voice on me now. "You better go."

I felt strangely flustered.

He walked me out and thanked me for bringing his dog home.

"I'll see you around," I said.

"You will," he agreed. "I'll give you a ride home."

"No, thank you, I want to walk."

I set off down the old highway. Stars were beginning to emerge against the darkening sky, and I hurried to see my way before it was completely dark. When night fell out here in this remote neighborhood, it got really dark. I sometimes forgot about that.

A light shone across the dark pavement, and I turned. Nick was walking toward me, carrying a flashlight.

I didn't feel annoyed to see him.

I paused a moment to let him catch up with me. I thought about how he had taken my hand impulsively even though I had already refused to come in, and he had led me up the steps into his house, and I wondered why I had found that so oddly . . . compelling.

"Thought I'd walk you home," he said.

He walked beside me all the way to the inn. We stayed on the road and entered the property at the parking area. When we reached the front porch, he stepped away. I said good night and he raised his hand in a swift salute, and was off again.

I watched him walk away, and it occurred to me that Nick was rather attractive, as Paula had suggested. I had scoffed at the idea then, but I had to admit it had become reasonable to me during the weeks I had known him. He was nothing compared to Eli, though, in my mind. And yet something about the real human vitality and warmth of Nick struck me in its contrast to my vague dreams of Eli. Pipe dreams, undoubtedly.

I was not one to dwell in fantasy, or so I insisted to myself. Turning back to the inn, I resolved to think of neither Nick nor Eli.

HAVING learned the missing woman was a flesh and blood creature who had actually existed, I set out to discover more about her. I started with Addie, but she seemed to grow flustered when I asked her about it.

"Come on, Addie," I said. "Tell me what happened. Was she murdered? Nick said—"

"I really don't know much about it, Kelly," she insisted. "I'm afraid nobody does, really. There was no evidence of foul play," she added firmly, as if repeating something she'd heard and had taken to heart.

"Maybe Bill can tell me more, or Grendel . . ."

"Yes, maybe. But it might not be such a good idea, asking Grendel. After all, he is our tenant and we wouldn't want to disturb him."

I knew Addie well enough by now to know she hated any kind of negativity and had a remarkable ability to shut out any unpleasant thing she didn't want to think about. And if it reflected badly on someone or something she loved—like the Magic Mermaid Inn—she would be even more determined to deflect it. But she *did* have a point about keeping such talk away from our guests or, in Grendel's case, our tenant.

A couple of days later when I was alone with Bill in the office, I brought it up with him.

He hesitated. "I don't like to talk about it, because it disturbs the missus, you see. And talking about her won't bring her back. Yes, she was a spirited girl. We liked her."

"So you knew her well, then?"

"I can't say I knew her well. She was here such a short time."

"A redhead?" It seemed a trivial point, but I had to ask.

He nodded again, not looking at me. "Never did find out what happened to her. It remains a mystery."

Bill was shrewd. Without even seeing the expression on my face, he seemed to guess the direction of my thoughts. "Well, Kelly, we're running an inn here, you know. People come and go. That's not a crime. It's not like a body was ever found."

"What was her name?" I asked.

I was almost surprised when he gave me the answer.

"Alicia," he said, and I heard something tart in his voice. "Her name was Alicia St. Claire."

"Alicia St. Claire," I repeated. It seemed a fitting name for a beautiful, mysterious woman. "How long did she stay at the inn?"

"Not long."

"And when did she—"

"You see a lot of life," Bill interrupted, "running an inn like this for so many years." He seemed to be tired of my questions. "A lot of different characters coming and going, with all their different stories. Such a range of personalities and professions. We've had movie stars stay here, and United States senators. But it's not really that kind of place. Our favorite guests aren't celebrities, but regular folks. Families."

"Like Eli Larson's family, for example," I said.

"Sure. They're regular folks. Eli being the exception." Bill smiled.

"I understand Eli appreciates the inn just because it *is* rather . . . unprepossessing. That he has brought more than one young beauty here for a discreet getaway."

"Well, sure," Bill said, with a blush that suddenly flared up beneath the spots on the aged skin of his neck. "He's done that on occasion. But I think we can safely say that was the old days. He'll be married soon, and that'll be the end of that."

"Grendel said—"

"Oh, Grendel," Bill interrupted. "He's just a lonely bachelor. Don't you pay him no mind."

FEELING troubled by what I had learned about the missing woman as well as what I had heard about Eli, I nevertheless tried to take Bill's words as an endorsement of Eli. I slipped away to my cottage when I had a free moment, to collect myself. There was a feeling of unreality in the air, as if this person Eli Larson was a mythical being who had shown himself and then retreated back into the mists of legend, along with a beautiful redheaded girl named Alicia St. Claire. Not a week had passed since I'd last seen him, and yet he was already fading in my mind.

I went to the dressing table mirror to look at his photo, just to remind myself of what he looked like.

It seemed to me I was expecting something new to leap out at me from the photo, but his expression remained inert, if patently sincere. The only thing different that I noticed was a small dark spot on Eli's forehead, as if someone had dabbed a wet cotton swab against the newsprint just there. I tried to flick the spot away, but it was a stain, like a watermark.

I frowned at this mar on the face of my fantasy. I must have gotten it wet somehow. Maybe while shaking out my hair after a shower, or something.

But at least now I remembered what Eli's face looked like.

Chapter 12

PAULA returned with the boys the next weekend. As she had hoped, Nick showed up on Saturday—without prompting. *I* hadn't said anything, anyway. The four of them were off to the beach together.

I watched them from Addie's geranium-bedecked balcony, where I sat in the shade of an umbrella with Bill, going over the inn accounts. They walked on the path below without noticing us sitting up there behind the painted railing.

Nick wore a blue volleyball T-shirt and baggy khaki shorts showing off his tanned legs and arms. Rocky and Winkle, dressed in swim trunks and slathered with sunscreen, hurried to keep up with Nick's quick stride.

Then came Paula. The woman had a movie star's body and a tendency to overdress. But the thing about Paula was, no matter how far she went with her self-adornment, she carried it off because her personality was always even more striking than her appearance.

Nick was obviously under Paula's spell now; he had a huge grin on his face from something she'd just said to him. She fell into step beside him and she leaned her head in close to his, to hear his reply.

Nick glanced up at the balcony and for a moment we looked at each other, or I thought we did. He turned away and then I knew I must have been wrong. He would have acknowledged me if he had seen me. *Wouldn't he?*

As Paula's younger son trotted along at his side, Nick laid his hand absently on the child's head. Nick's touch was easy. Companionable. Protective. His hand rested atop the blond curls a fraction of a second, then dropped away. The boy's obvious pleasure in the older man's attention was precious; he held his chest high and proud, and scrambled to keep up with Nick's casual stride.

Now *that* is cute, I thought.

At that moment, watching them, I became aware of an unusual confusion in myself. I didn't understand the feeling; I didn't know what to call it. It was akin to the sensation of watching another enjoying that which should have been yours.

Like . . . jealousy?

But I don't want that man. And I don't want children . . .

So why should I feel this way? Why would it cause me a pang to see the four of them walk off together down the cliff path?

I was happy for them, wasn't I? I was *hoping* for this.

"You might want to keep an eye on those two boys of yours," I said to Paula when I found her in the parlor Sunday morning. She was sitting at one of the side tables, writing in her leather appointment book.

Anita was in the room, too, polishing the old woodwork around the fireplace.

"Why?" Paula looked up sharply, immediately suspicious. "What are they doing?"

"Nothing, don't worry," I assured her. "They're fine. They're right down on the front lawn kicking a soccer ball around. I'm just not sure it's such a good idea for them to be hanging out with that older one . . . I just don't trust him."

Earlier that day I had noticed Paula's young boys near the pool in the company of the teenager with the black hair and blazing eyes. The three of them had been huddled together closely, intently conversing.

"I have no proof, obviously," I said, "but I have a hunch he might have been the one who painted that graffiti on my cottage."

"Who? Are you talking about Zac?" Paula asked.

"Zac? Is that his name?"

"He's that beautiful boy with black hair and piercing eyes? Cruises around the inn on his bike?"

"Right, that's him." I said with a laugh, "Paula, I love the way you describe people."

Anita clenched her rag and walked out without a word.

"I'll keep an eye on them," Paula said. "But I wouldn't worry about it too much. Rocky told me Zac spent the better part of an afternoon the other day trying to convince Rocky and Dean to become vegetarians."

"Well, if that's the worst that happens, well . . ."

"Right. I think I could handle that."

PAULA and the boys left around two, and Nick stayed on to do some "prep work," as he called it, for the next day's painting. Twilight was gathering by the time he was packing up in the parking area. I walked across the yard to put some bills out at the mailbox by the road.

"So," I inquired politely, "did you have a nice day?

"Yep," he said, looking at me funny, as if I amused him. "You?"

I shrugged. "It was all right."

"Just all right?"

"You and Paula seemed to be hitting it off. Beachcombing with her boys."

"Oh, were you spying on me, then?

"Yes." I nodded.

"You were?" He perked up, delighted.

So he hadn't seen me watching him from the balcony after all.

"Why?" he asked.

"I was curious."

"Ah . . ." He gave me a sly look. "You saw me making out with Paula on the sand, didn't you?"

"What? You did?"

He laughed at my expression. "Kelly," he said patiently. "We took a walk on the beach with her kids."

"Okay, don't get all excited. I was just wondering if you owed me that dinner yet."

"No, I don't, but I'd be happy to take you out to dinner tonight, if you like."

"Let's just save it for the payoff."

"So how about you? Any progress on your end?"

"Progress?"

"With the tycoon?"

"Actually, yes . . . Eli told me he's going to break up with his fiancée, and then he's coming for me."

"Are you serious?"

I nodded, and he let out a low whistle.

"Fast work."

"I didn't do anything."

"You didn't do anything to stop it, either, did you?"

"Anyway, who knows what might happen? He might change his mind. And I don't know why I'm saying anything about it to you."

"You have to," he said.

"No I don't."

"If you want me to keep *you* updated, you do."

"I can find out anything I want to, from Paula."

"Not if I tell her not to tell you anything."

"You're evil."

"You think so?"

"Yes. Whenever I am with you, I come away feeling like I've made a pact with the devil."

He shook his head. "I'm not the devil. I'm your guardian angel, baby." He smiled at me, his teeth showing very devilishly. He finished packing up the truck and turned to me. "Hey, I'll see you tomorrow, all right, Kelly?"

HE didn't come back the next day. Or the next.

Paula called the inn late one afternoon when I was in the office. The TV was on in the parlor, and I was listening with half an ear to a news story on a local station about an elderly woman missing in the Santa Cruz mountains.

"I've been trying to get ahold of Nick," she said. "But he's not returning my calls. What do you think I should do?"

"Stop calling him," I said into the phone. "By the way, I haven't seen him around here, either."

I had thought he might be off with her. Apparently not.

"Well, hmm. I hope he's okay. Maybe you should check on him, Kelly, do you think? I would myself, if I didn't live thirty miles away. I'm kind of worried about him."

Do you know him well enough to be worried about him?

"Yeah, okay," I said. "Don't worry. If I don't see him soon, I'll check it out. I know where he lives."

"All right. Let me know."

Perfect, I thought, hanging up the phone. Now I've agreed to babysit Nick McClure.

HE showed up for work the next morning looking as if he had just come off a three-day bender. He was unshaven, stiff, and silent, and he made no apology for his absence. The several days' growth of beard shadowed his square, strong jaw, and the red rims around his eyes only made them look greener. There was a sleepy quality about him, like he'd just climbed out of bed.

I found him in the parking area, where he was unloading tools from his truck.

"Given what you charge me per hour," I said to him sternly, "I suppose I should be glad you chose not to grace us with your presence for the greater part of the week. But you know, you *did* say you were going to be here 'tomorrow,' and that was Sunday, as I recall. And then—"

"I know it's a cliché," he cut in, "but you sure are cute when you're mad."

I stared at him. *"What?"* I gave my head a shake, incredulous. "This is a *business* relationship we have here, Nick."

His grin faded. "I'm sorry, Kelly. I just like playing with you."

"I just think you should do what you say you're going to do. Or don't say you're going to do it."

He nodded. "You're right. Next time I'll call you."

"Next time!" I threw up my hands. "Whatever."

"You missed me, didn't you?"

I turned away, still shaking my head, refusing to speak with him anymore, but I was smiling. Damn him, I thought, amazed. He's right. I *did* miss him.

That only made it worse.

I need to fire him, I thought.

But how could I fire him? I needed ten more like him. Even with the excellent staff we had, I didn't know how I was going to handle the inn on my own when Addie and Bill retired.

"You know, Addie," I said heatedly a few minutes later when I found her in the office. "I like Nick, but I'm not sure I can—I'm not sure I can afford him. He's not very dependable, and he's got an attitude—"

"Nick?" Addie looked startled. "Oh, no, Kelly, Nick is *very* dependable."

"Addie, look." I cast about for a way to say it tactfully. Nick McClure, after all, was her choice, hers and Bill's. "Nick does nice work, I can see that, and the price is fair, I'm sure. But I need someone I can rely on. Someone who, when he says he's going to be here on Monday, doesn't not show up until Thursday looking like something the cat—" I caught myself and shut up. My grammar was suffering and so was my composure. Nick's appearance had been rugged and rough, but somehow it suited him. No cat had dragged him in. If he had looked burned out and haggard, he had also looked primal and sexy . . .

Okay, so that just proved how psychologically twisted *I* was. But I didn't have to let my neuroses interfere with business.

Addie laid her little hand on my arm. "Kelly, I want to show you something. Wait here a moment."

She went off into the parlor and returned with the morning paper.

"Have you had a chance to read this yet?" She waved the paper at me.

"No," I replied impatiently, wondering what this had to do with anything.

"I thought not."

She flipped through a few pages and laid the paper down, smoothing it for me to read. "See?" she said, pointing. "See?"

My gaze drifted over the images and words, and I'm not sure how many seconds passed before I registered what I was seeing.

I began to understand.

I was looking at a photo of Nick, who was wearing a jumpsuit and a backpack, flanked by Freesia and Maggie, both dressed in jackets distinguishing them as search and rescue dogs.

The headline read: "Search Team Finds Lost Woman.

"This is why Nick hasn't been here the last few days, Kelly." Addie's voice was patient. "He was helping to look for the lost lady. Eighty-nine years old. She wandered off from a nursing home in Scott's Valley a couple of days ago. Alzheimer's."

I looked for some mention of Nick's name, but there were no specifics on the rescuers in the story; the only name given was that of the rescued woman.

Looking down at Nick's likeness, I thought of how I had discovered Eli's true identity when I had seen his photograph in the newspaper, and it occurred to me that perhaps I had just discovered Nick's true identity in the same way.

"WHY didn't you tell me?" I confronted him, made him stop what he was doing to the window he was working on. He stood on a ladder, so I had to look up at him, which didn't help with my power stance.

"What?" he asked faintly.

"You go away all mysteriously and then you suddenly reappear, and allow me to vent at you about not being around here working, when you could have just said what you had gone to do." I held up the newspaper. "That's where you were, that's what you were doing, the first week I was here, too, right? Off rescuing people. And you let me think you were just a flake. Why? Why didn't you just tell me?"

He climbed down from the ladder. "Would it have made any difference?"

"Yes," I said, quieting my voice. "Of course it makes a difference."

"You're berating me again."

"Well, you're so exasperating."

"I have to get something from my truck," he said.

I walked with Nick toward the parking area, thinking of the night we had walked together on the old highway in the darkness, when he had caught up with me to light my way. My feelings for him were changing, and that worried me a little.

And yet here I was once again, annoyed with him because he never told me what was going on with him. Somehow this was reassuring to me. I *wanted* to feel annoyed with him.

But that strange, wistful feeling that had come over me at the sight of him with Paula and her kids—what was that about? That wasn't annoyance.

We reached the parking area just in time to witness the arrival of a vintage '50s convertible Cadillac with the top down. Paula was driving the car and—more surprising—Eli was riding shotgun. She took the corner into the parking area a little too fast and kicked up a spray of gravel.

She cut the engine and they jumped out to greet us, Paula hopping on one leg, trying to put on her shoes—spiky high-heeled sandals, which she had apparently slipped off while driving. Eli was grinning and draping his arms around Nick—a quick hearty bear hug; and then me, less hearty and more lingering.

I tucked the newspaper under my arm, afraid that if I showed the picture of Nick to Paula she would take it from me.

Nick and I were too surprised to say much, but it didn't matter, because Eli and Paula were full of noisy triumph about what they'd just done—having come to see us on a whim—and they filled the air with chatter, or rather, Paula did.

"We met for coffee at Buck's in Woodside to talk business, and I persuaded him to do this crazy thing," Paula explained, grabbing my arm in a chummy way. "Not that it was difficult. I knew he wanted to come, but he wasn't sure what you'd think. I told him it would be okay. Is it okay?"

"She said she was taking a ride over to the coast to check on Nick, and she wanted me to keep her company," Eli said sheepishly.

"And you said yes," I said, my voice too sweet. I felt cross with him, thinking of what Grendel had said. Was Eli really just a player? Kyra, me, and now Paula? Did it really matter with him?

I glowered at Nick. I wasn't too happy with him, either. What had he said to Paula about our competition? Our sordid little dare . . .

"And then Eli insisted that we take his car," Paula went on, "but he let me drive! It was so fun. And here you are, Nick, all in one piece; I needn't have bothered checking on you."

"Turns out he's a hero," I said. "Search and rescue worker. He was off saving people."

"Oh, yeah? Ha, ha!" Paula said. She thought I was joking.

"It's true. You can find his picture in the *Chronicle* today."

"Really? Awesome. I'll look for it."

Nick was flushed now. He turned away and tended to something in his truck.

"You two go on ahead," I said to Eli and Paula. "We'll see you up at the house in a moment."

Eli and Paula went off to the house. Nick shut up his toolboxes with a loud slam. I waited for him to look at me.

"What?" he asked.

"Never mind." I turned to follow Eli and Paula.

"Hey." Nick stopped me with his hand on my arm. "What's going on?"

"Nothing." I shrugged him off.

"I know," he said gently. "You're all freaked out, with them showing up here like this, aren't you?"

"No, I'm not."

"Look," he said, "I'm not sure what to do about her. I don't have time to socialize. I need to get some work done here. I need the money."

"Why, don't they pay enough for your rescue missions?"

"Our team is all volunteer. We don't get paid for anything. We supply all our own equipment, dogs, training, food, everything. And when I'm off doing that, I'm not making any dough here, if you get my drift."

"Hmm. That's tough. But you know, Nick, some things in life are even more important than money. And you wouldn't want to throw away *that* for an hour or two of *work*, would you?"

He leaned against the truck and studied my face. "I see your point," he said.

"Come on, then," I said, tugging on his arm, lowering my voice vampishly. "Let's go get 'em."

I found Eli and Paula in the parlor, sitting close together on the couch beneath the ocean-view window, laughing and chatting like old friends.

"All right, Kelly," Paula demanded when I walked in alone. "Where is he? Did he run off?"

"Nick's cleaning up his job site. He was trying to get some work done. You've distracted him."

"Poor boy," said Eli.

"And how is Kyra doing these days?" I asked him pointedly.

"She's stressed," he replied. "It's shaky. I want to talk to you about it, Kelly."

"We're all friends, here, apparently," I said. "Go ahead and talk."

"Kelly, you're not happy we've come, are you?" Paula said, her voice suddenly small, like that of a scolded child.

"Hey, Kelly and Nick are working," said Eli. "And here we come, barging in—"

"Nobody ever barges in, at an inn." I smiled, softening to them, feeling ashamed of my lack of hospitality. "You're always welcome."

"Look, Kelly," Paula said, "don't worry about us. If you're busy, we'll just hang out for a little while, then we'll get out of your way."

Nick came into the room and I could see Paula was getting a good look at him in his painter's overalls and his three days' growth of beard. She seemed to be weighing the sexy against the scruffy; Nick embodied a bit of both.

"Hey, Kelly," Eli said. "What do you say we take a walk on the beach?" He remained sitting beside Paula, waiting for me to say yes or no.

I couldn't help thinking that if it had been Nick, he would have simply jumped up, grabbed my hand, and we would have been gone. "Maybe some other time," I said.

I left them and went into the office. A few moments later Eli appeared in the doorway.

"How about it, Kelly? Walk on the beach with me?"

"I *do* have work here," I said, shuffling papers, not looking up. I was angry with him. How dare he show up with Paula in that sexy silver convertible! And what about Kyra, who was evidently still ignorant of her fiancé's plans to dump her? Strange, but it wasn't jealousy I felt where Kyra was concerned. It was something else . . . the feeling that I was being taken for a fool.

So did that mean I was jealous of Paula?

"I'm sorry, Kelly," he said softly. "I didn't want this. I vowed not to come back here until I was free."

"You broke your vows, apparently."

"Paula caught me in a moment of weakness," he said. "My golf game has been lousy, I can't concentrate . . . and it's all your fault."

This made me laugh, given his winsome expression. He was such a big, gentle man with his big boots and his broad shoulders. It was hard to ignore the power of his appeal.

He went on explaining. "So when I met Paula for coffee, and she came up with the idea, I couldn't help it, I said yes. Nothing's changed with Kyra, I haven't said a word, but she knows something's going on, I can't touch her . . ."

I breathed in deeply. "Oh, God, this isn't good."

"I know."

"Let me see if I can get Addie to cover for me."

WE walked along the cliff path and down the steps to the beach. Halfway down the cliff, where the stairs turned at the landing, he stopped and faced me. "You've got quite a stretch of beachfront property here, don't you?" He said it appreciatively, gazing across the land. "How many acres?"

"Quite a few," I said with a shrug, and I'm sure my pride shone through. "It's mostly open-space designated, you know, but that's cool."

He suddenly took me in his arms, a graceful, surprising movement. "Kelly," he said, "you don't know how I—" He pressed his lips against mine suddenly and I responded awkwardly; I had been expecting something like this, but somehow not just at that moment. His timing seemed slightly ahead of mine. But I was catching up fast. He kissed me expertly, with just the right slip of moist tongue between the lips.

"Eli, no . . ." I finally managed to say.

But he had already let go of me.

A kiss, I thought wildly. No harm in a simple kiss. *I can't let anything else happen, though . . .*

I was all ready to block the next pass, but he didn't try to kiss me again.

When we got down onto the beach I let him walk a little ahead of me in the sand for a moment so I could look at him. I had recovered a bit from the kiss. I breathed in the sight of his lovely male proportions, marveling at the height and breadth of him, the beauty of his long, full-muscled limbs, his wavy-haired action-hero head. His physical looks seemed a fitting manifestation of the power he handled as a mighty entrepreneur. I wanted to kiss him again, smell that semisweet spicy scent of him, get my hands on those long, broad muscles, get his hands on me. But I was determined to stick to my principles. I wouldn't cross the line with this man until he was free.

You have already crossed the line.

Oh, shut up, I told myself.

He turned to let me catch up with him. He held out his hand, but I shook my head.

"I'm sorry, Kelly," he said, dropping his arm. "This was a mistake. I shouldn't have come. I pride myself on my control. But you do something to me."

It struck me that he was hoping I would take charge of things. Call the shots. Frustration welled up in me. If he was waiting for a sign, we were in trouble.

"No harm in a walk on the beach," I said shortly.

If he had overwhelmed me with sudden unstoppable passion, that would be one thing. Or if he had withheld himself, aloof, reserved—I would have known how to handle it. But he had thrown me off balance.

I asked Eli about something I'd read in the paper recently about his business, a question designed to distract him, which it did. While he talked, I kept us walking, down the beach and back, and we returned in less than an hour to the inn.

Just before we went up into the house, he stopped and turned to me. "You'll wait for me, won't you Kelly?"

"It's you who's waiting," I said, not stopping.

He walked beside me up the steps. "I can't wait any longer," he said. "I'm going to break up with her. Tonight."

"You might as well stick to your plan," I said flatly. "It won't be long now, right?"

He sighed. "No. It won't be long."

NICK sat on the front porch steps talking to Paula, who lay draped over the wicker chaise, wearing a flared black and white miniskirt and big black sunglasses. The spiky black sandals were off, lying on the porch.

There was an awkward moment when nobody had much to say, then we all suddenly excused ourselves, saying we had to get back to whatever we had been doing.

Eli brushed his hand over the curve of my back as he said his casual good-byes to Nick and me. He took the wheel for the drive home.

"WELL?" Nick asked. His manner was subdued. "Your turn to walk on the beach, Kelly. You and Eli."

I raised an eyebrow. "Yes, we did take a walk on the beach."

"Anything you'd like to tell me?"

"Well, you know, there's this secluded cove with a little hidden cave, very private, just big enough for two people to squeeze into and, um . . ."

"Yeah, I know the one."

"I'll bet you do."

"So, Kelly, are you buying me dinner tonight? Is that what you're saying?" He looked at me, green eyes glittering.

I let the question linger in the air a moment, then shook my head. "No," I assured him. "I am not buying you dinner tonight, Nick."

"You're telling me he didn't try anything—"

"No, I didn't say that, but . . . a friendly kiss is a long way from . . . you know. Owing you dinner."

"A kiss, huh?" He frowned. "That's fast work."

"What do you mean, fast work? A kiss? A moment ago you were asking me if I owed you dinner."

"I guess I shouldn't be surprised."

"Oh, and you never kissed Paula?"

"I—uh, yes. No. I haven't."

"Well, don't worry, I don't think I'm much ahead of you. He hasn't broken it off with Kyra yet."

"That's not a good sign," Nick said hopefully.

"No, but he's already told me that he wanted to wait a few weeks before he breaks up with her."

"Why?"

I was embarrassed to answer, and wished I hadn't mentioned it.

"Why?" he repeated.

"Well, his grandparents are having this big fiftieth anniversary party, and he doesn't want Kyra to go ballistic and wreck everything for them, with the relatives all coming in, and . . . everything. He's going to wait until after the party to break it off with her."

"Hmm." Nick let out a grunt of disgust. "Well, if it were me, I wouldn't wait for anything."

His words touched me in a strange way. They annoyed me, which I'm sure they were meant to, but also I felt a touch of remorse that Eli didn't share Nick's philosophy of passionate recklessness.

"I told him to wait," I said loyally. "When he first brought it up. And I told him the same thing today."

It was true. I had. And I meant it. After all, reckless passion almost always spelled trouble.

"Well, if it were me," Nick insisted, "I wouldn't listen to you."

I blew out a breath of exasperation. "Nick, I don't doubt that at all!"

Chapter 13

I took the newspaper from where I'd stashed it behind the literature rack in the hall and brought it to my cottage. I sat on my bed and cut out the photo of Nick. When I finished, I tucked the photo into the edge of the mirror just below Eli's, and I looked at the two men. I couldn't help but compare them. Nick's full-body shot was caught in action—not much detail showing, but a ragged energy shone through. Sexy. Eli's portrait-face looked handsome and sincere, but rather vacant, staring into the camera with no expression.

Not a fair comparison, I insisted to myself. And there was that damned spot, right about where Eli's third eye would be, or a bit higher. It actually looked larger than it had before. What I remembered as a spot about the size of a raindrop was now a larger water stain.

My first reaction was to glance up at the ceiling, looking for a leak. How was this happening? There was nothing suspicious above me, only the white painted pine boards. I looked back at the picture. I must have misjudged the size of the stain to begin with.

I took down the photo of Nick and put it in the top drawer of my dresser. I didn't want him to walk in here to fix a leaky faucet or something and see his photo on display. And if there was something dripping on things, I didn't want it dripping on my picture of Nick.

The next morning Maxine stopped in for coffee and a chat with Addie as she often did, arriving in the office the same time as Grendel, who had come to pick up the bag lunch Arturo made for him to take to work every morning.

"Addie's with her visualization class," I told Maxine. "They had a field trip this morning to watch the sunrise from the bluffs."

Maxine laughed. "A field trip, huh? So she's still involved with all that New Agey whoo-hoo with Hazel?"

"Hazel? You mean the countess?"

"Right, the countess. To me she's just Hazel. I've known her since I was a kid—she used to be my babysitter. She was married to that count—if he really was a count—for about twenty minutes, back in the seventies. Do you even get to keep the title if you divorce the guy? Anyway, if Addie wants to give her money to Hazel, it's none of my business. If she's getting something out of it, good for her."

"Let's hope it's good for her," Grendel, who had paused in the doorway to listen to Maxine, said dubiously.

"What's the matter, don't you like Hazel?" Maxine asked him.

"Grendel thinks she's a charlatan," I said. "He thinks she's a con artist, bilking vulnerable Addie. Right, Grendel?"

"No, actually, I believe the so-called countess is perfectly sincere," he replied. "I have conversed with her on occasion, and I have even purchased one or two books in her establishment. But as for spiritual pedagogy, I have always maintained that the level of an educator's own perception necessarily determines the level of the material he or she is able to present and impart to the student. I must say I have my own opinion as to the level of the countess's perceptions."

"Grendel, honey," said Maxine, "I did not understand a single word you just said. All I know is, Addie didn't murder Earl and me when that little heifer of ours broke into her garden for the second time, so I guess she must be doin' a good job of visualizing world peace."

Grendel smiled. "That's the important thing, I suppose," he conceded graciously. He got his lunch from Arturo in the kitchen and went off to work.

"He's a character, isn't he?" said Maxine, watching Grendel ride away on a bicycle. "Earl thinks he's a loon."

"He's different," I admitted.

"At least he's a gentleman. Always so kind and helpful and clean."

"Yeah, that's the thing about Grendel. He has an air of peace around himself."

"Unlike my husband's hotheadedness. That man is an embarrassment to me. Good thing he has his welding to keep him occupied—he can pour out all his fire into that."

"What's he working on now?"

"Fence sculptures. He's doing a galloping horse for some friends of ours. But mostly he just fixes things. He loves it."

"You can't help but admire that passion."

"Passion! I'd like to wring his neck sometimes. Like that night he tried to start a fight with Nick after the community meeting. Thank goodness Nick's got a cool head."

"Well—it takes two to tango," I pointed out, eager to find fault with Nick. I felt myself drawn to Nick McClure more and more, and I didn't want to be. Besides, wasn't I just wishing Eli had more of Nick's passion? And here was Maxine, praising his cool head!

"Well, that's just it," Maxine insisted. "Nick chose *not* to tango. But it's true. Nick and Earl get along like Cain and Abel. Ever since that girl went off . . ."

"What girl?"

"Oh, a few years back—" Maxine stopped abruptly, as if she'd suddenly decided against that line of conversation.

"The girl who stayed at the inn? And then went missing? Alicia St. Claire, right?"

"Yes, that's right. I believe that was her name."

"Nobody will give me any details on what happened," I said. To me, the lack of information on the missing woman was intriguing in itself. Nobody wanted to say much about it. I had done some searching on the Internet and found nothing there, either.

"Well . . . we don't talk about it around Addie and Bill, because it disturbs them. But I sometimes wonder if the girl didn't stage her own disappearance. People do sometimes, you know."

"Did she have a reason to do that?"

"Well, she might have been trying to escape the past. And I think she had a few ghosts from the past who didn't *want* her to escape."

"You mean like a lover? A man?"

"A man, sure. Or *men,* was more likely with that one. She was an attractive girl, and don't think she didn't know it."

"So you knew her, then?"

"Well, I ran into her once or twice. Didn't get to know her well."

"Bill seems to think she might have been like any other guest. Stopped for a while, then moved on . . . Addie said there was no evidence of foul play."

"Oh, but *something* happened to her, all right," Maxine said knowingly. "If she didn't stage it herself, that is. Maybe it wasn't foul play, but something happened. Could be she slipped on the cliffs, fell into the waves. But you would think her body would have been found, eventually, in that case."

"You don't think maybe she just . . . moved on?"

"If she moved on, she forgot to bring her car with her," Maxine said with a hoot of laughter. "A nice enough car, too."

"Her car . . ."

"It was found abandoned, just a quarter mile or so down the road from here."

"So what happened between Earl and Nick?" I asked her. "You said after the girl went missing, they—"

"Oh, it was a . . ." She scowled and shook her head, looking away from me. For a moment, I didn't think she would continue. "Earl got a notion that Nick shouldn't be part of the search team looking for the girl. Nick didn't agree with Earl, as you can imagine."

"Why? Why would Earl feel that way?"

She shook her head as if she didn't know, but she had to know. I was sure of it.

"I mean, that seems odd, considering Nick does search and rescue," I said. "Or didn't he back then?"

"Oh yes, he was doing it then. This was only three years ago."

"Three years?" For some reason I had thought the woman had disappeared in a more distant past. Three years was *recent*.

Maxine nodded. "Same year Earl had his bypass surgery."

"So why didn't Earl want Nick to be part of the search?" I asked.

She didn't answer right away. "Well, now, you have to understand, Kelly, Earl is stubborn. And he likes to take charge of things."

The phone in the office began to ring, a shrill note that cut the conversation short.

"I'm sorry," I said. "I should answer that."

"Of course you should, honey. You've got a business to run here." Maxine pushed herself up from her chair. "I've got to get going anyway." She went out in a hurry, waving good-bye to me as I answered the phone, leaving me with the distinct impression she had been grateful for the interruption.

WHEN I was finished with my call, I went into the kitchen, where Arturo was sautéing garlic on the old gas stove, and I stood there, just breathing in the delicious smells that filled the room. Anita walked in and out between the kitchen and dining room, carrying baskets of napkins and silver. At one point we were all three of us in the kitchen together, and on impulse I asked them what they knew about the missing woman.

Anita, typically, did not respond to my question directly. She looked at Arturo, who turned down the flame under his skillet and turned to me, wiping his hands on his white apron. "We knew her," he said with a shrug. "She stayed here. What about it?"

"I just wondered what really happened."

"Nobody really knows," Arturo said. "She was here one day, and then she was just gone the next day." His voice was quiet, and hesitant. "I think she was trying to get away from a bad thing."

"And she run into something worse," Anita spoke up unexpectedly.

"So you don't think she just—left?" I turned to her.

Anita appeared to regret having said anything. She shrugged and didn't say another word.

"What was this bad thing she was running from?"

"A man who wanted her to get naked in front of a camera, I think," Arturo answered. "In Los Angeles."

"Did she tell you that?"

"I heard her say it to somebody. I don't remember who."

"What room did she stay in when she came?"

"She stayed in . . ." Arturo glanced at Anita for help.

Anita gave her answer to him, not to me, and in Spanish.

"She stayed in the motel when she came," Arturo translated. "She don't remember which room."

As the days went by with no further word from Eli, I tried to convince myself he had been using me. I knew I should just forget about him. But one little stubborn voice inside my head said Eli was sincere, and urged me to wait and see.

Esperar, I thought. To wait, to hope. Arturo was teaching me Spanish.

And I waited to see what would happen with Nick and Paula. Nick was in and out of the inn; besides his work with the search and rescue team, he had other jobs. I couldn't afford to have him around all the time anyway. When our paths did cross—literally, more often than not, on the walkways around the inn—we joked about "our competition" or "the dare" or whatever we were calling it that day. Usually one of us would ask, "So, do you owe me a dinner?" The answer, so far, for both of us, was always no.

The day of the big anniversary party would soon be upon us, and after that I would know if Eli was serious about what he'd said he was going to do. Would he break up with Kyra and come to me? Fortunately I was too busy to think much about it.

Chapter 14

"COME on, Kelly, the inn won't fall into the ocean if you aren't here to hold it up for a few hours." Nick stood with his legs spread slightly, looking down on me. I was sitting on the floor in front of open cabinet doors in the kitchen, trying to organize it a little better. Some beautiful old vases had been shoved to the back and looked like they hadn't been used for years.

"Addie already told you she was going to be in the office all afternoon. She doesn't mind if you go."

"Nick, what is it?" I turned and looked up at him, exasperated. He'd been nagging at me to take the afternoon off and go somewhere with him, but he wouldn't tell me where, or why. "Why do you always act so mysterious? Why don't you just say what it is you want me to do, and stop pestering me?"

"I want you to come with me to visit my great-grandmother, who lives in Boulder Creek."

"Fine. I will. Why didn't you just ask?"

"I did. I asked you to forget that you're mad at me, and be my companion today."

"I am not mad at you, Nick."

"Do you swear it?"

I looked at him to see if he was for real. He was grinning at me, happy that he'd talked me into going along with his scheme.

"Why were you so adamant about me going with you to see your grandmother today?" I asked Nick when we were on the road. I was driving my Honda. Nick sat beside me holding the vase I had filled with Addie's flowers.

"My great-grandmother," he corrected me. "'Cause she's old. She might drop dead any minute."

"Nick!"

"And then you wouldn't get to meet her."

"You are mental."

"She's a painter, Kelly, like you."

"You said my painting looked like a paint-by-number."

"Well, you really aren't very good yet, it's true. But there's something there. Some strange potential."

"You can see that, huh?"

"Yes. That's why I'm taking you to see Gran. She can teach you, if you want her to."

We left the ocean and drove inland, up the curving highway into the redwood forests of the Santa Cruz mountains. It was invigorating, the clean, crisp air tinged with the scent of wood smoke and the spicy essence of the earth in autumn. We let the windows down and turned up the music.

*   *   *

NICK's great-grandmother lived on the banks of Boulder Creek in a cabin speckled with sunlight and shaded by redwood trees in a clearing beside the river. I saw a small vegetable garden with some spent tomato plants and several rows of newly planted lettuce, cabbage, and broccoli, all wrapped in wire fencing to protect them, as Nick put it, "from the critters." Near the house, clay pots full of herbs and baskets of flowers hanging from the eaves gave the small shingled cabin a pretty, homey feel.

"Oh, great." Nick's expression changed to one of pain when he noticed an old Lincoln Continental parked in the driveway. "Cassandra is here. Damn. Usually she's working during the day."

"Cassandra?"

"My cousin Cassandra. Second cousin, actually. I guess you're getting a taste of the full-on clan treatment . . . all wrapped up in one cousin. Come on." He took my hand for a moment and smiled at me. "Hey, don't worry. You'll be all right."

WE went into the house and no one was there. I blinked, my eyes adjusting to the dark, pine-paneled front room, with its rustic stone fireplace and rocking chairs, and a big oval hooked rug on the clay-tile floor. The house smelled of dried roses and sage, wood smoke, and something like donuts or freshly baked bread, the smells all mingling together, earthy and heavenly at the same time.

Nick wandered around the little house, looking for his grandmother, and I followed him, carrying the flowers. In the kitchen, open shelves held dozens of bottles, hand-labeled jars of herbs, spices, and potions. Low exposed beams were crowded with bunches of plants and cut flowers hung to dry. In the hallway, a cat slept curled in a fluffy orange ball on a stack of magazines. In the bedroom a television was on, tuned to a soap opera, with nobody watching.

"Were they expecting us?" I asked, trying to be helpful.

"Gran always knows when I'm coming," Nick said offhandedly.

We walked outside the back door and there they were, off in the distance, moving through the long grass at the edge of the woods on a trail that ran beside the bank of the river.

"Nick!" They had spotted us and were waving.

"That's my gran," he said fondly. "The little one." She was a tiny old Indian woman in a flower print dress, with a long gray braid down her back. Beside her walked a younger and taller woman who also looked to have Native American blood, in baggy khaki slacks and a faded blue polo shirt, thick gray hair cut blunt at the top of her neck.

I realized then Nick wasn't having me on when he'd said he had Indian blood.

Nick introduced us and told his great-grandmother we had come to see her paintings. I gave her the flowers.

WE walked together to the studio, a low building with large windows, hidden in the woods, yet only a few steps away from the house.

The paintings were electric and naive, painted in psychedelic earth colors with slashes of neon—landscapes and portraits, paintings of animals and houses, all with the same fervid energy and vibrating color.

He was right to bring me, I thought, mesmerized. I could hardly stop staring at each canvas in turn—I did respond to these paintings, as an art collector, and as a painter. These paintings made me want to paint.

And I responded to the artist, too. Though at first diffident, the old woman seemed to feel my appreciation for what she had created—and she warmed to me.

While we looked at the paintings, the younger woman, Cassan-

dra, stood outside the studio near the doorway, smoking a ciga-
rette, looking bored.

"WELL, you made her day, you know," Cassandra said to me as we
walked up the path to the cabin afterward. Nick and his great-
grandmother had gone ahead.

"Really?" I said. "I wasn't sure at first. I didn't think she was
too happy about having a stranger looking around in her private
space like that."

"Yes, she is shy. I don't think she minded you, though, she
could see you were sensitive to her feelings. She's very sweet anyway, she loves everyone. She's a true healer and a medicine
woman. She sees the energy of the spirit around a person. She's
very generous with her gifts. She doesn't care if you're white or
Native American or a green Martian. It isn't always like that with
us, of course. Indian people don't want to share their knowledge
because they've been so abused. Whenever we—"

"Hey, Cassandra," cried a hearty voice. Nick appeared from
behind us with a mischievous air and he clapped his hands over his
cousin's eyes.

"Where'd *you* come from?" she asked with a laugh, prying his
hands off her.

"Out of thin air. Just in time to save Kelly."

"People need to hear the truth. Whether you want to hear it
or not."

"And I don't." He kissed her cheek.

"I wasn't talking to you anyway, Nick."

"IT's become rather a fad among white people nowadays, have
you noticed that?" Cassandra spoke with controlled passion.

"They seem to think Native American spirituality is some offshoot of their New Age pop philosophy, that they can hang a dream catcher from the rearview mirror in their car and suddenly they're all shamans. Incidentally, the word *shaman* isn't even—"

"Cassie, have some tea," the old woman, Nick's great-grandmother, said softly.

"Yes, thanks, Gran. Look, your pitcher is chipped, when did that happen? I'm sorry if I come across as angry, Kelly. I know people can't hear me when I speak from anger. But I am angry. Many Native people are. And rightly so, I might add. Since the first Europeans came to this continent, my people have had their lands systematically stolen away from them, and it's still happening in this country today, Indian lands are *still* being taken, to this day—dear, look, you spilled it. Never mind, I'll get a sponge." Cassandra rose and went into the kitchen.

I dipped a piece of fry bread into a puddle of maple syrup and smudged it with butter. I savored the rich, tender pastry. I looked up to see Nick's great-grandmother looking at me with a thoughtful expression. I smiled at her and she continued what seemed to be an open, frank appraisal of me.

"Nick never brings a girl to see his grandmother," the old woman said.

I recognized the cadences of her voice, which echoed Nick's deliberate, unhurried way of speaking.

Cassandra came back with a sponge and cleaned up the spill. "Don't get me wrong," she admonished us all, as if a lively argument was taking place in the room. "I believe positive change is possible. But reparations for the past must take place before we can move into the future. Gran, you will have to get a new teapot now. You're going to burn yourself with this one if you keep using it, because it drips. On a practical level, I do think we have made some progress, though not nearly enough. We're starting to see something very interesting happening in mainstream culture, aren't we? White people are starting to listen to mother earth." She added dismissively: "Though I do not hold with this business of so-called ancient prophecies foretelling of our ancestors returning to bring the medicine teachings to all cultures—by reincarnating into white bodies! That sort of thing makes me impatient—"

"Really?" Nick said. He was sitting in a comfortable, shabby chair in the corner by a window. "But maybe white ancestors are being reborn into Indian bodies, too. They're the ones building casinos."

Cassandra looked at me and shook her head. "He doesn't like to admit it, but he's Indian in his heart."

"I thought you said my Indian blood was hopelessly diluted by my white-man blood."

"You are misquoting me, Nick. Though I've probably said you *are* hopeless. You can be maddening at times."

"Nick, you know I've always considered you to be a true blue blood, seeing as you're descended from Native American chieftains on your father's side, and you—"

"I'm surprised at you, Cassandra," Nick said, "using an expression like blue blood."

"Are you? Why?"

"I would have thought you would be the first to say the concept of *blood* was an absurdity. Just a construct of all that race and class stuff you hate."

"And yet you can't deny the power of it. Blood. It's not biological so much as it is sociological. You once said yourself you thought your wife married you because of it."

"Did I?" His tone was suspiciously casual. "Funny. When she stabbed me in the back, I don't remember anything unusual about the color of the bleeding."

"She was more interested in social climbing than in keeping her marriage vows," Cassandra said, for my benefit. "She married Nick thinking he would give her an importance she lacked."

"Nick? Importance?" I acted astonished.

"The woman was deluded," he said lazily. He pretended nonchalance, but I knew he was embarrassed with us talking about him.

"His family connections were not enough, after all," Cassandra went on. She had a chin that reminded me of Eli's, for some reason. She seemed to lead with it. "Maybe those connections *would* have been enough, if Nick had cared to use them, but I think the more his wife pressed him, the more he withdrew from the whole high society *thing*."

"Family connections?" Now I really was perplexed.

"Well, yes." Cassandra seemed astonished at my ignorance. "Nick's grandfather was the son of a Scottish earl."

"You know," Nick said, "some Scots think a title is more a badge of shame than an honor. My dad used to say that knighthoods and peerages were handed out like dog biscuits to the drooling hordes of social climbing arse lickers—uh, sorry, Gran."

"And on his mother's side of the family, well . . ." Cassandra ignored Nick and directed her speech to me. She was now stirring milk into her tea. "Nick's maternal grandmother was the product of two wealthy old San Francisco society families—"

Nick rose from his chair. "What's happening in the garden these days, Gran?"

"Well, not much right now, but I think with the fences you put up for me, we might be able to sneak some leafy greens past the deer . . ." Nick's great-grandmother rose when he gave her his hand, and they walked outside together.

Through the front windows I could see them moving around the garden. He put his arm around her to steady her as they went down a few steps.

"You can imagine the shock and dismay when Clara fell in love with a poor Indian boy . . ." Nick's cousin went on with her story, unconcerned that she had lost two-thirds of her audience. "Of course the girl was forbidden to see the man, but Clara was your classic headstrong young woman. I might add that, while she's no longer young, she's *still* headstrong." Cassandra laughed. "She defied her parents and married the Indian—*her* son." She nodded out the window toward Nick's great-grandmother. "We lost my uncle years ago, alas. At any rate, when Jake and Clara got together, *our* side of the family wasn't terribly happy about it, to be sure, but *her* family disowned her. They didn't speak for years, not until she had a child." She raised her eyebrows and waited. It was a cue.

"Nick's mother?" I said.

She nodded. "Nick's mother. That girl was able to bring the family together. She grew up between her mother's wealthy old San Francisco family and her father's people on the reservation."

"Nick mentioned he had Indian blood," I said. "But he didn't say anything about old San Francisco society or Scottish nobility."

"You know, these days money will buy access into almost any society, but even now there are still a few enclaves in Hillsborough and San Francisco you can't gain admittance to without a pedigree, where lineage trumps coinage. That's the sort of family we're talking about. Quite a contrast to our side of the family. We had so little, materially. We had reverence for life and gratitude for each sunrise, and that's real wealth. Singing Water grew up knowing both sides of life, and she made sure her son Nick did, too."

"Singing Water!"

"Clara's idea of an Indian name, I suppose," Cassandra laughed indulgently.

"So . . . Singing Water met Nick's father . . ."

"Bruce McClure. Yes, she met him when she was visiting some relations up north. He was helping build houses on the reservation. He had come from Scotland. The grandson of a Scottish earl."

"Nick, great-grandson of an earl," I said. "Fancy that."

"Yes. Nick's father was a tradesman, a builder. An honest man, but no title and no money to speak of there. But people do love a connection to a title! And what with the money and social prestige on Nick's mother's side, well . . . Nick's ex-wife thought her dreams were coming true, and she was going to be a princess."

"But it didn't work out that way."

"No, not quite. Nick turned out to be an ordinary man. Or so it seemed to Juliet."

There was something exaggerated and theatrical about Cassandra. She clearly relished the opportunity to gossip and tell tales, and didn't apologize for it. I wondered how much of her story was embellishment. Quite a lot of it, would be my guess.

We walked outside to join Nick and his grandmother. I sensed Nick wasn't happy about us discussing his personal life, but Cassandra didn't seem inclined to drop the subject.

"Obviously, Juliet didn't deserve someone like our Nick," she said. "I think Nick is lucky he found out about her when he did. Before they had children. Still, it *is* sad."

"My ex-wife and her new husband have been together longer now than we were actually married," Nick said. "I hear they've got two little kids and a vacation home in Italy."

I studied him, unsure what to read in his tone.

"It's not for us to judge," Cassandra declared. "Everyone must follow his or her own path."

"Hey, I wish them well," Nick said, and now I heard the acid in his voice.

"The impulse to go after love is natural." Nick's great-grandmother spoke up unexpectedly, and we all turned to listen to her.

"We all seek love," she said. "That is natural and right. But when we steal someone's partner, we destroy something that person has created with another person."

"Which means Juliet and her new husband would carry into their relationship the karma of the past," Cassandra declared. "To bring themselves back into balance, they would need to do ceremony."

"They did a ceremony," Nick said flatly. "It's called a wedding. It came after the divorce."

THE old woman's words hit me hard and unexpectedly. I was thinking of Eli and Kyra. They had created something together. And I was working to destroy it, with my designs on Eli.

I haven't done anything, I insisted to myself. But I knew I was guilty.

"You take care of yourself, beautiful," Nick said, kissing his great-grandmother on the cheek before we drove off. "And thanks for making my favorite fry bread."

"Well, you know I don't make it too often anymore," the old woman said. "But my medicine told me you were going to come see me today."

"THANK you for doing that for me," I said to Nick on the way home. "Thank you for bringing me to meet your grandmother . . . great-grandmother."

"I didn't do it for you," he teased me. "I did it for her."

"I loved your gran. She seems so . . . transcendent. And something about her paintings reminds me of those Tibetan Mandalas, you know, you stare into them and you can go into another world. Does she . . ." I tried awkwardly to frame the question. "Does she practice Native American spirituality?"

"Actually, she's a Christian."

"And what about you, her favorite great-grandson?"

"Oh, I guess I'm the one who went back to my roots," he replied with a laugh. "I'm a Celtic Indian. Or an Indian Celt. It's a very Earth-based orientation. What about you? Earth gods? Sky gods? Which do you prefer? Or as Aaron likes to ask people, 'What *are* you?'"

I don't know why, but it surprised me when he turned the question on me. "Me?" I exclaimed. "I'm an engineer!"

He seemed to think that was funny.

"So what's the deal with Cassandra?" I changed the subject.

"What about her? She's my cousin. She's got a good heart and she loves to lecture people. A lot of what she has to say has merit, but she does tend to go on. And on."

"Is it true, all that stuff she said about you and your family, that you're like—what? Part royalty or something?"

"Yes, and we are not amused. She shouldn't be spreading the family secrets."

"Not even to me? Don't you trust me?"

"With my life," he replied simply.

"You mean, you don't trust me with your life—or you do?" I asked, confused.

"I do, and I shouldn't."

"Because you haven't trusted a woman in five years?"

"Right. Except for Gran, of course. And my mom."

"And now me?"

"Listen, even if I do trust you, I don't trust myself for trusting you."

"How about cousin Cassandra. Do you trust her?"

"I trust her to be annoying. Tell me about *your* family."

"My family is so normal and boring. I'd like to hear more about yours."

"Well, don't believe everything Cassie tells you about my family," he warned. "Which was *way* more than enough for today. It's your turn. How many brothers and sisters do you have?"

"One sister, Bethany. She got married to Troy last year, so I guess I have a brother now, too."

"Parents?"

"One mom and one dad. Mom's really into quilting. Dad's an engineer."

"Oh." Nick nodded wisely. "That would explain a lot."

"Hmm," I said. "I'm not even going to ask what you mean by that."

"COME on in and say hello to the pups," Nick said casually when we reached his house.

The dogs ran to greet us; when they calmed down a little, we could see Freesia was hopping with a noticeable limp.

"She's been having troubles," Nick said soberly, running his hands over the dog's flanks. "And it's getting worse. Nothing we've tried has worked . . . not my gran's herbal treatments, not the vet's medication."

"Is it hip dysplasia?"

"No, it's calcium deposits on her backbone. Cutting off the nerve action. Poor girl." He knelt down and stroked her gently. "I'm facing the fact that she's just not going to be able to work anymore. She's going to hate being left behind. And I'm going to hate leaving her. I've relied on her for so many years . . ." His voice trailed away, and I sensed he wasn't talking to me anymore.

Time for me to go.

"I'll see you guys later," I said to Nick and the two dogs.

I touched my hand to Nick's head for a second, tempted to stroke his hair the way he was stroking the dog's fur. His hair, dark and thick and unruly where it was starting to curl at his neck, was surprisingly soft to the touch.

I walked away, went outside, and let myself out the gate. The stars were out in profusion—the fog was offshore. It was a clear night on the edge of the ocean. I almost danced to my car, high from the long, offbeat day, from meeting Nick's great-grandmother, being with Nick, discovering new aspects of him, his goofy rude humor, his affection for his family, his soft gentleness with the old dog, and the old woman . . .

All at once I felt an urgency to be gone from there, certain Nick would follow me outside to my car, and suddenly I didn't want to see him anymore. I jumped in my car, started it up, quickly threw it into gear, and drove off. And as I climbed the hill to the old highway, I caught a fleeting glimpse of him in my rearview mirror, coming out to see me off, or to say one last thing to me before I left, or to stop me from leaving, or who knew why—maybe he'd just come out to pick up the newspaper. But he had followed me out, as I had known he would.

Chapter 15

WE had a party coming in toward the end of the week for Thursday and Friday nights; I noticed the name Larson written in the book, and of course I thought of Eli. But according to my records, Eli was always just "Eli" in the inn's antiquated, handwritten reservation system, and this party had reserved three cottages. I felt certain I had nothing to worry about—not that I would worry, anyway . . .

Grendel forgot his lunch Thursday morning, and since I was going out to do the shopping anyway, I told Arturo I'd take it to him. I knew, from reading his file, that Grendel worked just off the coast highway on the way into town. I thought he would be easy to find.

He wasn't. I finally discovered the place after driving up and down the frontage road several times until I spied the modest sign over the front door of the nondescript block building: Cielo Shores Clinic.

I parked my car and went through the front entrance into a waiting room that was noisy and alive with people, mostly Hispanic women and small children.

Across the room, a woman in a blue coat appeared in a doorway, holding a file. She had pale skin, short, curly carrot-red hair, and a drill sergeant's voice. "Martinez?" she barked out over the din.

One of the mothers gathered up her children and followed the woman in blue into an inner hallway, and the door swung shut.

I made my way through the little crowd to the counter, where behind windows with frosted glass I could see someone moving about. I knocked and the windows slid open.

"I'm looking for Grendel," I said. "That is, uh—Jerry Greenfield? I have his lunch."

"Dr. Greenfield is with a patient," said the receptionist, a young woman with striking dark eyes and two long black braids.

Dr. Greenfield?

"Well, maybe I could just leave his lunch with you."

"Of course." She took the bag from me and shut the windows.

A wail went up from a toddler who had tripped over a toy car and fallen on her heavily padded bottom. Gingerly I stepped over children and made my way around the parents who were standing because all the chairs were full.

I was almost out the door when I heard my name.

"Kelly?"

Grendel had just come into the waiting room from the inner doorway. Over his usual whites, he wore a blue cotton smock with little elephants printed on it. A stethoscope hung from his neck.

"I brought your lunch," I explained.

"Oh, I was late this morning, I ran out without thinking," he said. "Thanks, Kelly, that's so nice of you. Come, I'll walk you out to your car."

We walked outside the building, which was a cinderblock rectangle. Only the glassed-in waiting area had any windows to speak of. It would be a depressing place to spend a lot of time in, I thought.

"That's quite an operation you having going in there."

"Yes. We keep pretty busy."

"So—Dr. Greenfield is it? I didn't realize you were an M.D."

"Yes, I'm a doctor." He sighed, smiling. "We're actually a private research institution for longevity and wellness studies, but I devote the facilities to the vaccination clinic three days a week. There's such a need for it. And even then I feel like most of my time I spend writing grants, trying to fund the place."

"Well, I'll let you go. I can see you're busy."

"Yes. Some other time I'll show you around, give you the tour."

"Okay," I said.

"Thanks again, Kelly."

Grendel may have been a doctor, but he certainly didn't seem to be getting rich off his profession. He didn't drive a fancy car or live in a big fancy home. You could see from the look of the clinic that it was pretty much a nonprofit outfit. As I started up my car, I thought back on my aspirations to get more money for his cottage. Now I wondered if I should cut him a break in rent.

As I was driving out of the parking area, I waved at Zac, who was coasting up to the building on his bike. He didn't wave back; I'd taken him by surprise.

In my rearview mirror I saw him throw his bike down by the door of the clinic. There was something beautiful and yet sinister about him, like a young raven.

He pushed open the glass door and went inside.

THE big SUV pulled into the parking area around four o'clock. I watched two older couples disembark and I guessed the Larson party had arrived.

Then the third set of doors on the vehicle slowly opened, and a young couple emerged. It was Kyra and Eli, both looking utterly bewildered.

"IT's so nice to meet you, Kelly," Eli's mother said warmly. "Eli has talked about you so enthusiastically."

He has? My heart thrilled and danced. *He's told his parents about me!*

"And you're such a pretty young thing. I hadn't expected that. He said the inn had recently changed hands, but not to worry, he met the new owner and she loves it just as much as we do. I suppose he's mentioned to you how we've been coming here for years and we just love the place?"

Okay, so he hadn't really told them about "me" after all.

If I had been surprised to see Eli and Paula show up unannounced in a convertible Cadillac, I was utterly astonished by the arrival of Eli and Kyra and their parents in that big SUV.

"I'M telling you, I only found out this morning my dad and mom had arranged this so-called surprise with Kyra's mother!" Eli, looking stricken, tried to explain, taking me aside after his mother had checked them all in.

"So-called surprise?"

"Well, definitely a surprise. They asked us months ago to keep these dates free so we could do something together when they came into town for the anniversary party. God knows I had no idea they were thinking of *this*. Kyra didn't know about it, either. They wanted it to be—well, a surprise! And was it ever. We didn't know where they were taking us until we turned onto the old highway."

I couldn't believe this was happening. But Mr. and Mrs. Larson were wandering around, exclaiming with delight and wonder at how little had changed since they'd last visited.

"How long has it been, Ed?"

"Well, it's got to have been at least a few years, wouldn't you say? Boy, time does fly, doesn't it?"

They were eagerly showing Kyra's mother all their favorite things about the place.

In spite of my apprehension, I was charmed by the older folks, especially Eli's dad, who was a retired army major, an older Eli with the same jutting chin and enormous vitality. Eli's mother was talkative and lively, and wonderfully enthusiastic about the inn, so I got along great with her. Kyra's mother, by contrast, was quiet and wary looking, not sure if she really wanted to be there. She was the youngest of the parents, with smooth skin and shining blond hair like her daughter. The man she was with was not Kyra's father, as it happened (no one mentioned *his* whereabouts) but a German businessman she was dating, who didn't say much and went immediately to their room.

It was obvious that Eli had yet to mention the idea of a breakup to Kyra, or anyone else, for that matter; but with one or two guarded expressions of longing he gave me to understand that was still the plan. The anniversary party, he very casually let it be known, was this coming Sunday. After that . . .

It struck me that if Eli really wanted me to have a future with him, *I* should be the one at his side during the family festivities, not Kyra. Grendel's words of warning came to mind, unwelcome. And I thought about what Nick's great-grandmother had said about destroying that which another couple had created.

If I were smart, I said to myself, I would avoid the Larson party as much as possible. And so I did, finishing my work in the office, then slipping away to my cottage to hide from them all.

Paula and the boys came the next day.

"Where's Nick?" Paula asked me in a low voice when the boys had taken off. They had just arrived, but they were already headed to the pool.

"I have no idea."

"You know, Kelly," she said, leaning toward me over the desk in the front office. "I am finding him more and more . . . fascinating."

I realized with a start that I was, too. Nick intrigued me, and kept me wondering, and he was, I had to admit, a sexy, elemental man.

If I weren't so hung up on Eli . . .

But I was. Seeing him again more than confirmed it. And yet it also confirmed that he was still very much attached to his fiancée.

"So he's not around?" Paula was disappointed.

"Haven't seen him around today. So, what's going on between you two, anyway?" I asked, casual.

"Not much, I'm afraid. But I'll tell you what," she said, lowering her voice. "I'm going to turn up the heat this weekend. I have a plan. And I was wondering if I could ask you a huge favor."

"Sure, you can ask . . . what?"

"I was wondering if you could watch the boys for me for a couple of hours tonight. Like, between nine and midnight?"

"Of course," I said. "I'd be glad to." I liked Paula's boys. And it wasn't like I had anything else going.

Through the window I could see the man in his bowler hat standing on the lawn below the porch, staring out to the ocean. His name was Mr. James and he stayed with us at the inn quite often, but he never talked to anybody, never even seemed to be enjoying himself much.

"They can just stay in the parlor, playing chess or watching TV or whatever," Paula was saying. "They won't go to bed until around midnight anyway. You don't have to worry about staying up; they'll be okay—just as long as there's someone responsible around, in case of emergency, you know?"

"Sure. No problem."

"Oh, perfect!" She clapped her slender hands together. "Thank you, Kelly."

"So . . . what is the plan?"

"Oh, you mean with Nick? Well, I had been *hoping* he'd call me—I gave him my number, twice. But he didn't call, leaving me no choice but to take matters into my own hands. So I'm going to chat with him during happy hour this evening, and I'm going to casually suggest that he take me back to his place, you know, show me his digs. I'll tell him I have to be back by midnight, like Cinderella, so he won't be scared. But that will give me plenty of time."

Plenty of time! Well, it appeared Nick would soon best me in our competition. Perhaps it would be accomplished this very night. Paula didn't seem one to pull any punches.

A drag of regret weighed me down. I was sorry our game was coming to an end; I realized I enjoyed comparing notes with Nick almost as much as I did generating them.

"Well," I said to Paula. "I hope he shows up this afternoon so you can set your plan in motion."

"Not to worry," she said slyly. "If you see him, tell him I'm at the pool. Speaking of which, I told those boys not to go in the water till I got there, so I'd better get going . . ."

WALKING through the kitchen garden in the afternoon, I came across the three boys, Rocky, Winkle, and Zac, half-hidden behind an arbor, deep in conversation. I heard Rocky's voice, intent and sober: "And the police won't treat it as a murder, 'cause they never found a body, but—"

"Are you talking about Alicia St. Claire?" I asked softly, startling them all.

Rocky blushed. Zac's eyes darted about, like those of a cornered animal looking for a way to escape. Winkle looked up at me with a charming smile and said, "Hello, Kelly. We're going to find the mooderer!"

"Shut up, Dean," said Rocky mildly. "There's no evidence a murder ever took place."

"But Rocky, you seem to know a lot about it," I said, thinking a little flattery might encourage the boy to say something revealing. At the same time, I felt a sense of shame stealing over me for using kids to further my own morbid curiosity.

But Rocky, challenged by an adult, appeared to back down on his claim that he knew anything at all, and would only laugh and shrug his shoulders. And if Zac had any information, he wasn't sharing it with me.

HAVING them there, Kyra and Eli and their parents, all sitting on the wide front porch, sipping wine at happy hour, was surreal. Addie and Bill, who usually didn't come out at happy hour, made a special appearance in honor of their favorite old-time guests, the Larsons. Grendel emerged from his lair, which had become a habit for him at this time of day, and he poured me a glass of wine. I accepted the glass and raised it to him. We turned to greet Paula, who was coming up the steps with the boys.

If Nick comes, I thought, the scene will be complete.

Paula appealed to me directly. "How do I look?" she whispered.

She looked great, of course, in a short denim skirt, a wide white belt, high-heeled boots, and a tight black T-shirt.

"You look ready to ride," I teased her. "All you need is a cowboy hat. Here, this is for fortitude." I handed her my glass of wine.

I felt a tug on my hair; it was Nick, sneaking up behind me. He was looking at Paula, and she set the wineglass down on a table, and they greeted each other with an embrace and a social kiss—his lips on her cheek.

Hmm, I thought. He's never done that elegant, affectionate, and flirty greeting thing with *me*.

Nick greeted Eli and Kyra. Introductions were made, and Nick sneaked me a look of comical questioning.

Yes, I said to him silently, defiantly, Eli is here, his fiancée is here, and both their parents are here! Paula is here, and as you can see, she's ripe for the picking. Enjoy!

I acted cool and unconcerned about all of it.

Paula retrieved the glass of wine I had given her, and I helped myself to another. Though it was my custom to have a glass of wine with my guests and then leave them to themselves, on this particular evening I didn't slip away from the social scene on the porch.

I was excited because Eli was there, and I got a perverse pleasure from being with him, despite the fact that his fiancée was present. And for some reason, the fact that Nick was there excited me, too.

Kyra sat slumped in a wicker chair, making no effort to socialize. Eli sat beside her, looking as if he were in pain. The parents for the most part were oblivious and chatty, though Kyra's mother, twirling her bracelets around her slender tan wrists, kept asking Kyra if she was all right.

"I'm *fine*, Mother," Kyra snapped, growing exasperated with her.

Grendel came to stand beside me, a wineglass in his hand. "Are you surprised to see them here again?" he asked me in a low undertone.

I looked at him sharply. "Why?"

"Somehow I just didn't expect to see her back." He nodded toward Kyra, camouflaging the gesture with a swipe of a hand over his smooth bald pate. "I don't think we're her kind of people."

I relaxed a little. "Oh, yeah, no, me neither. But I don't think she had a choice in the matter."

"Poor angel," he said with a hint of sarcasm. He smiled at me, and I appreciated it; he was letting me know that he thought the inn was special, even if Kyra didn't.

I watched to see if Paula was making any progress with Nick. She was holding her glass of wine and peering at him over the rim with her huge dark eyes. Their heads were close when she whispered something to him. Her legs were crossed toward him; her hand ran up and down the long bone of her shin as she laughed at something he said; she leaned against him, and he didn't draw away from her.

At the sight of Nick McClure in combat courtship mode—his head turned, his smile broad across his square, clean-shaven jaw, his cheek dimpling, sun rays beaming from his eyes—something caught on something, deep in me.

I looked away from the sight, uncomfortable with a new awareness that I was harboring some possessiveness about Nick, which was rising up strong, now that Paula was making her move.

It's not that I really want him myself, I thought. But I didn't want anyone else to have him, either. It was natural enough to feel that way about a friend, wasn't it? A platonic jealousy. Was he becoming a friend to me?

No, we didn't know each other well enough to be friends yet.

And this stirring in me, when I looked at the man, wasn't platonic, if I were to acknowledge the truth.

Sitting there in some confusion, I noticed Grendel staring at me.

"Kelly, are you all right?"

"Yeah, I'm good!"

"Sure?"

"Sure."

I looked up and caught Eli's gaze. He looked miserable, which I found strangely satisfying.

Eli was handsome, big and rugged and casual, yet with the subtle polish of money—a worn Gucci belt, a tousled haircut that probably cost hundreds of dollars in the city, and loafers he had custom-made in Milan, as he mentioned to Paula when she admired them.

I wondered if I'd ever be able to look at him without seeing his net worth. To his credit, he didn't seem to think about it at all, except to enjoy its benefits and find ways of using it to make other people happy. He doted on his parents. He was deferential to Kyra and her mother, ready to provide anything necessary for their comfort. He tipped generously. He bought presents and did favors. Paula had told me he had sent her boys new computers—one for each of them.

"Okay, then, we're on for nine?" Paula said to Nick, who was getting up to leave.

"See you then," Nick said, and went off.

So Paula's strategy had been successful. So far, so good.

I avoided looking at Nick as he was leaving. I didn't want to see the triumph in his expression.

Eli and Kyra and their parents had a dinner reservation, and soon they left, too. Addie and Bill vanished; a few other guests lingered awhile, and then only Paula and Grendel remained. The boys had gone inside to play chess.

We sat and chatted, Paula and I, Paula doing most of the talking as usual, Grendel watching us quietly, adding little to the conversation. Paula seemed strangely loose; she finished her glass of wine with a languid slurp. I hadn't noticed her take a second glass, but she did seem to be feeling the affects of the alcohol. She must have been drinking in her room before she came up to the house.

I began to be concerned for her. I had never seen Paula so drunk; in fact, I had never seen her drunk at all until this evening. But now she was making very little sense, and when she stood, she swayed and nearly fell.

"Whoops!" she cried, laughing. "Better not try that again."

She sat back down, then thought better of it, and lurched to her feet. She picked her way across the porch and headed to the stairs with an alarming lack of coordination. She stopped, confused, clinging to the railing.

"This isn't good," I whispered to Grendel.

"Maybe we should put her to bed."

"Yeah, I think so. I'd hate for her boys to see her like this."

She collapsed onto a wicker chair and closed her eyes, her head lolling to one side.

She must have gotten herself overexcited about her big night with Nick and went a little too far with the drink. I felt guilty about handing her that first glass of wine. If it *had* been the first.

We escorted Paula to her room and put her to bed. Grendel was gentle, calming, and helpful, supporting the limp woman as we walked with her to her cabin. In her room, he turned away as I loosened Paula's clothing and covered her with a blanket. He opened the window an inch for fresh air and set the thermostat to keep the room warm, and then we walked back to the house together.

The boys knew nothing of their mother's condition; they were happily unaware, playing chess in the parlor.

Grendel paused before going off up the path to his cottage.

"Would you like to come up with me to my place for another glass of wine?" he asked cordially, pleading with his beseechingly beautiful blue eyes. "Or—coffee?"

I glanced up at Grendel's cottage, the farthest away from the house, a narrow, crooked-looking shack in silhouette against the evening sky, partially obscured by two large dark pines. It almost seemed to lean off the side of the cliff.

"I shouldn't," I said quickly, grateful that I had an excuse. "I'm keeping an eye on the boys for Paula. I'd better stick around the house."

"Right." He waited a beat, for an invitation from me, perhaps, but the moment passed, and he turned to walk away.

It was just too bad the way things worked, I thought. I had been aware for some time that Grendel looked at me in a certain way. But for this gentle, kind, available man, I felt nothing. My heart yearned for Eli Larson, who was as of yet unavailable. And I found myself attracted to Nick McClure, who was completely unacceptable.

Nick! I frowned, annoyed at him, annoyed by how he continually crept into my thoughts lately. I knew why. No doubt it was just that *he* was no longer available, either. Not without stepping on Paula. The mind is funny that way, I thought. Seems we always want what's just out of reach. Always want what we can't have.

I do not want Nick.

But some part of me did. It was beginning to disturb me a little. But that was okay. As soon as they got together, Paula and Nick, that would be that. I'd let it go. I'd get over it, real fast.

If they got together. Maybe Paula had sabotaged the evening because secretly she didn't want to go through with it. Maybe it just wasn't happening between them.

But that didn't ring true to me. Paula had been excited about this evening. She had *wanted* to go out with Nick.

Speaking of Nick . . .

He still didn't know his date had passed out.

*   *   *

He showed up on time, which impressed me, for Paula's sake. He must have walked, because I didn't hear his truck come in. Through the parlor window I saw him mounting the front steps, looking around uncertainly; the inn was quiet.

"Hi, Nick." I stepped out on the porch and shut the front door behind me to keep the heat inside. I stood on the welcome mat, my arms crossed to keep myself warm. The wind was blowing in from the ocean, tinkling the wind chimes hanging from the porch eaves.

"Hey, Kelly." His voice was strangely quiet, in keeping with his silent arrival. He seemed preoccupied.

"Looking for Paula?"

"Yeah, you know where she is?"

"I'm sorry to have to tell you this, Nick, but she's, um . . ." I wasn't sure how best to put it.

"What?"

"Well, she's sleeping."

"Sleeping." He didn't seem to believe me.

"Yeah, I mean, she was—she's passed out."

"Are you serious?"

"Afraid so, cowboy."

"I didn't see her drink all that much. She must have partied on after I left."

"No," I said, "she really didn't . . . but she sure got blitzed. I've never seen her that way before—it was actually kind of strange."

I began to wonder if Paula was all right.

Nick stood there frowning, uncertain.

"Maybe I should check on her," I said. "It seemed to happen so fast."

He walked with me along the path to Paula's cottage, and he waited outside while I went in and checked on her. She looked like a model on a punk rock album cover: smudged eyelids, long lashes, shaggy black hair over her pretty, sharp-featured face. She had tossed off the blankets, and the line of her body was long and slender and completely relaxed; her breath came steadily, deep and slow.

"She seems to be sleeping peacefully," I said to him when I came back outside.

We walked back on the path toward the house. The veil of mist parted slightly and the moon, almost full tonight and glowing pale, emerged galloping, racing the clouds.

"So your date has stood you up," I said.

"Perhaps all is not lost, and *you* will walk with me instead," Nick suggested, his voice deep and impish. "Come out walking with me in the moonlight, Kelly."

We were already walking together in the moonlight, but I didn't point that out to him.

"No, I don't think so," I said, shoving him off playfully when he accidentally-on-purpose bumped into me. "I'm not into being second choice."

"You're not my second choice," he replied, looking at me directly.

"So what am I, then? Third? Fourth? Seventh?"

He didn't answer. He stared at me without flinching until I couldn't take it any longer, and I whirled away.

We didn't speak for a few moments.

The energy between us settled a bit and we drew together again. Ahead the pathway continued on down to the main house, but another path branched out in the direction of the cliffs, and the cypress wood on the hill.

He reached out for my hand. "Come on, Kelly," he said. "Come with me."

Our hands clasped for a moment, but at the fork in the path I resisted him and he let go of me.

"I'm watching Paula's boys tonight," I said. "I really can't go anywhere."

He nodded, and we walked back to the house in silence, side by side.

When we were nearly to the front porch steps, he stopped me just before I moved into the light, taking my hand again. He gently tugged on me, and I turned into his arms like a dancer in a spin.

"Kelly . . ." His voice near my ear, though a murmur, sounded hoarse.

The front door opened and Eli stepped out onto the porch. Over Nick's shoulder I could see him there above us, peering out into the night.

I stepped away from Nick at once, but my hand slipped out of his almost reluctantly. I was feeling strangely torn.

Nick looked around and saw Eli, and didn't seem concerned. He turned back to me, and he held his head with a sort of haughty pride, and gave me a look, intense and quiet, and I started to wonder if I'd walked into some weird alternate universe where I'd rather be in Nick's arms than Eli's.

"Ah, there you are, Kelly!" said Eli, and his hearty voice broke the spell. "Hey, Nick, how you doing, man?" He came down the stairs to shake Nick's hand.

"About the same," said Nick.

Though I was wrestling with a sudden rush of guilt for my fickle heart, it was clear Eli had no inkling that he might have a rival for my attentions. His confidence might have been sexy, but I felt a little offended.

Nick should have walked away. He should have walked away down the hill through the parking area, and kept on walking out to the old highway, all the way back to his house. Instead he stood there with me, one booted foot resting on the bottom step, and there was an awkward moment when the three of us weren't quite sure what to do with one another. As the innkeeper, my instinct was to start up a congenial conversation; but somehow my role here was not that of an innkeeper.

"I'm worn out," I said. "I'll see you guys later. I'm going to check on Paula's boys, and then I'm going to bed."

"Good night, Kelly," the two men said in unison.

As I climbed up the steps, I saw the man in the shadows, sitting in one of the Adirondack chairs on the lawn, a still figure in the dark moonlight, recognizable only by his round hat.

FOR a long time I couldn't sleep. I felt so strange. It was a wonderful feeling, like flight, physically strong and free. Feeling the desire of men. Tasting my own desires.

And the slightly bitter aftertaste of uncertainty and confusion.

In the middle of the night, I awoke suddenly. A deep soft voice was calling my name outside the bedroom window. I was instantly alert, and it seemed I had been waiting for this.

I switched on the bedside lamp, got out of bed, threw on my robe, and opened the door.

"You're so beautiful," Eli whispered.

Wearing jeans and a dark turtleneck sweater, he was a tall, graceful figure, standing in my doorway in the dark.

What if someone sees him on my doorstep in the middle of the night?—I motioned him quickly to come in, and closed the door. Inside the small cottage the bed loomed large and I felt uncovered; I dove back in like a seal into dark waters, to protect myself. But then I thought maybe getting into bed while alone with Eli in the small dark room wasn't so smart. I pulled the blankets up to my chin.

I hoped the room was too dark for him to notice his picture on the mirror.

He moved closer and looked down on me. Slowly he knelt beside the bed, like a knight of old in a pool of moonlight, and now we were looking deeply into each other's eyes. Our hands joined, our fingers laced. He closed his eyes. "It won't be long now, Kelly," he murmured, ending with my name on a soft groan. Once again I had the unconfirmed impression that Eli wanted me to move things along, that he was waiting for me to press on physically with him.

I kept thinking of the old Indian woman's words about destroying something someone else created. Eli was still promised to Kyra. She lay sleeping in a cottage nearby. He was supposed to be there at her side.

I pulled my hand from his and drew away from him. "Eli, you have to go."

"Yes, I know I have to go," he said. "I just had to see you alone for a moment . . ." He leaned down to kiss me. I felt his lips cool on my forehead, swift and chaste. "Good night," he said.

"Next time I hope you won't have to say good night, Eli."

"Kelly . . ." he breathed in a rush, and with that, he seemed to lose control, and he kissed me on the mouth, less chaste now.

The moist kiss was like a teasing, partial quench of thirst.

This isn't good. This isn't right. The voice called to me from somewhere far away inside my brain—laughably easy to ignore. I found myself wondering how much the illicit nature of the encounter added to its undeniable thrill.

"No, Eli," I gasped. "Stop." I tried to wriggle out of his grasp.

"Kelly, don't make me go," he moaned. "Let me stay. Just for a little while. I'll tell her, I swear it."

"Go tell her now, and then come back," I said sarcastically, straightening myself out.

He seemed to collapse into himself, his shoulders hunched in frustration. "I don't blame you for mocking me," he said. "And you don't know how close I am to doing just that."

"I am a fool," I said to myself out loud. "This is a ridiculous situation."

"If you say the word right now, Kelly, I'll do it. I'll walk over to that cottage, wake her up, and tell her—"

"Yeah, do it right now, in the middle of the night, with both sets of parents sleeping nearby. When Kyra starts shrieking and wakes them up, you can introduce me as your new girlfriend. A most auspicious beginning for our relationship. Your parents would really take to me if we did it that way, wouldn't they?"

"Well, maybe now you understand my dilemma," he replied, looking stung. "I have to think about the timing. I want this to work out for us, Kelly. Don't you get that? Look, it's not my fault I was dragged here. What was I supposed to say? Hey, sorry, Mom, we can't stay at the Magic Mermaid Inn because the girl I've fallen for in a big way happens to be the Magic Mermaid herself, and I can't stand to see her because I can't see her without wanting to put my hands all over her, and I can't do that yet because of Kyra, and I'm waiting for the right moment . . . the right moment . . ."

Suddenly the window above the bed shattered with tremendous force. The bedside lamp fell over and burned out with a pop and a flash of light.

"My God—" Eli sprang up from the bed.

"What was that?"

"I think it was a rock through the window."

We were still for a moment; we didn't know what to do. Then he squatted down on the floor and began looking around the bed.

"Here it is." He handed me the rock, a chunk of granite, maybe, from the hard, rough feel of it, the size of a man's fist. He edged to the door. "I'll take a look around outside." He slipped out and I heard him walking around the cottage, then his voice at the window. "It's all clear," he said quietly.

I didn't answer.

"I better get out of here," he whispered. "Good night, Kelly," he called softly. I still didn't answer. I heard him crunching away on the gravel path.

How could he just leave me like that, after such an attack?

I got up and turned on the overhead light, drew the curtains over the window, and turned up the heat in the room. I righted the lamp and changed the broken bulb. I pulled the bed away from the window and shook a few bits of glass off the bedspread and swept up the shards on the floor, though most of the pieces remained stuck in the window frame.

It was a mild night; I wouldn't freeze. The break in the window was fairly high up, an irregular circle of jagged shards. No intruder in his right mind would try to crawl in that way.

After a while, I went back to bed, drew the blankets up high again, and burrowed down into them. I had a crazy urge to call Nick. He was my window glazer, right? He would fix my window for me.

It was the middle of the night; I couldn't call him now. But I wanted to.

Chapter 16

I woke early in the morning and sat up, feeling bleary and sore. As I reached out to push aside the curtains, I felt a pull of pain and I gasped at the sight of a long, bloody gash down the inside of my arm.

The blood was dried and made the cut look deeper and more severe than it really was. Probably it had happened during the excitement of the window shattering. I drew back my blankets, which were stained with blood, and found I had slept all night beside a six-inch shard of glass.

PAULA sat in the parlor, curled up in the wing chair with a cup of coffee, staring at the cold fireplace with a scowl. It was eleven in the morning, which was late for her to be just getting up and having coffee. The boys had walked off down the road to look for fossils. Addie and Bill were in the office, taking care of the Sunday morning checkouts. I went into the parlor and sat down near Paula.

"What happened last night?" she asked me flatly.

"I was going to ask you the same question."

"The last thing I remember is sitting with you, talking, after Nick left. We had a date for later . . ."

"Yeah. I think you were excited about that, maybe had a little too much to drink."

"Kelly, I didn't have that much to drink."

"I know, but maybe it just hit you harder than usual. You were keyed up, you know, alcohol is so unpredictable—"

"No, you're not hearing me. I never drink more than two glasses of wine. Never. That's my self-imposed limit, otherwise I would drink too much and it's way too fattening. Two glasses. I can get tipsy on that much sometimes, if I haven't eaten, but I don't get fall-down dead drunk. Not ever. Kelly, I don't even think I had a second glass of wine last night. I think there was something in that wine you gave me."

"Paula," I said softly, "nobody else felt any ill effects from the wine."

"There was something in my drink, Kelly."

"I hope to hell you're wrong, Paula."

"I'm not wrong." She looked at me oddly. "Did you pour that wine?"

"No . . . Grendel poured it for me."

"Grendel?"

"He often pours me a glass of wine at cocktail hour."

"The wine was meant for you?"

"Yes, it was mine, and then I saw you, and I gave it to you."

"Did you drink any of it?"

"No, not a sip."

"I think maybe someone meant that little potion for you,"

Paula said. There was a hard glint in her expression. "Who would do that to you, Kelly?"

Who would want to drug my wine? Who would want to shatter my window?

"Who was here last night?" Paula asked.

"Lots of people were here last night," I said crossly. I wasn't happy about the way this conversation was going. If she wasn't accusing me of providing drugged wine to my guests, she was suggesting someone had tried to drug *me*.

"Who would want to do that to you, Kelly?" she pressed.

Indeed, I thought, who would want to slip me a date-rape drug? That's what we were talking about, here, right? A chill passed through me.

I thought of Eli, coming into my room in the middle of the night. Had he expected me to be inert, unconscious? The thought made me shudder, and I realized how little I really knew Eli. And how little I knew of Nick. Or Grendel. It could have been any one of them.

What about Kyra? Maybe Kyra knew what was going on between Eli and me. Maybe she had meant the dose, of whatever it was, to be dangerous, or even lethal . . .

The memory of the impact of shattering glass above my bed shook through me again; I couldn't stop thinking about it, hadn't stopped thinking about it all through the night, even in my dreams, when I was finally able to sleep again. And the fear lingered into daylight waking, into the morning. My heartbeat had not returned to normal for a long time after Eli had left me.

It was unnerving, to think that I might have an enemy. And uncomfortable, honestly facing the fact that I might have brought this upon myself.

"Kelly, can I talk to you?" Eli was standing just inside the door.

Paula waved me off. "Go," she said.

I followed Eli outside onto the porch, troubled, wondering what to think, what to say to him. Everybody was suspect. I didn't even know if Paula was telling me the truth.

"Where's Kyra?" I asked him.

"Down on the beach with her mom. Listen, Kelly," he said in a low, urgent voice, taking my hands, sitting me down beside him on the wicker chaise. "I felt terrible about leaving you last night. I want you to know I was watching out for you. I watched your cottage, from a distance, practically all night. I want you to know that. I had to leave you, because it's possible that someone may be spying on us, and if they find us together—"

I withdrew my hands from his grasp. "Who? Kyra?"

"I don't think Kyra knows anything. It's probably something much less personal."

"Oh . . ." I was beginning to understand. "You mean like paparazzi?"

He shrugged off the word, but he didn't argue with it.

"I suppose in your position you must get people trying to take advantage of you," I said. "Trying to take your photograph in a compromising position. Trying to dig up the dirt on you."

"Unfortunately, it goes with the territory. Now for me, I don't care, it doesn't matter, it'll all be over in a few days with Kyra, so what have they got to hold over me? Nothing. But for you, it could damage your reputation, and the reputation of your inn. It was bad enough I risked it, coming into your room as I did. I'm so sorry, Kelly."

His words flooded me with relief and happiness. I had been shaken almost as much by his leaving me as by the "attack" itself. I had wanted him to stay in my cottage with me. To make me feel comforted and protected. But his explanation made sense, and his actions certainly seemed more sensible than what I had wanted him to do.

He was looking at me with such a stricken expression, I was moved to cover his hand with mine. "Thank you, Eli," I said, "for watching over me."

A movement at the doorway had us both startled and I quickly pulled my hand away. Nick was standing there, watching us.

I rose, aware of a great affection welling up in me at the sight of Nick, and a corresponding anxiety, wondering if he was to be trusted.

"I got your message this morning," he said to me coolly. "You said you had a problem of some sort?"

"I'll show you." Turning to Eli I said, "I'll see you later?"

"You can be sure of it," he said.

Paula came out of the house as Nick and I were about to go down the front steps.

She blocked his way when he would have gone past her. "Nick, can I talk to you?"

"Sure," he said, as frosty with her as he was with me. "What's up?"

"Well . . ." She hesitated, looking from Nick to me and back again. "I wanted to apologize for last night, obviously."

"Paula thinks her drink was spiked," I said.

A look of annoyance passed over Nick's face. He didn't seem to be in the mood for jokes, and he thought we were joking. "Yeah, right," he said.

"I'm quite serious," Paula said. "That wine was drugged."

He took in the two of us and our troubled faces.

"Can I talk to you?" she asked him again. "In private?"

"Okay," he said. "Let me look at this thing for Kelly, and then I'll meet you back here, if you want."

"I want," she said.

*   *   *

NICK and I left Paula on the porch and walked off in the direction of my cottage.

"Do you believe that!" he said with a sneer. "Her wine was drugged!"

"Well, it was rather strange, Nick. And she tells me she never drinks more than two glasses of wine."

"Whatever."

What's going on with *him?* I wondered. He seemed so cold and surly.

We walked around to the back of my cottage.

"Nick," I said, "the wine she drank was meant for me."

"So what are you saying? You think someone has it out for you?" His voice was sarcastic.

"Look." I pointed up at the broken window. "This happened in the middle of the night. Somebody threw a rock the size of your fist through the glass."

He looked at the hole in the window, then looked at me. "Jesus," he said. Dark brows slashed down over unsmiling eyes. The sun ray lines were gone. He said softly, "You must have been scared, Kelly, all alone in there in the dark."

"I was scared," I said hesitantly. "But I wasn't . . ." I felt somehow obliged to tell him. "I wasn't alone."

He nodded. "I see." Nick turned away and focused his attention on the glass; he reached up and pulled on one of the shards sticking out of the window frame.

"You should have gloves on to do that," I said.

"Yeah, you're right. I should."

"Aren't you going to ask me if I owe you a dinner?"

"Let's just skip the dinner," he said.

"Nick . . ."

"I don't have much of an appetite for it anymore, to be honest."

"If you—"

"I'll have this fixed for you in an hour or two. But first, I'm gonna go talk to Paula. I'll see you later, Kelly."

I followed after him, intending to call him back, to make things work between us again. I quickened my pace and nearly collided with Anita, who was coming around the corner of a building with her cart piled high with linens.

I apologized, feeling flustered, laughing, hoping she'd laugh, too; but she merely looked at me with her expressionless eyes and waited for me to pass before going on her way.

Recovering myself, I thought better of chasing after Nick. *If he wants to be sulky, let him.* I should worry about my own problems.

ELI, Kyra, and their parents checked out later that morning. The anniversary party was to take place on Sunday evening.

Monday morning I began to wait, nervous, to hear from Eli.

As far as I knew, Paula hadn't met up with Nick again over the weekend. I wondered what had become of their "talk." Were they going to give it another try?

I saw Nick on Monday afternoon, but he seemed in no mood to be asked.

I wasn't feeling so great, either—it was now twenty-four hours since the big anniversary party and I had yet to hear from Eli.

By now I should have been convinced that Eli was a fraud and had no intention of breaking up with his fiancée, probably never had, but for some reason, I believed in him.

Most of my time was spent working and my mind was full of the inn—learning the ropes of running the business, making plans for upgrades and improvements, dealing with the guests, the buildings, the staff. I hardly ever thought of Eli during the day.

It was only late at night when I lay alone in my bed, listening to the ocean play below the cliffs, that I wondered what might become of us.

AND then he called me.

"Well," he said with a long sigh. "It's done, Kelly." He sounded worn out. It was Tuesday morning.

"Eli, are you okay?"

"Sure, I'm fine. Really, I'm great. I feel free, Kelly. So free. I'm just tired. I'm in Tokyo."

"You're what? You're where?"

"Yeah, I had to take care of some stuff here. It's been planned a long time, and I really couldn't get out of it. Unfortunately, I'm going to have to be here a couple of weeks. I was hoping I wouldn't have to go until I could see you again—but it didn't work out that way, and so here I am. But it's done, Kelly. I broke up with her."

I paused to take a deep breath and let it go.

"When?"

"Yesterday—or let's see. Was it the day before? I'm sort of wiped out. It was after the party, after all the relatives finally went home."

"How did it go?

"Well, she seemed to be in shock. I don't know. I was sort of glad I could get the hell out of there, to tell you the truth. But before I left, I told her that when I come back, I'm not going back to our apartment in the city. I'm going to move into the Woodside house."

"Wow. This must be so hard for you. And for her."

"Yeah, but I'm convinced it's the best thing for everyone. I wasn't making her happy. She actually took it surprisingly well. My mom cried when I told her, though. That made me feel kind of bad."

"Oh, Eli. I'm sorry."

"Now don't say that. If you're sorry, then I'm done for!"

"You know what I mean."

"Yeah, I do." His voice softened. "And I thank you."

Now that he had finally done it, I tested my own feelings.

I was glad Eli had followed through on what he had said he would do. What a relief. I had believed in him, deep down, and yet I'd felt like a fool because I did.

I felt unhappy for Kyra's sake, and for being an instrument of destruction. I felt guilty. I wanted to feel excited, looking forward to see what the future would bring. But mostly I felt scared.

"Kelly, I want you to come here and be with me," he said. "I'll have a plane waiting for you this evening, if you'll come."

There was a short silence. I realized he was completely serious.

"Eli, I can't," I exclaimed, with a laugh that sounded slightly hysterical to me. "I can't just leave the inn right now."

Even as I said it, I asked myself, *Could I?*

"I can't wait to see you, Kelly. How am I going to wait? I won't. I'll come see you—now. I'll just come back. To hell with the merger!" He laughed. "Who cares about making money?"

"No, Eli," I said. "Don't do that. It'll be different now. The waiting will be different. And it's not just about money, is it? It's your work. I have my work, you have your work."

"Yeah."

"Do a good job, Eli."

"I always do. And I'll come to you as soon as I can."

Hanging up the phone, I remembered something Nick had once said to me. *If it were me, I wouldn't wait for anything . . .*

Nick! Sometimes I cursed the day I met the man.

FRIDAY afternoon a present came for me, special delivery, a necklace with diamonds and emeralds, fit for a princess.

Nick came into the office while I was opening it. We had hardly exchanged a word all week.

"Great," he said when he saw the necklace.

I knew I should have waited until I was alone in my room to open the package. Holding the necklace up to the light, I watched the gems sparkle. "What do you think?"

"You can wear it to the hoedown," he said.

"The what?"

"The hoedown. Tonight, at the old church."

"Oh, right, the community hoedown . . ."

"You're going, aren't you?"

"No, I don't think so . . ."

"Don't you like to dance?"

"Well, yeah, but—"

"I've already asked Addie and Bill, and they're not going. So there's no reason you can't. Come on, Kelly. You know you want to. I'll pick you up."

"No." I shook my head.

"Come on. It'll be fun."

Maybe it *would* be fun, I thought, if Nick was going . . . "Okay, maybe I will come to the hoedown," I said. "But I'll drive myself."

THE place was packed, but looking quite different without the folding chairs all set up in rows for a meeting. Lanterns hung from the rafters and straw bales lined the walls. Musicians tuned up their instruments on a platform stage, and people were dressed up country casual, swingy skirts and bolo ties.

I was surprised by how many people I knew there. Arturo was there with his wife and their two little girls. I saw Arturo's assistant, Juan, talking to Irma and Maria, my housekeeping staff. Earl and Maxine were there, as was Bernie, who paced near the doorway in his uniform, a grim expression on his face. Zac was standing with some friends outside the back door, and I saw the crew from the general store, who greeted me and called me by name. I realized I was starting to feel a familiarity with my new little community.

I didn't see Nick, and after a while I began to wonder if he had decided not to come. Then I spotted him across the room, looking fresh-scrubbed in a clean white shirt and jeans. His hair was less shorn looking than after he'd first cut it, and though it was still short, it was starting to curl around his forehead and down the back of his neck.

He was looking around the room as if searching for someone. When he saw me, he smiled and looked away quickly.

So everyone is here, I thought, satisfied and happy I'd come. The party had started.

OFFICER Bernie Hollinger looked lonely standing by himself near the entrance while everyone else was dancing in the main room or eating out on the back deck. As I wandered by I started talking to him. He seemed in the mood to chat, so I casually brought up the missing girl and asked him what he knew about her. I told him I was sure he must know more than anyone, being an officer of the law. Flattery seemed to work better with Bernie than it had with Rocky.

"Well, she had gone to Los Angeles looking to be a star," he said. "Same old story. Met a producer who sweet-talked her and made her feel special; he shot some film of her, coaxed her into taking off her clothes, and by the time she realized what she'd gotten herself into, she owed some people money. Those who were in charge of the investigation concluded the St. Claire woman was probably running from creditors, not porn producers. Though the porn angle makes a better story, no doubt. So we turned our attention to the local area. We had our suspicions . . . I won't name any names. Innocent until proven guilty, etcetera. Well, it's not something I can get into with you at the present time, I'm afraid."

"Why, is it still under investigation?"

"Not officially." He gazed off through the doorway at the crowd. "But I *would* advise you to always keep your doors locked at night."

Officer Bernie was just too much for me, with his tone full of importance and his chest thrust out like a rooster's. I had the same impression of him I had when I asked Eli about the subject—that he knew nothing, really, but he didn't want to just come out and say that.

EARLIER in the evening, Earl's nephew Lewis had played DJ, something for everyone, but now we were going to be treated to some live music. George from the feed store played guitar, Maxine sawed away at her fiddle, and on drums, the president of the city council kept the beat, which was rollicking. The room swelled up with dancing.

Suddenly Nick took my hand and swung me into his arms.

It must have been a combination of the music, the mood of the crowd, the stout ale, and the wind in off the sea; I was breathing deeply and laughing, twirling and turning. His hands were arrogant and skillful, confident and strangely gentle, moving me, guiding me. It was the most fun I could ever remember having on a Saturday night.

The old-fashioned country dancing allowed us to move together, arms entwined, hands clasped. I could smell his clean, damp hair and his fresh skin, which was taking on a sheen, like the gleam in his eyes when he pulled back a little and looked at me. A moment opened up in the middle of it all when time stretched out like warm taffy and he was staring into my eyes in a new way, deeply serious, searching, the laugh lines fading away, leaving only the clear color streaming toward me through the whirling air between us.

When the musicians stopped playing to take a break, I left him and floated to the refreshment table, where an older woman stood watching me with a cunning expression.

I plucked a bottle of water out of a cooler, opened it, and took a gulp. I felt light and buoyant and graceful.

"He makes it seem easy, doesn't he?" She leaned against the table with her bony arms folded over her boyish chest, a beautiful, scowling woman with black hair streaked with white and eyes that followed Nick with a dark gaze.

"Who?"

"Nick, obviously. Just like my first husband, Adhemar. He played tennis professionally. I used to play tennis occasionally, for fun only. I wasn't very good. But when I played with my husband, he would return every shot right back, pop, pop, pop. It went on and on; you wouldn't have to chase the ball at all. You would start to believe you were a great tennis player. But it isn't you. It's him. You couldn't do that with anyone else."

It was true, I'd never danced like that with anyone else. What was she saying? That my joy in dancing was merely an illusion? That Nick charmed women into believing he was wonderful?

There might be something to that, I thought, watching Nick laugh at something Anita was telling him. They stood by the open door, with the stars behind them. She flashed him a huge smile. I had never seen her smile like that.

"You're the new owner of the inn, aren't you?" The older woman reached for my hand, as if she intended to shake hands with me, but instead she turned it over, staring down intently at my palm.

"Good Lord!" she exclaimed.

I pulled my hand away sharply; it was necessary to yank it from her, she held it so tightly.

She looked offended. "Hasn't Mrs. Addie told you about me? The countess?"

"Oh," I said. "You're the countess? I pictured someone . . . different," I confessed.

"Different how, may I ask? Please be honest."

"Well, *heavier*, I suppose. And also—not that she ever used either of these words, now that I think about it, but—*older.*"

"That's right. Everyone thinks of me as older than I am. That's because I'm an old soul."

I had my doubts. Still, I knew Addie adored her and was enjoying her visualization classes, so I thought I should give her a chance.

"So, the count played professional tennis?" I asked her.

"No, the count was my third husband. A most disagreeable man. We never did *anything* well together—well, except for, you know . . ." She let out a deep murmur of laughter. "I'll let you fill in the blank yourself, my darling. As for my second husband, I suppose he fit me too well, it was all rather dull, actually. But when he passed on I *did* miss him terribly . . ."

She was oddly entertaining, but my attention kept wandering back to Nick and Anita. Anita's body language was offering, I thought, her black hair loose, tumbling down past her hips. She always wore it tied back at work.

But if Nick noticed an invitation, he gave no indication. After a few minutes he came across the room to stand with me and the countess.

"What are you drinking?" he asked me suspiciously.

"Water," I said. "I already had some of that punch, which is spiked."

"Of course. These community hoedowns rock."

"I had no idea."

"It's pathetic, really," said the countess. "In our small seaside hamlet we have no clubs or singles bars. A forum for human social interaction must be provided. Look around—I feel positively *surrounded* by young people trolling like sharks, everyone looking for that special someone with whom to mate and procreate."

"Everyone?" I looked out at the crowd, which seemed to me a pretty mixed bunch, old people, kids, middle-aged marrieds, a couple pairs of newlyweds, and yes, young singles. A few older singles, too.

"A great majority of them," the countess argued. "The ones that aren't already spent or spoken for. All driven mindlessly to breed."

"All but our Kelly here," said Nick. "She doesn't want kids."

"Is that so? Not looking to procreate?" The countess looked at me, surprised. "Odd, looking at your palm, I would have thought perhaps—"

I was embarrassed by this turn of the conversation, and Nick sensed it. "Come on, Kelly," he said, interrupting. "Let's go dance some more."

I smiled apologetically at the countess as Nick pulled me out to the middle of the room.

We danced, and I forgot about the countess, and Anita, and although the specters of Eli and Paula hovered about us, neither Nick nor I mentioned their names.

"Sorry about that," he said. "I didn't mean to bring up your personal life with her. That wasn't cool."

I nodded, patting him on the shoulder. His shirt was damp. "That's okay," I said.

I was on the verge of telling him about my secret change of heart. That I was beginning to have thoughts about maybe having children of my own someday. About marriage, even. Actually they were more like feelings than thoughts—but as an engineer I attempted to translate them into some kind of structure. Eli had come into my life, and suddenly I was thinking about having a family of my own someday. The correlation seemed obvious. And why not? When you meet the right person, that's when everything changes, right?

No, I thought. I can't tell him about any of that. I didn't want to prove him right, that I would change my mind so easily the moment Eli paid me a little notice. Though strangely enough I had first noticed these—feelings—the morning I had seen Nick walking with Paula and her kids down to the beach.

"What?" Nick was watching my face. "You were going to say something."

"Let's just dance," I said.

Chapter 17

HE was running his hands over me. Down my arms. Up my back. His lips were on my ears, on my neck. I felt my eyes close, my brain running rapid. We were at a party after the party. It was late and we were alone together in a dimly lit room.

Tell me, Kelly. Tell me what you need.

Need. What a strange concept.

I shook my head, and my strength ebbed as his powerful hands squeezed me against his body. The only need I had, in that moment, was for what he was doing to me. But I knew better. Even in this state, I knew better.

No, Nick, I murmured, falling against him. *This can't work.*

Why? Why can't it work? His voice sounded so sad. *You want someone else, is that it?*

I just . . .

You've got your sights set on something else.

Yes, but I . . . I was shaking my head, confused.

I tried to get away, but he wouldn't let me escape. He blocked the way with his body.

It became a crazy frenzied encounter. I was fighting him at first. Fighting with all my might, which only served to provide him with writhing flesh to press himself into, to plunder and feed off. Our kisses were attacks, and he was the superior in strength in this battle. Struggling became supplication as a new kind of response emerged, no less passionate. The wildness and hunger was so powerful, it was . . .

It was . . .

A dream.

No . . . I heard myself moan. *I don't want to let go of this.*

It was only a dream. There had been no party after the party. I knew that. I had slipped away from Nick the night before around midnight and driven myself home to my cottage.

I opened my eyes to find Grendel gently shaking me, his hands on my shoulders. Through the dreamy haze I noticed a painful-looking rash speckling his wrists on both arms, disappearing beneath his sleeves.

"Kelly, Kelly," he said soothingly. "You're having a dream."

"Grendel?" My voice cracked.

"You were crying out in your sleep," he explained, looking down on me, his beautiful blue eyes regarding me kindly.

My eyes adjusted to the late-afternoon sunlight on the porch. I sat up.

Nick McClure. I had meant to sit and read, but I kept thinking about him. Thinking about how it had felt, dancing with him last night. I had fallen asleep, thinking of him.

"Were you having a nightmare, Kelly?" Grendel asked me solicitously.

I shook my head and laughed, embarrassed. "No . . . not a nightmare."

"Ah . . ." His face registered understanding, a faint smile flickering over his lips. "One of *those* dreams."

He laughed gently and sat down on the bench across from me.

I was silent, staring off at the silver line of the horizon.

He seemed to understand what I needed right then, and his voice took on a vaguely professional, yet fatherly tone: "So, Kelly, are you seeing anyone in particular these days?"

"Well . . . Eli Larson recently called off his engagement, and we've been in touch . . ."

"I see." And he did see. I didn't have to say anything more; which only made me wonder how obvious we had been, and who else knew what was going on between us.

"Well, then that's fine, isn't it?" he pressed. "If he's made a clean break."

"I hope so," I answered, though I wondered: Is any break ever really clean?

"Well, he's a great guy," Grendel said. "And you deserve the best."

"You warned me about him. You said he was a cad."

"*Was* a cad. Past tense. Why would he want any other when he's got you?"

I went into the office and found a delivery had come for me while I was napping; another gift from Eli, no doubt—they were coming at the rate of about one a day. Seeing another present from Eli increased the sense of sin I was carrying around along with the sensual glow of my dream.

Flowers, it appeared. He hadn't sent flowers since the first bouquet of pink roses.

But when I opened the box, I was puzzled. In black tissue lay a dozen long-stemmed roses—black roses—all dead, the heads nearly severed, each of the dark buds hanging on a thorn-studded stalk by a single tendonlike strand of the stem. This wasn't a pretty dried arrangement, fragrant with floral oils and tied with silk ribbon. And no, there weren't a dozen of them—I quickly counted—there were thirteen.

I snatched up the card that had accompanied the delivery, ripped it open, and read:

If it's because of you
You're in for a big surprise.

There was no signature.

What a stupid cliché of a dirty trick, I scoffed to myself. Dead roses. But I was shaken.

In late October the rains came after days of heat. Softly at first, in a gentle sprinkling. But one night it rained hard. Lightning opened up the sky in brilliant flashes. Huge explosions of thunder had my heart beating fast as I sat alone in my cottage. Sheets of water began falling out of overflowing gutters.

In the morning I walked the property, which seemed none the worse for the storm, besides needing a good cleanup. I dragged away branches and swept up the leaves covering the pathways. Bill was sweeping off the decks, with Anita and the maids pitching in to help.

Nick showed up midmorning with a few days' beard, wild dark curls poking out from the rim of a knit cap, his green eyes trimmed in red. In the days since I'd seen him last, my dream infatuation hadn't completely worn away, and I looked at him carefully. He seemed so normal in some ways. So average. Yet even when he wasn't looking his best, like right now, the sight of him raised a deep heat in me.

"Haven't you gone to bed yet, Nick?" I asked him.

"Kelly, I have a monster favor to ask you. My truck is AWOL with a broken water pump and I need to drop Freesia off at Aaron's in Half Moon Bay in a quarter of an hour and meet my crew."

"You mean your rescue team?"

"Yep. There's been a huge mudslide in the foothills and a bunch of houses are covered. It's a bad scene and I gotta get to it." He paused long enough to shine me a cocky grin. But the sun rays around his eyes hardly deepened at all, the way they usually did when he smiled, and he was serious again in a flash. "Would you give me a ride into town?"

"Sure," I said, "Just give me a minute . . ."

I conferred quickly with Addie and Bill, who were only too happy to help Nick's cause.

We drove to his house and picked up his gear and the two dogs, then we were off.

"You know," I said, "I'm surprised you didn't ask Paula to drive you."

"Well, she lives kinda far away. And she'd hate it anyway, having the dogs in her car. She doesn't get along too well with the mutts. We took them out to Dog Beach the other day, and I think she's had enough for a while."

"So . . . you've been seeing quite a lot of each other, then?"

"We've gone out a few times, with the boys. To the beach, the Pumpkin Festival, stuff like that."

I said casually, "So, do you owe me a dinner, Nick?"

He glanced at me, his expression sharp. "I thought *that* deal had been broken a long time ago."

"Nothing was broken on my side, if that's what you're implying."

I took one hand off the steering wheel and flicked him under his chin. "Nick, I know you think I've already gone to bed with Eli, but you're wrong. I haven't."

He looked as if he would rather ignore the subject altogether, but he could not help saying angrily: "Kelly, you told me he was with you in your cottage, that night your window was broken—"

"Eli came to my room that night. True. And nothing happened."

"Nothing?" he repeated incredulously.

"Well, not *that*. I told you nothing was going to happen until he was finished with Kyra."

He stayed silent, still scowling.

"Look, I can't honestly say what *might* have happened that night. I'm only human, after all, and he took me by surprise. But when that rock came through the window, that was it."

"That was it?"

"He shot out of my room like a bat out of hell. He told me later he was afraid for my uh . . . for the reputation of the inn."

"Makes sense," Nick conceded grudgingly. "That's Aaron's house, there on the end of the block, with the boat trailer out in front."

We reached the house and I parked.

"Aaron's at work right now, so I'll just put Freesia in the backyard."

"Will she be okay with that?"

"Sure, Aaron's dog Shalimar is Freesia's buddy."

"So she's retired now?"

"Afraid so."

He helped the old dog out of the car, though she would have scrambled out without a complaint if he'd let her.

"Be right back. Maggie, you stay."

I waited, listening to the sound of dogs barking behind the house.

WHEN he came back I had already taken his bag out of the trunk and was waiting by the car to say good-bye.

"Thanks for doing this, Kelly," he said. "The guys will be here in a few minutes to pick me up, if you want to get going."

"You still haven't answered my question," I said.

"What question?" he asked, his face innocent for a moment, like a boy's. "Oh—you mean, do I owe you a dinner?" He lingered in the silence before he answered, and now the sun rays were deepening around his eyes. "No. It's never even been an issue, not with her kids around. But I think she's closing in on me."

"Yeah?"

"Yeah. She's staying at the inn this evening, as you probably know, and her ex isn't bringing the boys down until tomorrow. She made sure I was all clued in on that."

"So tonight was supposed to be the night."

"Afraid so."

"I'm sorry. You must be terribly disappointed."

"I'll deal. So, Kelly, tell me. Apparently my perceptions have been off—just what *is* going on with you and the robber baron these days?"

"Well, I haven't seen him since he was here with his parents. Actually, he's in Japan right now. But he broke off his engagement with Kyra. He is officially a single man again."

"For real?" Nick looked skeptical. "He really ended it with her?"

"Yes, he really did."

"Wow. So he actually went and did it." He sounded amazed.

"Well, they were having problems anyway."

"He didn't exit his engagement till he met you, Kelly. He traded up."

"Traded up?" I said scornfully. "Hey, I don't have what *she* has, Nick. Kyra is picture-perfect beautiful, she has money and social connections—she's thinner than me, she's younger than me, and she drives a better car!"

"But there's one thing she isn't, and will never be."

"What?"

"She's not you."

I kicked at some pebbles on Aaron's driveway. I was torn between feeling insulted—by the way Nick had used the phrase *traded up,* as if I was some sort of commodity, like a car—and touched, by the sweetness of his words. *She's not you.*

The sweetness won out. I walked back to him and we stood together quietly a moment, and to fill in the silence I said quickly, nervously, "Well, it's too bad you lost out on your chance with Paula tonight."

"You think so?" His tone was challenging. "You really want me and Paula to get together, huh?"

"Of course, if that's what *you* want."

"Apparently you think I should want it."

"Oh, please. Anyway, what's wrong with that? You're the one who told me I should pursue Eli."

"Looks like you took my advice."

"I have never *pursued* him."

"No, I guess you probably didn't have to."

"Are you trying to pick a fight with me, Nick?"

"Yeah."

"Why?" I asked.

"To make it easier to leave you."

A large white van came rumbling down the street and pulled up to the curb. Nick's ride had arrived.

He stepped up to me and laced his fingers together behind the back of my neck, and brought his forehead to rest against mine. It was a gesture that lasted only a moment, so graceful and swift, I had no chance to respond.

He murmured, "Thanks for the ride, Red."

The other team members emerged from the van. There was a rapid bustle of greetings and loading of gear, and dogs mingling and sniffing.

I stepped away. Nick was focused now on the task at hand. He finished loading and jumped into the van and the door slid shut as I walked to my car. The van rolled past me and I looked up; there he was, leaning out the window, his eyes on me, his expression ambiguous.

He had something in his hand, and he raised it to show me, and then he flung it out to me, a small glittering golden disk sailing through the air. I caught it without thinking.

"Take care of that for me," he called out as the van moved slowly down the street and disappeared around the corner.

It was his father's brass compass.

What is he doing?

I looked down at the compass I held in my hand. He's crazy, I thought. If I hadn't caught it, the old compass might very well have smashed on the ground. His father's compass! And didn't he tell me this compass was his backup, in case something happened to the state-of-the-art modern compass he carried? That he never got lost when he had it? What if he needed this compass? He was on his way up to the foothills now. Why had he wanted me to have his compass?

My fingers rubbed the smooth cool brass, my eyes delighting in the beauty and simplicity of the piece. Holding it, the weight of it felt right, like fine jewelry. Precious and meaningful. As a symbol. With meaning. With a message.

But what message?

To you I entrust my direction.

When I got home I laid the compass on my desk so I could glance at it while I was working. I realized with a jolt that I was more taken by this impromptu gift of Nick's than I was with any of Eli's gorgeous, expensive presents.

It was weird. I hardly knew Nick McClure. But I *did* know him. He was a paradox. This man who once merely annoyed me and exasperated me now fascinated me and turned me inside out.

Paula had said something similar—I remembered her words suddenly, as if waking up. *I am finding him more and more fascinating . . .*

The old Indian woman's face came into my mind. Nick's great-grandmother.

Oh, God, I thought. Here we go again. What was I thinking?

Nick was Paula's territory now. Nick and Paula were dating. I had no idea what they had between them, really. It might have gone further than I even imagined, despite what he'd told me.

Did he really want her? Did she really want him? Messing with Paula's feelings was the last thing I wanted to do.

I set them up, for God's sake.

So what was I doing, thinking of him? Why wasn't I thinking of Eli?

Because I was too busy thinking of Nick.

His unexpected sweetness. His humor. That pirate's smile of his, those green eyes. The way he moved when he was working, standing on a ladder, stretching up to reach the eaves, or playing with his dogs down on the beach, throwing sticks for them to chase, his body graceful and loose.

Why was I thinking about that?

*   *   *

"HE somehow manages to evade me every time I think I'm going to get my hands on him! Rescue mission, huh?" Paula laughed heartily. She was philosophical about her cancelled date.

Nick had asked me to let her know he'd been called out, so I broke the news to her.

"He couldn't call and tell me himself?" she asked with a wry smile. But she didn't seem too discouraged. "To tell you the truth," she exclaimed, "I'm very proud of him."

"So . . . is he your boyfriend now?" I asked her.

"Actually, no. It's not like, *you* know. It's not like that, not yet. Maybe he will be. I wouldn't rule it out. But it's not like we're not dating other people, still."

"Nick's dating other people?"

"Well, he hasn't told me he isn't."

"And I thought *you* were finished with men, until Nick—"

"I know. It's all suddenly blossoming for me again. There's this guy who works in my department . . ." She blushed. "He's so nerdy, but I don't know. It suits him. But we work together. So right now, I'm just okay with being free." With a saucy lift of her chin, she added, "Playing the field."

Her face softened and she leaned toward me. "Seriously, I would love to find someone. Someone who would love me, and accept the boys. You know? And Nick is really good with the boys . . ."

ADDIE was in the office catching up on paperwork. I was going into the parlor to pick up the newspapers and I saw what I thought was a dirty napkin on the floor near the entry hall. As I knelt to pick it up, I found it was actually a thin strip of yellowed newsprint with a tarnished paper clip hanging off it.

The clipping had been trimmed so there was no date at the top of the piece.

POLICE CALL OFF SEARCH FOR MISSING WOMAN

Pescadero, CA. Coast guard officials announced yesterday the search for missing Los Angeles woman Alicia St. Claire will be suspended.

St. Claire, 26, was last seen at the Magic Mermaid Inn on the Old Coast Highway, where she had recently taken a part-time job and temporary residence. Employees of the inn said she had moved from Los Angeles several weeks earlier.

Police have no conclusive evidence of foul play in the disappearance. But owners of the Magic Mermaid Inn, Adelaide and William O'Mally, said they were doubtful St. Claire would have left without notice, and (continued on page 5)

"Whatcha got there?"

I looked up, startled, at Paula, who had come into the parlor behind me.

"Oh, hey, Paula . . . it's . . . it looks like part of an old newspaper clipping."

I checked the impulse to stuff it into my pocket, out of her sight. But she was already peering down at it.

"Oh, my God," she said. "It's about that missing girl. I'm terribly fascinated by her."

"Me, too," I said, giving up the clipping for her to read. "But the locals will hardly talk about it. Even this newspaper story is only half here!"

"Where did this come from?"

"I found it here on the floor."

"How did it happen to be here on the floor?"

"That's what I'm wondering." Goose bumps ran over my arms.

A movement in the doorway had me jumping.

It was only Addie, looking in from the entry hall. I seized the clipping from Paula, marched over to Addie, and held the yellowed bit of paper out for her to see.

"Is this true, what it says here, Addie? You didn't think she would leave without giving notice?" She couldn't very well keep pretending she didn't know anything about it now.

"Yes, it's true," Addie said defiantly, after taking a good look at the clipping. "And it also says what I said before. There was no evidence of foul play."

"But Maxine says her car was found by the side of a cliff . . . Would the woman just abandon her car like that?"

"The bank was about to repossess that car." Addie smiled sadly.

"Then wouldn't she have left the car at a bus station, or an airport?" Paula spoke up. "Would she just leave the car by the cliffs and disappear into thin air?"

"Good point!" I exclaimed. "I mean, I guess she could have caught a ride, hitchhiking, or something, but—"

"Oh no, I hope not." Addie frowned. "That would be so dangerous." After a beat, she laughed at herself. "We were afraid she had drowned," she said. She sounded tired now. "But she was never . . . We never found out what happened to her."

"It says here she had recently taken a part-time job at the inn," said Paula.

"Well," Addie said with a sigh, "that's not really true, but, yes, we were talking about her working here. She took over the desk once or twice for me. She was so friendly, the guests loved her. She paid for a month in advance, and talked about staying for at least several months, working for room and board. Except she didn't stay very long, as it turned out . . ."

"How long *did* she stay at the inn?" I asked.

Addie thought awhile. "It seemed longer than it actually was, I think. Probably not more than a few weeks . . ."

"Did she leave anything behind when she left?"

"There might have been a few things." Addie had a faraway look in her eyes.

"And she stayed in the motel, right?"

"Yes, she stayed in the motel, at first. But then we moved her into the water tower unit, because it's got the kitchenette. It was different in those days, you know. Much nicer. We've let the place go, I'm afraid. I didn't want anyone staying there for a while after she disappeared . . . so we just let it go. Began using it for storage."

I thought of the day I had gone into the water tower and found Nick and Anita in there alone together.

I said, "Alicia's things are still in there, aren't they?"

"Where?" Addie looked blank.

"In the water tower."

"They might be," Addie said evasively. "There's so much junk in that old unit, I've forgotten what's in there. I thought you were going to have Anita and Nick help you clean it out."

"No, I haven't touched the place. The one time I was in there, I found several bags packed with women's things. And—and where did this clipping come from?"

"I don't know how it got there on the floor," Addie replied, "but I know where it came from. I have a whole scrapbook of things I've saved, related to the inn, over the years. Though after that incident, I wasn't so keen on keeping up with the scrapbook . . . I let it go, too, I suppose, just like the water tower . . ."

"Can I look at it? Can I see the scrapbook, Addie?"

Addie, resigned, walked to the bookshelves flanking the fireplace and knelt to the bottom shelf, where she kept the vast collection of photo albums she and Bill had amassed over the years.

"I'm sure I keep it down here . . ."

But after several minutes of searching, Addie shook her head.

"I'm sorry, I was sure it was here . . . How funny. And you just found that clipping on the floor?"

She went back into the office to assist a guest who was checking out. Paula and I walked outside on the porch together.

"She doesn't want to talk about it," Paula said as soon as we were alone.

"I know. But it makes more sense now, why she doesn't. Addie hates anything negative, and always tries to find the good in everything. This one is just a little tough for her to manage."

"Hmm."

"But I have to wonder how that clipping ended up there on the floor, for me to find like that. And what happened to that scrapbook?"

"It's probably in Addie's apartment," Paula said. "Most likely she was just looking in the wrong place. I say we check out the water tower. See if those things you saw in there do in fact belong to the missing girl."

"Alicia," I supplied the name. She was becoming more and more real to me.

"Alicia," Paula repeated soberly. "Right."

So we went to the water tower to check it out, like Nancy Drew and her sidekick Bess, or George.

But someone had been there before us. The suitcase was lying half in and half out of the closet, open, with its contents jumbled and spilling out over the sides onto the wood plank floor. The duffel bag was open and the little pink backpack was gone.

"I take it you didn't leave her stuff like this?" Paula said, surveying the mess.

"No." I shook my head. "I left everything packed up neatly, just the way I found it, in the closet."

We looked at each other, eyes large, and grabbed each other for support; we both suddenly needed it.

"Apparently we're not the only ones interested in Alicia St. Claire," Paula whispered.

TOGETHER we went through the suitcase and duffel bag, folding everything up and neatly repacking the bags.

"I'll bet it was just kids messing around in here," I said. I was thinking of Zac, possibly even Rocky and Winkle. The two younger boys seemed so bookish and pure, but maybe there was something more mischievous under that seeming innocence of theirs. "And I'm pretty sure something's missing."

"So what's missing?"

"There was this sort of tacky pink backpack. With nothing much in it, except . . ."

"What?"

"Except for some papers and makeup and a little beaded evening bag. I remember, because I liked it. I even thought about taking it."

"Well, why didn't you?" Paula asked. "You own this place now, and everything in it."

"I don't know. It didn't seem right, to just take it. Like the girl might come back for it or something. You know?"

Paula nodded. We surveyed the freshly packed bags, which sat together in the closet.

"Maybe she did come back," I added as an afterthought. "To pick up a few of her things." It was meant to be a joke, but we both shivered and hugged each other again.

*　　*　　*

WE left the water tower at dusk and walked together down the path to the house. The man in the bowler hat was strolling along by the picket fence near Addie's flower garden.

"There he is," I said to Paula in a low voice. "Mr. James. Why do I always feel like that's an alias? He's getting to be a regular, but we haven't exchanged a dozen words. He's very quiet. Always pays with cash."

"He looks harmless enough," Paula said.

"Not like a guy who would go through Alicia's suitcases, anyway."

"No," Paula agreed with a muffled laugh.

I finally had someone to talk to about the missing woman. About Alicia. Because Paula was a guest, I wouldn't have intentionally brought it up with her; but obviously she wasn't put off by it. She had been coming to the inn before I was around, and she had probably known the story long before I did. I was thrilled to have her companionship in this sleuthing game.

Chapter 18

My mind was full of the mysterious missing woman, and I often thought about her, even as I worked, hustling to help keep the inn running smoothly. Occasionally I thought of Eli, asking myself what might become of us; but I couldn't get Nick out of my head.

Sunday evening I went out and walked for a long time, wondering if I was "pursuing" the wrong man. Because I was pursuing Eli, wasn't I? Even if I pretended otherwise; that was a strategy in itself.

But in the last few days I was hardly thinking of Eli. Eli, who seemed like a figment of my imagination, like a crush on a movie star. I had spent a handful of minutes with him over the past two months. Nick was the one who really dominated my thoughts. Nick was real, flesh and blood, in my world. Nick made sense to me.

I walked down to the beach and up the cliffs near the highway to the north. On my way home I walked by his house. The sky had grown dark and I saw the light on in his kitchen window, his truck parked in the side yard.

So he had returned. We'd heard on the news that all the missing flood victims had been accounted for, but I had not expected him back tonight. Without thinking I pushed open the gate beside the driveway and walked up the pathway to the house.

Dogs started barking and by the time I reached the porch, another light had blinked on, and as I came to the top step, Nick opened the door.

He was completely expressionless, looking at me.

I was a little taken back by his demeanor; it was like he didn't quite recognize me. I matched his silence with one of my own, and the two of us stood quietly looking at each other for about three seconds. Three long seconds. This strange not speaking only increased the poignancy of the urgency of my mission.

I could no longer deny it. It was strumming in my blood. *I want him.*

He seemed to snap awake. "Come in, quick, Kelly—I'm gonna burn my supper."

I obeyed him and stepped inside. He slammed the door and sprinted off toward the kitchen. The house smelled spicy and warm. The dogs wiggled around me, happy to see me.

What am I doing here?

I wandered around the living room, looking at Nick's possessions. He had some beautiful things. I especially liked the beaded leather bag that had belonged to one of his ancestors. When he had showed it to me the first time, I had thought he was putting me on about his Indian ancestry.

I walked into the kitchen. He was stirring canned spaghetti in a pan on an old Wedgewood stove.

"You call that supper?" I laughed.

"Why, don't you like SpaghettiOs?" He turned off the fire and set the lid on the pan. He opened the fridge and got out two bottles of beer, popped the lids off, and handed me one.

He clinked his bottle against mine. "Let's go sit down on the back porch," he said.

"Aren't you going to eat?"

"The sight of you is all I need to sustain me." His words were teasing and gallant, but he seemed preoccupied.

Bad time? I wondered.

We walked through the kitchen to a glassed-in porch with a view of the ocean. The last faint light was dying out of the sky to the west and night was coming on. Nick lit a candle in a lantern on a table, and we sat down on canvas-covered chairs.

"I was just walking by, when I saw your light on," I said. "I would have brought your compass back to you, if I had thought I was going to see you this evening."

"Hang on to it for me for a while," he said. He sounded almost angry that I had brought up the subject of the compass.

I said softly, "Tell me about the floods."

"Oh, it was brutal, Kelly. There were entire houses smashed up, down in the river, just ripped off their foundations . . ." He sighed heavily. "We didn't find anybody alive, but one of the teams plucked a woman off a tree a ways down the river."

"You didn't find anyone . . . alive?"

"There are teams who specialize in looking for the dead. They use cadaver dogs."

"Cadaver dogs!" The name to me conjured an image of terrifying, half-dead beasts.

"Yeah. They're a subspecialty of search and rescue, the ones who look for the dead. But sometimes these things overlap . . ." He stared away at the ocean for a moment.

I listened to him talk about his work, what he had been doing the past few days. He spoke casually about what to me would be mind-blowing situations.

I wondered if he could feel the questioning heat simmering off me; he didn't seem to. I had become obsessed with him and he had no idea.

He stopped talking and a strange stillness gathered around us. The urge to fill in the spaces of the silence was strong in me, but I was so aware of him, of being alone with him, that I could not come up with any trivial conversation.

I wasn't sure what it was, exactly, but I sensed in him some uneasiness or agitation that I hadn't noticed when last we had been together. I wondered if it was because of what he had gone through, up in the foothills. He got up and wandered outside on the deck, leaving the door open between us. I sat for a few moments alone, then I got up and followed him. He stood at the railing, listening to the soft roaring of the ocean.

How ironic it seemed to me. *Here I am, pursuing Nick McClure, of all people. Literally pursuing.*

I came up behind him and laid my hands on his back. He wore a thin cotton shirt, soft to the touch, though what lay under the soft fabric was hard, and I felt a flinch of muscle beneath my fingers.

"Aren't you cold out here, with no coat?" I asked him, my voice low behind his ear.

"Nah," he said, shrugging, "I'm not cold."

I let my hands fall, but I didn't move away. He turned to face me, looking at me solemnly. "Are you?" he asked.

I nodded.

We stood close enough to touch; if one of us were to take a step forward, our bodies would be pressed together.

He wasn't tall, but he was staring down at me, his mouth and mine a feather's breadth apart.

He was looking at me as if he wanted to burn my image into his brain for all time. He brought his hands up to cradle my face; but then he let them drop away again, fisting at his sides. He was breathing hard and his forehead was creased in a scowl. He gave his head a shake.

Suddenly I realized he was calling upon the same sort of restraint he'd used when he chose not to punch Earl in the face the night of the community meeting.

He's trying *not* to do this! I thought, struck with wonder.

But by then it was too late. Neither of us could help ourselves. Though it only lasted a moment, the kiss was deep and it seemed endless. His mouth was warm and unfamiliar, the taste of him intoxicating, the smell of him—cotton and clean sweat and the faint lingering essence of wood smoke—was like the scent of home.

Like in my dream, only completely different, his hands swirled over me. But now there was no instinct urging me to flee. I wanted more.

Suddenly, abruptly, he let go of me.

"I can't do this with you, Kelly," he said in a strangled voice. He gazed beyond me like a soldier with a painful duty.

I must have looked like I'd been struck.

"Let's go in," he said. He walked past me into the house.

For a moment I just stood there, stunned, then I trailed after him mutely.

In the kitchen he opened himself a second beer. He offered me another, but I was still working on the first one.

Nick drank deep, as if he had a great thirst.

He became chatty and funny and he repeated a work-related story he'd already told me a couple of weeks earlier, adding a few new details.

This gave me a chance to pull myself together, which I did, taking a few deep breaths.

Actually, I was a little relieved. Me—and Nick? What was I thinking? What had come over me, anyway?

I deserved . . . this. Rejection.

I finished my beer quickly and dropped the bottle into the recycling bin outside the back door, calling out to him that I was heading home.

Without saying anything—I would have discouraged it, and he must have known it—he took it upon himself to walk me home, falling into step beside me, still chatting away about his work to fill in the empty space between us.

I was saddened by this. He'd never had to do that with me before. But once we reached the road, he grew more quiet and we walked together in silence.

I wondered what had happened between us. Not just this evening—well, *that* was obvious. I had offered, and he had refused. Clear and simple. What confused me was that I had been so sure he was interested; in fact, I felt certain he had been about to make a move on me once or twice before—only the timing wasn't quite right, or we had been interrupted—

I *felt* it with him.

Or so I had thought. I wasn't sure what had gone wrong with my instincts, but he had made it clear. He didn't want to go there, not with me.

He has made a commitment to Paula. He likes me, but he's decided he likes Paula better. That's fine. That's good.

Confused and hurt, I wondered how I might salvage my dignity.

We reached the inn. Nick and I walked into the yard, and there was Eli.

Eli! How long had it been since I'd last seen him? Seemed like another season. He stood on the porch in the glow of the lamp, looking relaxed and worldly in jeans, a thigh-length coat of dark leather, and shiny calf-high boots. He must have just arrived.

Home from Tokyo. A luminescent silver Jaguar sat in the parking area.

"Kelly!" he cried. "There you are! Thank God." He hurried down the steps and crossed the parking area with his long, confident stride.

"Hey, Eli." I walked toward him swiftly, trying to hide my confusion at seeing him there at this particular moment. He looked even more handsome than I remembered him, big and well groomed, and he embodied the image of subtle money, an admittedly effective aphrodisiac. Best of all, at this particular moment, his eagerness to see me was obvious, and I sensed his greeting would have been even more potent had we been alone. As it was, he grabbed me up in his arms and squeezed me passionately.

When at last he released me, I stepped back from his embrace, dizzy, glancing at Nick, who stood motionless a few paces away, watching us.

The two men shook hands in the aggressive, forceful, two-alpha-males-in-meeting mode that I had seen before—between Nick and Earl, the rancher.

Having been summarily rejected by Nick, I have to admit I found it gratifying to have him walk me home to this surprise reunion with Eli Larson. The freshly single Eli Larson.

Stealing another look at Nick, I became aware of an evil urge, to make some snide or insulting comment, not so much with words as with a gesture, or an expression—perhaps one of haughty contempt, or better yet, withering scorn—but I didn't. I had the strange feeling that for him it had been no easy thing to pass on my pass, which only increased my perplexity at what had just happened between us. What *hadn't* happened between us.

Before going up into the house with Eli, I glanced at Nick again—it was an accident, I hadn't meant to look at him at all. I'm not sure what he might have seen in my expression—nothing, probably. I think I was in a state of shock. But he was looking at me so mournfully, I was left bewildered. *Why did he reject me when I know he wants me?*

The door shut behind us and I was alone with Eli.

For the first time, Eli sensed he might have some competition. He asked me directly: "So, Kelly, should I be worried about this guy Nick?"

"No, Eli," I said in a voice that sounded detached from my body. "I don't think you have to worry about Nick."

Now that Eli was there in the flesh, I began to focus on him again. I had been spurned and rejected by Nick, which was puzzling and hurtful to me, but I decided it was mainly just my ego taking a bruising, not any great love lost. I would get over it soon enough.

And yet Nick had done something to me. He had messed me up somehow. My physical and emotional defenses had rolled up around me. I was too deep into Nick, at the moment, to suddenly give myself to another man.

Eli was smart, as it turned out, and sensitive. He didn't push it too hard. It would take me time to let go of myself with him, and he seemed to know that. Maybe it wasn't easy for him, either; he'd been with only Kyra for years . . . unless what Grendel had told me was true, that Eli had lots of women, all the time. That he knew how to play them, knew what they wanted to hear, knew what they needed . . .

He certainly seemed to know what *I* needed. In any case, now that we were finally free to be physical with each other, we were strangely chaste. Aside from a few tentative kisses, nothing much happened between us the night he returned. I was standoffish and he was tired.

We just need a little time. After all, we hardly know each other.

It had been a close call, I thought, with Nick. I might have done something foolish. Something I'd be regretting now.

I would have blown my chances with Eli . . .

The more I thought about it, the more I realized I must have been temporarily insane.

THERE was no question. The spot was growing.

Eli appeared to have a cancerous growth that was spreading over his eyes and up into his hair.

Days had passed since I'd last seen him, and I turned to the photo, as I often did, to assure me of his presence; to convince myself he existed, somewhere, in the world.

I examined the room. How was this happening? There had to be some logical explanation.

I yanked the photo out of the mirror frame and threw it into the top drawer of the dresser, where I had stashed the photo of Nick. I picked up Nick's picture, half expecting to see a similar effect on his image. But it was just a black and white photo, neatly cut from the newspaper.

For a while I simply looked at Nick's body, with its lanky, low center of gravity, the economical cut of his features in profile. A form in movement, yet somehow seemingly solid.

He's my rock, I thought. I hung on to him, feeling him hard and solid in my mind.

But he's not. He's not for me.

I was eager to show Nick that nothing of consequence had happened the night we had shared that one swift and endless kiss, so I went out of my way to be casual and friendly when I saw him. I called him to schedule the next project for the inn—as if nothing had changed. Things were strained between us, but I was sure it would only be a matter of time before we were back to our old sarcastic selves.

As soon as I could get the four of us together, I had Nick and Paula to dinner at the inn to prove I wholeheartedly supported their union, which I did. Even if Nick had the audacity to choose Paula over me.

Eli would have preferred it to be just the two of us that evening, I think, but he was a gracious cohost. Arturo catered the meal; barbecued Santa Maria tri-tip and garlic mashed potatoes.

"We should serve food like this at the Magic Mermaid every evening, like a real inn," Arturo said in his dusky voice, watching me taste the dripping meat hot off the fire. I practically swooned whenever he fixed me something to eat, and he loved cooking for me. He wanted to expand our services to include dinner. Arturo had ambition: He envisioned feeding multitudes. He thought the inn's large formal dining room was going to waste.

I thought we had enough going on already, but I didn't exactly discourage his dreams.

As I savored the meat, I noticed Grendel moving about in the little patch of growing things near his cottage. I was struck with a sudden rush of guilt; here I was throwing a dinner party and I hadn't invited him. Hadn't even thought to ask him. I considered setting another place at the table and calling him to come over, but he'd know he was an afterthought; there was nothing remotely vegan about this meal we were about to consume. Even the salad was full of chunks of blue cheese, sliced hard-boiled egg, and bits of shaved salami.

Bill and Addie had dinner in their own apartment, as usual. I had yet to actually come right out and tell them about me and Eli; I wasn't sure they would approve of the situation.

Eli spent most of dinner on the phone, talking business. He was using my cell phone because he had mislaid his own somewhere. I tried not to imagine the extra charges I was racking up while he talked to someone in another country.

While Paula, Nick, and I were eating in the dining room, Eli stood outside on the porch, and I could hear the occasional word or phrase. It reminded me of Kyra and her one-sided telephone conversations.

"Look, Lou, I'm all for giving to charity—especially when it's tax deductible . . . Well, that's what you're asking for, isn't it? We are businessmen, my friend. You know me. I'm in it for the deal and I never forget that. If we can't get it at three and a half percent, I don't want it."

No doubt you don't get to be one of the most successful guys in the world without sacrificing something, I thought. In this case, most of a tri-tip dinner with friends.

"So how are you and Paula getting on?" I asked Nick. We were alone in the dining room, finishing up a bottle of wine. Paula had left early to pick up the boys from her ex, and Eli was outside, talking on the phone again.

A couple of weeks had passed since the night Eli had returned from abroad, the night Nick and I had come together on his deck overlooking the ocean.

Not for the first time, I wished I could take back what I had done.

But it was nothing, really. A quick kiss.

Nothing.

We had just about returned to normal, which was a relief, though it seemed to me he was generally more subdued with me than he once was.

Just to prove how unaffected I was, I asked him lightly, "You probably owe me that dinner at Charlene's by now, right?"

"No, it hasn't come to that," he replied. He didn't joke about it, as I had expected. "We have to be really careful, you know, with those kids involved."

"I suppose it's difficult, finding time for the two of you alone."

"No, it isn't that. It's . . . I have to make sure I don't start something leading to false expectations, especially with Rocky and Dean." He turned the subject on me abruptly: "What about you? As I recall, the deal was whoever was first."

"Yeah, well, don't look at me."

"I wonder how much I can even trust what you say these days, Kelly."

There was an edge to his words that startled me. And why would he say such a thing?

Then I asked myself—when I did finally make love with Eli, would I report back to Nick?

I was silent, pondering this, and unexpectedly he apologized to me. "Hey, I'm sorry, Kelly," he said. "You've never given me reason not to trust you."

The way he turned from sardonic to serious affected me more than I would have liked, sometimes. Disarmed me when I would have preferred to stay armed. I said irritably, "Anyway, to answer your question, I'm trying to take it real slow with Eli, too. You know? Because I like him, and I think it could work out."

"Of course that will only make him desire you more," he said sourly.

"Thank you, Coach. Any more tips?"

Eli came into the room, looking flushed and happy. He flung himself into the big wing chair and called to me. "Oh, Kelly, come here, you pretty thing."

I rose hesitantly and crossed the room to him, and when I reached him, he grabbed me and pulled me down on his lap.

"Eli, are you drunk?" I asked him.

"I am not drunk. I haven't had time to get drunk yet. Put your arms around me," he commanded.

I looped my arms around his neck. I didn't look at Nick.

"That was quite a feast, wasn't it?" Eli sighed contentedly. "Arturo is the man."

I nodded and sighed. "You said it."

"I may have to hire him away from you."

"You wouldn't dare!"

A pitiful wail rose from the doorway; we looked up with a start to see Kyra standing there with her mother. I dropped my arms from Eli's neck and I tried to get up, but he held me fast.

Kyra turned to her mother, livid. "So. I now see how it is. And you knew it, didn't you, Mother? Whatever possessed you to bring me here? You *wanted* me to walk in on this?"

"I wanted you to see that I was right, Kyra Lynn. He's already got another woman and I was also right about who she is."

Kyra said tightly, "Well, if she really makes him happy, I'm not going to stand in his way. She can have him." She turned like a dancer, graceful and dramatic, and sailed out.

Her mother set after her, scolding, "Kyra, don't you walk away from him like that. Don't you just give up without a fight, do you hear me?"

I hear you, I thought.

I eased out of Eli's lap, shaken and speechless. Now we could hear Kyra's mother's voice through the front window. "If you are to have any chance at all of redeeming this situation, you are going to have to listen to me, and do exactly what I say . . ."

Her voice faded and we didn't hear anything more until we heard the spin of tires in the gravel.

I walked out to the porch to assure myself they were really gone. I couldn't help but wonder if it was my imagination, or had Eli held on to me extra tightly so Kyra would be sure to get a good look at us in that position? And how did Kyra's mother know she'd find Eli and me together this evening?

I looked around for Nick, but he had disappeared.

AND so the scandal, such as it was, went public—apparently some quiet guest of the inn had observed the scene and had informed the right people. Or maybe it was Kyra herself, or her mother. I opened the *Chronicle* one morning and found my own name in print, paired with that of famous local tycoon Eli Larson. Eli was portrayed as a two-timing playboy cad and me as a home-wrecking slut.

And there's some truth in that, I thought miserably.

At first I felt like I'd been punched in the gut. My life seemed to be turned upside down, my privacy shattered. But as the initial shock wore off, I discovered the notoriety was great for business. The inn had acquired instant cachet, now that it was known as the place where the rich and shameless went for trysting. We suddenly had a whole new clientele, more chic, more upscale. It was what I had always wanted.

Bill and Addie seemed a bit dazed by it all, but they took things in stride.

Eli worried that I would be unduly disturbed by the sudden spotlight on my life. He seemed terribly concerned for my well-being, and he warned me not to pay too much attention to gossip or what was written and said about us.

He sent me presents constantly, but there was only the occasional phone call or stray e-mail message from him; for a software magnate, he was oddly inept when it came to using the latest technology himself. He was always losing his phone, or whatever communication device he was currently using, but he called when he could, which was enough for me.

The important thing in all this, the only important thing—he wrote in a rare e-mail one day from Hamburg, where he had gone for an international technology conference—*is you and me.*

I clicked on the next e-mail message and found this one from Zlot67: GOD will Damn you for yout sins you Hwore.

And, from HoMgrrlJEeeP@hotmail.com: There goes another overpaid executive with his trophy girlfriend, dumping the tried and true for the new thang. And you are that. You are it. Girl, why you goin go and let yourself be used like that? You be her awhile, pretty soon u r last yearz model, then what?

The same afternoon I found another note, handwritten on an elegant white card.

For Kelly.
Whenever you need to get away from it all—you can go there fast, in this. Please always come to me.
With my love, Eli

This note was attached to the steering wheel of a sleek Mercedes SL65AMG, which I discovered sitting in the parking area after a small, mysterious box appeared in my office, a box containing a key with the distinguished logo on the keychain, and a little map directing me to walk down into the parking area. There it was, sitting in the shade of the trees, looking smart and sassy, its glossy silver coat and convertible top already peppered with eucalyptus debris.

"I can't accept that car, Eli," I exclaimed when he called me that night.

"Don't you like it?" He sounded hurt. "Is there something you'd rather have? There's this trick BMW you would absolutely love—"

"No, God, no, it's a beautiful car. It's—amazing. But I can't accept it. It's too much. You know I can't."

"Listen," he said. "The deal is done. Your name is on the title."

"I can't, Eli—it's crazy. What am I supposed to say?"

"Say thank you."

"No! I mean, yes, *thank you*, but—what am I supposed to say to my family and friends? How can I explain it? They'll think I'm a drug dealer."

"Tell them it was given to you by an admirer, which is the truth. Hey, if you don't want the car, Kelly, sell it. Push it off a cliff into the ocean. Make it into a planter box. The point is, it's yours. To do with as you will. That's my final word on it."

It was a nerve-racking, heady time, being wooed by a man who was not only immensely wealthy, but generous—as well as funny, handsome, and kind. Physical intimacy was developing between us as we became comfortable with each other, but I still didn't owe Nick that dinner.

For some reason, the spark I had felt with Eli had been the hottest in the beginning days, before he had broken up with Kyra. The irony was not lost on me, but I was confident that we could regenerate the excitement, given the right moment and the proper setting. Because Eli and I lived and worked an hour apart, and because he traveled so much, there was a natural buffering of time and distance between us that worked to our advantage, the way I looked at it, helping us to take it slow and easy, and I reassured myself that was best, if we were to have a future together.

We didn't see much of each other, and I almost worried about how little it bothered me. But in truth, I was enjoying my life. I lived and worked by the ocean, something I had always dreamed of doing. I loved having people around me, and I was growing attached to my little inn family—Addie and Bill; Arturo and his assistant, Juan; the shy young maids, Maria and Irma; sweet, neurotic Grendel; and even icy Anita, who always took care of me even if she didn't seem to like me.

And Nick was often around. I depended upon him more than I wanted to admit; he was always fixing something for me. Always solving some problem. We were back to normal, or at least we pretended to be. Without ever discussing it, we had reached an implicit understanding never to mention what had happened between us the night he returned from the floods.

Eli wanted to fix things for me, too, though on a somewhat different scale. He had seen to it that the inn office was computerized, and we now had a sophisticated, elegant, and easy-to-navigate website. Addie didn't like the computer, and she refused to use it. I decided not to push it; she and Bill would be retiring soon, and I was beginning to realize their handwritten system had an appealing simplicity.

There were other changes, too, because of Eli. We were so busy because of the sudden notoriety that we had to turn many of our old-timers away when they called. The clientele was different, I found, but not necessarily improved. Now there were fewer families and more couples with monogrammed luggage who arrived looking for porters, whirlpool tubs, and full turn-down service. I missed some of the laid-back casualness of the place in its former incarnation.

I knew I needed more help. I couldn't imagine what I was going to do when Addie and Bill retired. I lived in perpetual fear that Anita would suddenly quit.

"No, I'm fine," I assured Eli, when he expressed his concern for me. Things were changing fast, and he knew he was the cause of it. But I wanted him to see I could handle it.

"It's crazy around here," I admitted, "but it's what I've always wanted." I didn't tell him I was beginning to wonder if what I had always wanted was what I really wanted. "Though I do wonder if people aren't coming to the inn now with the wrong expectations . . ."

"What do you mean?" he asked. One thing I liked about Eli, he really listened hard. Sometimes too hard. He wanted to hear me, to understand, and then move to action.

"Well, it's just that a lot of these people get irate if they can't use their computers in their rooms," I told him. "They expect fax machines and we don't even have phones in most of the rooms yet!"

This offhand remark resulted in a team of computer technicians showing up the next day to begin work on an elaborate wiring project, providing every unit with phone service, voice mail, dataport and fax capability, including all the interior wiring and hardware. By now I was becoming accustomed to Eli's magic, and I knew how incredibly lucky I was—more and more guests were expecting such amenities, and I hadn't planned to implement a system like that for at least a year or two. He didn't even give me the opportunity to reject the offer.

But when it was all set and ready to go, the experts couldn't get things up and running until Nick facilitated some necessary exterior electrical wiring, performing the final bit of magic that got it all working.

I was in Cunha's Grocery in Half Moon Bay one afternoon when I encountered Zac—he was just ahead of me in line at the check stand—and I asked him if he wanted a job. It was an odd impulse, given that I didn't quite trust the lad.

"I need help," I explained. "Someone to do small jobs around the inn. You know, like running errands, carrying luggage for the guests, washing windows, that sort of thing. Flexible hours. Fair pay."

"Nah," he said. He shook his head. "I'm not into supporting the commercial establishment. Nothing against you, personally, it's just not where I want to put my energy."

"Okay. Thanks anyway." Just as well, I thought. I didn't know him at all, and he didn't seem like a very good hiring choice to begin with.

The cashier rang up Zac's purchases, a bottle of orange juice and a small notepad.

"Would you be into doing this deal in trade instead of so-called legal tender?" he asked the cashier, a girl of about his own age.

"What?" said the girl, sounding mildly affronted. She was a lush creature with large brown eyes and long auburn hair tied back in a bit of raffia. "Zac, I am not paying for your stuff again."

"You did not pay for my stuff," he replied, indignant. "I traded you two hours of working on your computer. That's a rather good deal."

"Just cough up the dough, Hernandez," said the girl. "There's people behind you."

Hernandez. That was Anita's last name.

Zac Hernandez was about to walk out of the store, when he paused, and as if his early parental training had been so thorough he couldn't help himself, he looked at me and said, "Hey, uh— sorry I can't help you out and thanks for the offer, okay?"

So I finally put it together. Zac was Anita's son. No wonder she had walked out in a huff when I told Paula I didn't trust him . . .

Chapter 19

ELI was out of the country on business and I didn't expect to see him for at least another week, so I was surprised when he called late one afternoon and asked if I was going to be around for a little while.

"I can only stay an hour," he said breathlessly right after he arrived. The sun had set over the sea as he drove to me, and in the gathering twilight he looked romantic and somehow fleeting, like a sailor. I had tried to think of myself as Mrs. Worthington, romantically pining away for her absent man, waiting for his return—but I'd never once had the impulse to go up and pace the widow's walk.

I laughed, amazed at him. "You drove all the way out here for an hour?"

"I *flew* about ten hours out of my way. I had to see you. It's driving me crazy. So . . . I made a slight detour. But I leave for Brussels tonight. Kelly, come with me."

I shook my head. I didn't doubt him anymore when he made fantastic requests like that. *Come with me to Brussels. Tonight.* He was serious. He would welcome me, truly.

But I was needed at the inn; we were already shorthanded. And I didn't *want* to jet off like that, didn't want to leave my work here, not right now. I wanted to be an innkeeper. I wanted to see who my next guests would be. I wanted to work on this funky motel, these quaint cottages, this sweet old Queen Anne farmhouse. I wanted to clear out spent flower beds. I wanted to drink in the sea air and feel the wind off the ocean.

But I wanted a man's hands on me just as badly. I was definitely torn. Or maybe just wearing down. I took his hand in mine. *Let it not be said that I don't know how to appreciate what I am given in this blessed life.*

We drifted without further discussion to my cottage, where he pulled me into his arms, and he was clearly planning to avail himself of my flesh during the scant hour we were allowed, and I couldn't think of any reason why he shouldn't.

We left the lamps on in the cottage glowing softly.

He stripped off his shirt. His skin was golden and gleaming in the muted light. He was a beautiful man. My heart was full of affection for him; my body full of need—but I found the affection and the need somehow disjointed. Physically, I wanted release, and emotionally, I wanted love, and to feel love; I wanted it all to blend in this moment, in this room, in this bed, with this man.

But I wasn't in love with him.

I wanted a man's hands on me, but which man? Was Eli the one? I wasn't sure, and that troubled me.

I'm jumping the gun here, I thought. We're about to make love, and I don't love him. Shouldn't love come first, then lovemaking? *Not necessarily. Not always.* I tried to convince myself it didn't matter—I had never been one to look for more than was actually there, in any relationship. And love grows. Infatuation, in any case, was usually suspect. For now, trust and friendship were enough.

But Eli was clearly of a different mind, and that made it strangely worse. That night for the first time he used the word *love,* repeating, "I love you, I love you so much, I love you, Kelly," over and over as he touched me. Once again, I thought, our timing was off. I wasn't ready to hear it yet.

I began to worry that he might ask me if I loved him. How would I answer that?

Naturally, all this thinking wasn't doing much for the mood. I might not have noticed when the power suddenly went out, had I been more engaged in the moment. But I noticed immediately; we were plunged into complete darkness, and a vague electrical hum I wasn't even aware of suddenly subsided, and all was dark and silent.

"The power just went out," I whispered.

"We don't need electricity," he replied. "We'll make our own."

"*Please,* Eli," I said sharply, pressing down a flare of irritation. "I need to know. Is it a power outage, or is it the electrical supply for the inn? If it's the inn, I need to deal with it."

"Later . . ."

"Let me just check, real quick. It will only take me minute. Then I can relax."

He sighed. "All right."

I buttoned up my blouse and ran outside.

There was a turn in the path where I could see out to the old highway and the faint glow of a lone streetlight. So there was power out at the road. On the hill across the gully, the motel sign glowed neon. Only the house and cottages were dark. I picked my way between the cottages on the unlit path. I came around the corner behind the laundry cottage and was startled to see a disk of light bobbing around at the main electrical panel.

"God, you scared me," I said, laying a hand over my pounding heart.

It was Nick, in silhouette, holding a flashlight, looking into the open panel.

"Was it *you* who turned out the lights, Nick?" I questioned him, only half joking.

"No," he answered curtly. "*I'm* the one who's trying to get them back on."

"What are you doing here, anyway? Isn't it a little late for you to be working?"

"I'm here tonight on pleasure," he said, peering into the electrical box. "Not business. Or so I thought."

"Date with Paula?"

"We're just hanging out."

"Sure."

"I noticed a Lamborghini sitting in the parking lot," he said. He squinted at the breakers lined up inside the panel. "Who drives a Lamborghini, I wonder?"

"Um . . . a guy who doesn't have much time," I said. "Do you have this under control?"

"Do you see any lights on?"

"No."

"There's your answer. Sorry, my sweet. But the two of you don't need lights, anyway, do you?"

"Ha. That's what he said."

Nick clicked something in the panel and a hum rose as the ice machine suddenly kicked on, and light blinked and shone from the old amber fixture under the laundry cottage eave.

"All systems go," he said. "I think."

"Hooray," I cheered. So Nick had gotten things working again. Sometimes I wondered what I'd do without him.

"The strange thing is," he mused, "the electrical appears to have been tripped on purpose."

"On purpose! Why do you say that?"

"It's been . . . what do they say? Tampered with."

"Who would do that?" I looked at him, my brows tense, wondering. Suddenly it struck me: What if he was lying?

But why would he be?

Why would anyone mess with our power?

Most all of my time with Eli must certainly be over by now, and I needed to get back to my room. But I was troubled by the questions this power outage had raised—if it was true, as Nick had suggested, that it had been done maliciously, by human hands—who would do that, and why bother?

What if it was Nick? He, of all people, could have done it with ease. One or two basic maneuvers, and he could plunge the place into total darkness. Then he could claim it had been "tampered with."

But why would Nick do such a thing? What motive could he possibly have?

Jealousy? Resentment?

I thought of his snide tone when he mentioned the car parked out front.

Perhaps Nick resented Eli, simply because Eli was Eli.

Sure, it was possible. But it didn't make sense. I just couldn't see Nick letting it bother him overly much, what wealth or status another man had. And it wasn't like he was jealous of Eli because of *me*—he'd had *that* opportunity himself, and had passed on it.

He closed up the panel and turned to me. "Well, hadn't you better be getting back to him, then?"

"Yes, and I suppose you'd better be getting back to her."

"I suppose."

"Nick, what do you think is going on here?" I blurted out the question, impetuously, seriously. "A tampered-with electrical panel. Rocks through my window. That spiked drink of Paula's . . ."

A muscle clenched in his jaw. "It's probably just coincidence, Kelly."

"What?"

"The things you mentioned. One of the boys probably threw that rock through your window accidentally, and was too scared to fess up. And—"

"The electrical panel? Was that kids, too?"

"I don't know." He looked at me somberly.

We heard a door shut, and a husky female voice calling out for Nick.

"I'm here," he shouted back.

Now came the click, click, click of her shoes and then Paula appeared, strutting along the path in black high heels with the toes cut out, wearing only a long, loosely belted black silk dressing gown.

"Just hanging out, hmm?" I muttered, looking at her.

High heels and a bathrobe? It was over the top, and yet in a weird way the shoes kept her from appearing inappropriately dressed outside in polite company. I truly admired Paula, wearing those shoes. She was a tall woman to begin with, and in her heels she was several inches taller; she didn't seem to give a damn if she towered over a man—or anybody else. She always wore her high heels.

"You were successful," she said to Nick when she caught up to him. She looped her arm through his.

"Yep," I said. "Nick is a handy guy to have around."

"I said we didn't need the lights on anyway," Paula said with a wink at me. "In fact, I preferred the darkness. But he wouldn't listen to me." Her manner was light and easy, and friendly toward me, though she didn't seem to be completely happy with him.

"I think I said the same thing," said Eli, who had suddenly joined us. "But Kelly wouldn't listen to me, either." His shirt was back on, mostly all buttoned up. He had his coat slung over his shoulder.

"Well," Paula said. "Here we are again, the four of us. How does this keep happening?"

"I'm afraid it's only for a moment," Eli said. "I've got to get out of here. I have a meeting in Brussels in a few hours." He sighed, and the regret in his voice was real. "You all be well, now."

I walked him out to the car, and he was his usual gracious, gentlemanly self, though I sensed he was ready to erupt with frustration. We stood a moment beside the car, looking at each other.

"I'm sorry, Eli," I said.

"I shouldn't have been so eager and greedy, anyway," he said with a stressed smile. "When we make love for the first time, it should be relaxed and unhurried, when we have all the time in the world."

"Ah, Eli." I grasped him, and hugged him hard. "Sometimes you know exactly what I need to hear."

I was grateful to him, and relieved we hadn't gone any further. We had the future to look forward to, and I was glad he was such a good sport about it. I felt cheered, and amazed at my good fortune to have found someone like Eli.

But as I walked back to my cottage alone, I looked over at Paula's cottage, knowing Nick was probably in there with her. He might already be running those calloused hands of his over Paula's smooth limbs. Might be pressing his sardonic, sexy mouth on her cherry red lips. Where were her kids tonight, anyway?

I tried to think of Eli, to remember in detail his loving caresses.

Eli shouldn't have left me like that, I decided crossly, contradicting all the nice things I'd thought about him a only few moments earlier. *He should have stayed until he made me his own.*

Nick's truck pulled out of the parking area a few minutes later, and I felt a puzzling relief as I watched the headlights of his truck beaming up the old highway.

If Eli would stop taking no for an answer, I wouldn't be thinking about Nick at all.

With Nick, I explained to myself, it was purely animal attraction that played off my unslakened desires. But deep down I knew I had been relieved that Eli had left when he did. Something was wrong with me. Or maybe I just needed more time.

Beneath (or on top of) everything else, I felt this nagging uneasiness, a constant, low-grade fear, wondering who had tampered with the electrical panel. Who had thrown that rock through my window? Who had sent me those dead black roses? Who had rifled through the missing woman's suitcase and bags in the water tower? Who had drugged my drink?

Who was messing with me, with my inn, and with my mind? And why?

It was about that time I started to question whether my curiosity about the missing woman and the mysterious harassment were somehow related. At first I had assumed the dirty tricks were done by Kyra, or her mother, or some fan of hers and Eli's who didn't like thinking I'd broken up the golden couple; or maybe even some member of the tabloid press, out to incite a story. But after a while I began to wonder . . .

Addie and Bill were away from the inn, and I was busy in the office for several hours, greeting guests, getting them settled in their rooms and cottages.

Night was coming on early these days, and it was dark before

I had finished. I looked up to see Nick coming into the office with some copies of receipts I had asked him to bring me.

"Here you go, boss," he said.

"Thanks, Nick. I appreciate it. I know how you hate anything to do with paperwork."

"You're welcome. I think."

I stopped a moment, listened. "What is that?"

"What?"

"That sound."

It came again, a low call of distress. Nick looked at me.

We walked outside together.

The bawling was louder now, out by Addie's garden.

"It's the calf," Nick said.

"Not *again*."

We found the distressed animal mired in the muddy bog that had once been Addie's prized cutting garden. We'd had a couple of days of rain, and this latest visit from the heifer had pretty much destroyed what was left of Addie's flowers.

"She's stuck in good this time."

"Should we go get Earl?"

"We can deal with this ourselves, I think," Nick said. "If you're game to try."

"Sure I am."

"Where's Addie?"

"She's with Bill, in Carmel. It's their fifty-third anniversary."

"Good. 'Cause this ain't gonna be pretty." He looked at me. "Better take off that purty sweater, darlin'."

I looked down at the green cashmere, an old favorite I'd nicked from my dad. Nick was right. I peeled it off, ran up and tossed it up on the porch, and ran back down to the garden. Beneath the sweater I wore a simple black cotton camisole; with that and my jeans, I was ready for a mudbath.

"You'll freeze in just that," he said disapprovingly, his eyes roving over my suddenly bare skin.

"What about you? Afraid of getting dirty?"

"You think I'm afraid of getting dirty?"

We stepped into the mud and slowly approached the calf. I got ahold of her shoulders while Nick tried to move the bony rear end.

"She's really stuck, isn't she?" I gasped.

"Careful, we don't want to break her leg or something."

"I'm more concerned about my legs than hers, to be honest."

"This is it—heave-ho—"

The astonishingly strong animal threw her head up, and with a plop and a splash, I was suddenly sitting in the mud.

Nick let out a bleat of laughter before he had the presence of mind to shut up. This fired me with fierce determination. I scrambled to my feet, only to slip and fall in again, this time completely into the drink. I was rapidly becoming as mired as the calf. I half sat, half lay in the shallow mud puddle that was once Addie's garden. I looked up at Nick's face and burst out laughing.

Nick let go of the calf and sloshed toward me; he reached down to help me up and I gave him my hand, but when he tried to pull me up he lost his footing, and he slipped, too. With a big muddy slosh and an exaggerated grunt, he landed on top of me.

It was like slow motion, feeling him come down heavy on me, startling, sensational.

"Sorry," Nick murmured, his mouth close to my ear; but for a second or two he just lay on me, letting his heat settle into me, and I felt his heavy body pressed against mine and the mud against my back.

He slowly raised himself above me. As the dark water showered down off his body, he lingered a moment, braced on his taut arms, poised over me like a shelter, looking down into my eyes, staring at me with a look of intense sadness.

And then he was sitting up, and he helped me sit up, giving me his hand. For a moment we sat there in the mud, looking at each other.

"Did you mean to do that?" I asked wryly. "Search and rescue technique?"

He grinned. "Yep. That's how we do it in the field."

We were both drenched and dripping with mud. I was shivering. The calf, spooked by the strange antics of the humans, had pulled herself out of the mud with a squishy sucking sound and loped out of the garden, back home through the latest hole in the fence.

"I don't get how that keeps happening," Nick said with a frown, looking over at the fence. "I thought I fixed up that section of the fence to be ninety-nine percent indestructible last time."

"That cow is one percent smarter than you, N-Nick," I said, my teeth starting to chatter.

"Come on," Nick said. "Let's get you inside." He threw his arm around me, and we helped each other up out of the muddy hole. His body felt hard and slick, sliding smooth against mine as we bumped into each other with the dark, slippery mud all over us. It was like wearing nothing but mud. His hands glided over me, over my back and my arms, as if unable to resist stroking. "You go on inside and get warm," he said, his voice husky. "I'll board up this fence."

I hurried down to my cottage, hoping none of my guests would see me in this condition, covered with mud, shaking with cold.

Reaching my cottage, I kicked off my shoes by the door and reached out for the door handle, and hesitated. The door was ajar.

I had left it closed, and locked.

Well, these old doors didn't always latch properly. I pushed the door open and looked inside, but I didn't step over the threshold.

Someone had been in my room. I was sure of it. I wasn't sure how I knew.

Nick, I thought. I wanted Nick . . .

I turned around quickly and was startled by Nick himself, who had apparently followed close behind me.

"Kelly, what's going on?" he asked, seeing my frightened expression.

"Somebody's been in my cottage," I gasped.

He sheltered me in his arms for a moment, pressing me against his heart. We were both dirty and wet, but somehow he was warm. "How do you know?" he asked.

"It's like . . . it smells different. And the door was open."

"I'll check it out," he said calmly.

"Wipe your feet."

He went inside. It was such a small cottage, it was easy to determine that nobody was in there now.

"The coast is clear," he said.

Tentatively, I walked into the cottage and took a quick inventory. Stereo. Jewelry. Anything of value would have been easy to find and grab.

Nothing was missing.

"What's been taken?" he asked me.

"I don't know," I said. "Nothing, I don't think."

"Then what—"

"That blouse!" I said suddenly. "I didn't put it there. I didn't hang it up on that hook. It was dirty. I left it lying on the floor."

"Okay, I believe you."

"I know that sounds weird. Why would someone come into my house and hang up my blouse? Or you're thinking I just forgot and hung it up, right?"

He didn't answer, walking slowly through the little cottage, looking around like a police inspector.

He's just humoring me, I thought. But I knew something wasn't right. I couldn't get my goose bumps to smooth out, and it wasn't just because I was drenched and cold.

"Kelly," he called out.

He was standing in the kitchen, peering beneath the curtain at the window over the sink. The sash had been jimmied open and the screen was broken.

"Looks like you were right."

"What's that?"

"One of my screwdrivers," Nick answered. "It was lying here on the counter by the broken window."

"They used that to pry open the sash?"

"Looks like it."

"Where'd they get your screwdriver?"

"I guess it wouldn't have been hard for someone to grab one of my tools while I was working around the place. Or maybe I left it lying around."

I shook my head, bewildered. I knew Nick was always very meticulous about putting his tools away at the end of a work day.

"And nothing's been stolen from your cottage?" he asked.

"No, nothing. That's what's creepy about it."

I went to my dresser and grabbed a pair of jeans and a shirt out of a drawer while he stood in the doorway, watching me. "I'm getting out of here," I said. "I'm going to take a shower in Addie's place. Come on, you could use a shower, too."

"What?" He sounded alarmed.

"We'll take turns," I said firmly.

"All right. Let's just get this cottage secured. And I'll make sure that calf can't come back tonight."

After he left, I wondered why he had followed me to my cottage. It was strange; he had been there right when I needed him.

While Nick boarded up the fence, I took a shower in Addie and Bill's apartment, washing off the mud. Standing there beneath the warm spray, I suddenly thought of the infamous Bates Motel—and wondered if a shower was such a good idea after all.

Rinsing off as quickly as I could, I got out of the shower, dressed, and went downstairs. From the lost-and-found basket in the office I dug out a pair of men's sweats, a T-shirt, and a sweatshirt, and I brought them up to the apartment. When Nick came in, I ordered him into the bath. While he was showering I ran downstairs again to help some late-arriving guests.

When I came back up to the apartment, Nick was in the kitchen, out of the shower, damp and clean in the clothes I had given him, assembling the ingredients for a supper of scrambled eggs and toast.

"Better than SpaghettiOs, eh?" He grinned at me.

I turned away, blushing. Ordinarily neither of us made reference to that evening.

Outside, the night was utter darkness, and I pulled the curtains over the windows. Inside it was cozy, and we ate at the kitchen table.

He tried to get me to laugh, but I was a tough sell tonight.

"What is it, Kelly?" he asked later. We were at the kitchen sink, cleaning up after dinner. "You don't want to go back to your own place, do you?"

I shook my head. "No, I don't. I'm going to sleep here in Addie and Bill's tonight. They suggested it anyway, so I could be closer to the front office while they're gone."

"Which anniversary did you say?"

"Fifty-third."

"Wow. That's pretty cool."

"Yeah. They're an inspiring couple."

"Won't be long now till they move out, huh?"

"I know. What am I going to do without them?"

"Are you going to move in here, to the apartment, after they go?"

"I guess."

"You sound thrilled. Why, don't you like puke-colored carpet and baby blue floral wallpaper?"

I smiled. "I'm not worried about that."

His expression changed to one of alarm. "You mean you *like* the wallpaper and the carpet?"

I laughed. "Why, don't you? I've arranged to keep the framed Scottie dog silhouettes, too. Addie didn't want to part with them, but I made her an offer she couldn't refuse."

"Don't worry, Kelly, I'll fix it up really nice for you. We'll strip off the wallpaper, throw down some new flooring. Hang some new windows, put up some nice moldings. Paint the place up."

I nodded. "Yeah, that's what I'm thinking. It'll be okay."

"I mean, look at that view. It's like my house, you know, you can see the bluffs and the mountains, and way down the coast."

"I like your house. It is a lot like the inn, isn't it? Last century."

"You're a little more grand, but yeah. We're the same vintage."

"The inn house is bigger, yes, but yours is all yours. You have your house all to yourself."

"There's room for more," he said, looking at me with a shy smile.

I wondered if he was talking about Paula. Would she move in? Her kids would love Nick's place. We would be neighbors.

"Hey," he said. "Cheer up."

"I'm okay. But who broke into my cottage? And . . . I wonder . . ."

Funny, I thought. I had done everything I could to keep my fears from Eli. Because I didn't want . . . what? I wondered. To burden him? But I was grateful to be able to talk to Nick about it.

"Am I supposed to think it was you?" I asked him.

"Me?" he frowned.

"Why did you follow me up to the cottage? You were going to stay and fix the fence . . ."

"I can't remember," he said slowly. "I think I was going to tell you something. I don't know." He looked at me quizzically. "What are you saying?"

"I'm saying—it points to you. Same with the electrical thing. It could have been *you*, Nick. The screwdriver I found belongs to you. You have the tools, and the skill."

"I have enough skill with the tools that I wouldn't have to make a mess of the window like that, if I wanted to break into your place. I could easily break into any of the cottages or rooms on this property and nobody would be the wiser. And I wouldn't leave my screwdriver behind as a calling card."

"Unless you wanted me to know someone had been there . . . if you had done it deliberately . . ."

"Do you think I'd play those kind of games?" he asked with a sigh.

"No. But . . . it's funny. So many things seem to point to you, and yet I . . ."

"What?" he asked faintly.

"I just have this feeling of trust when I'm with you," I said, my voice quiet. "It's like something you said to me once. I feel like I shouldn't trust you . . . but I do."

"Hey, there, Kelly," he said. "You're not alone here, you know." He pulled me into an embrace. He offered comforting shelter, and for a moment I closed my eyes and let him support me. But only for a moment.

We went into the living room. I covered the parakeets' cage for the night, and we settled down to watch an old movie on TV.

SOMETIME during the night I woke up in Bill's recliner, wrapped in Addie's pink and white afghan. Nick was asleep on the couch. He looked sweet and vulnerable, which was not how I usually thought of him. I covered him with the afghan and went into the bedroom and lay down on the bed.

Nick spent the entire night on Addie and Bill's lumpy couch. I knew he had stayed to make me feel safe. I woke at six and checked on him. He was still there, sleeping. I went back to bed, got up at seven, and he was gone. But from the window I could see his truck was still sitting in the parking area.

I went out on the deck, leaned over the railing, and caught sight of him down on the beach, standing with his arms raised to the sky, looking south. He lowered his arms, then flung something into the wind, yellowish powder, sand, or crumbs of some sort. I cocked my head, trying to figure out what he was doing.

He turned to face the west, raised his arms, and did the same thing, flinging the crumbs. Then he turned to face the north, and repeated the ritual.

He turned to the east, and suddenly he seemed to notice me, standing above him, leaning over the balcony railing, watching him. He didn't break his rhythm, or if he did, he flowed back into it, regaining it so neatly, I hardly had time to notice.

He finished, lowering his arms and pressing his palms together.

I realized, awkwardly, that he was making his morning prayers. I moved away from the railing and went inside. I uncovered the parakeets' cage and gave them fresh food and water. I put on coffee and Nick came up the stairs. He was still wearing the sweats and T-shirt I'd found for him in the lost-and-found basket. I wore Addie's flowered bathrobe and my feet were bare.

We ate a simple breakfast of coffee and toast, and a perfect pink grapefruit we cut in half and shared. There was something homey about us, comfortable and easy.

As Nick was leaving, Grendel came down to the house to get his lunch.

Grendel, ever the perceptive one, cast me a questioning look.

"Yes," I teased him in a low voice when we were alone in the office. "Nick spent the night. And I'm not charging him."

Grendel looked stunned. "Sorry, Kelly, it's just that I thought it was . . . Eli Larson."

"I'm messing with you, Gren," I said with a laugh. "Nick slept on Addie's couch. I took the bedroom."

He seemed embarrassed, and I was sorry I'd said anything. "Someone was in my room yesterday evening," I hastened to explain. "I was kind of upset about it, and Nick hung out to watch over me."

"Nice of him," Grendel murmured. "But what do you mean, someone was in your room?"

"Someone broke into my cottage. Nothing was stolen, but things were moved around. And Nick's screwdriver was lying there, by the window, which was broken—"

"Let me get this straight. The window was broken. With Nick's screwdriver." His expression was stern. "And you picked Nick to watch over you?"

He didn't scold me, but his expression was enough.

Chapter 20

I was glad to be getting away for a few days, and I was indebted to Addie and Bill for letting me take the time off. To my family, too, who weren't too happy about me missing Thanksgiving dinner.

Strange to remember back to Nick's challenge, months earlier—I had accepted the proposal so blithely, never seriously imagining this outcome. But here I was on my way to Eli's ski house for a couple of days, and I knew that sometime during the weekend winter wonderland, sex was supposed to happen. We had taken it slowly, but even so, the time had come. Eli was ready, and I thought I was getting there, too.

Sitting beside Eli in his Gulfstream jet on the way to Aspen, I thought about how it would be when we returned, two or three days hence. I would finally have something to say to Nick, if he were to ask if I owed him a dinner. Not that he would ask; he hadn't brought it up in a long time. And I realized, as I considered this future conversation, that I dreaded the idea of finally confessing the thing.

But why? I should be proud to have a lover like Eli. He seemed to be all things a man should be, and he was good to me. Most of the world thought we had already done the deed. Nick would figure out how things were, eventually, whether I said anything about it or not. Eli was already talking about us living together.

But the idea of going to Nick and claiming some sort of victory had a hollow feel to it. It wasn't respectful of Eli, for one thing. Eli had been more of an abstraction when I'd made that silly pact with Nick. Eli was a fully dimensional person to me now, and he was my friend.

But the truth was, I just didn't *want* to tell Nick. I didn't want to talk to him about it. Which was weird, because we used to be able to talk about anything together. But now a certain politeness had grown up between us, and it had the effect of closing off certain topics.

Then I began to notice that Eli was acting strange. The closer we got to our destination, the more moody and tense he became.

THE Aspen house was huge and magnificent, a log cabin fit for a king. The sheer scale of it was impressive and daunting, like a medieval castle, built stout for defense. Immense iron and antler candelabrum hung suspended on chains from painted ceilings supported by immense timbers. The paneled walls and floors had been polished until the wood gleamed like sun shining through honey.

High transom windows of stained glass over larger panels of clear glass opened up endless views in every direction. All the rooms were furnished and decorated in a style that combined rustic cabin-in-the-woods styling with posh comfort.

Like Nick, Eli had an impressive display of authentic Native American artifacts. In fact, if quantity and dollar amount was the standard of value, Eli's things were more impressive than Nick's, with Pueblo pottery, woven baskets, Navajo rugs, and antique Hopi Kachina dolls displayed in glass cases. When I commented on his collection, Eli waved it off. These beautiful objects didn't seem to interest him, except as finishing touches on his architectural masterpiece. He told me his interior designer had chosen and purchased each item, and that he considered fine Native arts a good investment.

"That thing up there on the top shelf?" he said, indicating a lovely and intricate woven basket. "That's already made me about thirty-five thousand dollars. Which doesn't begin to offset the cost of this cozy chalet, but what the hell."

"Cozy chalet." I laughed drolly. We had it all to ourselves, Eli and me, all twenty bedrooms.

"I'VE had two rooms made up for us," Eli had said when we arrived. "But I don't think I've made any secret of the fact that I'd rather share just one bedroom with you."

I ignored the vague apprehension creeping over me, knowing that simply by being there with him, I was accepting certain terms. He had been patient with me, and would be patient longer, if need be, but I had no desire to lead him on.

I replied, "I had been thinking that maybe one room would be enough."

"There is something I need to talk to you about, Kelly, before you decide," he said slowly.

Oh boy, I thought. What's this?

"Come sit with me."

He led me through the house to an enclosed sunporch, a well-appointed room with retractable glass walls to show off the spectacular views in any kind of weather.

Gazing out at the snowy mountains, I thought of Nick's glassed-in porch overlooking the ocean. Eli's place was much bigger and more sparkling and spacious and up-to-date, with a state-of-the-art entertainment center hidden in some rustic cabinetry. But Nick's place was cozy, and with the old square windowpanes that framed views of the sea, it was like being inside a ship riding over the waves . . .

We sat down and Eli was silent, staring out the window, his arms draped around me. Whatever happened between us, I thought, I was certain of his genuine affection for me. And mine for him. So what could it be?

"This isn't easy for me, Kelly."

I waited, nervous.

"Kelly, I know you've talked about not wanting marriage, or children . . ."

Oh my God, I thought. He's not going to propose! It would never have occurred to me, but his timing had been off before . . .

"Do you still feel that way?"

"I always thought I would never want either," I said carefully. "Marriage or children. I still can't imagine either any time soon, but it's funny—lately it's not so distasteful to me, the idea of it all, as it once was—"

"I'd like to think that's because of me," Eli said.

"Probably just my biological clock alarm going off. Breed before it's too late, you know?" I tried to get him to laugh, but he stayed steady and serious, and pulled me into his arms.

"Whatever the reason, Kelly, I'm glad to know it. If you would just consider the possibility . . ."

"Well, sure. Like I said, it's something I've been thinking about lately, getting to know Paula's kids, and wondering what it might be like to have my own family. I guess I'll have to give it some time, see if it's not just some passing thing, but—"

"Kelly, we might not have all the time we need."

"What do you mean? What is this all about, Eli?"

He loosened his hold on me, sober, and searched my face. "Kyra says she might be pregnant," he said.

The sound I let out was something between a howl of despair and a hoot of laughter.

"She called me just before we left for Aspen, said she had something to tell me. I was blindsided."

"How far along is she?" I inquired, my voice surprisingly steady.

"I don't know. Not very, I guess." Eli took my hand. "Look, Kelly, it wouldn't surprise me a bit if this is a false alarm. Kyra tends to be nothing if not melodramatic, and it isn't beyond her to grow something in her own mind. I know it sounds serious, and maybe it is. But I think we need to take a wait-and-see attitude here."

A wait-and-see attitude. Huh, I thought. Was it something growing in her mind—or in her belly? Big difference there.

It was disturbing to think that he must have been having intimate relations with Kyra even after he had claimed to have fallen for me. I had assumed he had stopped having sex with her, and he had led me to believe this was so. Hadn't he? But it was hardly surprising that he had been with her. He was living with her at the time, sleeping with her every night, probably, and *I* hadn't promised him anything. We weren't committed to each other then.

We aren't committed to each other now, I reminded myself. I knew *I* hadn't made any commitments.

"Tell me it doesn't matter," he said urgently, squeezing my hands. "Tell me whatever happens with Kyra, it won't change anything with us."

"But it *will*, Eli. It would *have* to. You would want to raise that child with her, wouldn't you?"

He looked at me, distressed, and he hesitated as if afraid of giving the wrong answer. "Yes." He nodded. "Yes, I would."

"Of course you would. It's your *child*. And that would affect my life, if you and I were together. And you would be tied to Kyra forever. That changes everything."

"I know. Look. We can work this out, no matter what, but let's just wait and see what happens. Okay?"

"Okay," I agreed. There was nothing else to be done, in any case. We let the subject drop and neither of us mentioned it again that weekend. We pretended it wasn't hanging there between us, and we had fun together and played and cuddled and though we did sleep together, that was about all we did in bed together—sleep.

ELI drove into the yard at the inn and parked. We sat there in the showy red Ferrari, silent for a moment. The weekend had left both of us feeling wrung out. The trip had been exciting and glamorous, and the scenery spectacular, but I had missed my family on Thanksgiving, and I felt stalled with Eli.

"All your other cars are silver," I said with a yawn. "Even your motorcycle is silver. Why is this one red?"

"Because it's a *Ferrari*."

"Ah. I see."

"When can I start referring to you as my girlfriend?" he asked me suddenly.

The question made me laugh.

"You're murdering me, Kelly," he said. "You know that."

"Eli, what are you asking of me?"

"Tell me you won't see anybody else but me." He fumbled

under his seat, and in the darkness I saw him open a small box. He took my left hand.

"I want to give you this."

He was attempting to thrust a ring onto my finger.

I stilled his hand and put in on myself.

I lifted my hand and gazed at it, adorned as it was now, with a giant ivory pearl in an antique gold setting. It was beautiful, in a dazzling, decorative way. The idea of wearing such a thing seemed impractical, but receiving it as a gift had certain attractions all the same. It was obviously valuable, and pretty, if rather out of its element on my work-roughened hand.

"I want you to accept it," he said petulantly, as if afraid I wouldn't. I realized then that I shouldn't.

I looked at the ring, troubled. If I accepted it, I would be agreeing to a commitment. Was I ready for that?

Yet if I refused to take the ring, I would be rejecting Eli, and I wasn't prepared to do that, either. I wanted the relationship to continue, to see where it might lead . . . to see if this new desire of mine for a family of my own would develop into something real, something that had to do with Eli. I wanted to wait, to see if Kyra was pregnant, and whether or not it would make any difference . . .

Eli's timing, again, was off. Or maybe it was just me.

"Please, Kelly, take it. Do whatever you want with it." He sounded tired.

"It's beautiful, Eli," I said, kissing his cheek.

I returned to find the inn plunged in mourning. While I was gone, Addie's parakeets had disappeared. They had flown the coop, literally. Addie was so upset, she could hardly talk about it. Grendel filled me in on what had happened. On the Saturday after Thanksgiving, the weather had been so mild and warm that Addie had put the birdcage outside. Bill had installed a hook in a sheltered spot just outside the kitchen door just so she could hang the cage there. The parakeets seemed to like it.

But later on Saturday afternoon, when Addie went to bring them inside, she found the cage door open and the parakeets gone. She was always so careful, it was almost certain someone had deliberately let the birds out, either to steal them or to set them free.

"I like to think the birds might have been set free," Grendel confided to me at happy hour on Monday. "I never liked seeing those birds in that little cage."

I thought of Addie's fat, pampered blue parakeets, and the coming winter, and said nothing.

"So how was your Thanksgiving weekend?" he asked. "Wasn't that Eli who dropped you off last night?"

"Yes, we've been seeing a bit of each other," I said evasively.

I didn't tell him about Aspen. I wanted to change the subject. I made him tell me all about the special Thanksgiving feast Arturo had prepared for the inn. Though he hadn't been able to eat much of it himself because of his strict diet, Grendel told me in detail about each dish that had been laid out on the sideboard for guests and staff in the large formal dining room.

While Grendel and I were talking, Nick had come up the steps to the porch and was now helping himself to some crackers and cheese. I thought of the last time I'd seen him, the morning after he'd slept on the lumpy couch in Addie's living room, just to make me feel safe. Or maybe he had simply fallen asleep and was too lazy to get up. I thought of Grendel's expression when I had told him about finding Nick's screwdriver near the broken window, and I wondered, again—should I be more afraid of Nick than I actually was?

"So tell me about your weekend, Kelly," Grendel prodded.

And why didn't he say hello?

"What?" I turned to Grendel.

"I want to hear all about your big weekend."

"Oh, well . . ."

"Grendel, can you help me?" Addie called from the office. "Bill's got cactus thorns stuck in him again!"

"Duty calls!" Grendel said with a laugh, and he left Nick and me alone on the porch together.

"Well, don't you want to hear about my weekend in Aspen?"

"Uh . . . sure," Nick said.

"Ski cabin. Palace. Huge beams, stone fireplaces, trees, snow. The whole bit. Very romantic."

He scratched vigorously at the back of his neck, staring out at the ocean. "You can skip the details."

"He asked me if I wanted to share a bedroom."

"Why don't you just cut to the chase?" Nick's voice was cool, but he couldn't hide the fact that he was curious.

"But then he says, before I decide, there's something he has to tell me."

Nick looked at me intently. "What?"

"Kyra says she's pregnant."

He winced. "Whoa. With Eli's kid, I take it?"

"Yes, that's the idea."

"Wow. I guess that's the last thing you want to hear. You don't even want kids."

"Well, it does complicate things, doesn't it? If it is a sure thing."

"Is it? A sure thing?"

"Eli doesn't seem to think so, but . . . I guess we'll see."

Nick reached out and touched my shoulder, a sympathetic caress. His hand dropped away slowly, his fingers brushing lightly down my arm. It was weird how his touch always made me want to lean against him, purring and arching my body like a cat.

"I'm sorry, Kelly," he said. "You know I don't wish you any pain."

"But you know, Nick, I find the idea of having a child doesn't seem as foreign to me as it once did. For the first time in my life, I'm actually thinking that having a baby in my life might be . . . nice."

He said guardedly, "Maybe it's the perfect thing for you, Kelly. A child you wouldn't have to see all the time."

"Sounds pretty pathetic when you put it that way! Actually, to tell you the truth, Nick, it's been bothering me to think that if it does come to pass, and Eli is a dad, the child wouldn't be *mine*. I've actually been feeling sort of jealous of that."

"Well, I guess it's only natural for you to feel jealous of Kyra, if she's having a baby with Eli, if you and Eli are, uh . . . together."

"Yeah, I know. But that's not what I meant. I think I'm having baby envy. I've been thinking I might want a child of my own, Nick. Someday. I never thought I did, but I'm beginning to think maybe I do."

"Are you serious?" He let out a short laugh, like he thought I was joking with him.

"Yes. I'm serious. And it's like, I'm suddenly seeing the whole thing, how it could be. Having a kid, raising a family, marriage, the whole bit."

"Your eyes are shining, woman," he said, and looked away, scowling.

I've embarrassed him, I thought.

He glanced at me again. "This is all about Eli, isn't it? This sudden, um, change of heart?"

"He thinks it's all grown out of my feelings for him." I smiled, thinking of Eli with affection. "But I don't really know."

"My guess is, it's all grown out of your increasing awareness of Eli's net worth."

"Yeah, that's it." I laughed, but I felt offended. My feelings were hurt, but I decided to pass the comment off as a joke.

And yet his dark expression made it difficult to take the comment lightly. And he went on: "How quickly we throw away our convictions and sell out when it comes to the almighty dollar—"

"Is that really what you think?" I cut in, incredulous.

"Well, it *is* rather a coincidence that you're suddenly thinking about marriage and children, don't you think? Hey, don't look like that. All's fair in love and war, right? And you're certainly not the first gold digger that got herself a rich chump."

"I am not a gold digger and Eli is not a chump." I was barely able to get the last word out. I set my wineglass down on the table and walked away from him.

TEARS burned in my eyes as I climbed the path toward the cypress wood. I was so hurt, and angry. At Nick, yes, but mostly at myself.

Why should I give a damn what Nick thinks? I asked myself in frustration. I know my motives are innocent. I know my motives are pure.

Didn't I? Weren't they?

I caught sight of someone moving along the path near the top of the hill. Idly, I looked up to see a woman with tight carrot-colored curls cut close to her head, and a soft, rounded body in a short, pale, flower-print dress. She had a determined, jaunty air. I knew I had seen her before, but I didn't remember her checking into the inn.

She surprised me by walking up and knocking on the door of Grendel's cottage. She waited a moment, then opened the door and went inside. I knew Grendel was still in the office with Addie, and for a moment I wondered if I should warn him that somebody had just gone into his place. But there was nothing furtive about the woman's behavior, and she looked harmless enough. In my own turmoil, I forgot all about her and continued briskly up toward the woods.

Nick came after me to apologize. I heard him behind me as I walked along the cliff path.

"Hey, hey—come here," he called after me. "Hey. I'm sorry, Kelly."

He caught me by the arm and turned me around to face him. "Forgive me."

"It's okay," I mumbled, easing out of his grasp.

"No, it's not. I was way out of line. First off, any guy who gets you is no chump. Second—"

"Shh, Nick." I put my fingers against his lips for a brief moment. "The worst thing is," I said, "I wonder if maybe you're right. It's hard to think straight sometimes. Maybe the money *has* influenced me. Maybe it has. I can't say I haven't thought about the money, daydreamed about what it might be like. But I really don't think it's about the money. It's something else."

I looked out toward the headlands to the north, frowning. "As a matter of fact, it was when I was watching you with Paula and her boys, walking down to the beach one day, that I first realized I felt this . . ."

"What?"

"I don't know. Almost a jealousy. Like I suddenly wanted something I'd never wanted before. It was just never something I desired. I never thought I'd need or want a family of my own, but maybe I do. Maybe I do want that." I turned and looked straight at him, expecting him to laugh at me.

He was staring at me strangely, as if I were someone he didn't quite recognize.

"What?" I asked.

He didn't answer.

"Nick?"

"Yeah, so, um . . . so Eli might be a father. And you think you might want to be a mother. I—I wish you well, Kelly."

"Well, I'm going to see what happens. If she's not pregnant, it's not an issue, and life goes on, and if she is . . . we'll see."

"No chance you'll stop seeing him, then?"

"Why, because his ex might be pregnant?" I pondered the question, not for the first time. "Well, *you're* seeing someone who is a parent, aren't you? It's not stopping *you*."

"And you're not going to let it stop you."

"No, I don't think it would stop me, not if—not if I really wanted the guy."

"And you really want the guy? Forever and always?" Nick's voice curved up into a question.

I didn't answer at once. Put that way, I couldn't wholeheartedly say yes. Not that I would say no, either. I just hadn't been with Eli long enough to know. But the desire had been awakened, for something. And that something was new for me. Maybe that's just what happens when you meet the right person, I thought. I struggled to explain it. For some reason it was important to me that Nick understand.

"I'm not sure about Eli," I admitted. "I'm not sure about any of it. But it's only natural that I might change my mind about wanting kids, isn't it? I'm only human. Do you think it's crazy? That I could change my mind like that?"

"No. I don't think it's crazy," he said quietly. "After Juliet left me, I was sure that I was never going there again. Never getting married again. Ever. That's what I thought then."

"What do you think now?"

"Now? Let's just say I understand how you can change your mind about certain things."

"Ah," I said. "So how are things with Paula? You really like her, huh?"

He nodded, thinking about it. "Yes, I like her."

I couldn't bring myself to ask him if he owed me that dinner. I was afraid that he might just owe it to me by now, and I didn't want to know. Didn't want to hear it.

He guessed what I was thinking. "So, Kelly," he said softly. "Would you like to raise the stakes, as we once discussed?"

I knew what he was talking about. Not merely bedding Eli or Paula. But marrying them. It sounded absurd, but being Eli's girl-friend once seemed absurd too.

Nick's phone began ringing in his pocket. He pulled it out and looked at the screen. "I gotta take this one, Kelly," he said, and answered the phone. "Yeah?"

I watched him.

"Okay. I'll be there in twenty minutes . . . Yeah. Later."

He shoved the phone in his pocket and looked at me. "Missing hikers. Couple of kids, teenagers, down near Big Basin."

I nodded, solemn. "Kids, huh?"

"Don't worry. They'll probably walk into camp before I get there," he said. "They'll be starved. We'll bring chocolate."

"Do you want to bring your father's compass?" I asked him. "I'll get it for you . . ."

"No. Hang on to it for me until I see you again."

WAITING to find out if Kyra was really pregnant, sometimes it struck me as ridiculous. If I truly loved Eli, it didn't matter. And if I didn't love Eli, then it didn't matter, either!

But I kept worrying at the problem. Especially late in the evening, when the guests were all tended to, and I was alone in my cottage.

We needed to see each other more often, I decided on one of those lonely nights. There was too much "out of sight, out of mind" in this relationship. And that was my fault. He was always asking to see me. Usually, that meant he was offering up some sort of luxury transportation to bring me to wherever it was on the planet he happened to be doing business.

On impulse, I opened the top drawer of my dresser. I needed to see Eli's face again. I'd taken some photos on our trip to Aspen— I had some good shots of him on the computer in the office, but for the moment the newspaper portrait would do.

I reached into the drawer and pulled out the picture, looked down on it, and nearly dropped it.

The spot I had first noticed as a small dot on Eli's forehead had somehow spread over his entire body, like some sort of acid, and it had completely eaten away the image of his face.

Chapter 21

NEVER one to let myself rise on flights of fancy (or so I kept telling myself) I could not help but allow into my thoughts the possibility of supernatural forces at work in the dark corners of this creaky old collection of cottages. Of course I sought a natural explanation—that some sort of corrosive liquid had spilled on the paper—but it seemed to me that if this were the explanation, the damage would have been done almost at once, and would not continue on slowly like this, week after week.

Perhaps one of the maids—Anita, for example—had come into my room to vacuum, and had decided to vandalize Eli's photo. Just to mess with me. But why go to the trouble?

And my mind would wander again to the realm of malignant spirits and demons. People throughout history have believed in such beings, and I was beginning to understand why.

But after considering the situation, I became convinced that I was the victim of a systematic, deliberate attempt to terrify, and that my tormentor was a corporeal, flesh and blood human being. And my fear crystallized into anger, along with a determination to beat this opponent at his—or her—own game.

I was torn between tactics. My impulse was to gather Addie and Bill and our staff in a meeting, lay it all out before them, and demand cooperation in apprehending the culprit. But I was stymied by the nature of the problem. A photograph with a growing spot? A broken window sash? A rock through a window? *Please.* They would think their boss was mad. Or at least paranoid.

"It's getting to me, guys," I admitted one morning when both Grendel and Bill happened to be in the office with me and nobody else was around. "The electrical panel was tampered with deliberately. Somebody threw a rock in my window, and one of our guests thought her wine had been drugged. I got a delivery of dead flowers with a threatening note—"

"Jesus!" Grendel exclaimed.

"And somebody opened the birdcage and let the birds go," Bill added somberly. "Not to mention that calf getting loose—"

"Yes." I nearly laughed out loud, I was so relieved they didn't just scoff at me.

Bill was clearly angry. "Not only that, but I've had the distinct impression someone's been sneaking around the place at night," he growled.

"Really?" I was surprised to hear this, and puzzled by his vehemence.

"This is an inn we're running here," he said. "I realize people wander about at all hours; that's fine. But on more than one occasion, I've heard noises, and gone out to see who's out there, and—there's no one!"

"Maybe the place is haunted!" I gave way to laughter. "Mrs. Worthington pacing the widow's walk, scanning the horizon, waiting for her husband, who will never come home."

"Aye," Bill said, nodding, " 'tis probably the unhappy lady herself causing the problems. We've been neglecting her, I fear, and she doesn't like it one bit! Besides which, you know, she hates change." Bill's anger faded as his natural showmanship took over. Try to seek out some information about a real-life missing woman, I thought, and nobody wanted to talk; but people did seem to love a ghost.

BILL knocked on my cottage door that evening. He had a look of mild embarrassment on his face and a baseball bat in his hand. "Kelly," he said, "I'm not one for keeping guns around—too many innocents get hurt accidentally, you know—but I'd feel better if you'd at least keep *this* in your room. Who knows? Might be some protection for you."

He held out the baseball bat and I accepted it gravely, touched by his thoughtfulness. "Thanks, Bill," I said. "I'll keep it right beside my bed."

IT was good to think I had Grendel and Bill in my confidence. But I decided to take it a step further. The next afternoon I went into the police station in town. When I saw Bernie behind the desk, I wanted to turn around and go home. Something about him bothered me. But I was there, and he'd already seen me come in. I sat down with him and told him about all the things that had been happening to me.

He didn't laugh at me, as I half expected he would. In fact, he seemed very interested.

"A stalker, huh?"

"Well, I'm not sure if—"

"Listen, in your position, that's not something to be surprised at, is it?"

My position?

He shook his head and then resumed writing. "Guy like Eli

Larson might have to consider an increased security presence. Might provide the same for the, uh, little lady in his life."

I sighed. I suppose it wasn't unexpected that he knew about me and Eli.

I couldn't figure out what it was about him, but I really wished I hadn't come to the police station. By the time we were finished I felt I had wasted both my time and his. And to be fair, what did we have to go on? A bunch of random weird events.

Maybe Bernie was right. Maybe it just went with the territory when you lived in an inn and were dating a famous and rich play-boy tycoon.

"Before I go," I said, "I was wondering. Have you made any progress on the case of the woman who disappeared several years ago? Alicia St. Claire?"

"Well, as I think I told you before, it was concluded that the woman was running from creditors, not bad guys. Not to say that nothing bad happened to her, necessarily, but if something happened, it might very well be out of our jurisdiction anyway. The woman was a transient."

"Did she leave any family behind, or—"

"Look, that's all I can tell you. I suggest you ask Nick McClure, if you want to know more about her."

"Nick?"

"On second thought, maybe you'd be better off avoiding the subject all together. Seriously." He laid his hand on my shoulder. "Let it go. No sense dwelling on bad times. The people around here are trying to forget. This place doesn't deserve that kind of reputation, and you don't want to stir it up."

He would say no more about Nick or the missing woman, but he did promise increased police presence in the neighborhood.

*　　　*　　　*

I walked into my cottage after meeting with Bernie and immediately I was beset with the feeling again: Somebody had been in my place. There was an actual scent in the air, and it was a scent I recognized. Like cinnamon and flowers. But it was subtle and I couldn't think of why it seemed familiar.

I threw open a window, and I saw the paper on my bed.

I grabbed it up and saw it was a note, printed from a computer. *Kelly, I know you're scared. This will help.* At the bottom of the note was a Web address.

I went over to the office, sat down at the computer, clicked onto the Internet, and typed in the address. I was so startled by what came up on the screen, I literally jumped back in my chair. The first three words were printed in all caps, twenty-point boldface type and bright red.

FOR EMERGENCY SITUATIONS:

BEFORE PROCEEDING FURTHER

IF THE PERSON HAS DIED, COOL HIS OR

HER HEAD IMMEDIATELY!

FILL A PLASTIC BAG WITH ICE, CRUSHED

ICE, OR WATER ICE

COVER THE FRONT, TOP, BACK, AND SIDES OF THE PERSON'S HEAD COMPLETELY

CLICK HERE if death HAS NOT YET OCCURRED

CLICK HERE if the person HAS DIED ALREADY

For a moment I sat there stunned. I read it again.

I didn't know what to do. There were no other identifying notes on the screen.

My hand was trembling on the mouse.

There was only one link at the bottom of the page: *Home.*

I clicked on it.

*   *   *

My heartbeat began to calm down some as I navigated through what appeared to be a website for a legitimate cryonics facility near San Jose.

I had to give the opponent points for originality. This was terrifically creepy and yet so simple. Direct someone you want to freak out to a webpage that pops up on your screen with horrifying words in big red and black letters. Doesn't cost you a thing, and yet it's very effective.

I read through the home page of the website, horrified and fascinated.

Cryonics is the widely misunderstood practice of using cold temperature to preserve human life. Cryonics strives to maintain the body until such time as the preservation process can be reversed, and the patient restored to full health. At this date, reversible cryonic suspension for adult humans is only a goal. But human embryos in cryostasis have been restored and went on to become living, breathing people. That was unthinkable only a few years ago.

There was a list of prices and descriptions of services. Facts about Cryonics. Cryonics Myths and Misperceptions. Nanotechnology and Science. There was a photographic tour of the facilities, and photos of the facilities manager, and the president of the organization, Charles Shannon, M.D. Both rather average, normal-looking guys. There were even photos of the cryostats, the containers where the "patients" were stored in liquid nitrogen. They looked like industrial shipping containers.

So who left the note directing me to this website?

Who was doing this to me? I wondered.

Kyra, I thought.

But was it really Kyra? I kept thinking about how it seemed that the more I asked about Alicia St. Claire, the more strange and threatening things happened. When I went to the police, I had come home to this latest prank.

I went back to the website and got the phone number and name of one of the contacts at the cryonics facility and made a phone call, asking for Dr. Shannon.

"I'm sorry, Dr. Shannon is out at the moment," said a woman's voice. "May I give him a message?"

"I'm calling in regards to woman named Alicia St. Claire."

I heard a weary sigh. "Yes? How may I help you?"

"I wondered what connection she might have with Dr. Shannon and your, uh, organization."

"I'm sorry, we cannot give information about our patients."

I felt a thrill of excitement. "So she *is* a patient of yours?"

"I'm sorry. I can't release that information."

"Are you aware Alicia St. Claire disappeared from the Half Moon Bay area three years ago?"

"There is no one by that name under our care," she interrupted me sharply. "I hope that's enough to satisfy you, because that's all I can tell you."

I kept thinking about it. I wanted to pursue this further, but Eli was taking me to a party in the city that evening; he was coming to pick me up in an hour, and I was trying to get some chores done. I asked Arturo to help me move a heavy table out of the entry hall.

"*Es muy* . . . How do you say *heavy*?"

"*Pesado,*" he said.

"*Pesado,*" I repeated. "*Es muy pesado.* What's that down there?" On the floor where the table had been was a scrap of yellowed newsprint.

Arturo bent down to pick it up. He looked at it and then handed it to me.

It was the second half of the newspaper story I had found earlier about the missing woman.

SEARCH SUSPENDED (from page 2)

they expressed concern for a possible drowning.

A local contractor, Nick McClure, was held briefly for questioning on Tuesday. According to sources in the police department, McClure was found in a room at the inn with the manager of the inn's housekeeping staff, Anita Hernandez, and a large amount of cash. McClure, who is responsible for maintenance on the inn property, was reportedly romantically linked with the missing woman.

Police are asking the public to call with any information regarding the disappearance of Alicia St. Claire.

I stared at the words, rereading them again. And again.

Nick? I thought. Nick was "romantically linked with the missing woman." What did that mean?

I knew what it meant.

. It shouldn't have surprised me. Especially after Bernie's comment. It shouldn't surprise me, I repeated to myself. But I felt shocked.

I heard Addie's voice in the office, and that of another woman. Maxine.

But wouldn't Nick have told me, if he had been going out with Alicia?

Looking up from the clipping, I saw Arturo watching me.

"Thank you, Arturo," I said. "That's all I needed."

*   *   *

"WELL, yes," said Maxine. She glanced at Addie. They both seemed uneasy. "It was Nick she was seeing. Among others."

I should have guessed. And Nick should have told me himself.

I said, "Is that why Earl didn't think Nick should be helping out with the search?"

"Earl was suspicious of Nick. Still is. Thinks he's up to no good."

"What do *you* think?"

Maxine rubbed her eyes as if she were tired. "I think maybe they're somewhat alike, in certain ways. I like Nick. I'd like to think he's good people. But I can't tell you, 'cause I just don't know for sure."

"What do *you* say, Addie?" I asked her.

"I—I didn't know!" Addie replied, flustered. "I didn't realize they'd dated. I thought they were just friends."

"But you knew what was in this newspaper story, didn't you?" I said. "This clipping came from your scrapbook, didn't it?"

"Well, yes," she admitted guiltily. "But I just can't believe that Nick . . . that he'd do anything to hurt anyone."

Me neither. Or maybe I just didn't want to believe that of him. Not for the first time, I wondered about Nick. Something was going on with him.

I can't trust him, I thought.

I ought to avoid him altogether.

Was he the one shutting off the electricity? Throwing rocks through my window?

I'll stop calling him for work. I'll ask Paula not to see him here.

BUT it was no use. Nick was too strong a presence for me to simply turn him off like that. Thirty minutes after my big decision, I changed my mind. I would go ask him what the hell was going on.

I found him down on the beach, throwing the Frisbee for his dogs. He wore faded jeans low on lean hips, and only a thin T-shirt on this cool, bright December afternoon. He moved with a careless, lanky grace, flinging the disk, and the baseball cap he wore got knocked askew and fell to the ground as he ran, releasing a handful of unruly dark curls. His hair was getting long again.

He swiped his cap up from the sand.

I marched toward him and confronted him directly. I held up the snippet of newspaper clipping.

He jammed his hat back on his head and stood there a moment, his eyes scanning the clipping. It seemed to take him some time to figure out what he was looking at. Admittedly, it was the second half of a three-year-old news story. But he didn't have to ask what it was.

"So you were seeing her."

He handed it back to me and said, "We went out."

"Why did you hide this from me?"

He shrugged it off. "Anything I could have said to you about it would only have made it sound even more bizarre than it was, Kelly."

"Bizarre, how?"

"Not bizarre. I mean, coincidental. You being so interested in her . . ."

"And what about this? You and Anita alone in one of the motel rooms, with all that cash—"

He laughed. "It's not illegal to have cash in your wallet. And Anita and I *have* been alone in a room together, from time to time, as you know." He gave me a look that was downright pirate-like. "And yes, I did go out with Alicia St. Claire. Guilty as charged."

"You slept with her?"

"I dated her once or twice. Maybe three times, something like that. I don't know."

"You can't recall," I said sarcastically.

"Right. Actually, one of those three times, I went with her and some other people to the Pumpkin Festival that year. I don't know if that qualifies as a date."

"Ah, the Pumpkin Festival again."

"Yeah. I take all my women there, before I off 'em."

I backed away from him.

He laughed softly. "Are you afraid of me, Kelly?" He took a step closer to me. He asked me again, coming at me with mock menace, clamping his hand around my wrist, towing me in closer. "Are you afraid of me?"

It infuriated me, being held this way, and being restrained roused in me an elemental determination to fight, to escape him— yet it also excited me strangely.

Our struggle lasted only a second or two. I yanked my hands from his, and we stared at each other. I felt my pulse shaking me, my heart was beating so hard.

"Are you afraid of me, Kelly?" he asked yet again, very softly now.

"No. Not in the way you mean," I said dully.

He looked surprised. "In what way are you afraid of me?"

"I just don't understand you, Nick."

"You understand me too well, I think," he said with meaning.

"No." I breathed in deeply and looked him straight in the eye. "You act like you want me sometimes, but . . . I don't think you really do."

"Why on earth would you think . . ." He laughed painfully. "Give me a break, Kelly. What are you doing?"

What *was* I doing? That wasn't what I had meant to say at all . . .

"I have to go," I said, holding my hands to my temples.

"No, don't go, Kelly." He came to me and would have laid his hands on my arms but I twisted away from him.

"Eli and I are going to the city tonight, and I'm going to be late unless I—"

"What's in the city?" he demanded, as if it were any of his business.

"Calvin Aronson's birthday party. He's the mayor's—"

"I know who he is."

"Eli's picking me up in about twenty minutes."

"Have fun."

I turned and walked away from him, trying to hurry, but the sand was deep and dragged heavily at my legs. It was like trying to run in a dream. Walking away from him, I felt panicky, as if I had narrowly escaped something. Something that was still pursuing me. But I almost wished he would . . .

Wished he would what? Come after you?

I didn't know what I wanted.

WHEN I returned to the inn, Paula was in the office with Addie.

"Paula!" I said, surprised to see her. She had no reservation for the weekend.

"Hi, Kel. I just stopped in to get my phone charger, which like a dunce I left here last time."

"Nick's down on the beach, if you're looking for him," I told her.

"That's okay. Next time. I have to fly." She blew the two of us kisses and went out. I followed her out and down to the parking area.

"So what's going on with you two?" I asked, unable to hold back any longer.

"You mean, with me and Nick?"

I nodded.

"And here I thought he told you everything!" The look she gave me was almost pitying, and I wished I hadn't asked.

"Never mind," I said.

"Well, I'd love to tell you all about it, Kelly, and I will, but I don't have time to get into it right now. Let me just say that I think . . ." She considered her words carefully. "Things between Nick and me are moving to a new level."

She looked so pleased with herself, I felt like slapping her.

"Kelly, my life is good—I'm in love! I'll tell you everything next time, I promise!"

Chapter 22

"HELEN of Troy," said Eli. "You are the mortal woman all the gods want."

I laughed, staring at myself in the mirror, but suddenly I knew exactly what he was talking about.

You might wonder what difference twelve thousand dollars makes in the price of a dress; I know I always did. Now I understood, at least partly. When I put on this gown I suddenly looked like someone else. A sophisticated, sensual siren.

He had picked me up at four and we drove up the coast to his hotel in San Francisco. Though I had assumed he was a paying guest, I found out later that he owned the hotel. He presented me with a gracious suite of my own, with a private Zen garden and dipping pool.

"I have half a mind to skip this party and keep you here all to myself," he murmured in my ear, when we had arrived and settled in. "I never have enough time with you. I'd love for you to spend the night tonight, here with me."

Though he was staying in the city for a few days and had wall-to-wall meetings all week in the financial district, he had insisted upon driving down to pick me up at the inn.

"Eli, I told you, Addie and Bill are going to their granddaughter's birthday brunch tomorrow. I can't stay over—"

"I know." He smiled and patted my cheek. "I know. I know you have to get back before you turn into a pumpkin. I understand."

"I should have brought my own car. You have to work in the morning, too."

"It's no problem. I had to come pick you up, because I couldn't wait another minute longer than necessary to see you. And I will make sure to have you home by dawn, as I promised. Okay? Listen. Forget about all that. Right now I want you to relax and let yourself be pampered. Okay?"

"Okay."

A rack of evening dresses, each costing more than the down payment on a house, stood waiting for my perusal. A woman appeared to do my hair, another to tend to my hands and feet. A jeweler inquired as to which dress had been chosen, then reappeared later with several large velvet cases.

The finished product, me, was really quite astonishing. Irish setter hair upswept in a graceful yet modishly messy neo-beehive, complementing the Olympian flavor of the gown I had chosen, which fell like a shimmering bronze waterfall from one shoulder. The effect was as if a breath of silk had simply draped itself over the curves of my body. As an engineer, I was impressed with the graceful marriage of aesthetic enhancement with structural efficiency. As a woman, I was thrilled with the results.

Wow, I thought, gazing at myself in the mirror with admiration. I wish Nick could see me now.

Not uncommon, such thoughts, ever since Nick had rejected

me. I merely wanted to remind him of what he had passed on, I assured myself. The impulse was only natural, if not laudable.

Of course the one I really wanted to look good for was Eli.

THE house was a surprise to me. I was expecting overdone gilt and heavy marble, but it was understated, classic architecture, comfortable furniture and jaw-dropping art, impressionist landscapes on huge canvases, abstract pieces and old masterworks. The oak floors were glassy herringbone, and the lofty windows framed a three-bridge view of the San Francisco Bay.

But the gorgeous surroundings couldn't make up for the dullness of the event. The party guests stood around stiffly in small groups, sipping club soda. I had attended kitschy suburban barbecues that had more pizzazz than this well-heeled birthday extravaganza.

"Don't worry," Eli whispered in my ear. "The amusing ones are always late."

A waiter passed by with a tray of martinis and Eli picked off one for me.

"There," he said. "You see? The party is improving already."

I made the best of it, and I had to admit I was enjoying it, walking around in my gorgeous gown, draped in chunky emeralds, a martini glass in my beautifully manicured hand, gazing over the lights of the city, feeling proud of myself for not being completely overwhelmed by it all.

Eli was right: Gradually the place filled with people who were increasingly more fun and interesting, or maybe I had drunk enough vodka by then to make them seem so.

Around ten o'clock I was dancing with a scorchingly handsome black gay man when I looked up idly to see pair of latecomers walking into the ballroom. They appeared in the doorway, a beautiful couple in evening dress, graceful and elegant.

The man reminded me of Nick, if Nick were to dress for a party like this.

I cursed myself. Can't I not think of him for an hour? I wondered. A minute? A second?

Nick?

My astonishment, when I finally recognized him, was complete. He paused for a moment before making his entrance, arm in arm with a young woman in a white sheath shimmering with seed pearls. If I was Helen of Troy tonight, this was Aphrodite, the goddess of love and beauty herself, a tiny, wonderful-looking girl with huge eyes almost as green as Nick's, dark hair pressed to her head '40s style, dark red lipstick and a seam down the back of her leg, which could be seen through the slit in her dress as she walked. And she possessed the perfect sweetly slinky attitude to carry it off.

She was a riveting sight, but even more so, to me, was Nick. I stared at him, openly gaping over the shoulder of my dance partner.

As dazzled as I had been with myself and my own transformation for this event, I was even more impressed by the sight of Nick in black tie. I couldn't stop staring at him. He looked dashing and elegant, and his hair, which he usually kept cut short or covered with hats or bound back with bandannas, had been tamed somehow, and it lay glossy and dark, combed off his suntanned forehead, sleek and smooth, except where it was curling over the back of his collar.

He caught me staring at him and stared back.

What are you doing here? I mouthed at him.

I could have sworn he mouthed in reply: Looking for you.

His being there was amazing enough; somehow after that, it didn't seem odd that Nick knew practically everybody at the party. Anybody who was anybody, anyway. And Eli had already made certain I knew who *they* were.

Nick graciously withstood kisses from a number of older

women who greeted him heartily and asked about his family, as well as a number of younger women who asked him why they hadn't heard from him in so long. He exchanged easy pleasantries with many of the local celebrities Eli had discreetly pointed out to me.

Gradually it dawned on me: Those stories Cassandra had told me about Nick, the product, on his mother's side, of Blackfoot great-grandparents and old San Francisco society—the stories I thought Nick's cousin had embellished, to say the least—turned out to be true. She wasn't even exaggerating.

I met Nick's grandmother that night, the famous Clara, who had defied her society family and "ran off with a handsome Indian brave," as she put it—"for love. It's been thirty years since I lost him, but Lord, how I still miss that man!"

She was a fascinating lady, imperious and beautiful in an old-fashioned gown of dark silk, and we clicked instantly.

"Ah, so you met my mother-in-law," Clara said when I told her about my visit to Nick's great-grandmother's house. "Isn't she marvelous? She is simply on another plane of existence. And you encountered our Cassandra, too, did you? Did she set you down and drill you about politics and the history of the clan?"

"Well, yes," I said. "Particularly the history of Nick and his marriage to Juliet."

"Ah, Juliet," Clara said in her gravelly, patrician voice. "Nick's wife was a lovely girl. But she expected too much of his connections. She wasn't content with a contractor husband, which of course is how he makes his living. Is that what Cassie told you? Well, it's true. Juliet thought she would marry Nick and use him to further her social aims. My daughter—Nick's mother—has never been drawn to the glamorous existence, either. Maybe that's where

Nick gets it. He just isn't interested in that sort of life, I don't think."

She waved a hand, and the gems on her wrist and fingers sparkled beneath the faceted lights. "This sort of existence," she added with an ironic smile.

"And yet, here he is."

Nick was walking toward us in his dark suit.

"Oh, yes." Clara smiled. "He can mingle with the best of them."

Nick stopped before us, bowed over his grandmother's hand and kissed it, then turned to me. "Are you going to dance with me, Kelly?" he asked.

"You're a fraud," I whispered in Nick's ear.

"Why? 'Cause when you met me, you thought I was a lowlife, right?"

"That's right. I thought you were so clever, getting along with everyone, making them accept you as an equal, but turns out you're one of them."

"I'd be their equal in any case," he said darkly, and I knew he was thinking of Eli.

"Nick," I murmured, "you have no equal."

Eli had been outside on the terrace for the last half hour, flattering a starry-eyed young vice president of a competing software business into sharing his company's secrets.

Nick and I were dancing the tango. It was like the night we had danced the swing at the community hoedown, but with an added, unrestrained intensity, almost an anger between us. Nick was a very good dancer, and not just country-western and swing dancing, apparently, but also the foxtrot, the rumba, the waltz—and the tango.

"So who is she?" I asked pointedly. "The girl in the white sheath?"

"My cousin. Cute, huh?"

"Yes, very."

I tilted my head, regarding him. "And where is Paula tonight?"

"Home snug in her bed, I would think."

"Why didn't you bring her to the party?"

"I decided to go with my cousin instead. Were you surprised to see me?"

"Not really."

"You weren't?" He looked crestfallen.

"I know all about your high-society connections."

"My wife left me because I refused to play this game." He looked around the room with an expression of distaste.

"So I've been told."

The dance ended and a polite applause for the orchestra rose from the dance floor.

"So why did you come here, then, tonight?" I asked him. "If you hate it so much?"

He plucked a glass of something from a passing tray and tilted it up, taking in the entire thing in one gulp.

"I'm thinking maybe I was wrong about the whole *scene*," he said, smacking his lips. "This could be fun. Who knows? Maybe I'll give it another try."

IN the wee hours we ended up alone in an antechamber outside the grand ballroom. I lay slumped against one arm of a sofa, with Nick leaning against the other, both of us drunk.

"I lied," I confessed. "I was surprised to see you tonight, Nick."

"I'm an idiot, trying to surprise you."

"Are you?"

"Am I what? An idiot, or trying to surprise you?"

Our legs accidentally touched. I was in stocking feet, my shoes lying on the floor. I could never rival Paula in that respect—even the most expensive Italian shoes hurt me when the heels were that high.

"Kelly, what did you mean today, this afternoon on the beach, when you said sometimes I act like I want you but you don't think I really do? Why did you say that?"

I drew my legs up beneath me. "I shouldn't have said that. It was a crazy thing to say. Just forget about it, Nick, okay?"

He pushed himself up out of his attitude of repose and leaned toward me. "Kelly, please. Tell me."

"Are you trying to completely humiliate me, Nick?"

"Kelly, you know that night you came over to my place . . . You know the night . . ."

I nodded. My heart started loping. I couldn't believe he was bringing it up. That one hungry kiss. I had almost convinced myself it had never happened.

"When you came to me and—"

"And you turned and walked away from me."

"So you do remember."

"Uh, yeah, I remember. And you remember it, too, apparently."

"You think I could forget?" he cried.

Good thing we were alone in the room. Where was Eli?

My bare arms felt shivery with cold. "I don't know," I said. Where had I dropped my cashmere shawl?

"You were standing there on that deck," he said, his voice dropping low. "Looking at me with those oceany eyes of yours. I had to turn away. I was afraid I was going to pass out."

"You're drunk, McClure," I said.

"See, I had been thinking about you, Kelly, the whole time I was gone on that search . . . you know, after the flood . . . It's funny," he said sardonically, " 'cause usually I prefer girls who like me. And you didn't seem to like me much, at first. But I told myself I would convince you somehow. I kept looking for signs."

"Signs?"

"Yeah. At first I figured it was just wishful thinking, but I thought maybe you were starting to thaw out a little with me."

It was true. I was.

"But anyway, while I was in the foothills, I went through the whole thing in my mind. Over and over. All I did was think about it. I just kept thinking: I want to be with her."

Nick leaned back and closed his eyes. We sat like that for a long time, and I thought he had passed out.

Then he suddenly spoke again, opening his eyes. "I knew I was up against Eli Larson. And that he was a formidable rival." His words came slowly, his voice thick with weariness and alcohol. "But there was something about you, Kelly, made me think I could slay dragons. Like the poor guy that has no shot at all at winning the hand of the beautiful princess, but he wants her so badly, he manages somehow to accomplish it."

Nick stopped talking and stretched out his arms, reaching out in front of him, then above his head. His black jacket shrugged up above his shoulders. His tie was pulled sideways. He blew out a breath and went on. "But there was one big problem, even bigger than the Eli Larson problem, and I couldn't figure out any way around it."

My gaze was fixed on him. "What was that?"

"You told me you didn't want kids."

He let that hang there for a moment. I frowned, not understanding at first.

"Didn't want to get married, which is okay, I guess, but no kids? I just couldn't see my life without kids."

For some reason, I wanted to laugh. I found this absurd and delightful. That's what stopped him kissing me? Because I'd said I didn't want kids? Out of consideration for his serious expression, I held back.

"And I knew better than to try to change someone's mind about all that," he went on in the same grave tone. "Because I saw this very same thing wreck my father's second marriage. She wanted kids, and he didn't. She thought he would change his mind eventually, but he never did. It broke them up."

From his expression, and the tone in his voice, I could see this had really affected Nick.

"So I thought about it," he said, "long and hard, and I could only come to one conclusion. Two conclusions. One, I wanted you. And two, I wanted a family. I had to make a choice."

I found this confession extraordinarily touching; but my feelings were jumbled. Why was he saying this now, now that we were both involved with other people?

"I told myself, you and me, we would have to be just . . . friends." He went on, a rush of words. "That's why I turned away from you, Kelly. I had made up my mind that I could never have you, and it wasn't even going to be a question. And I was pretty much convinced that you would never have me anyway. You were going for Eli Larson, and that was it. And then I got home and you came to my house and you put your hands on me, and I almost came apart."

He's drunk, I reminded myself. We both are. Otherwise he wouldn't be saying all these things to me.

"I mean, if I wasn't so gone on you, Kelly, it wouldn't have mattered. We might've hooked up, kept it casual. Why not? But it seemed to me that if we were to go there, you know . . . for me, I had to go the distance. Not just physically. But in every way. All or nothing. 'Cause anything else with you . . ." He blew out a long, deep breath. "It just wouldn't work. Because I was falling in love with you."

I was amazed, listening to him.

Is he really saying these things to me?

Only because he was drunk.

"That night, when we kissed . . ." He closed his eyes and seemed to be reliving the moment all over again. "I came this close to losing it." He groaned. "This close to throwing away my better judgment . . . or what I *thought* was my better judgment."

He laughed bitterly, opened his eyes, and looked at me again, his eyes hard now, shards of emerald. "So I walked you home and there was Larson, waiting for you. I thought I should just go home and shoot myself. And then the final ironic twist, later, when you told me you were starting to think about having kids of your own."

And it's too late now, I thought. *You're with Paula. And I'm with Eli . . .*

"So where does Paula fit into all this?" I asked.

"Paula?" He frowned at me, puzzled, as if wondering what she had to do with anything he had just been telling me.

"After that . . . night," I said, "you picked up with Paula, and you've been seeing her ever since."

"Yeah. I wish I could say she helped me keep my mind off you. But I still couldn't stop thinking of you, all the time . . . I'm sorry. I know I've told you too much."

I said sharply: "Paula informed me this afternoon that you two have decided to take things to another level. She says she's in *love*."

He sighed, staring off into the corner. "Well, life goes on."

"Nick," I said, after what seemed a long time, my voice somewhere distant, calm and resonate, someone else's voice, "you know I want you to be happy and . . . everything. I know you wanted to find the right woman. To have a family with, and . . . and to be happy." I was stammering.

"Like you've found with Eli?"

"Y-yeah . . ."

He was quiet. I was quiet, thinking about him and Paula.

"Kelly," he said, "about Paula. There's something I've been meaning to tell you."

I waited, as my heart reared and galloped away. I braced myself. *This is the moment that changes everything between us.*

"I know you were suspicious, and I wanted to tell you before, but—" He stopped. Started again. "What I mean to say is—"

"What?" I asked, impatience winning over dread.

"Kelly, I owe you a—"

"Hey." It was Eli, coming in through the doorway leading out to the hall. "Helen of Troy. I've been looking for you."

"You have found me," I said. *So he has done it. Nick finally owes me that dinner. Well, I guess I won't be far behind.*

A wave of sadness rose over me and I went under without moving a muscle. It was pain so unexpected and sharp, it was almost sweet.

"Do you think you'll be ready to leave soon?" Eli asked me politely.

"I'm ready now." I stood, cool and calm all of a sudden. Not even feeling drunk anymore.

Yes, Eli, I thought savagely. Let's go back to your hotel. I had a couple of hours before I had to head back down the coast. Eli would appreciate that.

"Your cousin's been looking for you," Eli said to Nick. "I think she's ready to go home."

"Uh, I don't think so," said someone behind us. "Looks like Katie is going to the hospital."

Nick's cousin had broken her leg, having fallen on the elegant stone steps leading down from the terrace to the swimming pool. Somehow it worked out that the four of us went to the emergency room together—I think it was because Eli was the only one fit to drive.

After a couple of hours we emerged from the hospital, Nick's cousin hobbling on crutches. By the time we got her home, Nick was sober enough to drive, and it was nearly dawn. Though Eli raised his objections, it only made sense that I should go back with Nick.

IT was a stiff, uncomfortable silence we shared, driving along the edge of the ocean in the dark.

I couldn't stop thinking about it. Nick was sleeping with Paula. Why did it bother me so?

It made no sense; Nick owed me no allegiance, but the fact that he'd had been intimate with Paula was turning me inside out with grief.

Like it should have been me. Not her.

Damn it all. I didn't want to feel this way. I was with Eli now. Why would I feel this way, feel this regret for Nick?

Why couldn't I just let it go? I had told myself many times that when I finally heard the news I would be able to open my hands and watch him fly away with her, and I would be proud, like I'd helped create something good. If you could destroy what another couple had created, you could help another couple build something, too, couldn't you?

Creation, the opposite of destruction.

But it was me who was devastated, jealous, and dizzy with all the things he had said to me.

Drifts of fog came in from the ocean. On the outskirts of Half Moon Bay, we passed a small café lit with a string of white Christmas lights.

Charlene's Café. There was a Closed sign in the window.

Neither of us said a word.

Finally, after an interminable ride, Nick turned off onto the old highway. The headlights shone on the heavy fog. We drove slowly past his place.

We were halfway to the inn on the old highway when we came to a roadblock. A uniformed police officer approached us like a vague apparition through the white mists.

"Sorry, you'll have to drive around. Road is closed." When I heard his voice, I recognized Officer Bernie Hollinger.

He nodded at Nick as he walked up to the driver's side, and he noticed me in the passenger seat.

"Hey, Bernie," said Nick with a sigh. He looked tired. "What's up?"

"Fatal accident. Victim wrapped his Mazda around a tree sometime earlier this evening."

We peered through the foggy white darkness to the mangled chunk of metal. I was glad we couldn't get a very good view of it from where we'd stopped.

"DUI. Found a mostly finished fifth of tequila in the backseat," he went on.

"Well, at least he didn't take anyone else with him, huh?" Nick's voice was weary.

"But you know what?" Bernie leaned against the rim of the window and craned his neck so he was looking in at me. "The twist is, and this is pretty bizarre—even considering some of the strange stuff I've seen on this job . . ." He glanced from side to side, as if to make sure nobody else could hear him but us. "Check this out. The body was fairly intact, considering the guy's chest was completely crushed, from the impact, you know? But his *entire head* is gone. It's completely missing."

Nick and I looked at each other.

"I know what you're thinking. Decapitation, yes, it sometimes happens in freakish ways, in certain kinds of accidents. But this was done surgically. The head and the spinal chord were cut out, clean."

Another car was approaching and Bernie straightened up. "I'm afraid you're going to have to turn around and go back up to the highway, and come back up from the southern end."

It would be a five-minute drive through the thick fog back up the old highway, and then another five minutes down to the southern junction and back—or a five-minute walk to the inn. And the idea of continuing on in that silent car with Nick was unbearable.

"You know what?" I said as he turned the car around. "I'm just going to walk. I'll see you later, okay?"

He stopped the car for me; I was already opening the door. I jumped out, slipped off my high heels, and began walking down the road, past the roadblock.

"You know, young lady," Bernie called out after me. "You really might not want to be walking alone out here tonight, what with what's been going on. I can't guarantee your safety."

He was right, but there was something about Bernie Hollinger; I just couldn't take him without a huge grain of salt, and his claims, that the accident victim had no head—it just seemed preposterous.

I averted my eyes from the sight of the mangled car and the knot of technicians working around it

For a minute or two, I walked alone.

Nick had the truck. He couldn't follow me. Which was a relief.

But it wouldn't stop him, anyway, I knew that. He wouldn't let me walk alone through the night, not with a madman lurking in the dark.

Unless *he* was the madman. I thought of the yellowed newspaper clipping.

Nick had been seeing the missing woman . . .

I heard his footsteps falling behind me, and I began to hurry.

A wave of panic rolled over me—the same excited fear I'd felt hours earlier, on the beach, when I walked away from him. The feeling that I had to get away from him, for my own safety. But if I broke into a run, it would be futile; he would chase me, and he would catch me.

I continued walking briskly, waiting for him to catch up. But the footsteps stayed just behind me.

What if it wasn't Nick? What if someone else was following me?

I turned, and there he was, walking along behind me with an odd tilt of his head, watching me.

I stopped, heart pounding. I waited.

"Well?" I demanded.

"Just thought I'd walk you home," he said meekly. He came up beside me. We walked together, side by side. My feet were freezing; I had to put my shoes back on. He balanced me, my hand on his arm. I swayed on one high-heeled foot while putting on the other shoe.

We left the old highway and walked through the woods to the rear entrance of the inn property. I went along slowly on my stilts and Nick patiently kept pace. When we came to the old wooden gate, I expected him to let me go on alone, but he came into the yard with me. The inn was silent and dark. There was a faint lightening of the sky over the hills to the east.

We reached the passageway to my cottage and I thought he would leave me there, but we continued on down to the doorway, where I stopped, took out my key, and hesitated.

I said, "Well, good night, then. Thank you for seeing me home."

As I turned and reached out to put the key in the lock Nick slammed his hand against the door.

I looked up at him, startled, and his expression burned into me so that I gasped and stepped away from him, bumping into the wall against my back. He had me trapped.

"How could you think I don't want you?" He laughed and groaned at the same time. "Hell, you know I want you."

He held me against the door and kissed me. The kiss was brutal and full-bodied, and it made of us together something of the same substance, molten and rising to find release, Mercury in heat. With his hands ranging over my body, I thought, *My God, the strength in him, in these hands*—I would not be able to resist him, if he decided not to allow me to resist.

The warmth of him, the smell of him, the sheer physical force of him, the intense expression in his eyes, the curious tone in his rough voice—all combined to make me lose my reason.

But didn't he just get finished telling me about him and Paula, and how they were taking it to another level? He knew I was with Eli. Why was he doing this?

He tried to kiss me again, but I grabbed his wrists and held him away.

"I know what you think I am," I said coldly. "Which is the only reason I can think of, that you could treat me with so little respect. I'm sorry to disappoint you."

He dropped his arms to his sides and gazed at me uncomprehendingly, looking heartbreakingly forlorn in his rumpled black tie.

"Kelly . . . ?"

I jammed my key into the lock, opened the door, and threw him one last turbulent look.

"Good night, Nick."

I flung myself on my bed and moaned out loud.

What have I done? I had very nearly slapped his face, when I really just wanted to drag him into my room and voraciously consume him. But how dare he think he could use me that way! And what kind of a man was he, anyway, making new commitments to his girlfriend, then turning around and making a pass at another—me! And he knew I was with Eli. All that mushy stuff he had said to me at that party, was that just some guy thing, a Casanova technique? Preparation for seduction?

I was surprised. I had thought Nick was different.

Chapter 23

WHEN Nick came to work on the plumbing the next day I avoided him, and he seemed glad of it. This annoyed me greatly; I wanted to treat him with cold disdain if he would only give me the chance.

Grendel found me staring pensively off to the ocean at sunset, and with his usual perceptive kindness, he asked me what was going on.

"Oh, I'm just a little tired," I said. "What's going on with you? You look like you've had a hard day."

"Yes, it is true, I have," he sighed. "A very long day. Some prankster set our dumpster on fire down at the clinic. Of course we all ran outside, and while that was going on, someone came into the lab and stole some materials I was planning to use for research."

"That's terrible, Gren!" I said, concerned for him. He really did look rather pale. "I'm so sorry."

"Well, it's not a big deal, really. We were able to get the fire put right out, and as for what was stolen . . . I suppose it will be easily replaceable. It just puts me behind schedule in testing some equipment, that's all. Mostly it's just that feeling of violation, you know."

I understood.

"ARTURO," I said, "Once this plumbing project is completed, I'd like to see if we couldn't find someone else to use for the maintenance around here instead of Nick."

"Instead of Nick?" Arturo looked at me with surprise. "But we're lucky to have Nick!"

"Yes, well, I know," I said with a sigh. "But it's getting to where I just don't know if I can rely on him."

Arturo shook his head. "I don't get it."

"Arturo, you were there when I found that newspaper clipping in the parlor. You know what it said about Nick, right?"

"Yes," he nodded, frowning.

"And so," I concluded, "I think we might want to look for someone else. I need to be able to trust people."

When I finished, Arturo nodded. He seemed to have fallen deep into thought, and he didn't say anything more.

I went into town to do some Christmas shopping the next day and it was arranged that I would bring Addie home after her visualization class at the countess's metaphysical book shop.

When I arrived, the class had just let out. The shop was small and dark, lit with candles and smelling of sweetly pungent incense. Through a curtained doorway, I glimpsed a larger meeting room where people were still mingling and chatting.

Addie waved. "I'll be ready in a minute, honey."

"Don't worry about it. Take your time."

I wandered around the tiny shop, looking at the books and knickknacks displayed on shelves. Crystals, candles, incense, little statues of Buddha.

"Kelly, hi. Welcome." The countess presented herself to me. Draped in swirls of silk, skirts and scarves, she held her slender form erect and her grip was startlingly strong when she shook my hand.

"Nice shop," I said. "I like that big hunk of crystal there, the way you have the light shining through it. Beautiful."

"Smoky quartz. Very good for clearing negative vibrations from a space. You might want to take some home with you."

"Uh-huh," I said.

She appraised me with a shrewd expression. "It wouldn't hurt to do a cleansing on that old inn, either, you know, during this time of transition. Once Addie and Bill are gone, they'll be taking a lot of their protective spirits with them and you'll be left alone to manage that old ghost town of an inn all by yourself, at least until you can rally the devas and sprites of the place to your cause. Not that you don't have protection, you do. I sense a very glowy being sitting right there, on your shoulder. Nope, other shoulder. But you still need to gird yourself, my darling. And I do suggest you conduct that thorough cleansing. I can help you with that, if you like. Addie and Bill are wonderful people, and they've made that inn into a loving haven, but even good pure souls can get lazy and let the energy stagnate in dark corners. When longtime issues aren't resolved, and tragic incidents are simply ignored, realities never faced and processed—well, that never makes for a clean flow of chi, does it?"

"What issues are you talking about?" I asked.

"Well, can you imagine what it must be like? To have someone you care for vanish like that, right out from under your nose. And they doted on her."

"Yes, so I've heard," I said encouragingly. Here was someone—and a bona fide old-timer—who was apparently more than willing to talk about Alicia St. Claire. I asked in a low voice, "And you don't think they ever . . . faced what happened?"

She turned thoughtful, introspective. "I'm sympathetic, believe me. Due to the nature of the situation, you want to hope. So you hope. And you keep hoping. But I don't believe they did enough to find out the truth."

"And after several years, the trail gets cold, I guess."

"Yes, so you can imagine how cold it's become after thirty years. And yet trauma and anguish linger in the ethers, that is, in the very aura of a space, and it can—"

"Thirty years?" I said blankly.

"That's how long it's been," she said, dropping her voice to a near whisper. "Almost exactly. She vanished at Christmastime."

"Who?" I asked, astonished. "Aren't you talking about Alicia St. Claire? Wasn't it just about three years ago—"

"Oh, I'm afraid I don't know much about *that* incident," the countess said modestly, laying her beautiful, bony hand on her chest. Her nails were long and lacquered, her fingers covered with large rings. "I was on sabbatical in Italy at the time it occurred. I never met the young lady. But that's just another example of the latent energies that have permeated the actual timbers of that old house and those cottages—"

"There was someone else?" I interrupted her again. "Another missing woman?"

"Yes, but it *was* thirty years ago. Darling girl, haven't they told you the story? She was only twenty years old when she disappeared. I was very fond of her. *I* would have adopted her in a heartbeat! I could never have children of my own, you know, and my second husband, he was simply—"

"She stayed here, at the inn?"

"Of course. She was the—oh!" A pair of ladies were standing at the cash register, signaling for the countess. "Excuse me, darling, I must tend to my customers. Lovely to see you."

Addie appeared and as we walked outside, and I said to her excitedly, "Wow, Addie, did you know that another woman went missing from the inn, like thirty years ago or something?"

She let out a bleat of nervous laughter. "Oh, dear," she murmured. "You've been chatting with the countess!"

I tried to nudge her into saying more, and I tried to remember if Addie and Bill had owned the inn that long ago. I was pretty sure they had owned it for at least thirty years . . .

We were getting into the car when another car pulled up in the parking area beside us.

"Look, there's Anita and Zac!" Addie cried, waving.

I looked over and there they were, getting out of a Toyota Corolla.

"I wonder what they're doing here," I said.

Anita and her son were walking into the countess's shop.

"I hope they're getting some counseling," Addie said. "I recommended it."

"Counseling from the countess?"

Addie smiled at the dubious note in my tone. "Well, Kelly," she said with an air of wise understanding, "sometimes you just need an honest mirror, and the countess is rather good for that."

ELI broke a date with me when he couldn't get home from a business trip as early as he'd expected; he seemed to be more unhappy about it than I was.

"As soon as I tie up all the loose ends of this merger deal," he assured me, "we'll be able to really spend some quality time together, okay?"

The media reporting on Eli's current business maneuverings referred to it as a hostile takeover, not a merger, but I decided not to mention that.

"In fact," he went on, "I have some dates near Christmas that I must absolutely have you clear your calendar for, okay? Promise me? Three days. Will you give me your word I can have you then, all to myself?"

"For what, Eli?"

"It's to be a surprise, okay? All you need to pack is your bikini. Okay?"

"Well . . ." I felt silly for even hesitating. It would be nice to get away for a few days. Get away from the inn, get some perspective. And since he was giving me notice this time, I could easily arrange things to suit Addie and Bill. . .

"Will you give me your word?"

He was so adamant and intense, demanding this promise from me, that I couldn't help but admire what must surely be the driving force behind his phenomenal business success. But by the time he had extracted the agreement I had begun to feel a strange sense of unease, as if I had just signed away my soul.

"Go on," said Arturo sharply. "Tell her."

Anita looked at me, something she did only when necessary, her brow a dark slash over hostile black eyes.

"Tell her."

"Nick gave me money," she said. "When my brother came from Mexico. I got a call, my brother is in San Jose. Coyotes have him locked in a warehouse and if they don't get three thousand dollars in two days they gonna kill him."

"This really happened?" I asked, shocked.

"Yeah," she said, emotionless. "I got some money, but not that much. Who could I ask? Arturo has no money, he just bought a house, and he has a family. So I asked Nick to lend me the money."

"When was this?

"Last time? In September. You came into the room, in the water tower, remember? Nick was giving me the money then. And he gave me money before, when my other brother came."

"When was that?"

"Three years ago. My brother paid him back for that already."

"Why are you telling me this?" I asked.

"Because of what happened three years ago," said Arturo. "And what they said in that newspaper."

"About the woman who disappeared?" I asked.

He nodded. "The police came to the inn to check it out. They found Nick and Anita in a room in the motel where she was cleaning, along with several thousand dollars in cash. They got suspicious."

"Nick knew I didn't want the police to know he was giving the money to me, and for why," Anita explained grudgingly. "So he didn't say too much, and they thought maybe he killed the woman for her money. Later they found out that a half hour earlier he took out the same amount of money from his savings account, which is not against the law. And they never found the body, so they couldn't blame him for a murder. But for a while they thought he did it."

"Did *you* think he did it?" I asked her.

"I know he didn't do it. That's why I asked him to meet me in the water tower last time. I didn't want somebody to see us again, and nobody ever goes in there. But then *you* came and found us!"

She glanced at Arturo like he was her defense lawyer, to see if there was anything else she was required to say.

Some unspoken agreement passed between them and she slipped out of the room. He turned away as if to follow her, then thought of something, looked back at me, and remarked, "They *did* pay him back, you know. And the new brother is paying his share. He's the kid who helps me in the kitchen."

"Juan? He's Anita's brother?"

"Sure. And Maria and Irma, the maids? They're cousins—"

"I see."

"Irma's brother trims the trees, and Anita's sister works in Grendel's clinic as a receptionist."

And of course all the social security numbers they provided for our records were completely legitimate.

"Anyway, I just wanted you to know. Nick is a good man."

ONE afternoon a day or two later I got a call from Nick. His voice sounded shaky.

"Kelly, I need your help. Can you drive me to the vet? This puppy I've been taking care of got out of the yard and was hit by a car. I need someone to drive me while I hold her still."

"Sure, I'll be there in a minute."

I got Addie to cover for me, grabbed the keys to the Mercedes, and ran out.

I pulled up in front of his house and ran in. He was coming to the door with the dog in his arms, wrapped up in a blanket.

"I wrapped her up," he said, "but the leg was just dangling."

I helped him into the car and reached across him, pulled the seat belt over him, and fastened it. I tried to ignore the heat of his body. I held my breath so I wouldn't breathe in his scent.

"There," I said. "You're all set."

"Nice car," he said drolly.

"Yes," I mumbled. "Isn't it?"

I ran around and jumped in, started up the engine, and we were off.

The young dog, a German shepherd with a black face and one loppy ear, looked about apprehensively, panting heavily, but stayed still in Nick's arms.

"So what happened?" I asked.

"Damn, I don't know. I put her out with the other dogs and gave 'em dinner, the next thing I know I hear this screech of tires out at the road. I looked outside, the gate was open and the dogs were gone. I ran up there and some guy was standing beside an idling Camaro looking very distraught. But it wasn't his fault—how did those dogs get out? This isn't the first time. It keeps happening. And it's not just my yard. Earl and Maxine's gates are found standing open. That calf who keeps coming into Addie's garden—"

"And Addie's parakeets," I said.

"Yeah. Addie's parakeets! Who keeps letting the animals out?"

"So this is a new puppy of yours?"

"This is Heidi. She belongs to a friend of mine. I was trying her out, seeing if she has the makings of a search and rescue dog. I thought I'd keep her for a few days, get to know her. I'm thinking of buying her."

"You break it, you buy it."

He laughed in spite of himself. "Right. I guess she's mine now for sure."

We had reached the highway. "Which way?" I asked.

"North. Juliet's office is in Half Moon Bay."

"Juliet? Your vet has the same name as your ex-wife?"

"My vet is my ex-wife."

"You still use your ex-wife as your vet?"

"Yeah. Brilliant, aren't I?"

"Why do you go to her?"

"Because she's the best."

THE receptionist and technicians gushed and fawned over the puppy, but the doctor herself remained dispassionate and cool— with the dog and with her ex-husband. Juliet was a neat, professional brunette. She performed a quick, skillful evaluation, gently and expertly examining the frightened dog with the help of a young male technician.

"I'm going to get some pictures," she said to us. "You can wait here." She went out, the technician following behind her, carrying the puppy. "Don't worry baby," he was murmuring. "You're gonna be all right."

Juliet came back to the little examining room where Nick and I waited. The expression on her face was unreadable. She clipped the pictures up for us to see.

"Well," she said. "There it is. You can see the bone is shattered."

It was. Even to my untrained eye, it looked bad. The bone was broken into shards.

"Basically," she concluded, "fixing up this girl is beyond my capability. I can't help you unless you want to amputate. I can give you the name of a specialist who can do the kind of surgery required to repair the leg. Or you can have her put down."

The doctor's lovely face remained impassive. Nick, on the other hand, looked as if he was about to cry.

"Well, give me the name of the specialist," he said, and cleared his throat.

"He's in the city," she said, writing something on a tablet. "And he's very expensive."

She seemed to emphasize this last point. There was a cold silence in the room, and I remembered the story of Nick and his marriage. His wife had wanted someone with more social cachet. Someone, no doubt, with more money.

Juliet handed Nick the phone number she had written down. "I'll have the leg bandaged up so she can't make it any worse," she said. "Then you can take her home and decide what you want to do."

"I've already decided what to do," he said curtly. "But she's not my dog yet. I gotta give Rick a call," he added, looking at me. "Let him know what's going on." He dug out his cell phone.

"Reception's better just outside," Juliet advised.

"I'll be back in a moment."

Juliet and Nick went out opposite doors. I sat in a plastic chair, staring at a cinderblock wall and a poster depicting the complete life cycle of the canine heartworm.

Juliet came back in a minute later.

"Barry's fixing the puppy up for travel," she said to me, attempting a new note of friendliness. "Don't worry, I'm sure it will all work out. She looks very strong and healthy."

"Well, if anyone can do right by that pup, it's Nick. He's got a rapport with dogs."

"This is a serious injury, and fixing it is going to take more than a rapport with dogs. But you're right. Nick has something special with animals. I saw that the first time I went out with him. I had this huge black monster rotweiler who was my baby, but he hated anybody putting his hands on me, which didn't go over well with any of the men I'd been dating, as you can imagine. Either they were afraid of him, or they tried to strong-arm the dog in some way. Nick was the only one who ever took the time to get to know Colonel. He won him over with charm. He spent an entire hour on the floor of my entry hall that first time, just getting the dog to trust him. I think my decision to marry Nick was based in that first hour. Crazy, huh?"

"I suppose there are worse reasons to marry a man."

"Well, look where it got me!" She tried a smile, but it went flat. "Right back where I started. Taking care of his dogs."

"He says you're the best."

"Well, I'm good at what I do, but I don't do the kind of surgery that pup requires."

"I am impressed that you and Nick get along well enough to do business together."

"It's more than business with me, with the animals. Freesia is like one of my own kids. But thank you. We try. Things worked out fine between us when we realized the dogs were the only thing we have in common. So," she said. "I take it you and Nick have plenty in common."

"I have a car," I said. "Nick needed a ride. That's what we have in common at the moment."

Nick came in and we went out to the lobby. The technician led Heidi in on a leash. She came hopping along beside him on three legs, one hindquarter completely wrapped in white, and began squirming with happiness when she saw Nick.

"Keep her quiet," said Juliet. "Don't let her run around."

"We won't," I said.

Nick gave me a funny look.

Well, I thought, I guess he's thinking it's none of my business.

HEIDI lay asleep in Nick's arms on the drive home. I didn't speak, and neither did Nick. I wondered if he was thinking of his ex-wife.

"Kelly, what the hell is going on with you?" he finally asked. From the sound of his voice, it seemed he had finally lost his patience with me. "You seem really angry with me or—something. Because I kissed you, which I guess I shouldn't have done—and I won't do it again, I promise—but what did I do to make you hate me?"

"Nick, I don't hate you."

"But you're all stirred up, and you won't forgive me. Why?"

I sighed. I had asked myself the same question. It was hard for me to put into words what I felt. "I don't know," I said. "I guess it just made me feel used."

"When I kissed you? Why?"

"You know I'm seeing Eli. Not that you necessarily have any loyalty to Eli, but what about Paula? Where is your integrity?"

"My what?" Scowling, he pressed his forehead into parallel creases, obviously perplexed. "What are you talking about?"

"She told me that day—after I talked to you on the beach—she told me you two had decided to take it to *another level*." I snapped out the last two words. "And when I told you that, you didn't deny it. That night at the party in the city. You agreed you were taking it to a new level with her."

"Yeah," he said. "A new level, like, down a notch or two."

"Down!" I exclaimed. "You mean . . ."

I glanced at him. He had on his amused expression.

"Oh," I said. "I thought she meant . . . You mean you two broke up?"

"We were never anything to break up, Kelly."

"Well, how is Paula doing with this?"

"She's okay. She's the one who called it quits."

"She was? So you wanted to keep seeing her?"

"No. Like I said, I didn't realize we had anything to end until she told me she didn't want to see *me* anymore."

"And yet it was necessary to call it quits."

"We hung out, Kelly. Did stuff together with her boys. A few dates, one or two kisses, that was about it. There was never any commitment of any kind."

"You—kissed her? That's all? But you told me you slept with her!"

"I did not." He laughed. "I never said that."

"At that party. We were talking about you and Paula taking it to the next level and you said there was something you'd been meaning to tell me about Paula. You said you owed me a—" I stopped.

"I owed you what?" he asked.

I suddenly realized he had never actually said what he owed me.

"Oh! I get it. You thought . . ." He grinned devilishly. "I see how it is. No, I'm afraid you misunderstood me. I owe you an apology is what I was going to say, if I remember rightly. But I think we were interrupted just then, weren't we?"

"Yes, I think we were."

"I wanted to apologize for telling Paula about you and Eli."

"What about me and Eli?"

"I told Paula, that you had encouraged me to go out with her, and that I had sort of challenged you to go for Eli, and that we had a bet. Well, not a bet, but a dare. Or a competition. I don't know what you'd call it."

"A pact with the devil, is what *I* call it. So you told her about that?"

"Yeah. But then I thought maybe you wouldn't want it put out there like that, in case it got back to Eli or something, but by then it was too late. I meant to tell you . . ."

I was silent, pondering this. I wondered if it *had* got back to Eli.

"So you thought I was saying I owe you a dinner. Didn't you?"

Nick was looking at me intently.

I turned my face away, trying to concentrate on the road.

I reminded myself the point wasn't him and Paula—the point was, I had felt used when he kissed me.

At any rate, it would seem Nick had decided not to try again, whatever he had been thinking, whatever his motivation. He had promised he wouldn't kiss me again.

Thank God! I said to myself. But I realized, if I was honest with myself, that if I had felt used when he kissed me, I had also felt thrilled, electrified, and vibrantly alive.

And I longed for him to break his promise and do it again.

My guilt made my head ache. These thoughts and emotions of mine were a betrayal of Eli. Where was my loyalty? *My* integrity?

"What is it?" he asked. "You're so quiet.

I felt mixed up and emotional, and worried about what I might say. "Juliet is cool," I said.

"Ah—she is that."

"And she had some nice things to say about you."

"She did?" he looked dubious.

"I admire your cordial relationship. I'm serious. I know there are still some bad feelings there, and yet you manage to get along, and work together. That's impressive."

"You know, Kelly, when I saw her today, something strange happened. I realized I only want good for her. I'm not mad at her anymore." He seemed surprised by his own admission. "That's nice."

I said, "That *is* nice. And you know what else is nice? What you did for Anita."

"What?"

"Helping her with her family. Giving her money, and all that."

He looked uncomfortable. "It was just loans. No big deal."

I reached out and laid my hand on his arm. But the touch seemed to startle him and he shrank away from me.

We were silent again the rest of the way home, and after that he seemed to withdraw from me, even more profoundly than before.

Chapter 24

THE puppy had her operation and was doing fine. I offered to transport her to and from the hospital, or help care for her, but Nick declined my assistance. He said he already had a support system in place for this sort of situation. I wasn't needed.

Eli was out of the country. I kept busy, but I couldn't shake the feelings of emptiness and dread that came over me at times. Grendel picked up on my mood, and one morning when he came in to pick up his lunch, he said, "Okay, Kelly girl. What's going on?"

I said with a laugh, "Grendel, you know me so well."

"Talk to me, Kelly," he said patiently. "Does this have anything to do with Eli Larson?"

"I really like him, Grendel. He's a great guy."

"He must be, to have you."

I squeezed his arm for the compliment, but he was missing the point. "He's got it all, you know? And he really likes me, too. I know you were afraid that he isn't trustworthy, but I really don't think . . . Anyway, he's just . . . practically perfect in every way. Like Mary Poppins."

"And yet there's a problem."

"It's crazy."

"What's crazy, Kelly?"

"I am." I scowled. "It's maddening. I can't stand it."

"You want to explain that?"

I shook my head. "No. I don't. Grendel, tell me about yourself. Distract me. Tell me about your love life. There must be something."

"Well . . . as a matter of fact," he said, trying not to smile too largely, but not succeeding. "There *is* someone in my life. Someone very important to me."

"Someone new!"

"Well, we've known each other for a while now. But lately we've been getting closer. I have a really good feeling about the future."

"I think I've seen her," I said.

"You have?" He looked surprised.

"Short red hair, really curly? Pretty face. Kind of . . ." I rounded my arms and was about to say *pear-shaped*. I merely shrugged my arms.

He burst into laughter and nodded. "You *have* seen her, haven't you? Isn't she cute?"

"Yes, I saw her come to your cottage once."

"Did you?" He seemed a little flustered. "Ah, yes. And we thought we were being so discreet."

"So, Gren, how did you meet your true love?"

"Ellen and I work together."

"That's right, I thought she looked familiar. I saw her at the clinic, that day I brought your lunch."

"We have quite a bit in common. Of course there's the work.

And she's become a vegan, under my tutelage. She's extremely intelligent, and she gives great back rubs." He gave a rather evil snicker at this last bit, and I stared at him, shocked. This side of him was new to me, but somehow it made him more likeable.

"Well, congratulations!"

"Thanks, but I don't want to jump the gun here."

"Well, if you work together, you're often together, you get to know each other, don't you?"

"Yes," Grendel said. "Rather like you and Nick, eh?"

I nodded. "I've wondered if that has anything to do with it. I hardly ever see Eli. And Nick is always around."

"You're not saying you're thinking of *Nick* . . . in *that* way . . ."

"Yes, doctor, that's exactly what I'm saying. Not that he's even . . . or that I—" I stopped. "I'm so confused."

He stared away pensively. "He may be a bit wild, but Nick is a good man," Grendel said at last. "But about your situation. It sounds to me like you probably shouldn't be putting your energy toward either of them at this time, Eli or Nick, if you're feeling that confused."

"Well, you're probably right," I said.

Trouble was, I was already entangled with both men, and I wasn't sure how to untangle myself.

THROUGH the white sheen of fog, a strange sight appeared: a line of drummers marching down the old highway toward the inn. It was the fourteenth day of December.

I stood on the porch, watching them. The drummers wound their way into the yard and came to stand beneath the porch, beating out their chant. They were a mixed bunch, all carrying their drums as they walked, young and old, men and women, all dressed differently but in a theme of red and green, with elf hats and Santa hats. One of them had green boots with bells on his curled, pointed toes. They played their drums for a few minutes, then moved off slowly in a jaunty line.

I counted twelve of them. They drummed and drummed as they moved down the road, and slowly they faded, first from sight, then from earshot, into the distance.

"Addie, did you just see that?" I called to her excitedly.

"What, dear?" she appeared at the railing of her deck with her hair up in a towel.

"Drummers!"

"What was it?"

"Drummers, drumming!" I laughed. "Twelve of them! Twelve drummers drumming!"

She had been in the shower, and hadn't seen them. "I thought I heard something," she said.

"That was so cool." I ran outside again, and found the drummers had left something: a small Christmas tree with a red envelope attached. I took the envelope and opened it. There was a note inside on green paper.

Nick's truck pulled into the parking area, dog faces peering out the back.

I ran to him, full of excitement, forgetting, for a moment, the polite distance we were keeping between us. "Did you see that? Did you see the drummers?"

"Yeah, I saw them. What was that all about?" He got out of the truck and told the dogs to stay.

"Weren't they great? Twelve drummers drumming!" I glanced down at the note I held in my hand.

"Your true love sent them to you, perhaps?" he said sourly, his eyes on the note, though I was sure he couldn't see the words written there.

To my true love: Happy first day of Christmas.

"*You* didn't send the drummers, did you, Nick?"

"Hell, no, it wasn't me."

The way he said it, the derisive tone of his reply, hurt me. After all, I was only joking. I stuffed the note into my pocket and rubbed my hands up and down my arms. I suddenly felt the chill of the wet December air, my excitement fading into the mists that swirled around the inn.

"Technically, you know, the real first day of Christmas isn't actually until December twenty-sixth, Boxing Day," Nick said. "But a guy like Eli Larson can make up his own rules, right?"

"You're being pretty petty, aren't you?" I scowled at him. "Worrying about technicalities like which is the real first day of Christmas."

"He must be going in reverse order—counting down the twelve days to Christmas." Nick absently patted Maggie's nose, which she had thrust out the window of his truck. "Tomorrow, eleven pipers piping," he went on in his lazy voice. "That'll be interesting."

"I'm freezing," I replied. "I'm going in." I turned around and walked up the steps and into the house, letting the door shut behind me. He'd follow me if he felt like it. He always did.

If he felt like it.

I checked the thermostat in the parlor, though the temperature in the house was fine. Through the front windows I could see Nick standing outside near the garden in his cambric shirt and his dark blue ski cap, hands jammed in the pockets of faded jeans. He looked cold; why didn't he come in?

I walked about the room picking up newspapers and magazines.

HE came in as far in the doorway between the parlor and the hall. "I gotta go," he said. "I just wanted to tell you I'll be away for a few days."

"Rescue mission?"

"No, I'll just be on call. I'm covering for a friend of mine who has to be in Southern California for a few days. He's with a team I worked with a few summers ago, in the Sierra near Desolation Wilderness."

"Desolation Wilderness!" The name sent shivers through me.

"Chances are it will be uneventful. Anyway, I just wanted you to know I'd be gone for a little while. No more than four or five days."

I regarded him, perplexed. He had finished the plumbing and had tended to all the little odds and ends on my latest list. There was always more I could have him do for me, but he owed me no explanations about his whereabouts. And yet, he had come to me, to let me know.

How sweet it would be, I thought, if I could step up to him, embrace him, and kiss him good-bye, as a friend. But I still felt the antagonism that had sparked between us a few minutes earlier when we had been talking about the drummers. And all the way back to the strange chilly distancing that had come about after he'd walked me home the night of that drunken confession in the city.

"Who's taking care of Freesia? And the puppy?" I asked.

"Aaron's going to watch them. They'll be fine."

"Leg's healing okay?"

"You'd never know what she's been through, except for where her fur is growing back around the incision."

I nodded. "Good. Well, good-bye and good luck, Nick," I said.

"Thanks." He turned and was about to go out the front door.

"Oh, wait . . ." I called to him. I called to him so he would turn around and I could look at him again, look into those clear green eyes with their sun ray lines and expressive dark brows and that unfathomable expression.

"Yeah?"

"Um . . . never mind. I forgot."

"Well . . . see you, then."

I went into the office and stood looking at the pile of paperwork on my desk. But I wasn't thinking about work. I was thinking about Nick. I thought of him driving up those steep winding roads into the mountains where it was already deep winter. He could be called to set off into the mountains with his dog, right into the same conditions and places that had brought the people he searched for into mortal danger.

Desolation Wilderness.

I thought of him never coming back.

His brass compass lay on my desk, a softly gleaming golden disk.

As I heard his engine start up, I grabbed up the compass and ran out, down the steps to the parking area.

He looked out through the open window of the truck, surprised to see me.

"I want you to hang on to this for me," I said. "Until you come back to me." I passed it through the window.

He accepted the compass gravely.

I stood there a moment, awkward. "Well, good-bye again," I said. I thrust my hand through the window, offering a handshake, stiff as a salute.

He grabbed my hand and held it tightly. We were face-to-face, looking into each other's eyes, and then suddenly, through the open window of the truck we were sharing a kiss, hard, sudden, and heated, lingering with lips slightly parted, and then it was finished.

"I made a promise I wouldn't do that again," Nick said darkly.

"I know. But I didn't."

He pulled me in for another kiss, his hands fisting in my hair, his mouth hot on mine. I felt the edge between us dissolve. He

moved against me slowly, his tongue delving into me, at first tentatively, then deeply. Finding the resistance, the surge.

Finally I broke away from him because I would have slid down
the side of the truck in a warm puddle if I hadn't.

I staggered backwards, staring at him, and he held my gaze a
long time, his eyes troubled and lips parted as if he were about to
say something, but the only sound that came out of the truck was
from the radio.

Then he gunned the engine and the truck leaped and he was
rumbling away.

I ran into the house. *This is ridiculous!* I said to myself. *This is
crazy.*

I paced the empty parlor, across the worn Persian carpet and
back again.

I must finally face it. I could not lie to myself any longer. I was
so much more attracted to Nick, physically, than I was to Eli, that
I must acknowledge something to be very wrong. That good-bye
kiss had shaken me to the depths. I had never felt anything like
that with Eli.

Nick, Nick, Nick. I couldn't stop thinking about him. Not just
today, not since the first scorching kiss, but ever since . . . I don't
know when it all began. I searched my memory, looking for the
moment it had turned for me. There was a time when he annoyed
me and I wanted to avoid him; now I craved his presence. Somewhere in between then and now, something had changed.

But I was still telling myself it didn't mean anything. It was a
crush. An infatuation. I'd get over it. He had annoyed and irritated
me in the past, he would do it again in the future.

Nick, I told myself, was merely a symptom of a larger problem.
The big question, the problem I must focus on, was the issue of Eli

and me. What was I doing, kissing another man when I was supposed to be working on something with Eli? I had already congratulated myself on not screwing up, not doing something with Nick that I'd only regret later.

Why was I trying to wreck what I had with Eli?

He called me that night to see how I liked the drummers. The drummers were wonderful, of course. I told him how much I loved them. But really the drummers only made it worse. If you can't fall in love with a man who pulls a fantastic stunt like that just to show you he cares, who the hell are you going to fall in love with?

So why wasn't I falling in love with Eli?

"All right, Kelly," he said. "You liked the drummers. But you don't sound very happy to hear from me."

My guilt pained me; he was so sweet and sensitive. "I don't know, Eli," I said. "To tell you the truth . . ."

"What?"

"I'm guess I'm really having some serious doubts."

"Doubts."

"About you and me."

"Kelly, look. It's because we're in limbo here, waiting to see if Kyra is really pregnant. Isn't that it?"

"Maybe." But that wasn't true. Or was it?

"Tell you what. Let's assume she *is* pregnant. Okay? Say she is. So what. It doesn't change the way I feel about you. Does it change the way you feel about me?"

I considered the question. "No," I replied honestly, "it really doesn't. But—"

"It doesn't?" A note of hope sprang into his voice. "So . . . what is it, then? What's really bothering you?"

"Well, for one thing, I think you might decide to go back to her if she is pregnant."

"Not a chance."

It cheered me a little, to have suddenly thought of this excuse for my ambivalence. Maybe it was true—maybe I was waiting to see how he reacted to the definitive news before I let my heart go.

"I don't know what the hell to do." He bit at the words savagely. "She refuses to give me any kind of proof that she's pregnant. I could just kill her. God, I swear I could."

Something in his voice scared me a little. I had a fleeting memory of Eli holding me fast on his lap, Kyra standing at the parlor door beside her mother, shrieking, Eli's arms tightening around me . . .

"Sometimes I wonder if it's even mine," he mumbled.

"Do you really?"

He was silent. "No," he said at last. "If she's pregnant, the kid is mine. I know Kyra *that* well, I think."

"I better go. I know it's late there."

"Kelly. Please. Don't give up on us. Not yet."

I think I knew for certain in that moment. Breaking it off was the right thing to do, and I felt instinctively the best way to do it would be to do it on the spot, then and there, cleanly and simply. But I hesitated, like a diver on a diving board, and Eli jumped into the pause and began to plead with me.

"Give me another chance to show you how good it's going to be, Helen of Troy. You and me together, we can do anything. Anyone you want to be, you can be with me. Do you get that?"

"Eli . . ."

"Don't answer me yet, Kelly," he whispered. "Wait until we're together again. Just promise me that much. I'll make it worth your while."

"But if—"

"Please. You've already promised me this weekend. Give me that much."

"Okay. All right." I felt obligated; he had asked me earlier to clear my calendar, and I knew he had something special planned, and I had promised . . . I had given him my word.

With a tremor, I remembered the feeling of disquiet that had come over me when I had made that promise. That feeling had returned.

"No pressure, I promise you, Kelly, I will take it as slow as you need me to go. I'm very okay with that. Sexually frustrated, but okay!"

I smiled into the darkness. Ah, Eli. I was truly fond of him. Couldn't that fondness grow into passionate love, given some proper nurturing?

"You can have all the time you need, my love," he insisted. "Forever and a day."

FOREVER *and a day.* A quaint expression.

Would he really wait that long? I didn't think so.

Why should he?

Forever and a day; it made me think of something Nick had said, how he had thought of himself as the guy in the story who would do anything he has to do, to win the princess.

I was falling in love with you . . . His words sent me into a sizzle every time I recalled them.

I wondered when I would see him again.

Forget Nick, I said savagely to myself.

But why? The mischievous and familiar voice inside my head persisted in making my thoughts into dialogue. *Why should I forget Nick?*

Because I just agreed to give this thing with Eli another chance, that's why! I roundly admonished the part of myself that I regarded as my dark side and was pleased to think I had the power to ignore whenever appropriate. *And it's only a physical attraction thing with Nick. You know you don't really want Nick, not really.*

But I do want Nick . . .

The voice of my dark side was surprisingly wistful.

ELI had taken my attempt to break up with him as a challenge, and he was treating me to a billionaire's version of the Twelve Days of Christmas. He had started it all off with the drummers drumming, and indeed the next day eleven pipers piping appeared, flitting about the inn grounds like a bunch of oversized elves.

The prospect of ten lords a-leaping alarmed me a little, but I needn't have worried. On the "tenth day" a delivery arrived in the office addressed to "My True Love." It was a hand-painted wooden box that fit in the palm of my hand, with little drawers that opened all over it. Out of each drawer popped a small jack-in-the-box, or rather a lord—they all had crowns—each holding a tiny wrapped gift. Foil-wrapped candies, exquisite gems, bangles, and charms.

Our date was scheduled for the ninth, eighth, and seventh days of Christmas, as Eli was calling them. We flew in his private jet to his newly remodeled beachside estate in Maui, where nine ladies dancing gave us a private and sensual hula show.

The next day we hopped over to another island in a small plane that Eli piloted himself. When we landed, we climbed into a waiting Land Rover and drove up to a farm on a plateau overlooking the ocean. There we found eight sturdy maids a-milking eight rare Ayrshire cows at a small dairy.

"It's for you, Kelly," Eli said, looking at me with a shrewd expression. "It's all for you. " He gave me a large envelope, and when I opened it I found the deed to the farm in my name, all the paperwork tidy in a plump legal-sized folder holding the documents on the property.

"It's a small organic farm that makes a fair profit and is completely self-running. There are seven full-time employees and some seasonal labor. The foreman, or I should say forewoman, is a Hawaiian lady whose family has farmed the land for generations." He added with a grin, "Some of the eight maids a-milking were hired for the day. It's all automated nowadays, you know."

It was a whirlwind tour. He was deliberately showing me what he could give me, if I would have it—if I would have *him*.

And he was deliberately keeping the relationship chaste. He had changed his tactics, and he was making it clear that if I wanted it, I was going to have to come and get it.

"God, look at this place," he exclaimed, gazing out of the Land Rover as he drove the fast, narrow road. We had been traveling through fields of sugarcane with the backdrop of purplish green pointed mountains emerging from a rainbow-tinted mist; but then we had entered the jungle again and now the sweet fermented odor of rotting fruit permeated the air.

Eli flipped off the radio.

I glanced up at him, wondering why he'd done that. He met my glance with a gleam of intensity.

"Now watch this," he said in a low voice, quiet but holding restrained excitement, like a TV sports announcer calling a play. "Down into this little rainforest canyon. Around the curve. Into the little stream, getting our feet wet, see if our brakes work, oh yeah, up a rise and—there. The sea comes into view again. Sparkling and vast. And the towers stand in dramatic relief to the ocean."

I saw what he was talking about. Several large hotels dominated the horizon where the mountains plunged down to the sea. The buildings were graceful and beautiful, with the setting sun gleaming off their cylindrical sides, but I couldn't help but feel a sadness for the landscape, for the primeval world now gone.

With a shock of memory I suddenly realized I had been in this place once before. I had visited this island with my parents and my sister a few years earlier. We had piled into a rental car and took off for the less populated side of the island, and this was where we'd come, where the road ended. It had been nearly pristine then, though not untouched by humans. A narrow road had curved alongside the ocean, threading its way along the edge of the cliffs. A few huts on the ridge. Surfers on the waves below the volcano . . .

Only the shapes of the mountains were the same, and the smell of the jungle.

It was so changed, I almost hadn't recognized it. I was about to comment on all this, but something stopped me, and I remained silent with my thoughts. I didn't tell Eli that I had been there before.

We drove down into the complex of buildings, which were admittedly striking, structures any engineer would admire, rising above us like immense rocketships ready to launch, pointed toward the sky. I quickly realized why my instincts had warned me not to speak out, to express my feelings of sadness and dismay about what had been done to the land. This massive hotel and retail complex was one of Eli's "projects."

"We had a hell of a time getting through the green tape on this one," he said with a modest chuckle. "I had to buy about a million acres of coastline and give it to open space, you know, just to make it happen, but I don't mind that. I'm an environmentalist. Kelly, I wanted you to see this because I want you to think about the possibilities. We could do things with that prime California beachfront property of yours that will turn it into Boardwalk and Park Place covered with red hotels. I've checked it out. You have real acreage there—"

"Yes, but most of it is zoned—"

"Forget it. Forget everything you've heard about what you can do, or what you can't do. You are looking at the Wizard of Ahhs. And I do mean ahhhs . . ." He reached out and ran a finger over my cheek.

Then he let his hand drop away, as if remembering his vow to make me beg for it. Or at least ask nicely. "I mean, dear lady, that anything you can dream of, you can do, with me."

"What would you do with my place, if you could do anything?" I asked him curiously, a bit fearful of what he might say.

He hesitated. "I'd do whatever would make you happy, Kelly."

Good answer, I thought.

"And if I may be so bold . . . I could help you come up with ideas you probably haven't even thought of. Give you an idea of the scope of a project, the scale of which you probably never imagined. I repeat: Whatever would make you happy. There are no limitations in my world, Kelly."

"But the coast has such strict rules about building . . ." I thought of the ongoing controversy regarding land use along the coast. Even someone like Earl Johnson might object to behemoth luxury hotels rising up over our bucolic shores. Nick's calm, intelligent face came into my mind. "The locals would give you hell, you know—"

"So would my mom," Eli said with a laugh. "If I tried to change anything about the Magic Mermaid Inn. Yes, it will be a challenge, even for me. But I welcome a challenge. I thrive on it." His eyes glittered as he rested his gaze on me for a moment. "And just wait until you see . . ."

"Until I see?"

"Just you wait."

ON the seventh day of Christmas he brought me back to his estate in Woodside. He had never taken me there before.

We blew in on the front edge of a storm. By the time we landed in California, the winds and rain were lashing at the jet and we had a tense descent and landing. An umbrella opened over us as we stepped off the jet onto the tarmac. I heard the rain patter on silk as we ducked into a waiting limousine.

I was familiar with Woodside, a rural, horsy neighborhood, quiet and peaceful, oak woods and meadows, acres of paddock land and orchards and open space, forest and fields rising into oak hills, the ridges fringed with dark redwood forests. The residences were set back from the narrow roads and could be glimpsed through the trees or behind stone walls; most of them were rambling ranch houses or modest mansions.

Eli's place was something different right from the beginning. A uniformed sentry, staying dry beneath the eave of a gatehouse, nodded politely as we passed through the main entrance. The car swung around one graceful wooded curve of the road, and then another; a second gate opened silently as we approached. Suddenly the oaks gave way to an alley of giant date palms. At the end of the palm-lined alley was another gate, purely decorative, twin pillars built of what looked like volcanic rock topped with burning torches, the fires buffeted by the wind, flames leaping in the pouring rain. Iron gates crafted to look like bamboo poles opened automatically as we approached.

Eli's estate was more *island* than the islands we had just visited. Wide-eyed with wonder, I stared out through the rain at a man-made lagoon with a white-sand beach surrounded by banana trees and wind-threshed palms. A waterfall spilled down from the heights of what looked like a miniature active volcano, steam rising from its peak. Near the lagoon was a thatched cabana, pool house, and bar. But the best part was the full-sized eighteenth-century pirate ship that dominated the lagoon, half in and half out of the water, as if it had sailed right into Eli's property and had run aground, right there in the oak meadows of Woodside.

I quelled the urge to speak out and compare the scene to Disneyland, sensing Eli would not appreciate such a comparison.

"Well, there they are," Eli exclaimed, pointing out some masses of white fluff huddled on the far shore. "Seven swans. Supposed to be a-swimming, you know, but looks to me like they're merely roosting. Imported from Holland or someplace, just for your pleasure. They're beautiful when they wake up."

"Eli, you're crazy."

"Crazy about you. Stay with me here tonight."

"I thought you were leaving for Belgium tonight, Eli."

"I'll change my plans if you'll stay. The captain's quarters in the ship are quite comfortable and very romantic. We'll dine by oil lamp and I'll show you what's inside my treasure chest." He wiggled his eyebrows.

"Eli, you're incredible. But you know I've got to get home. I'm already behind on work as it is."

"You know, Kelly, if you want, you'll never have to work again a day in your life."

My expression made him laugh.

"Your generosity is amazing, Eli, and I thank you, but . . . it's just that I want to work, I—"

"I know. I know. You think I don't understand that? I live for work myself, you know that. I just mean, you don't have to worry about it. You can do whatever you want to do. Be whoever you want to be. You can own and manage a five-star hotel in Paris if you want. Just say the word. I want to give you it all."

"Eli . . ." I didn't want to sound ungrateful, but I was overwhelmed. I didn't want to be wondering how I could possibly accept a gift like a farm in Hawaii . . . and what about these swans? Were they my responsibility now?

"It's the fifth day of Christmas that I am really looking forward to," Eli was saying, almost like he was talking to himself. "You know, whoever wrote that song had the right idea. Why should a man give a woman only one golden ring? After all, she's got five fingers—on each hand!"

He was excited and happy.

"God, I wish you didn't have to leave. And I wish I wasn't taking off again, or I'd come with you. But I'll be back before Christmas, okay? I'll be able to be home a lot more after the new year. And tomorrow—six geese a-laying, Kelly. You know what they say about the goose who lays the golden eggs, don't you?"

"Don't kill it?"

"Eggs-actly." He was looking at me with the shrewd expression I was beginning to recognize. He wasn't just joking around with me.

"What are you saying, Eli?"

He pulled me into his arms. "The playing hard to get thing is terribly effective, sweetheart, and you are a master." He was murmuring the words against my ear. "But enough is enough, hey? You got me already." He kissed me softly, gently, on the lips. "And you don't want to make me mad."

He sent me away in a black limousine. I felt as if I had escaped something.

As the car passed Nick's house on the way home to the inn, I peered down his driveway to see if his truck was there.

He should be home from the mountains by now. Shouldn't he?

But I saw no sign of him, no truck, no smoke curling from the chimney. I saw only the rain, slanted against the roof, falling hard.

I went into the office when I got back and checked my messages. Addie came in, greeted me warmly, and asked about my trip with Eli.

"It was great," I said. "I've never experienced anything quite like it." But I couldn't muster up much enthusiasm. The trip to the islands was one of those things I was glad I had done. We had galloped Arabian horses over black-sand beaches and climbed up the flank of a volcano in Eli's open-topped Land Rover. We'd had the finest in local entertainment, food, and drink. Eli was a charming man who was constantly showering me with attention, presents, compliments—everything a girl could want.

I could even appreciate the zero tolerance sex policy he had employed. Unfortunately, having figured out what he was up to, I had felt only relief, not the increased physical frustration that might have resulted in passionate surrender and an outburst of wildly abandoned lovemaking.

"Addie, turn on that overhead light, will you? It's so dark in here."

"Oh, the light is out again," she said. "I don't know why, it just doesn't come on. I changed the light bulb."

"That's it," I said decisively. "I'm going to have Nick take a look at it."

Addie shook her head. "Nick is still in the mountains," she said. "There's a boy missing from a ski resort, and they're looking for him. I don't think Nick will be back for at least another day or two."

The dismay I felt hearing this news struck me with its forcefulness. I wanted to see Nick; I wanted to tell him about my adventures, even though I knew he wouldn't want to hear about my trip, because I'd gone with Eli.

I wanted to share with Nick how it felt, flying over the Hawaiian Islands in a private plane, seeing the limpid sea and the waterfalls and mountains from above. It seemed to me I had never fully finished with an experience until I had told Nick about it.

He's my best friend, I thought.

And he was off in the mountains again. Being a damned hero.

Chapter 25

I was on the edge of a dream that night, in and out of sleep, when I heard a sound outside my cottage. I snapped awake, sat up, and looked out the window just in time to see a woman in white gliding through the rain. She disappeared behind one of the other cottages.

Did I really see that?

She appeared again, coming around the corner, moving toward me through the windy, rainy darkness wearing a long white gown and carrying a large knife.

I grabbed the baseball bat Bill had given me, ran to the door, and flung it open. The woman was standing on my doorstep, a ragged, slender witch with huge blank eyes and small hands, one of which clutched a big kitchen knife.

It was Kyra, disheveled and dazed. She had lost weight.

"What the hell are you doing?" My voice rang out, loud and sharp.

Her arm fell limp and the knife clattered to the ground. She burst into sobs, crying pitifully.

I lowered the baseball bat.

In between hiccups and gulps she explained to me how she had gotten out of bed in the middle of the night, and without stopping to change out of her nightgown, she picked up a knife from her kitchen and drove down the coast from San Francisco to the Magic Mermaid Inn, to find me.

"Where you planning on killing me?" I asked her.

"No," she squeaked with a sniffle.

"Then what?"

"I don't know. I didn't think that far ahead."

She was crying so pitifully, all I could feel, after my heartbeat had settled a bit, was sorry for her. I brought her to the main house, gave her a towel, a box of tissues, and a glass of brandy, and we sat together in the parlor, talking.

"Kelly," she said tearfully, "I've come to a crisis moment. You and Eli are together now and I just need to learn to accept that."

"It's not right between Eli and me," I said. And it was true. I was certain. "It's just not happening. I can't tell you what he's going to do or how it will work out between the two of you, but for me . . . I tried, but I just can't. And he doesn't even know it yet."

"He hasn't loved me for over two years," Kyra said. She wasn't listening to me. "Dutiful, was what he had become, instead of passionate. I always had to initiate everything. Sex. Conversation. Whether to go out to dinner or a movie. Everything. It wasn't like that in the beginning. We used to have such a good time together. He took me places. Did romantic things. He was so generous. And so creative. Or so I thought, anyway. Turns out he hires this service to come up with gimmicks, you know, romantic presents and gestures, they think it all up and they take care of everything for you. Very impressive stuff they come up with, too. All Eli has to do is give them a budget and sign a check. It really wows his business associates. And it got me, too, I have to admit. I was impressed by the man. All his presents. Now I know there's more to life than things, and money."

"What about the baby?" I asked.

"The what?" For a moment she looked blank. "Oh. There *is* no baby, Kelly," she said coolly. "I thought you would have figured that out by now."

"Kyra," I said, "you know I am sorry about everything that happened, that we hurt you." It was true. Going out with Eli had been the experience of a lifetime, and I couldn't say I regretted it— but I was sorry I had hurt Kyra.

"No, it was really nothing to do with you." She wiped her nose. "Eli was just looking for an excuse to get rid of me. I realize that now. I just feel so damned angry all the time. I realize it's Eli. He's the one I'm really angry with. It's not you.

"Kelly," she said to me before she left to go home, "there's something I need to tell you. You know that service I mentioned, that Eli uses, to think up creative gifts for people? Well . . . I had them send you some black roses."

"Oh," I said. "I wondered if that was you."

"I am sorry. I feel really bad about it now."

"Well, thanks for telling me. It was creepy, especially not knowing who sent them."

"I know. I'm such a drama queen. What a dumb thing to do."

"The website was brilliant."

"The what?"

"Setting me up to find that cryonics website . . . It scared the hell out me. Please tell me that was you, too?"

She shook her head. "I don't know about a website. All I did was send some flowers."

"Are you sure?"

"Kelly, you know that day we showed up, my mom and I, when Eli was here with you? Well, somebody had called my mother an hour earlier and told her you two would be together. Somebody wanted us to see you together."

"Who? Who called her?"

"She wouldn't tell me. Actually, I don't even think she knows. Whoever it was probably would have called me direct, but my number is unlisted. So they called her, I'm guessing. I know it doesn't mean much, coming from me, but I think you should be careful."

"Hmm. Probably was just some low-grade gossip rag reporter, camped out in the bushes, trying to get a story . . ."

"Yeah, probably. So anyway. I'd better get going."

"Good luck, Kyra."

"Thank you, Kelly, for being so great about all this. You take care of yourself."

It was the middle of the night in California, but where Eli was, in Belgium, it was probably midmorning. I called Eli's cell phone and on the sixth ring, I got his assistant, Karl, sounding very sleepy.

"I'm so sorry, Karl," I apologized. "I've woken you up. I thought it would be morning by now, where you and Eli are."

"I'm here in California," he explained. "But I've got Eli's phone."

"He forgot it, I suppose."

"Right-o. He's going to be furious he missed you. You can try leaving a message on the Woodside line. He checks it from time to time, but no guarantees. You have that number?"

"Yes, Karl, thanks. And—if you hear from him, would you please tell him to call me right away? It's important."

"Of course. Anything I can help with?"

"No, thank you, I just need to talk to him . . ."

I hung up, frustrated. I needed to talk to Eli. Now.

I would prefer communicating with him face-to-face, but the important thing was to finish it with him, once and for all, as soon as possible.

I called the house in Woodside. When the answering machine picked up, I nearly left it in a message: *Eli, it's over between us.* But no, I thought. I couldn't do that to Eli. Over the phone was bad enough, but he deserved to hear it straight from me, not from a recording.

"Eli, it's Kelly," I said into the phone. "Call me, please."

I dressed warmly and went outside. A pink light was just beginning to tint the night sky above the eastern hills. I left the inn by the rear gate and set off down the old highway toward Nick's house.

Having made my decision to end it with Eli, I felt so free, I broke into a run and ran all the way to Nick's.

I slowed and walked up the long driveway to the front porch. Well before I reached the steps, I knew he wasn't home yet. His truck was gone.

Headlights shone as a vehicle turned down the driveway, and my heart leaped with hope. I stepped out into the light.

But it wasn't Nick's truck, it was a Jeep, rolling up to the house.

Aaron emerged from the vehicle, looking harried and not even surprised to see me there.

"I'm leaving the key for my sister," he said breathlessly, running past me and slipping the key under the door mat. "I'm supposed to be keeping an eye on the place for Nick while he's gone. But I figured I'd better go see if I can help him out."

He would have rushed back to his idling Jeep, but I stopped him. "Aaron, wait," I called, following him. "Help him out how? What's going on with Nick?"

"Uh . . ." Aaron caught his breath, blinked. Evidently he thought I already knew. "Nick's missing," he said.

"What do you mean, missing?"

"His team lost contact with him in the mountains yesterday."

A chill rippled through my body. "Are you sure of this?"

"Yeah. The team leader called me, asked me to let Nick's family know. I called his great-grandmother's house and told her. She'll tell his cousin Cassandra and then everyone will know." He attempted a smile.

"My God," I murmured. For a moment, it seemed I couldn't breathe.

"Hey, I gotta go."

"Aaron, wait. Take me with you."

He looked at me and decided not to take me seriously. He blew out some stressed laughter and turned toward his Jeep.

"Never mind," I said. "Just tell me where he—where are you going?"

He jumped into the Jeep. "Here," he said. "This is a copy of the directions to the base camp of the search operation. See? You can have that. But don't worry about it, Kelly. He's probably already turned up, safe and sound. And we're getting all excited for nothing."

I nodded, unable to speak.

He must have been moved by the look of worry on my face. "You know, Kelly," he said, "when I told Nick's gran he was lost in the mountains, I was all freaking out, right? I'm trying not to let it show, but she picks up on it right off, and she says to me, very calmly, 'Aaron, there is no need for you to get so upset. Nicholas has never been lost in his life.' "

I had to smile at that.

"Look, I've got my phone with me. I'll give you the number." He wrote his phone number on the printed directions.

"Thanks, Aaron. And let me give you mine . . ." I quickly scribbled a couple of phone numbers on the corner of the paper, ripped it off, and handed it to him. "This is my cell number and this is the office line. Someone usually answers that phone," I said. "Please call when you find out anything."

"Okay. Don't worry, Kelly," he said, taking the scrap of paper and shoving it into his pocket. "I'll keep you posted." For the first time he really stopped and took a good look at me, then he simply smiled and patted me on the shoulder.

It was beginning to sink in, what Aaron had said. Nick was missing.

And the weather was getting worse.

I tried to work, but underneath I was tense and nervous, waiting for the phone to ring.

A few minutes later a call came in, asking where I wanted my geese delivered.

"Geese?"

"Six Faience geese. We need an address for delivery."

"Faience geese?" I repeated. More fowl from Eli?

Six geese a-laying.

What the hell would I do with geese?

"Faience geese?" Addie perked up.

I covered the receiver with my hand. "Addie, what are Faience geese?"

"Oh, they're lovely ceramic figurines. There's a pair of them at the Oak Woods Heights Retirement Village."

"How do you think would they like six more?"

"You're not serious?" She seemed delighted at the idea. "Faience geese are valuable, you know, Kelly."

"Give them the address," I said. "And please hurry. I'm expecting a call."

I handed her the phone and turned around, and Paula was there on the other side of the counter, looking at me with a funny expression on her face. She had a large tote bag strapped over her shoulder.

"Hey, Paula!" I exclaimed, surprised to see her there on a weekday morning.

"Hi, Kelly. I was hoping, if you're not too busy, that you'd have a little time to hang out with me. I really need to talk to you."

WE went into the parlor. Paula walked over to a small table in the corner near the fireplace and slid the tote bag off her shoulder, letting it thump on the floor.

Arturo brought us coffee and then left us alone. For a moment the room was quiet, with only the sound of the flames snapping over the dry logs in the grate, and the rain spattering against the windows.

"How are you and Eli doing?" Paula asked.

"Funny you should ask. We're not."

"You dumped him!"

"Well—"

"Thank God. I mean, I didn't want to tell you this while you were with him, but I sometimes felt I should warn you. He's a snake, Kelly. He's charming and friendly and personable, and I do think he cares about people, on some level, but deep down it's all about business for him."

"That might be slightly harsh, Paula."

"That day we came to visit you, Eli and I, remember? On the ride over, we talked about our work. I could tell he was really interested in what I had to say. He just listened, mostly. I mean, I babbled on and on about all my ideas. And now I've come to find he's launched a takeover bid for our company."

Another one? I was awed and impressed, if a little appalled. *He never rests.*

"All that friendly networking we were doing? He was basically spying on my company through me. I could lose my job; I'll probably lose it as a result of this takeover, anyway."

"I'm sorry, Paula."

"Don't worry about me. I'll land on my feet. But anyway, I didn't come here to talk about Eli. I came here to talk about something else."

"Okay," I said warily.

"Where's Nick?"

"He's . . . in the mountains. They don't know where he is." My voice caught in my throat.

"You look worried. How long has he been gone?"

"They lost contact with him yesterday, I think."

"Well, he's very capable. I wouldn't worry about it just yet."

"I know. But I can't help it. It's all I can think of."

She gave me a long look. "You're really hung up on him, aren't you?"

"Paula, I'm sorry—I didn't ever mean to—"

"Kelly, stop. Before you say something that I'm really going to regret. The truth is, *I'm* the one who needs to apologize. To you. Because I haven't been completely honest with you."

"Well, you know he—"

"I'm not talking about Nick now."

She got up and crossed the room, closed the double French doors that led onto the entry hall, and turned to me.

"Kelly, my name is Paula Watson, but that's my married name. My maiden name is Paula St. Claire."

She let that sink in a moment; she must have found me a bit obtuse, because it took me a moment to get it.

"Alicia St. Claire. The missing girl. She's my sister."

I stared at her.

She came back and sat down near me. "She disappeared three and a half years ago and I've made it my cause to find out what happened to her. You think you're obsessed? Honey, it's been all I could focus on for years. When it happened, when she disappeared—well, there wasn't much I could do then, and you know what they say. Time is of the essence."

"Paula . . ." I was shaking my head in disbelief. "My God, I'm so sorry. Your sister?"

"My little sister. I was living in Boston at the time, when it happened, when she disappeared. I had two young children and no money. Blake was going to school. My parents are gone, and my brother is in and out of a halfway house, and we have no other family. There was no way I could just come out here and investigate, look for my sister when the trail was fresh, though I've often wished I had. Anyway, I resolved that I would, when I could.

"We moved to California about a year ago, as you know. I got a good job and Blake found something, too. But our marriage didn't survive the changes. I told you I started to stay at the Mermaid so that the boys wouldn't be bouncing off the walls of my apartment. That was true, but it was also an excuse. Truth is, I came here to find out what happened to my sister. I came here looking to set a trap." She smiled. "A trap for Nick."

At the look on my face, she laughed. "Well, see, I was pretty sure they'd identified the right guy, this Nick McClure, even if they didn't have enough evidence to nail him. And when time went by, and it was obvious they weren't going to do anything about it, I decided I'd smoke him out myself. I began to entertain the idea of using myself as bait. And after meeting him, I decided to try it. Believe it or not, I don't always flounce around in showy clothes and high heels! And the funny thing is, Kelly, you played right into my hand. You set me up with him. It was just the cover I needed. That way it didn't seem like it was my idea, you know? And for a while, it looked like he had taken the bait, and I was sure I would get him. But now I'm back to square one, because it wasn't Nick . . . I know at least that much."

"How can you be so sure?"

"Well . . ." She pondered a moment. "The more I got to know him, the more I saw that Nick is Nick. He's not kidnapper. He's a little mysterious, but I think that's because he's sort of shy, and doesn't want to admit it—"

"Good God, Paula, weren't you afraid for your life? And for your boys? If you thought Nick was a—"

"Well, I figured if he tried to hurt us, I was ready. I was ready to cut off his balls, if I had to. And I had Ben."

"Ben?"

"Benjamin James. My discreet bodyguard. Older African American gentleman, always wears a . . . ?" She mimed putting a hat on her head.

"A bowler hat!" I cried. "Oh, my God. Paula, I just don't believe all this!"

"See, Kelly, I thought Nick knew what happened to my sister. And I thought that if I got close enough to him, *I* would find out what happened to her."

"Were you ever actually interested in him?"

"Oh! Don't get me wrong. Obviously he's sexy as hell. Which made it all the easier to play out the charade. I was telling the truth when I said I think he's a doll. That I love his eyes. In fact, I could fall in love with him. I could. But I wouldn't let myself. Because you're the one he wants. I could see *that* from day one."

I turned my face to hide a blush.

"And besides, I've found the real deal. Didn't I tell you about him? We work together. His name is Edward, he's gorgeous, he gets along well with the boys, and he thinks I'm wonderful."

"Well, you are," I said.

"Of course! But how many men really get that?" She winked at me.

"Do the boys know? That she was your sister?"

"I think Rocky knows something. He knows my sister died several years ago, that it happened in California, and that something wasn't right about it . . . though I don't talk to him about her. I know he's talked to Nick, prodded him with questions about the woman who disappeared. I don't know how much of a connection he's made. By the way, that newspaper clipping you found on the floor? I must have accidentally dropped it there that day. I'd been poking around in the bookshelves, and I found the scrapbook. I took it to my cottage to look at it in private, and apparently that particular piece fell out."

"Well, it's good to know," I said. "I thought somebody had deliberately left it for me to find."

"And I should tell you it was me, I was the one who went through Alicia's things in the water tower."

"So . . . you were the one who beat us to it." I laughed ruefully, shaking my head.

"Well, *you* got there first, didn't you? Anita had told me Claire stayed in the motel, which led me to a dead end."

"Same here."

"But later I found out from Irma and Maria that she had moved over to the water tower and was staying there before she disappeared. So I went in there one afternoon, and I found her things. I was so excited, Kelly, I almost came and told you about everything then . . . But I wondered about you and Nick, and where your loyalties were . . . Anyway, I started going through her things, and then I heard a noise. I got scared—it sounded like someone was moving around upstairs—and I panicked and ran out, leaving everything messed up, and I didn't go back."

Like someone was upstairs. Rats in the rafters, I thought.

"But I took this."

She bent down and opened the tote bag, and pulled out the little pink backpack.

"I just thought it would be all right . . ." Her eyes beaded with tears. "I wanted something of hers."

"Paula, she's *your* sister; *all* her things are yours."

"But I want you to have this." From the pink backpack, Paula withdrew the little beaded evening bag I had admired. "I know you like it!"

"I do like it," I said. "But maybe you should—"

"No. I want you to have it. And I want you to look at this. This is all the research I've done." She picked up the tote and set it down beside me. "You can give me back the stuff in the folder after you look at it. The scrapbook is Addie's, of course—if you'll just discreetly return it to its place on the shelf in the parlor after you look at it . . . Oh, what the hell, you can tell Addie I took it, and you can tell her why."

"Why don't you tell her yourself?"

"Well, maybe I will."

I was about to ask her if she had heard of the other missing woman, the one who had disappeared thirty years earlier, but something stopped me. I decided I'd find out a little more about that before I started spreading more unpleasant stories about my inn.

GRENDEL came into the office, and it was obvious from the flushed glow of his skin something was going on with him. "Kelly," he announced solemnly, "I have some news that you might not like hearing."

"Okay." My heart set up a trip-hammer rhythm. Could it be

some word of Nick? But why would Grendel have information on Nick?

"So," he said. "Well, I did a little checking. And . . . those dead black flowers you received . . ."

"Yes." I let out a huge sigh, relieved this wasn't bad news about Nick.

"It seems that delivery was charged to the account of . . ." He paused for dramatic effect, then pronounced the name in hushed tones. "Eli Larson."

I nodded.

"You . . . don't seem surprised."

"No, I just found out about it myself. Kyra confessed to me she sent the dead flowers, charged them to Eli's account."

"Oh. I see." He seemed curiously deflated by this.

"That's pretty good detective work, though, Gren," I said. I appreciated the energy he'd put out, even if he did appear to be rather disappointed to find Eli was not the guilty party.

The phone rang—it was Aaron, calling from base camp. There was no news. Hanging up the phone, trembling, I tried to pull myself together.

"Everything okay?" Grendel asked when I hung up, seeing the expression on my face.

"God, Gren, I just can't stand it."

"What's going on, Kelly?"

"Nick. He went on a search and rescue mission in the mountains, and now he's disappeared himself . . ." The words squeaked out of a throat choked up with emotion.

Grendel laid his hand on my shoulder. "This is a little more than just the concern of a friend, isn't it, Kelly?"

"Yeah," I admitted.

"If you forgive me asking, Kelly, what is your current status with Eli Larson?"

"We're finished."

"Ah." His response was unreadable. I couldn't tell if he was pleased or disappointed. "Are you certain?"

"Quite certain."

"You appear to be rather less confused than you were last time we talked on this subject. Does that mean you are as equally definite about your feelings for . . . Nick?"

"You know, Gren, I kept telling myself that that I really didn't want to be with Nick, or if I did, I shouldn't want to be, and I had all these reasons why I shouldn't, but they just keep falling away . . ."

"So it's not about the wealth and prestige, obviously."

"The what?"

"Well, a woman like you has the right to expect certain standards in a partner. I suppose I'd have to agree with you that when it comes to character Nick is by far the better man. But he does rather lack in worldly attributes, doesn't he? My dear, he is a handyman. Of course the search and rescue business is all very admirable, but you must admit it would have to be considered a liability on the balance sheet. It's rather like an expensive hobby, isn't it?"

"If Nick's value to me is to be measured by the standards you're suggesting," I replied coldly, "then let me list his assets. He's there for me whenever I need him to keep my business running smoothly. He gets along well with everybody—guests, staff, management. And he he makes me laugh. That all adds up to priceless."

"Well, I don't know that he gets along well with *everybody*," Grendel replied, stung. "He—he really doesn't get along all that well with Earl Johnson."

I started laughing, a little embarrassed by my own sudden outburst of passion in defense of Nick. "No," I conceded Grendel's point. "You're right. Nick really doesn't get along very well with Earl."

*   *   *

THE widow's walk was narrow and slippery from the rain. I was a little concerned about the condition of the balusters. I wondered, did Mrs. Worthington really spend so much time up here, looking out to sea? Waiting? Hoping?

From this vantage I could see—on a clear day—far out into the ocean and up and down the coast. I could see the roof of Earl and Maxine's ranch house peeking out of the trees across the old highway. I couldn't see Nick's house, though I kept gazing across the top of the woods, scanning the hillside as if I had missed something. A curl of smoke from his chimney. His familiar truck moving down the road.

I couldn't see his house, but I knew he was still gone.

The weather had suddenly calmed, but I felt the deception in the stillness. It was the eye of the storm.

Chapter 26

I couldn't wait any longer. I packed a bag of clothes. I made sure Addie and Bill had Aaron's cell phone number as well as my own, and I set off.

But before I left town I called Eli's house in Woodside and when the answering machine picked up I left him a message, breaking up with him.

I'm sorry, Eli . . . sorry to be doing it like this, on the phone, but I can't get ahold of you and I can't wait any longer. It's just not working with us. We both know it's true. And you deserve better. We have to end it. So that's why I'm calling.

I hesitated, trying to think of something else to say.

We can talk when you get back, if you want . . . but my mind is made up, so . . . anyway . . . call me, please. I need to know you got this message.

The skies had clouded up again, with dark, menacing, wind-whipped clouds coming in from the sea. I drove through the rain, my hands tense on the leather-clad steering wheel of the Mercedes, trying to convince myself it wasn't foolish, what I was doing. I was no mountaineer, but I could hike, and I was determined I would join the search party somehow and help look for Nick and the missing boy.

But when I joined up with Aaron at base camp and he showed me a map of the back country where Nick was last seen, I felt the hopelessness of the situation. The sheer enormity of the wilderness daunted me, not to mention the steep, avalanche-prone mountainsides. The weather was so bad, I had barely made it there in my car, even with chains. Even the search teams couldn't go out.

I had hoped to be of help with the search operation, but it was already a well-oiled machine and now I feared getting in the way. And I was suddenly hit with my own fatigue. What with Kyra's middle-of-the-night visit and my own anxiety about Nick, I hadn't slept more than two hours in the last two days. I was lacking sleep.

Lacking sleep! I thought angrily. How much sleep has Nick had?

But I couldn't do anything for Nick if I didn't take care of myself. I rented a room in a motel near base camp. I didn't think I could sleep, but I thought a hot shower might help me wake up.

It was cold in the small, rustic room. Ordinarily I would have been looking around, comparing this room to one in my inn. But I could only think about Nick.

I went to get a few things from my car, and when I opened the trunk I saw the grocery bag Addie had given me to bring along. She had packed sandwiches and Arturo's fudge brownies, and Grendel had included a bottle of champagne "to celebrate Nick's safe return." Afraid to tempt fate, I decided to leave the champagne in the car for the time being.

Darkness had fallen. It was so cold, even in this room. What was it like for Nick, wherever he was? I turned up the heat and sat on the bed, waiting for the room to warm up before moving again.

What had happened to him? Was he all right?

Will I see him again?

I pulled the bedspread around me and curled up on the mattress. The heater rattled on the wall.

I awoke with a start. I realized at once, with a sickening lurch of the stomach, where I was, and why I was there. I couldn't believe I had fallen asleep, and so soundly. The sun was shining outside. The glare off the snow made the light in the little room brilliant. Throwing off the bedspread, I jumped up, grabbed my coat, and ran out.

"WELL, we'll be here until about noon, but after that I'll give you a call."

I was walking down the sidewalk, which was cut into a dirty snowbank on the edge of the street, when I heard the woman talking into a pay phone on the corner. She was about my mom's age, with brown wavy hair, worn jeans, and expensive hiking boots.

"Yeah, so I guess he just walked down off the mountain with the kid," she was saying excitedly. "Apparently he dug a snow cave and kept the boy warm until the snow stopped coming down and they were able to get out. The chopper pilot saw him on his first flight in this morning; the weather had finally cleared enough so they could get out there—"

"Have the missing people been found?" I rushed up and interrupted her.

"Yes, yes." She grinned at me. "The helicopter's bringing them in now. They'll come in at the field on the north side of town . . ."

When I asked her for more precise directions, she said to me, "Hold on a sec, I'll give you a lift."

*　　*　　*

WE arrived just in time to watch as the helicopter came in. A small crowd was waiting; the boy's family, rescue support, and a couple of news reporters. People were sobbing and jubilant. It was truly a sublime moment. The boy, a twelve-year-old who looked to be rather sunburned but otherwise healthy, was one of the first down out of the helicopter, practically into his father's arms, with his mother right there, reaching out.

I saw Nick, emerging behind the others, watching the reunion happen, with his hair whipped by the wind of the chopper blades. Maggie was at his side, her tongue hanging out of her smiling mouth. Somebody slapped Nick on the shoulder.

Nick didn't get very far from the helicopter before he was surrounded by people, officials and family and press. I couldn't hear what anybody was saying, it was so noisy. Nick looked exhausted, worn, relieved. He dropped his pack where he stood, and Maggie lay at his side, equally exhausted. Aaron came up to him and gave him a big bear hug.

Nick reached down into his pack to pull out a hat, which he jammed down over his unruly dark curls. He looked up and I saw him notice me as I walked slowly through the crowd toward him. He faltered a moment with what he was saying to someone, looking at me strangely.

The sight of him moved me deeply. The red-rimmed green eyes, the curls poking out of the bottom of his dark blue knit ski cap, the dark stubble on his chin and his cheeks—

He practically shoved aside a reporter who had pushed a microphone at his face, and he strode across the field straight to me. I thought of how I would explain my presence there, but he wasn't interested in explanations. We went into a bungling embrace, his shoulder smashing into my chin; he was hugging me so hard, he almost hurt me.

Then he took my face in his hands and kissed me roughly. His mouth tasted like snow. It was intense and it lacked finesse, but it was bliss, to feel him real and tangible and there. My feelings threatened to overwhelm me, and I drew away from him, but he wasn't giving up that easily—he pulled me back to him and was kissing me with ferocity and a lack of sensibility to the fact that we were surrounded by a lot of people.

For a moment my spirit seemed to rise above me, looking down on Nick and me and everything around us, witnessing it all—but then I was back on earth, back in my body, and I was finding this unshaven, dirty hero quite hot and rather irresistible . . .

Somebody called out his name.

He paid no attention. I pressed my hand to his heart and murmured, "Nick . . . "

He pulled back and looked at me with a strange, searching expression.

"Nick!" Someone else was calling him.

"The team vet is going to check out Maggie," he said. "Don't—go—anywhere!"

"I'm at the Enchanted Inn, just up the road, number seven," I said. "Come when you can."

He nodded, still fixed on me with that wide-eyed searching look.

THOUGH he had looked a little gaunt, he had looked damned good, I thought as I walked back to the motel.

I got the grocery bag with the champagne out of my car. I was touched by the gesture, and Grendel's show of confidence that Nick would be coming back. I couldn't wait to open it and celebrate with him. I hoped it wasn't frozen.

The knock came softly at the motel door. I let him in and shut the door behind us. He hardly waited for me to turn around before he practically fell upon me and we were warm in each other's arms, just holding each other. Maggie lay down in a corner near the heater, watching us with mild curiosity.

"God," he said, "you're all I thought about, for the last—"

"Tell me about it," I urged him. "Tell me what happened on the mountain."

"Later." He tried to kiss me again, but everything was suddenly changing so fast. I resisted him playfully.

"I was so *scared*, Nick. But Aaron said your gran told him that you've never been lost in your life."

"Not until I looked into *your* eyes."

I snorted laughter, but he grabbed my arms tightly and just looked at me.

I said shyly, "I've got a bottle of champagne for us."

"I don't want champagne, I'm just thirsty for you . . ." He quickly stole a warm, greedy kiss, then he seemed to wonder if he might hurt my feelings if he didn't accept some champagne. He let go of me and picked up the bottle, and with his eyes fixed on me, he twisted off the wire and thumbed it open. When it popped, he cupped the stopper in his hands, and held the bottle neatly and cleanly as it steamed like dragon's breath. He poured the sparkling wine into the glasses and we clinked.

"Never too early in the day for champagne," I said. "Grendel sent it along so we'd have something to celebrate with, you know, a successful rescue . . ."

"You know what we're drinking to, though, right, Kelly?"

I nodded slowly.

"To us," he said. "You and me." He lifted his glass to mine once again. "It *is* you and me, isn't it, Kelly?"

I nodded. "Just you and me."

He drank the champagne quickly, like he wanted to finish it fast. He downed the flute and poured himself another.

I had barely taken a sip, when he got me in his arms again.

* * *

His excitement was overwhelming. I was afraid. Afraid I would come apart, the energy was shaking me so hard.

He pushed me against the bed, pushed me down on the mattress, and he climbed onto the mattress with me, knocking over the champagne bottle and my nearly full glass and sending a sparkling waterfall over the edge of the nightstand. I let out a cry that he stilled with his mouth suddenly gentle on mine.

He murmured something in my ear, his voice completely gone, so hoarse, I could hardly make out his words. The kiss turned hungry again, and desperate. His shirt was unbuttoned and down off his shoulders, his chest naked; he still wore his jeans, low on his hips.

"Nick . . . are we about to do what I think we're about to do?"

"God, Kelly," he gasped, "at this point that is entirely up to you."

"What about protection?"

"Yeah. Uh, I got a condom. But it's at least a year old. It's been a long time for me."

"About the same here, for me," I confessed.

He raised a brow, skeptically. Obviously he didn't believe me.

"Why do you look like that?" I challenged him, incensed.

"What about Eli?" He propped himself on an elbow and picked up his glass of champagne. He offered it to me.

I shook my head.

"No, you don't want the champagne, or no, you never got with Eli?"

"No champagne, and no . . . *no.*"

"Okay." He sounded dubious. "What about Grendel?"

"Grendel!" I was puzzled at the question.

He drank from his glass of champagne. "And Arturo?"

"Arturo?" I laughed. "No, of course not. He's happily married. Why would you think?"

"Grendel told me you'd slept with Arturo."

"He did?" I looked at him, incredulous. "Why would he say that? And he told you I slept with *him*, too?"

The set expression on Nick's mouth and in his eyes was too serious for me to doubt. But I could not believe it.

"Why would he say that?"

"I don't know. It doesn't matter. Anyway . . ." Nick took one last gulp of champagne and set down the glass on the bedside table. He was getting impatient with the talk. Evidently he didn't care whom I'd slept with, if he was the one I was with now. But I couldn't just dismiss it like that.

"It does matter," I insisted.

By now the mood was irrevocably altered, which I deeply regretted, but we needed to talk about this.

He leaned back against the pillows and stared off dreamily.

"It's just that," he said with a sigh, "you seemed so self-contained, and yet so free and easy, as if you liked pleasure and didn't deny yourself. I liked that about you. It also made me nuts. Yeah, Grendel told me you had a go with him. I was certain you and Eli . . . And he said you and Arturo . . . Everyone but me . . ."

As he spoke, his voice was slowing down and he was making less and less sense. The fatigue he was battling—he must have hardly slept for days—had thickened his tongue and dragged down the lids of his eyes. The alcohol probably wasn't helping, either. He was beginning to sound drunk.

"It made me sad," he said. "Because I didn't want to be just one of the many. I wanted to be your one-and-only. I wanted to marry you and live with you in a house with a white picket fence and have kids with you. I already tol' you that."

I tilted my head, amused at him, and a little perplexed. He was practically mumbling now.

He sat up suddenly, looking at me with spacey eyes and swaying slightly.

"Nick, lie down," I commanded.

He looked at me, and I'm sure he would have shown surprise, if he had any strength left at all. Just before collapsing into the blankets, he turned to me. "Where are you going?" he asked.

"Nowhere."

"Okay. Good." And that was the last thing he said.

HE passed out on my bed and lay there limp and heavy.

I didn't know what to do. I felt for him, I really did. I could see how tired he was. And he was wonderful, and he had done a marvelous thing. He deserved to rest. And yet I couldn't help it—I was a little hurt that he had fallen asleep right when we were finally on the verge of intimacy. And it wasn't the first time he had avoided such a moment, which made it even more humiliating and perplexing. Was I seeing a pattern?

I got up and dressed, cleaned up the champagne with the skimpy motel towels, threw the empty bottle into the little plastic trash can in the bathroom, and went outside for some fresh air. Aaron was walking up the street toward the cabin.

"Looking for Nick?" I asked.

"I was looking for you."

"Me?"

"There was a message on my voice mail for you from someone at the inn. They've got some problem at home. Said it was an emergency."

"Really?" I pulled out my own phone and looked at it; I had no messages or calls. My phone wasn't getting a signal here.

"I didn't get the whole message," he said. "My phone died. But it sounds like you're needed back at the inn as soon as possible."

"Was it Addie who called?"

"I didn't get a name—like I said, the reception was bad—but it was a man's voice."

"That would be Bill . . ."

If it had been Addie, I would have suspected some exaggeration. But if Bill said it was an emergency, it probably was.

"Well, it sounds like I had better go . . ." I realized I was glad for a reason to leave. Now that I knew Nick was safe, I could go home. I didn't want to wait around for him to wake up. It could be hours, or even days, from the looks of it.

"Hey, do you know where Nick is, by any chance?" Aaron asked me.

"He's sleeping in the motel, in room seven."

"Oh, yeah? Whose room is that?"

"Mine."

"Son of a gun."

I blushed.

Aaron's eyes narrowed to shrewd slits. "This sounds like quite a scoop for the *Sunflash* gossip column," he said. "Search and rescue hero holed up with Eli Larson's girlfriend in mountain hideaway—"

At the look on my face he laughed and threw his arm around my shoulder. "Nah, don't worry," he said. "Nick would castrate me if I did a story like that. Besides, the *Sunflash* doesn't really have a gossip column."

I grinned at him, relieved. "I sure hate to wake Nick up now, just to tell him I'm leaving."

"No problem," he said. "I'll explain when he wakes up. I need to recharge before hitting the road myself. I'll just throw my sleeping bag down in my Jeep."

"The cabin is warm. The door is unlocked. You might as well make yourself at home in there. Would you tell Nick that I . . . that I had to leave?"

"Sure. I'll tell him."

I came home to a gift box in which were nestled five golden rings, each more beautiful than the one before, and a note that contained, if not an actual proposal of marriage, certainly an implied promise of a proposal of marriage. With a dull ache in my gut, I realized Eli had not yet received the message I had left on his machine in the Woodside house.

"THEY'RE okay," I assured Addie when I joined her in the office. "Both Nick and the boy. They're okay."

"Thank God!" She pressed her hands to her heart. "But—I didn't expect to see you back so soon."

"Isn't that why Bill called me?" I asked, perplexed. "Didn't you need me to come back to deal with some problem?"

"Well, we did have a problem with the heater in Sea Horse. But I never called you. And Bill already fixed it."

"Bill didn't call me?" I asked her. "On Aaron's phone?"

Addie shook her head. "No, I don't think so."

"But someone called me and said you needed me back at the inn."

"Are you sure?"

"Yes, I'm sure," I said. But I was wondering just exactly what it was that Aaron had said. Maybe he'd gotten it wrong. Or maybe I had.

* * *

In the evening I was out in the kitchen garden, cutting some rosemary for Arturo. Grendel came out to greet me. He had already heard from Addie that Nick was okay.

"I'm so glad," he said warmly. "So our Nick is a hero once again!"

"Yep," I said.

"Did you two enjoy the champagne?"

"We had your champagne, yes," I said, balancing my basket on my hip. "And while we were sharing that champagne, Grendel, Nick told me a few things that surprised me. He said that you told him that you and I . . ."

"What?" His expression was genuinely innocent.

"That we've slept together."

He looked puzzled.

"And he said you told him that I've slept with Arturo, too—"

Grendel slowly shook his head. "I think Nick must have misunderstood. I can't fathom . . . I wonder if . . ." He scowled, pondering. "All I can think of is that it might have something to do with something I said once about . . ." He faltered, clearly uncomfortable. "About what I *wish* would happen between the two of us. You and me. That's the only thing I can think of. If I was somehow indelicate, I apologize, Kelly," he said gravely. "I never meant to bother you with unwanted attentions. I hope you realize that. I only want your happiness. And it's all worked out for the good anyway. I've been blessed with happiness of my own. Or at least I feel I'm closer than I've ever been."

"Have you thought about moving in with her?" I asked.

He seemed startled by the question; then, emboldened, he said, "Yes, actually it is something I have considered."

"Well, good, because I think you should know that I plan to convert number nine to a vacation rental sometime later this year. No hurry, I'm not asking you to leave right now, but . . . I just wanted to let you know."

"No problem. I understand completely." He laughed. "Oh, hell, who am I fooling? You want me to go? Really? *Damn*. That hurts. I must confess, it does hurt." He looked out at the ocean and threw up his hands. "She wants me to go!" he shouted, startling me with the sudden, violent sound. I'd never seen such a passionate outburst from Grendel. "She's kicking me out!"

"Hey . . ."

"Don't worry." He grinned, panting a little. "I'll be fine."

"I know you will, Gren."

"Kelly, there's something I need to ask you." He was looking at me keenly.

"What?"

"If you . . . if you woke up tomorrow and found yourself in a strange alternate world, and everything and everyone you knew was gone—and the only constant between your new life and your old life was me . . . do you think you would—could you consider me as a suitor?"

I was astonished. What a peculiar question.

"Sure, Gren," I said. "Why not?"

THAT night, when my work was done, I cast about for something to keep my mind off Nick. I kept wondering how long he would sleep, and when he would return. I thought of Paula and the bag she had left with me, and I decided to look through Alicia's things again. Not that I expected any great revelations. Somehow I figured if Paula hadn't been able to find any meaningful clues in these things she had collected, why would I?

It was all just as I remembered. Some cheap jewelry. Cosmetics turning oily in their jars. From the pink backpack I pulled out some pieces of linty tissue, an old Chinese take-out menu, and a piece of folded colored paper, which I nearly disregarded. But something made me pause and take a better look.

The Speran Institue.

I opened up the brochure. I realized at once that I was already acquainted with the Speran Institute. It was the cryonics facility that had come up on the website my mysterious enemy had directed me to visit.

A coincidence?

Hardly. A strange excitement filled me. There had to be a link between the Speran Institute and Alicia St. Claire.

I didn't sleep well that night, my thoughts alternating between Alicia St. Claire and Nick.

When would he come home?

Late the next morning I left the inn and drove over the hill, passing Nick's place on the way out. Still nobody home.

Chapter 27

THE building looked like thousands of other commercial structures in the valley, a low rectangle faced with brick, surrounded by bare trees. A deserted parking lot. A small sign near the entrance read: The Speran Institute. Please Call for Appointment.

The place seemed to be locked up tight. I felt almost relieved, telling myself it was a ridiculous whim anyway; but really I think I was afraid that if I went inside the building, some mad scientist would put me into a deep freeze.

As I was about to turn and leave, I noticed the doorbell beside the entry door, almost hidden by a spray of ivy growing up the brick wall.

"HI there, can I help you?"

He was a tall man in his forties with thin, sandy blond hair, gold-rim glasses, and a big slouchy sweater. He smiled at me with friendliness when he appeared, coming around the corner of the building in apparent response to my ring. He was polite but guarded.

How can you help me? I wondered, and all the rehearsing I'd done for this moment on the drive over the hill seemed a waste of thought. I'd expected something different. A secretary behind a desk, or something.

I introduced myself.

"I've been investigating the disappearance of a woman named Alicia St. Claire," I said, more stuffy and official-sounding than I'd intended. I showed him the brochure for the cryonics facility. "This was among the few things she left behind. I wonder what you might know about her?"

"Are you a police officer?" he asked. "Private investigator?"

"No, neither. I just recently bought the inn where the woman was last seen. I've been hearing all these stories floating around. I just want to find out what really happened to her."

"You've called before, haven't you?"

"Yes, I have. And I'll keep calling and bothering you people," I added with what I hoped was a winning smile. "Until you help me."

He looked at me, biting his lip. "Why don't you come inside?"

"Don't worry, it's just coffee. No liquid nitrogen in it or anything." He smiled at me wearily, and I suspected he was reading my mind. The whole idea of cryogenics or cryonics or whatever they called it gave me the willies. I wasn't at ease being in the building, or—as he had correctly divined—even drinking the coffee.

We were sitting at a table in a small conference room that adjoined a kitchen with white painted cabinets and a speckled Formica countertop.

"Patient's privacy rights are critical," he said. "Particularly in a situation like this. There is a great deal of misunderstanding about what we do. Even now, in the twenty-first century, there's still so much fear and distortion in the mind of the average person. It's ignorance, really. The media tends to portray what we do as grotesque or ridiculous, though that's changing. But in any case, patient privacy rights come first."

"I've been told she's not a patient here," I said. "And if she's not a patient, you're not stepping on that patient confidentiality thing, then, if you talked about her, right, Doctor?"

"I'm not a doctor. I'm the facilities manager."

"So what do you do, as facilities manager?"

"Everything," he said with a modest laugh. "Everything in regards to maintenance of the cryostats."

"Those are the tanks where the people are . . . stored?"

"Right. I design and engineer them, I build them, test them, do all the maintenance, you know, top them off regularly, everything."

"Can I see these tanks?"

"For reasons of security and privacy, we don't let the public tour the facilities. But if you were a prospective member, you could arrange . . . Anyway, if you've seen our website, you've seen photos of all the rooms, and the cryostats, and everything. There really isn't anything secret about what we're doing. We basically store people in large thermos bottles at liquid nitrogen temperature, and we'll keep them safe and sound until the time when the disease or condition that brought about their death is treatable."

"But you can't bring them back . . . yet."

"We can successfully preserve and revive human embryos, viable human embryos. We can take 'em down, and we can bring 'em all the way back. It's only a matter of time before it's the whole person."

"And that's what you do, preserve the whole person? Are they really frozen?"

"Or vitrified. Right now, the best preservation technologies, like vitrification, can only be used with single organs. Vitrification is an ice-free process. Most of the water in the cell is replaced with protective chemicals. Instead of freezing, the molecules just move slower and slower until all chemistry stops at the glass transition temperature. And unlike freezing, there is no ice formation or ice damage in vitrified tissue. But if you want vitrification, it's just going to be your brain. So for that reason, only the brain and spinal column of the patient are preserved. And for reasons of protection, mainly, the brains are stored in their skulls. We treat full-body patients and neuropatients at this facility."

Neuropatients.

"Do you know where Alicia St. Claire is?"

He sighed heavily. "No," he said finally. "I have no idea where she is."

"But you know *who* she is."

"I never met the woman."

"But you know something about her."

"All hearsay, I'm afraid. My understanding is, she was seeing one of the fabricators for a while. But he left around the time I started working here, so I don't really know."

"She was dating one of the—fabricators?"

"Yeah. The guy who built the cryostats before I came. Well, I think he would have liked to have dated her, let's put it that way. I don't think she wanted anything to do with him, not in that way. He got her interested in cryonics, and tried to get her to sign up for a membership, but she was young, and death was a long way off for her. Or so she thought. But I guess nobody really knows what happened to her."

Could it be Nick?

"Do you know his name? Of this, um, fabricator who used to work here?"

"No. Sorry."

"Why did he leave?"

"I'm not really sure. But my understanding is, there were philosophical differences between him and the other staff."

"Philosophical differences. Is that like 'artistic differences'?"

"Kind of."

"Is there anything else you can tell me? *Anything.*"

He called into the adjoining room: "Helen? You in there?"

A few moments later a grumpy-looking older woman came in. She did not seem happy about being disturbed. We were not introduced.

"This lady is asking some questions about the woman who went missing—remember the woman what's-his-name was dating? The guy who worked here before me?"

"Ah, yes, Professor Fate's girlfriend," the woman said. She poured herself a cup of coffee and sat down at the table. "What about her?"

"Professor Fate?" I said.

"Yeah, that's what we called him. Quite a character he was. He even looked the part—long wild hair, beard, intense eyes. He was a genius, truly, well ahead of his time. Introduced some important innovations. He was working on some interesting things, advances in vitrification technology, among other things. But he could have set us back years in public relations, with some of his ideas. You can imagine the image people have, of what we do. We're actually just a bunch of normal people who believe in what we're doing and hope we can educate enough people so we can keep on working, keep the bills paid, and keep the tanks topped off."

"But he was different?"

"Well, just like any profession, we have our deviants. Unfortunately, he started having visions of grandeur. He thought, not illogically, that if cryonic preservation is a good idea when implemented at the time of clinical death, how much more effective it would be if cryonic suspension was to take place *before* death occurs. Well, a lot of us argue the laws are too restrictive in that respect."

She sipped her coffee. "Sometimes the team waiting to take over the body after death waits for days while the patient is in a vegetative state, and we watch helplessly while the physical organism deteriorates, until finally the death certificate can be signed. We can't do anything until that death certificate is signed.

"I'm just saying, he had my sympathy. But he began to take it even further. Why not put the body into cryonic suspension *before* disease or old age even has a chance to take hold? It became something of a crusade with him. Which didn't go over so well with our membership and our financial backers."

"So he was advocating that living, healthy people submit to cryonics suspension?" I asked.

"In a word, yes. Oh, I don't mean that he went around looking for volunteers. It was more like what you just said—an advocacy position."

"What happened to him?"

"I don't have any idea. We don't keep in touch. Ours was not what you'd call an amicable parting of the ways. And I hope you're not actually a reporter out to get a story, because this is exactly the kind of hype that cryonics does not need."

A builder with long wild hair . . . and a beard. Nick's hair was long when I met him. And he'd had a beard. I took a deep breath, hardly daring to ask the question for fear of the answer. "Can you tell me his name?"

She sat back and regarded me unsmilingly. "Look, I don't know anything about you, or what you're going to do with this information, okay? So let's just leave it at that."

I glanced at my watch. I needed to get back to the inn, but I wanted to keep asking questions. I was beset with a strange certainty that I was getting close to some important connection.

I thanked them and got up to leave.

The manager showed me to the door. "You know," he said, "you're not the first one to come around here, asking about that missing girl."

"So . . . the police came and asked questions, too? After the disappearance?"

"No, this was just a month or so ago. And I don't think it was the police."

Whoa, I thought. This reinforced the feeling I had experienced on other occasions, that someone else was just ahead of me, searching for clues about Alicia. "Who was it?" I asked.

"Some woman. I don't think she gave her name. I remember she wore dark glasses and a scarf around her head, like she was a movie star trying not to be recognized. She was tall, slender—and she was asking the same questions you are."

Paula, I thought. It must have been Paula.

WHEN I returned to the coast it was early evening. Nick's house through the trees was dark, and I had to steel myself not to turn down his driveway to make sure his truck wasn't parked there beside the house.

I got to the inn and went to the office, stopping to take off my coat in the entry hall. "Hey Addie," I called out.

"Hello, Kelly," chirped the reply from the office. "You just missed Eli."

"You're kidding me," I cried out. "Really? He was here?"

"Yes, not twenty minutes ago," Addie replied. "But he had to go back up to the city."

"Damn. We keep missing each other."

"He didn't have time to wait," she said, "but he wants to see you."

"I want to see *him*, too. I *need* to see him," I added vehemently. I desperately needed to tell him it was over between us. I wasn't sure about what was happening with me and Nick, but I knew what was happening with Eli and me. *Nothing*.

I was about to go into the office when a movement caught my eye and I turned to see who was in the front parlor.

I stopped in the doorway, astonished to see him there.

"Nick!" I cried. "You made it back. And now you're here!" *Dumb,* I thought. Stop *babbling*.

He took a step toward me, uncertain. Gone was the wild impulsive maniac just come down from the mountain who had grabbed me up in his arms and kissed me passionately. This man was clean-shaven and cool, his eyes green and hard.

"I didn't have time to wait, either," he said. "But I waited." There was a dangerous edge to his voice.

Obviously Nick had heard what I'd just said to Addie about Eli, and he had taken it wrong. He didn't understand why I needed to see Eli.

"Let's go up to my place," I said to him.

I grabbed my damp coat off its hook, slipped it back on, and we walked outside. Amazing, how distant he seemed. The idea of touching him seemed nearly impossible. The air was cold and scrubbed by the wind. We walked together silently to my cottage.

"WHEN did you get home?" I asked him. I threw my coat over a chair and walked into the little kitchen. I turned the gas on under the kettle.

"I haven't been home yet. Surprised to see me?" he asked, his voice sarcastic.

"Nick, is something wrong?"

"I don't know."

"Well, I don't, either."

"I was a little surprised when I woke up to find Aaron sleeping in my room instead of you. To find you . . . gone. You said you weren't going anywhere."

I planted a fist on one hip, standing there, facing him. "Oh, you remember that?"

He ignored the rebuke. "I came to apologize," he said.

"What for?"

"For my rough handling of you . . ." His voice trailed away, and he spoke again with apparent effort: "And for passing out. I begin to understand how a person could believe they had been slipped some sort of drug . . . I would almost wonder if—" He shook his head. "Anyway, Kelly, I just wanted you to know that's not the way I meant for it to happen."

We looked at each other across the room. I studied him, trying to fathom something. I wondered if I would have to refuse him for the same reason he had once refused me. Because it mattered too much.

Like a sleepwalker I paced into the bathroom, shut the door, and stared into the mirror over the sink for a long time. My long red hair was disheveled, my skin was unnaturally white. My eyes were blue and large and filled with a tumultuous expression.

I had started to think of marriage and a family only after I had met Nick. It wasn't Eli, or his money, that had raised the desire in me. It was Nick.

I was learning something about myself. I didn't want luxury hotels around the world. I wanted to run this modest, charming little inn and these funky cottages and this kitschy motel—with Nick. And I wanted a child, yes. I wanted *Nick's* child.

When I came out of the bathroom he was standing by the table, looking down at the box with the five golden rings. The romantic note Eli had written was lying there beside the box of rings.

"He's made it quite clear he wants to marry you." Nick's voice was flat.

"Yes," I said.

"Have you given him your answer?"

"No, I haven't seen him yet."

"You seem to be rather eager to see him. Judging by what you were saying back there, to Addie." I heard the sarcasm creeping back into his tone.

"Nick . . ." I let out a violent sigh. He could still exasperate me. More than ever. He probably always would.

"But what is it you want?" he asked rhetorically. "I wonder. Is it the money? Is it, Kelly? Is that what you want? I think maybe it is. It's just too much to resist. You know, I remember I told you once that you were too good for him. Now I wonder if you two don't deserve each other."

His words hit me like a blow. "How dare you, Nick!" I hissed. "How dare you?" That he could hurt me so made me terribly angry. I was shaking with emotion. I didn't know whether to claw out those beautiful green eyes or turn and run away from him.

"Is that really what you think of me?" I demanded. "I think it is. You've said it before. You—"

"Kelly . . ." His voice softened suddenly. He strode quickly across the floor to me and tried to take me in his arms. "I'm sorry. Please, forgive me."

"No!" I shouted, shaking him off. "To hell with your apologies, if that's what you think. Is that what you think? That I'm all about the money?"

"No." He looked sheepish. "I know you're not . . . but . . . when he comes into the picture, it just makes me nuts. I'm sorry."

"Well, at least I know *he* really wants me," I said bitterly.

The expression in the clear green eyes grew severe. "And you think I don't?"

"Forget it."

He took a step toward me. "Are you asking me to prove something?"

"The only thing I'm asking of you, Nick, is to leave. Please. *Right now*."

"No," he said. "No, Kelly, I am not leaving. And I am not letting you get away from me again. Not this time."

"Leave me alone, Nick." I shoved him away, but he came at me again.

"No. I will not."

"You will, if you think all I really want is money."

"Kelly," he said, grasping me, holding me against him, his mouth on my hair. "I think all you really want is *me*."

"That's just the sort of comment an arrogant, narcissistic bastard like you would come up with!" I sputtered and gasped, trying not to let my mouth graze his. I shrugged him off violently and backed away from him. "And yes! Obviously you've had your chance with me, more than once. But that's in the past now and the offer is no longer—no longer—"

He came at me, backed me up until he had me pressed against the wall.

I was furious with him and determined that nothing would happen between us. But he was equally determined that it would. Wildly I sought escape, even as I longed to be cornered by him, to be conquered. What an odd and paradoxical metaphor for making love, this image of capture and incarceration—what I really wanted was to be set free. To be liberated, unbounded.

Why? Why am I fighting him? If we could just start over . . .

He made me kiss him, his mouth coming down hard on mine. His kiss was determined, hot, opening. All life issued from that kiss. All the world emanated from this. All conversation was forgotten. I couldn't remember what we had been arguing about. Only this thing that began with two mouths was real in the universe and everything else was a strand that found itself back to that, strands of color and music and fibers of feeling, shimmering scented chords I could taste. *Tastes like you.* His eyes in the half light. Green radiant darkness pulling me in, swirling around me. His fingers on the edge of my jaw, trailing down along the slope of my neck.

We sank down together onto the bed, our hands pressed together in a prayer. His arms encircled me and pulled me against his body. *He is so strong.*

"Look at me," he commanded.

Just because he was so authoritative I resisted, turning my head and twisting away from him. I crawled off across the bed, but he came after me. He pounced on me and we startled wrestling on the bed like lion cubs, playful and ferocious. I knew joy like a physical thing running through my blood, to feel Nick's body tumbling and rolling me, to feel his mouth searching out mine with a voracious, invasive need.

He grasped my arms and held me down on the bed, the weight of him keeping me still now. I stopped fighting him; he let go and pulled me closer with his hands running up and down my body, kissing me, exploring me tenderly, reverently.

His kisses were like the winds blowing in from the north just before a storm. His body was the onslaught of the storm, bending the bough, scattering clouds, leaves, and branches, garbage cans rolling in the streets, weather vane spinning. A deep moaning down from the canyons, ocean waves thrashing in a squall, thrilling and frightening and compelling.

I remember how he suddenly sat up and yanked off his shirt, and then he fell down on me again, kissing me and kissing me. It is the kissing that I remember. He was kissing me, kissing me so deeply, so continuously, I opened to him, let him in. I could not help it.

Even when I was burying my lips in his hair, his mouth was on me, pulling, greedy, opening me, opening me all the way through. He edged away but kept kissing me. The kissing seemed to be the refrain. What it all came back to. He shed the last of his clothing but wouldn't let me touch him. He slid down over me and I felt his mouth on my knees, just inside the kneecap, right where it dimples. I felt his warm hands on my thighs, warm and waiting, letting the skin heat and tease.

My hands groped for him. But he was holding me off.

AFTER awhile he couldn't think straight anymore. The only thing he wanted was to get inside me. So I kept playing with him, teasing him until he wrestled me down again, pinning my arms out to the side, coming down against me, only now there was nothing between us.

"Look at me," he said in a whisper. This time I obeyed him.

THE trembling began in my thighs, rippled through my womb, my belly, my heart.

Nick held himself still above me on strong sinewy arms. His galloping ceased for a moment and a throbbing pulsated through him and into me. I arched to taste him ever more deeply against the center of my soul. He lowered himself down to kiss me again.

*   *   *

"I like this dimple," I said, touching the little indentation on the left side of his mouth.

"It's not a dimple," he said. "It's a scar. I cut myself on a shard of granite, climbing."

"During a rescue?"

He nodded. "Yeah . . ."

"So, your cute little dimple is actually a macho scar."

"That's right."

"Nick . . . there's something I've been wondering about."

"What?"

"If you didn't want to take it to another level with Paula . . . I mean, you know, *really* take it to a new level with her . . . why did you challenge me to raise the stakes in our little, uh, competition?"

"I just wanted to see what you were aiming for with Eli."

"Oh."

"It killed me to think maybe you had decided to marry Eli after all, which I found ironic given that I had pretty much dared you to do that."

"Funny. You're the only one I really *pursued*."

"Looks like you finally caught me." He grinned.

WE woke in the morning to the sound of the phone ringing beside my bed. I ignored it until I heard Eli's voice coming in through the answering machine.

"Hi Kelly, well, damn, looks like we missed each other again. I'm in the city and I was hoping we could meet for lunch before I have to—"

I grabbed up the phone and said, "Eli!"

"Hey, there you are."

"Did you get my messages?" I asked.

"No, I lost my phone, and I just got this new one, but I didn't—"

"I need to see you."

"Okay." He sounded pleased. "I'll come down, or—can you come up to the city?"

"Yes."

"Ten, at the Fairmont? I have a meeting—"

"Sure," I said. That would give me just enough time to see him and get back before I went on desk duty at noon. "I'll be there."

"I'll meet you in the lobby. I can't wait to see you."

"I'll see you at ten, Eli."

I hung up the phone and turned to look at Nick. He was fully awake, propped against the pillow, watching me with his expressive green eyes. He was bare from the blankets around his hips on up.

"You're going to him," he said.

"I have to talk to him, Nick."

"You have to talk to him now?"

"Especially now."

He didn't say anything more.

I quickly dressed and he was up along with me, pulling on his jeans, slipping into his white oxford shirt. He wasn't happy about me getting out of bed to go be with Eli, and I knew it. I couldn't blame him, really, but I wished he could understand. Until I made a clean break with Eli, what I was doing here with *him* was wrong. Maybe I should have just ended it with Eli on the phone right then, but I couldn't, not with Nick lying there in my bed, listening to the conversation.

"You've got time, if you're to be there at ten," he said. "Come down to the beach with me for a little while before you go." Nick's voice, sounding vulnerable, rose into a request.

The fog hung just at the edge of the ocean, so that the morning sun lit the hillsides to the east, but the sea remained shrouded, and we walked together through a strange bright mist, as if we were moving between two worlds. I was so full of Nick, my heart, my body, my mind, so complete with him, any worries or concerns I felt for the future, or regrets for the past, simply didn't matter to me in that moment.

But he hardly said a word.

The tide was out and we came to the point, where the low rocks lay exposed, and I began to pick my way through the tide pools, looking down to see if I could find any starfish clinging to the slippery stone. I glanced at Nick, who was a little ways up the beach. He was scratching something in the wet sand with a stick.

It was time to be getting back. I was determined to get to Eli as soon as possible and finish things with him. I rejoined Nick on the beach and my eyes fell to the words he had written in the damp sand.

I love you.

Our hands clasped. Slowly we walked back up to the inn together.

He remained silent as I prepared to leave the inn. Before I went out to my car, I wrapped my arms around him and held him.

"I'm sorry, Kelly," he murmured. "I don't mean to be a jerk. I just don't want you to pick him instead of me."

"Nick, can't you see by now there's no way that's going to happen?"

"Yeah, but, I don't know. I can't help wondering if I'm taking you from the life you really deserve . . ." He looked at me searchingly.

"I've got the life I want, right here and now, Nick. With *you.*"

We shared a kiss, immensely tender and edged with rekindling passion. I couldn't wait to get back to him, and I hadn't even left him yet.

But he seemed so thoughtful and somber. I was a little worried about what was going on inside him.

Chapter 28

ELI asked me if it was Nick.

I nodded.

We were sitting together in the lobby of the hotel. I had refused his offer to buy me something to eat or drink.

"I knew it, in my gut," he said darkly. There was a touch of pride in the admission. "Well, he's a fine man," he added sincerely, if stiffly.

Then he blew up at me, his voice ringing with anger: "You shouldn't have led me on, Kelly. God *damn* it. You really shouldn't have."

"Eli—"

"No." He held up his hand, took a deep breath. "I know you tried to make it work with me. I know that. I just wish you had figured things out a little earlier."

"I am sorry, Eli."

"No—that's not fair, either; you did try to break it off with me earlier, and I wouldn't let you." He thumped his fist on the table. "You, know it's funny," he said. "Paula told me once that you and Nick had a little wager goin', a little competition to see which of you could score first. Hey, I didn't mind. I *admired* you for that. I intended to see that you won that competition, and I figured all that playing hard to get was just your modus operandi. But you played so hard to get, Kelly, you forgot what you were trying to achieve."

"I'll return all the gifts."

"You certainly will not."

"I brought the deed to the farm, and the keys to the car and the pink slip, and the jewelry—"

"Kelly." His voice was crisp. "Please don't add insult to injury."

His expression was so fierce, I dared not argue. We could talk about this later, when he'd cooled off a bit.

"Eli, for what it's worth, I think you're great, and I wish you every happiness—"

"Unbelievable," he said, and his voice was flat. "You really are going to choose that two-bit handyman and that shabby collection of huts on a cliff over what I can give you." It was beginning to dawn on him, what was actually happening. He seemed stunned.

"That's just it, Eli," I tried to explain. "You want to give me the world. You're wonderful, and generous, and I *do* care about you, very much. You say with you I can have anything. Go anywhere, be anybody I want to be. But I'm already who I want to be. I'm already where I want to be. I'm already doing exactly what I want to do."

"And he fits in with that," Eli said grudgingly.

"Yes. He does."

*   *   *

WHEN I got to my cottage Nick's truck was gone and there was a note on my bed.

> *Kelly,*
> *I need to see you. Meet me at Grendel's clinic as soon as you can. Don't tell anyone you're going there, and bring this note with you. I'll be waiting for you.*
> *Nick*

It was such a strange message, I read it again. It seemed so odd, so emotionless and demanding, especially in light of the passion-filled night we had spent together. And yet things had seemed unsettled between us before I had gone. We had made love for the first time, and then I had left him to go to Eli. He hadn't been pleased about that. But I thought I had managed to reassure him.

Grendel's clinic? Why would he want to meet me there? I began to worry. Why a clinic? What was wrong?

I walked over to the office, looking for Addie or Bill. I was supposed to take over the desk at noon, so I needed to get someone to fill in if I was going to slip away. I felt guilty about taking so much time off lately, so I almost hated to ask.

Don't tell anyone you're going there, and bring this note with you.

I kept thinking about how strange it was.

I found Addie on her deck watering her plants. I quickly explained that I had to leave, if it was all right with her, just for a little while—

Impulsively I showed her the note, feeling a little guilty for disobeying its request for secrecy. I felt the need to justify asking her to cover for me yet again.

"Don't worry, Kelly," she assured me. "If Nick needs you, I'm sure he has a good reason."

I drove down the road to the clinic, which looked deserted, the parking lot empty, unlike the day I'd come before.

I pushed open the door and went inside. I stood in the small, modestly furnished waiting area with the reception counter behind opaque windows. The windows were closed and the clinic was dark beyond the waiting room. I noticed a card with my name on it sitting beside an open bottle of wine and two wine glasses.

I opened the card to read:

Kelly,
Have a glass of wine and I'll be there as soon as I can.
Nick.

Stranger and stranger. Meet me at Grendel's clinic for a glass of wine? It was just after noon and I rarely drank wine at lunch, though I had to admit a sip of something alcoholic might just hit the spot about now. I read the card again. It looked like Nick's handwriting, all right, what little of Nick's handwriting I had seen.

Wine, I thought. What was it about wine lately? Paula had been brought down by a glass of wine, or so she claimed. Nick had fallen asleep, unable to stay awake after drinking the champagne Grendel had sent. I decided to hold off on the wine.

I sat down and waited. Nick didn't come. I grew impatient.

Outside. I would wait outside in my car. I got up and walked to the door. But when I tried the handle, I discovered I was locked inside the building.

I dug around in my purse, looking for my phone. I couldn't

find it. I dumped everything out on a chair, and put it back again. My cell phone was gone. I knew I had put it in my purse yesterday, before I drove over the hill to the Speran Institute. I hadn't taken it out.

I was beginning to get angry, and scared. The double glass doors of the entry were locked, as was the connecting door from the waiting room into the clinic. I walked up to the window over the reception counter, which separated the two rooms. The sliding panels were closed. I pried them open slightly and peered into darkness beyond a modest office area. I could see nothing. The place seemed deserted.

I waited another few minutes. The more I thought about it, the more wrong it all seemed.

Why was I here, in Grendel's clinic?

Grendel, who had lied to Nick about me.

I was feeling claustrophobic. I paced the small waiting area, perspiration forming around the edge of my scalp. I was about ready to throw a chair through the glass.

There must be another way out.

I pried the sliding windows apart and climbed up on the counter, slithered through the opening, across the receptionist's desk and down into the small, acrid-smelling inner office.

Hurrying down a narrow, dark hallway, looking for a door or a window, I passed several small, dimly lit, cell-like rooms, with strange lights and equipment hanging from the ceilings or stowed on wheeled carts. Some of the rooms had chrome examining tables that made me think of altars for human sacrifice.

At the end of the hall I came to a heavy metal door. *Locked.* I tried the heavy handle again, no luck.

I turned around and walked down the hall and back into the office. I flicked on a light, and the weak fluorescent struggled to life.

There, I thought. *Telephone*. I picked up the receiver.

The line was dead.

I heard a step behind me.

"I took the precaution."

"God, you scared me," I breathed. "I didn't hear you come in."

"I didn't come in," Grendel said pleasantly. "I've been here all along."

"Where's Nick?"

"Nick?"

"I got a message to meet him here."

"Called away to an emergency, I'm afraid."

"Well, I'm glad *you're* here, you can let me out. I've been trying to find a way out of here for the last five minutes. I got locked in somehow. I don't mean to be wandering around your office, but your front door was locked—"

"No problem. Why don't you have a glass of wine, Kelly?"

"Thanks, no. I just want to get going."

"Please. I insist."

"*No*. Unlock the door for me, Grendel."

"You're a little keyed up. Everything will go easier if you just have a drink, Kelly."

"What did you mean just now, you *took the precaution*?"

"With the phone. Made it so you can't use it. Yours, too. Did you notice it was missing? Don't worry, I've got it." He patted his pants pocket. "Right here."

"Let me out of here, Grendel," I said firmly. He stood between me and the front exit, looking at me lovingly.

"Please, Kelly, have some wine. It won't interfere with the procedure."

"What procedure?"

He blew out his breath, shook his head, and spoke to me like I was a naughty five-year-old. "Kelly, I was *hoping* to spare you all this. You aren't going to like it one bit, and it would be so much easier if you have your glass of wine. But that is one of the things I love about you. You're curious and feisty. That's why I was attracted to you in the first place, so I suppose I can't blame you when you display those characteristics *now*."

I weighed my chances of getting past him by rushing him; the odds were not in my favor. I turned my back on him and walked through the office and down the hall. I reached the heavy steel door once again and shoved on it, pushing the heavy handle down, and this time the door opened.

The room was large, cool, and the acrid smell of the building was most intense in here. I stepped inside, hesitant, afraid of finding myself cornered, but I was already trapped. What choice did I have but to look for another way out?

The room seemed to be a storage area for tanks of some sort, containers, some of them cylindrical, some of them rectangular, all of them large enough to enclose at least one man. In the center of the room several large cylinders stood apart from the others, strangely lovely structures constructed of some crystalline substance. That curiosity Grendel had just mentioned was stirred, but all that interested me at the moment was finding a way out.

I turned and saw more containers, smaller ones. Thank God, I thought. Not big enough.

Unless . . .

I couldn't even admit to myself what I suspected.

Not big enough, unless . . .

Grendel came in behind me, and the steel door clanged shut behind him. I dragged my gaze from the small containers and stared at him.

"Heads, yes," he said softly.

"What?"

"Heads. Sounds macabre, I know, but it's really very practical. The brain is, after all, the essential conductor of the personality. We can transplant or re-create almost every facet of the human body. Why not the entire body? Someday . . . and when the time comes, the unfortunate driver of a zippy little Mazda will have the opportunity to live again. You might call that a miracle, but it's actually basic cell biology."

"It's science fiction at this point in history, Grendel," I said.

What was inside the other tanks? Or rather—who?

"You're right, Kelly," Grendel said. "That technology is in the future. The *near* future, I am certain, but the future nevertheless. But now we have the technology to prepare for that future. Don't you want to be prepared?"

"I want to go home, Grendel."

He smiled mischievously and shook his head.

Now I knew I was dealing with a madman.

"Grendel," I said soothingly, "I know you're just trying to do good here."

"You're so right, Kelly," he breathed out, exuding happiness. "I knew you'd get me!"

"I'm surprised you're so secretive about it. Aren't you proud of the work you're doing here?"

He looked at me as if he couldn't quite believe his luck. "I *am* proud of my work," he whispered. "The only thing I ever wanted was to help people live longer, happier lives. Bless you for understanding. I have devoted myself to the development of a process by which the entire human body can be vitrified. It's cutting-edge stuff."

"Hey, maybe tomorrow you can come over to my cottage and we can talk about it more."

He considered that, frowning. "You have never invited me over to your cottage before," he said in a plaintive voice.

"I just think it's so interesting, and I'd like to hear more about your work, and maybe I could—"

"In fact, yesterday you said you wanted me to *move out*!"

"—maybe I could help you."

"You have already helped me more than you know."

"Grendel, I've had enough of this." I marched across the room, right past him, and nearly reached the door.

He placed his bulk to stop me.

"I'm sorry, Kelly. I didn't want to frighten you. You would have had a much nicer time of it, but you didn't drink your wine."

I turned and ran back through the laboratory, looking for a way out, or something I could use as a weapon. There were no windows, and there was only one exterior door, a large steel door like the one leading into the office hallway. Locked.

I turned and he was standing next to one of the large tanks. "You know who's in here?" he asked pleasantly.

"Grendel. Let me out. Please."

"You never wanted me to know how much she fascinated you, but I knew. I know everything about you. You're like her in so many ways. And yet so different . . ."

I've found Alicia, I thought, and I have found Professor Fate. So Grendel wasn't bald; his head was shaved. When he worked at the Speran Institute his hair had been long and wild . . .

He had left the cryonics institution when they balked at his "visionary" thinking, and he started his own facility. I almost laughed; here was the classic mad scientist.

But I was slated to be his next experiment. That wasn't so funny.

"Why did you do this to her, Grendel?" I asked him. *And why are you planning to do the same to me?*

"Why? Because I wanted her, and . . . she said I was bothering her, that I was beginning to scare her a little . . . That made me so angry. As if I would do anything to *harm* someone." His voice shook with repressed emotion. "It won't hurt, I promise you. I'd never hurt you. In fact, it's just the opposite. I'll help you live longer and better than you ever dreamed."

"People are supposed to be technically dead before the cryonics process begins," I scolded him genially, still clinging to the notion that I could charm him into letting me out of there.

"That's because of our archaic and misguided legal system," he explained earnestly. "Think how much better a chance the patient would have of revival if the cryonics process took place *before* the mortification process begins. Before clinical death." With his white, disjointed fingers he put rabbit ears around the word *death*. I saw, then, the rash on his arms. I had noticed that rash before.

"Well, it's all very fascinating," I said sharply. "But it's time for me to be back at the inn."

"Kelly," he said softly. "Don't pretend you don't know why you're here."

"Come on, Grendel. You and me, we're friends. I look up to you for advice. For guidance. You're not going to keep me here against my will. You *wouldn't*."

"First, Kelly, I am not going to harm you at all. But I understand your feelings. You're a free spirit and I am clipping your wings."

He paused, blew out a sigh. When he spoke again there was something hard in his voice. "But I can't let you turn me in to the authorities, which I know very well you would have to do, if I let you go now. It's time for you to accept things as they are."

Trying not to hyperventilate, I searched for something, something to say to turn his mind from this course.

"So you planned to drug me, so I wouldn't know—"

"I knew you would be distressed unnecessarily. I wanted to avoid that."

"It was you, wasn't it? It's been *you*. You left me that note, directing me to that cryonics webpage—"

"I knew you were scared. I wanted to reassure you, Kelly, that everything would work out all right. I knew if you realized that life can be extended indefinitely . . . much longer than you ever dreamed possible . . ."

"*Reassure* me? You scared the shit out of me."

"I know. I think I wrote down the wrong link, didn't I? My mistake. But nevertheless, didn't you see—"

"What else?"

"What?"

"What else did you do to me?"

"Nothing!" He sounded hurt. "I just tried to get you to see you were making a mistake with him. And wasn't I right? Aren't you glad you never let him violate you?"

"What are you talking about?"

"Eli Larson. I was looking out for you, Kelly. If it wasn't for me, it might have happened. If I hadn't tripped the power one night, you might have been completely seduced by him. You can't say you're sorry I kept that from happening."

"Was it you who called Eli's ex and told her when we would be together? So she would discover us together? What did you think *that* would accomplish?"

"I thought the sudden spotlight on your life might make you consider the gravity of what you were getting yourself into."

"You spied on me. You came into my cottage."

"Yes."

"You vandalized Eli's photo—"

"Childish, I admit . . . But every time I saw his face in your bedroom, I just felt so . . ." His voice was calm, but he was clenching his fists.

"You tried to make me suspicious of Nick!" I was very close to shouting now. "What else? Did you drug the wine that I gave Paula the night she passed out? Yeah? . . . And you *did* mean it for me, didn't you? Were you planning to do this to me back then?"

"No. I just . . ." For the first time a look of shame tinged his pretty mouth and eyes. "I suppose I just wanted to spend some time with you, getting to know you . . . alone. In private."

Getting to know me. Good God.

He looked at me pleadingly, desperate to make me understand. "I wouldn't have done anything, Kelly. You know I'm not like that. I just wanted to . . . *look* at you."

"I can't believe I'm hearing this."

"I knew it was your habit to come greet your guests at the cocktail hour; to have a glass of wine and return to your office for an hour or so. So I poured you a glass of wine, as I often did. And I was going to follow you when you went to your office. I would have noticed you looked tired, and suggested you take a short nap in your cottage. Offered to watch the desk for you while you rested. But you didn't drink your wine and go to the office like you should have. You stayed . . ."

He was right. Ordinarily I had one glass of wine and then left my guests to themselves. But I had been feeling spirited that evening. Eli and Kyra were there with their parents. Nick was there, which had filled me with almost as much excitement, though at the time I couldn't imagine why.

I had blithely accepted the glass of wine that Grendel had poured for me, as I did on many an evening. But Paula had appeared right then, and I gave it to her.

"After that I was afraid you might be suspicious," Grendel said. "So I dared not try it again for a while."

"Until tonight."

"Yes. Well, actually, there was another time . . . That bottle of bubbly I sent with you to the mountains." He giggled.

Ah, I thought. The champagne. The champagne Grendel had asked Addie to send along with me, to celebrate Nick's safe return. Grendel knew Nick and I were about to become lovers. He could imagine the situation.

"You managed to drug a bottle of champagne," I marveled. "How did you do that?"

"Child's play for someone with my technical skills, I assure you," he said with a touch of pride. "I put enough medicine in there to put the two of you to sleep for a good long time. I was hoping it would forestall any energetic physical encounter . . ."

"You'll be pleased to know it worked."

"It worked, but not for long." He shook his head. "We could have gone on like we were, Kelly, for a long time. But I know what you did. I know *everything* you did. Everything. I let you go to the islands with Eli because I sensed you were losing interest in him. But I also know that Nick McClure never left your place last night." He added in a pained whisper, "You should have kept yourself pure."

It made me sick to think he had been watching Nick and me.

"So you see you leave me no choice. I can't have you catting around with other men. That's understandable, isn't it? Put yourself in my place."

"I'm trying to, Grendel."

I bolted and ran. Out of the sickly sweet–smelling laboratory and down the hallway to the front office and waiting room. I knew there was no escape behind me. I ran, desperate and searching for a previously undiscovered window or doorway, or a weapon with which to defend myself.

He ran after me down the hallway and came at me and grabbed

for me and I fought him with my fists and feet and knees and elbows, yelling and screaming. My brain was quickly downloading every piece of self-defense advice I'd ever heard, and though he was good-sized and criminally insane, Grendel was basically gentle, and he wasn't the most powerful of men. For a moment I thought I might have a chance. But then I felt the sting in my thigh.

Even as I continued to struggle, I felt my strength ebbing away and my brain turning to paste.

Chapter 29

"KELLY, it's no use. You may as well relax and accept the way things are." He held me tenderly. I nearly gagged on his scent, something flowery mixed with cinnamon, subtle, but so familiar.

"Why are you doing this to me, Grendel?" I gasped.

"Because I love you," he replied. "It wasn't Ellen. It was you."

The drug slowly took effect. I began to slump against him. He held me until I stopped fighting him, and even then I resisted. Even after it invaded me, I fought the enchantment of the potion.

With his arms around me to support me, he walked me down the hall and into the large back room, the laboratory, securing the door behind us.

"But you've already got Alicia," I pleaded, trying to wrap my mouth around the words as the vitality slowly bled from me. "You don't need me. You've got Alicia."

"I know. I hate to be greedy. But the truth is, you're much nicer to me than Alicia ever was. And you're even prettier. You have blue eyes, like me. Think how pretty our children will be!"

Our children?

"But I'd be happy with you, even without children," he added sincerely.

"Well, *I* won't be . . . happy . . . with *you* . . ." It was getting harder and harder to speak.

"You have a long time to get used to the idea of *us*. And besides, you know I can't let you go now. Everything is fixed."

Suddenly Nick was there with me.

But I knew I was dreaming. God, I was so disoriented. Battling the deep, drugged emotion, acutely aware of the danger. But I could not move. I could not escape him.

He whispered my name.

His fingers on my skin, ripples of sublime sensation. Thank God we had one night together.

I wanted only to sink into this bliss of oblivion where he was waiting. But some part of me was still watching and witnessing and warning, and flashes of lucidity came upon me like exploding stars in my head shouting, *It's Grendel's voice, Grendel's touch, you idiot! Resist!* and I tried to scream and run, but my limbs were limp and my voice had been silenced.

"You asked why, and I must admit I have asked myself the same question, Kelly. I am aware I am not like other men."

From the cold slab where I lay motionless, I could see a bank of TV monitors on the wall, up in the corner of the room, all dark. And I could see Grendel's face as he smiled, hovering over me. "I'm going to be getting everything ready now," he said. "I'll be working here, right behind you."

He leaned down and kissed me softly on the lips. "Patience, my love."

He moved out of my line of vision. But I could hear his voice, amiable, chatty, as if we were sitting on the porch at happy hour.

"When I was a young child," he said, "my father took me away from my mother. I was only five years old when it happened, but I remember very clearly the notion that my father had *taken* me, was refusing to let my mother have me. It wasn't so much that he wanted me himself, but that he didn't want her to have something *she* wanted.

"We went off in the car. I remember feeling his disdain for me, because I was a puny, weak thing, and I was scared. We drove for a long time and I probably began to whine and get on his nerves. Finally we stopped at a roadside inn.

"The place was quiet, nearly empty. I remember being frightened by the sound of the ocean in the storm. My father made me wait by myself in the car while he checked into the motel. But I couldn't stand it and I defied his wishes and ran into the office. He probably would have beat me for disobeying his orders, but the pretty lady behind the counter made much of me and I suppose he decided it was to his advantage to have me there.

"We struck up an acquaintance with the lady who checked us in and gave us the key to our room. It was probably because of her that we stayed longer than my father had planned—he had said we were only stopping for the night. We stayed for what seemed weeks, to my child's mind. I began to miss my mother. I wanted to go home. My father would have preferred to be rid of me, I think, but he needed me to punish my mother. And he needed me to attract the pretty lady, who seemed to be as fond of me as she was of him.

"She would come to our room in the evening and play cards

with us. They let me play a little, then they put me to bed and played on, just the two of them.

"And then late one night I woke to the sound of them arguing, and she was crying, she kept saying that she wanted to go. But he was trying to talk her out of leaving, and he pulled her onto the bed beside mine, and held her down. I peeked out of the covers to watch. Even at that age, I understood what my father wanted.

"She wasn't so friendly anymore, and she kept fighting him. My father became enraged, and he wouldn't let her go. She refused to surrender to him, but he was much bigger and much more powerful. She continued to fight him, until finally he had his hands around her neck, gripping it . . ."

Grendel made a sharp, whispery sound, as if gasping for air.

"And after a while she didn't struggle anymore. I don't believe he meant to do what he did. He must have lost his mind. He was so full of rage, but I remember him crying afterwards. The limp body lying across the bed.

"I had pretended to be asleep the whole time, and he didn't seem to realize or even care that he'd had a witness. He left in the middle of the night, left me alone in the motel room with the dead woman's body. While he was gone I tried to stay awake, but sleep dragged me down eventually. In the morning the body was gone and my father was sleeping in the bed next to mine, and when he woke up I didn't ask him any questions.

"We went back home to my mother, and we waited. I remember it was Christmas. It wasn't long before the police came to our door. When the investigators asked me what I knew about the lady from the motel, I played dumb. I knew what was expected of me."

"My father left my mother and me not more than a year after that. Abandoned us, essentially. We heard of his death a few years later. I suppose I rather forgot what happened that night. Didn't think of him for years. Until one day I was driving up the coast, looking for a building to house my new facilities . . . and I took a detour off the main road on a whim and found myself on the old highway. And when I saw the motel, and I realized that what I had assumed was a persistent recurring nightmare was actually a memory of something that had actually happened.

"I found a suitable building for my work just down the road, and I took a cottage at the inn. I continued working at the institute for a while, commuting one or two days a week. I made myself useful to Addie and Bill. I felt it was the least I could do for them. After all, my father had murdered their daughter.

"They took a liking to me, or at least Addie did. And I was surprised when I came to be so fond of the place. You would think with the bad memories . . .

"At any rate, they let me stay. And I hadn't been living there very long when *she* appeared. A good-looking young redhead, and we all felt the similarity, even though so many years had passed, and we were all attracted to her, in one way or another. I did feel bad for Addie when I had to take the girl away. And I will feel bad for her when she realizes you aren't coming back either. Third time's a charm, they say. I'm afraid it'll break her. It's not what I want for her, and I'm not looking forward to it, but it will be interesting to document her reactions.

"This is what you need to understand about me, Kelly. I'm a scientist. And a rather brilliant one, if I may say so without sounding like a braggart. I went as far in the field of cryonics as I could, and then I went beyond. When I ran into opposition, when people, narrow-minded people, refused see the utility and beauty in my ideas, I struck upon a way around the problem. I decided then I must strike out on my own.

"So I worked day and night, getting my facilities up and running. And when my facilities were complete, I already knew who my first patient would be."

Alicia.

"Every aspect of the work I do myself, with minimal assistance from my staff. I do the research and development on the latest processes and storage units. I suffer from these rashes on my arms, from working with the chemicals. But it's little enough to endure for my work. And oddly enough, you know, the persecution I endured, and the fact that I was driven to do my work underground, all helped point me in the direction that would ultimately result in my greatest innovation."

"And now that it is ready, *you* will help me test it. As you can imagine, it's not easy to recruit for experiments of this sort, so it's rather a challenge to test! Funny how things work out, isn't it? But I have no doubt history will vindicate me."

I heard the familiar, startling sound of my own cell phone. Muffled.

It rang again, more shrilly now. He must have pulled it out of his pocket.

"I don't think we'll be answering your phone at the present time," Grendel said. He let it finish ringing.

"Now, for the purposes of trying out the equipment I've developed, we will think of this procedure as self-induced. Though I had planned for you to be unconscious when the procedure commences, I anticipated the possibility of your resistance and foresaw the possible need for restraints. I'm actually glad you will be partly conscious. This is really something we should share."

My phone beeped. Dear phone, I thought. Dear friend phone. *Help me.*

"Let's see," Grendel said. "You appear to have a message. Six, sixteen, seventy-one. Your sister's birthday. Your secret code. Do I surprise you?" he asked, and he had moved close enough so that I could see him smiling down at me. "But I know many things about you. What you have in your refrigerator and what your blouse smells like when you take it off after a long day. I know your bank account numbers, your Social Security number, and all your passwords." He sank into silence, listening to the message.

He repeated the message and listened to it a second time, and when it was finished he pressed the number for repeat once again and laid the phone by my ear.

"Kelly, hello, how are you, this is Addie. Kelly, I'm calling to tell you that Nick did not leave you that message. He never left a note for you. He came by a few minutes ago and I told him you'd gone to meet him at Grendel's clinic. He said he never left a message asking you to come to Grendel's clinic. Somebody else left that message. Kelly, I have a bad feeling about this, because of something Anita told me, about Grendel—I didn't want to believe it at first, but then I began to wonder—anyway, come home, please. Oh—Nick is coming down there to Grendel's clinic right now to get you. All right, then. I'm sure everything is fine. Bye now."

Thank God, I thought. Nick is coming.

"So you betrayed me," said Grendel, looking down on me. "You showed Addie the note. How could you do that? I thought I could *trust* you . . ."

His mind seemed to be rapidly shorting out.

"Now then," he said. "I had planned on this going differently. They will be curious now, and they will investigate. This does change things, of course. This means . . ."

He looked at me and let out a long sigh. "Plan B." He laughed weakly. "I see now that I shall have to accompany you, Kelly. My God. It is rather something to face, isn't it? But I have often asked myself if plan B isn't the better plan, in any case . . . Perhaps that was why I was careless . . ."

He moved out of my line of vision and resumed his work, his movements more feverish now. "Don't you worry, Kelly. It will all work out. By the time they can get in here, the procedure will be complete. Even though now I will have to prepare both of us for cryonics suspension—and without assistance, unfortunately. But I have designed it just for this purpose. My God! To really *use* the equipment I've developed—it's exhilarating." His voice quivered with excitement. "I do regret leaving my work now; there is so much more I could do; but perhaps it is my destiny to move on into the future and continue my work there. And now the world will know of my work . . ." He began to hum.

"We should have just enough time," he said, breaking off his song. "Those steel doors are quite impenetrable. Not even your Nick has the tools to get through them, not in time. Even if he was convinced you were in here, which he won't be when he doesn't see your car parked outside. Yes, I took *that* precaution, too. The towing company should be just about finished up with that by now— let's just see."

The bank of dark monitors above me blinked on, each one trained on some part of the exterior of the ugly gray building where I was being held prisoner. In one of the monitors I could see my car slowly rolling out of the parking area, hanging off the back of a tow truck.

"All right, all right, then," Grendel said, sounding giddy. "Time to get down to it."

From where I lay, I could see little but the bank of monitors, which were now showing only static images of the building's exterior. Grendel hurried about behind me, humming. I forced myself to stay awake.

I dragged my eyes open. On one of the monitors I saw Nick's truck pull in beside the clinic and slam to a halt.

Nick jumped out and his dogs jumped out with him, Freesia

and Maggie. He was now walking around the building. I saw him first on one monitor, then another, with the dogs.

Grendel, who had been clattering and humming behind me, was suddenly silent.

"Oh golly," he murmured. "He's already here. Your Prince Valiant. He doesn't see your car, but he's going to take a look anyway . . . that's prudent of him. He'll see it's all locked up and dark and he'll figure you aren't here . . . and then he'll go look for you elsewhere."

Grendel went back to his work, but his hum was tentative. He stopped again, apparently looking up at the monitors and seeing what I was seeing.

"What are they doing? Oh, for crying out loud. The dogs! They know you're in here! Do you think he'll believe what they're trying to tell him?" Grendel chuckled. He didn't seem too worried.

Yes, he'll believe.

Presently we heard a faint echoing of sound. Nick was calling for me. His image was no longer on any of the monitors.

"He's made it into the outer offices," Grendel said as if to himself. "He must have broken in. Don't worry. He can't get into the lab. Not in time. The only way in here is through those locked steel doors. Nick doesn't have the tools to get through, not in time. Believe me, I know what he's got in his toolbox, and it isn't sufficient."

But Grendel wasn't humming anymore, and the sounds of his preparations took on a panicked, desperate quality. At one point something dropped on the floor with a jarring clang of steel on linoleum.

"Don't worry. He can't hear us in here."

Grendel ran some machinery. I couldn't see what he was doing, but it sounded like a vacuum cleaner behind my head.

"Just testing some things. You don't have to worry about maintenance, topping off the tanks, paying the bills, that sort of thing. Ellen will see to that. I've compensated her very judiciously, just to insure that she does. It's all set up already, in a trust. If anything bad happens to us, little Ellen won't get her allowance. There!" He spoke with satisfaction, and a touch of relief. "What did I tell you? He's leaving."

It was true. Nick had returned to his truck. I watched him on the monitor as he called the dogs into the truck and jumped in after them. The truck swung in a fast arc around the parking area and shot out toward the highway, out of the range of the camera.

"ALMOST finished." Grendel sounded relieved and happy. "I'm so excited, Kelly. This is a big moment for us."

One of the monitors sprang to life again. A big pickup truck was pulling into in the parking lot.

I knew that truck. It was Earl's.

The doors winged open and Earl jumped out of the cab on the driver's side. For a moment I didn't realize that it was Nick riding shotgun; seeing the two of them together was so out of the ordinary.

Now they were lifting something out of the back of the truck. It was Earl's welding torch, on its cart, with its tanks and valves—

"Oh, good Lord," Grendel moaned. "Now what's happening?"

Nick and Earl moved out of range of the camera, and then, seconds later, they appeared again in a different monitor. They were setting up the torch beside the steel door at the rear of the building.

Grendel came to stand beside me, watching. The men were working fast. Purposeful. Unified.

With a spark lighter, Earl lit the torch, which was fitted with a cutting attachment mounted on the end of the torch handle.

Earl turned to Nick and offered him the torch.

Nick looked surprised. He shook his head and said something.

We had audio, but it was muffled. Still, I knew what they were saying. Nick was arguing for Earl's greater skill and experience. *You know what you're doing.*

Now Earl was shaking his head and nodding at the door. *You can do it.*

This exchange took place in a split second and it was decided. They were no longer arguing. Earl motioned to Nick to put on the protection.

Nick pulled on the gloves and face mask and took up the torch. He stood with his body slanted to the door, out of the blast of heat from the torch. With his legs slightly spread he stood there, heating the metal, directing a stream of pure oxygen through the flame along the line to be cut.

"Oh, jeez." A tiny whimper squeaked out of Grendel. I almost pitied him. "Oh, Kelly. This is terrible. I thought I had planned it so precisely. I just didn't count on—but they can't *stand* each other!"

He stood beside me for another few seconds, watching the monitor in disbelief. He was shaking.

"Kelly, I do apologize. But now there isn't time, I don't think . . . not for both of us . . . I'm so sorry."

I could hear Nick calling my name.

"Jesus Christ," I heard Earl say. It wasn't an oath, it was a cry for help.

A loud whirring sound had started up. Behind me, I heard a clunk, like a hatch closing on a space capsule. Later I learned that was the precise moment Grendel had entombed himself in one of his precious tanks.

Nick was suddenly beside me. "Oh my God, Kelly," he was gasping. He took my hand. "Earl, call an ambulance, *now*!"

Nick is here, I thought. Now I can rest.

I gathered the last of my strength to squeeze his hand, then I let go.

Chapter 30

IT was early on a bright morning in late December, and most of the guests were still in their rooms. Addie and Bill were gone now, living in their condo over the hill; I was on my own with the Magic Mermaid Inn. Then again, I wasn't really on my own. I had Arturo and Juan, and I had Anita and the girls. I had Earl and Maxine across the road. And I had Nick.

I turned at the sound of footsteps, surprised to see Zac coming up the stairs to the porch. I assumed he had come to talk to his mother, but he stopped and nodded at Nick and me.

He came right to the point. "You once said you could use some help around here," he said, looking at me. "I know the veterinary bill for the dog was thousands of dollars, and I'd like to work to pay off the debt."

I studied him a moment. The blazing eyes, the beautiful bone structure of his face, the wing of black hair.

"Are you saying you're . . . responsible?" I asked.

"I let animals out of cages," he said. "I'm not ashamed of that. I'd do it again, if I had to. But I never meant for the puppy to get hurt."

I had pretty much surmised that Zac was the one who had tagged my cottage with the symbol of anarchy. I knew he was dedicated to the liberation of animals and had a tendency to set them free. And I blessed him every day for it.

Because Zac had figured Grendel out before anyone else.

Nick had told me later, after I had recovered a bit from my ordeal, what Zac had told the police. And some things he *hadn't* told the police. Zac had ridden his bike down to Grendel's clinic one afternoon to deliver a package to his aunt, his mother's sister, who worked as the receptionist there. He gave his aunt the package his mother had sent, and left the building. When he picked up his bike, he noticed several cages sitting out behind the clinic. Knowing that this was a research facility as well as a medical clinic, he wondered if the cages were for lab animals. He decided to keep an eye on the place.

One day he saw Grendel bring in a dog in a cage, a white, short-haired, mixed-breed mutt who looked through the bars of the cage with large and fearful eyes. Zac, watching intently behind the cover of the woods behind the clinic, caught a glimpse of the laboratory through the rear doorway as Grendel let himself in. Zac knew that Grendel had not just acquired a new pet.

So Zac started a fire in the Dumpster outside the clinic, and when Grendel and his staff ran outside to deal with it, the boy dashed into the lab and sprang the pup. But he had seen enough in Grendel's laboratory to start questioning things. It was strange, he thought, that no one seemed to know what sort of "research" Grendel was actually doing.

Zac did some research of his own on the Internet, looking for some laboratory procedure that would require the presence of large storage containers. His quest led him to the same cryonics website that I had visited.

But when Zac mentioned his suspicions to his mother she laughed at him, told him he was crazy and paranoid, and even his aunt, who worked at the clinic, said it was absurd. Zac continued to keep an eye on Grendel, cutting classes at school sometimes so he could follow the doctor's movements, mostly because he was determined to thwart any use of lab animals. And he saw some things he hadn't expected to see. He saw Grendel sneaking into my cottage, and he saw Grendel watching me much in the way he was watching Grendel.

Zac wasn't sure what to do. He thought of telling me, or Addie and Bill; but it would be his word against Grendel's, and he didn't think anyone would believe him.

But Zac's mother had taken him a little more seriously than he had realized. She had disregarded most of what he had told about Grendel's laboratory, and what he suspected was going on in there—it just seemed too far-fetched to her. But she could not dismiss what the boy had told her about Grendel spying on me and sneaking into my cottage.

Anita mentioned her concerns about Grendel to Addie just days before Grendel had made his move on me.

And Addie, dear, silly Addie—she was the one who put it all together. She was the one who advised Nick not to wait another moment to go down to Grendel's clinic and make sure I was all right. And she had helped convince Earl that Nick needed his help.

I considered Zac for a moment. "What are you coming to me for?" I asked. "*He* paid for Heidi's operation. *He's* the one you owe." I nodded at Nick, who was sitting at a table eating, with Freesia lying asleep under his chair.

"Yeah, I know," said Zac, "but you're his old lady, right?"

Nick stopped eating and locked his gaze on me.

"Well, you *are* his girlfriend, right?" Zac waited for an answer.

"Yes," I said. "I think I am, but . . . that partly depends on what *he* has to say about it." I shot Nick a quick glance, a shy smile. We had yet to actually define our relationship in so many words.

Suddenly unwilling to wait for a response from Nick, I looked back at the boy and said, "And anyway, Zac, you already know you have more than repaid your debt to me."

"And to me," Nick said.

I looked out on the lawn where Maggie and two half-grown pups gamboled together with the blazing blue ocean as a backdrop. One of the dogs was a young female German shepherd with a black face, so springy, rough and tumble, you'd never guess a steel plate was holding the bones of one of her hind legs together. The other young dog was a white, short-haired mutt with big brown eyes.

"Zac," I said, "it's because of you I'm free."

"Hey, I'll never stop working for the cause of liberation," Zac said with a faint smile. "So. When do I start?"

"My old lady? My girlfriend?" Nick turned to me when Zac had gone.

"Hey, what, you don't like the sound of that?"

"I just think I would prefer another word."

"What other word is that?" I asked him. "Mistress? Paramour? Courtesan?" I smiled. "Not *significant other*, please."

"*Esposa*," he said in his badly accented Spanish. "Wife."

*   *   *

WHEN I think of that strange and awful day in Grendel's laboratory I think of the miracle of connection, of people. Zac talking to his mom about his suspicions, Anita informing Addie, Addie advising Nick, Nick asking Earl for help . . . without any one of them I might not have made it.

I'll never forget the moment Earl said to Nick, "I was wrong about you, son. I apologize."

Addie and Bill wanted me to know about the past before they moved on, about their daughter who went missing nearly thirty years earlier.

"We feel now it was wrong of us not to tell you before," Bill said. "But we weren't really trying to keep anything from you . . ."

I understood. They found it difficult to speak of, even now.

They said I reminded them of their own daughter, Fiona O'Mally, who was murdered when she was twenty-four years old. And they admitted that perhaps they had befriended Alicia St. Claire for the same reason. She was a pretty young redhead who needed a place to stay, a new purpose in life. It was a terrible coincidence, they thought, that she had disappeared, too.

Addie and Bill had been vacationing in Europe when their daughter, who was taking care of the inn for them, had vanished. They told me it was a relief, in a sense, to finally know who had taken her.

Later Paula said the same thing about her sister. "It doesn't make it any easier to bear," she told me. "But at least now I can stop searching for her."

ON Christmas Eve, Nick and I walked on the beach together, holding hands, as the dogs raced back and forth along the wet sand and the sun dissolved into the sea.

"Well," he said. "Tomorrow's Christmas. I've been wondering

how I can give you anything to match what *he* could give you," Nick said.

"Nick, *you* are everything I want."

"Are you really sure about this, Kelly?" he asked me.

"Nick . . ." I tried to think of a succinct way to put it, to convince him once and for all. "There is something I want to tell you, all right?"

"Okay."

"You know when Grendel . . . when he had me . . ."

Nick nodded, looking at me with a sober expression.

"While I was lying there in that room, on that table, unable to move, I realized I might never again see any of the people I loved, you know? I thought about my mom and dad. And I thought about my sister, and all my good friends. And I thought about the man I had fallen in love with."

He was listening intently.

"And it wasn't Eli Larson I was thinking of," I said. "It was *you*, Nick. I was thinking of you."